THE GRASS IS ALWAYS BROWNER

MARTIN KNOX

The National Library of Australia Cataloguing-in-Publication

Author: Knox, Martin

Title: The grass is always browner

ISBN: 978-1-921731-69-3 (pbk.)

Subjects: Speculative fiction.

Dewey Number: A823.4

DEDICATION

Dedicated to the men and women everywhere, who create and use science and engineering while resisting manipulation by politicians, governments, corporations and religions.

ACKNOWLEDGEMENTS

I acknowledge assistance by the following people and groups:

Aborigines of various tribes, who are the original inhabitants of the Australian lands, which are the setting for most of this book; Delene Cuddihy, for encouragement and perspectives on spiritual, historical, Aboriginal, cultural and political matters; Elder Uncle Albert Holt and Pat Williams for communicating Aboriginal culture to me; Tiana Brockhurst for communicating an Aboriginal youth perspective; Helga Parl for cover graphics and reading of drafts; members of Fairfield Writers Group, Brisbane for reviewing my drafts; Dr Veny Armanno of UQ English Department for tuition; Roger Wooller for biological advice; Brisbane School of Distance Education's science teachers for their advice, interest and encouragement; Dr Zoe Knox of Leicester University for religion, politics and philosophy advice; Dr Tessa Knox of Nairobi for mosquito-borne disease dynamics and science philosophy advice; Dr Maciej Pomian Schredzinski for philosophy of religion in relation to science; Jessica McClymont for advice on processes of law; Kelly McClymont for advice on processes of medical prevention of disease, diagnosis and treatment; Megan Breen for advice on debating protocols; Zeido Franco for advice on computing; members of Yungaba Action Group for providing me with experiences of activism; members of The Immigrants Memorial Association for immigrant perspectives; Wayan and Nyoman Suwendra for introduction to Hinduism in Bali; Imam Ahmed of West End Islamic Society, Brisbane; Muslim people of Bedugul, Bali for their hospitality; student L for her explanation of Tao Buddhism in Australia; Linda Triasmono for Indonesian culture; Darren Godwell and Seleneah More of West End Community Association for Aboriginal perspectives; Elizabeth Gondwe, Librarian at Dunwich, Stradbroke Island, for Aboriginal culture and history; Vanessa Fisher for explanation of Indonesian Gamelan Band music; Peter Hosking, for advice on reconciliation methodology.

The opinions expressed in this book are those of the author alone and are not intended to resemble, criticise or lampoon any persons, partisan interests or religions.

AUTHOR BIO

Martin Knox was born in England in 1946. He became a Chemical Engineer and later a Management Scientist, researching alternative models of Government planning.

He worked in the UK, Canada, the USA and Australia in nuclear, tar sands, petroleum, coal and coal-to-oil industries.

He settled in Australia with his family, and at age 40 became a high school Science and English teacher.

He wrote full-time for several years a published course in Senior Multi-strand Science and went on to teach it on-line to distance education students.

Outside writing, he is active in public decision-making on development, population, growth, water and resources issues.

CONTENTS

CHAPTER 1

Neighbours

Abajoe had cared for them all their lives and yet they did not trust him at all. Sudden death was in their future. A white doe poised for flight, whiskers twitching and pink eye scrutinising his upper half, above the stable door of the lounge. What could she see of him? Tall, skin the colour of old hay, black hair, straight flat nose. Was his stillness gathering menace? Taking no chances, she thumped her foot once on the concrete of the fifth floor. It set off an explosion. Scratching claws shrieked on concrete as bodies hurtled into corners with percussive thumps. He squinted with pain as he watched 40 rossits pile up against the breakfast bar, clawing to bury their heads in the heaving mass of furry white bodies, like children hiding.

On this day in 2237, there were water restrictions, as usual. The water supply could only be used for drinking, hygiene, cooking and growing food. Since the Great Famine in 2220, when he was aged four, getting food had been Australians' top priority. The family's meat rabbits had died from disease and he had become a vegetarian. As an adolescent, he was a great success at growing vegetables but he grew tired of vegetables day after day and longed for meat. He experimented with a new disease-resistant animal, the rossit, with success. Today, at 21, he was proud to be preparing Australians for survival. He demonstrated his methods every week on the Government's 'Family Fare' self-sufficiency show.

"In a famine, people have nothing to share," he told their national audience. "It's every family for themselves. Self-sufficiency should be a lifelong strategy. Start a vegetable garden and a rossit hutch now! They won't let you starve!"

A rossit looked like a rabbit with a marsupial pouch and long bushy tail. They had engineered it with a possum's immune system, which was resistant to endemic rabbit diseases, along with a possum's reproductive system. Too bad, he thought, that rabbit genes for mob flight were integral with the genes for sociality. They were needed for intensive rearing and therefore couldn't be knocked out.

He let himself into the room, crossed to the corner and gently pulled apart the struggling mass, body by body. His ministrations seemed to calm them and they nosed around for food in the sawdust on the floor. He left them eating the vegetable peelings he had brought.

Then he inspected the bedrooms. One of the young does had her white chin hairs streaked with blood. In her terror, she had scoffed all her hairless, pink, blind kindle, born that day. Angry, he went to grab her by the ears to pick her up cruelly. Then he told himself she had behaved naturally, recycling protein that might be lost. He lifted her gently, with his hand under her heavy belly and took her to the buck in the next room. He watched him sniff her rear, mount her and, as she yielded entry, thrust once, then fall back and to the side. The protein would regenerate. 'Would she link the mating act with kindling again in 31 days?' he mused. 'What did sex mean to her?'

The Yabras did not need to grow their own food. His mother, Transcending One, famed for her dreaming and meditation, had been elected for a third term as Prime Minister of Australia the previous year. His father was Deputy. They received modest salaries. Their family's food-growing activities were broadcast to the nation as a model of self-sufficiency in a weekly nutrition show, 'Family Fare'. The show was based on the hydroponic gardens, poultry and rossits they grew in Family Fare Tower, the 80-apartment building their family alone occupied. His father had been deeply affected when his first wife had to abort Abajoe's half-brother in the famine of 2196. Since then, he had made sure his family would always have water and food. Marko and T One had bought the vacant building for next to nothing and transformed it into a model of self-sufficiency.

Poultry were on the ground floor. The four units on Floor One were his, his adopted sister Paula's, his grandparents' and his great-grandmother's. Floors Two, Three and Four were horticultural gardens. On the fifth floor were rossits. The sixth was storage. There were 14 empty floors above – no one had rented a unit during his lifetime. There was no electricity for the lift, and when they ran short of solar power for the pump, he had to carry water up from the basement.

They grew vegetables with water brought from lakes dammed by the embankments along the river. They prevented the sea from submerging the Meannjin River floodplain. The salt concentration from the breach had been diluted by storm run-off water and was low enough for hydroponics.

Their crops were safe in the building. Abajoe knew from experience that if he planted vegetables in the bare spaces between blocks, people would steal the produce. Civil society was still in disarray from the Great Famine. He had been only four, but he could remember the lines of people, who had come begging for water from his father's supply company and how he had shared their supplies until they went hungry themselves. Then he had guarded the building from the starving. Now, with the encouragement of the 'Family Fare' shows, Australians no longer crowded into cities and most people had a healthy diet of home-grown food.

His grandparents, Zelta, the former Prime Minister and Hugo, an energy consultant, had moved in when T One and Marko moved out to the prime ministerial residence at the stadium. Abajoe's great-grandmother, Charlotte 141, had been living there since she relinquished the Prime-Ministership to her daughter, Zelta, in 2185 after the Coal Wars. Her husband, Winston, had died three years previously, aged 131. Average age at death in Australia had risen to 136 and was still rising, due to ascetic and healthy lifestyles since the renunciation of materialism.

Abajoe and his adopted sister, Paula, grew food for all of them. Paula's parents had died in the Great Famine and T One and Marko had brought her up as his sibling. Also 21, she had studied with him, tutored by Marko and the elders and now helped with the animals and gardens for the shows.

Their weekly routine was to demonstrate the growing of vegetables and rossits and to research issues for the Middle Way Party (MWP) with John and Peter. They came to his flat every afternoon. As the nation's most eligible bachelor, Abajoe attracted a large personal following. The statuesque Paula had a segment on growing poultry and fruits. She was very popular, and fans, who at first had little interest in self-sufficiency, kept chooks and planted trees through admiration for her.

"Why don't more young people get into self-sufficiency, Chook?" asked Abajoe, using her affectionate name.

"Go on, tell me," she replied.

"They ain't figuring on starving!" he laughed. "It won't happen to us!" he mimicked the fashionable speech and pose of a 16 year old, born since the last famine.

He and Paula also broadcast from the family's market garden plot in a former football stadium nearby. T One and Marko lived there, in the prime ministerial residence under the grandstand. They occupied several former press boxes and studios built for football hype, that were now used for his mother's participation in virtual meetings of the Parliament. Most of the time, they were away visiting places that had requested help from the national government.

T One was mostly involved in making sure only essential developments went ahead because her Government had been elected to bring in a non-material, spiritually diverse society. Sudarta, who led the Opposition, had a different idea of the future lifestyle for Australia – a return to materialism. Her party, the Progress Party, wanted Australia to join the South East Union, which would bring population growth, industrial development and free movement of people between countries.

"Growth must be stopped," T One told the media. "We can't feed any more people – the drought could worsen. We have to prevent another famine."

"Food can be brought from overseas," said a journalist.

"By then it's too late. Ships take two months to load and sail here, and another month for the little that isn't stolen to reach the interior. Hungry people don't last that long."

"So how are you going to get food to them soon enough?"

"People have to be self-sufficient. That's why 'Family Fare' has been our major strategy."

"What else are you aiming to do this term?" It was two years until the next election.

"We will deliver on our promises. Anti-discrimination. Devolution. Population and water control. Co-ordination of the councils."

"What about defence?"

"There is an old saying that people with resources need never lack friends," she said. "On the contrary, we have resources and never lack enemies. We need good friends, who will come to our aid. I believe that we should share our resources with kin, people who will share their's with us. We can help each other against enemies."

Besides his work as an actor on 'Family Fare', Abajoe was learning and helping in the family business of national leadership through the MWP. He had inherited the Yabra's propensity for inclusive leadership of opposed factions. His genetic make-up was extraordinary and his take on most situations was radical and inspirational. He had been elected Leader of the MWPs Youth Organisation.

He was preparing his keynote address to the Annual Youth Conference and had almost finished.

"Australia has four times more land area than our neighbour, Bhakaria, with only one tenth of the population. Our population of 50 million is therefore 40 times less dense. It is the least dense of any nation. This may not be a good thing. Bhakarians feel sorry for Australians, their lack of community and the emptiness of their social lives. Lifestyles are quite different, neither better nor worse – It's a matter of what you get used to.

"Energy resources are also unbalanced. Bhakaria was once the world's greatest coal exporter but their resources are nearing depletion. Australia's precisely-known measured and indicated coal resources are ten times that of Bhakaria, or 100 times more per person.

"Australia's other mineral resources are also much richer. Mineral assets are 20 times higher in value, or 200 times more per person. Compared with Bhakarians, Australians are obscenely wealthy in mineral resources.

"We do not have to feel lucky or greedy or selfish about these disparities. The Australian environment is harsh and unable to sustain much development. However, Bhakaria is campaigning for sanctions against us for not rejoining the South East Union. Our membership of the regional economic bloc would give Bhakaria unhindered access to Australia's coal and other mineral resources. Their development could be sustained long enough for high profits.

"Joining the SEU would allow people to move freely between Bhakaria and Australia. If Bhakarians immigrate in large numbers, the possibility of famine could increase. Bhakaria has a thriving material economy and high density living. The immigrants may see the solution to be industrial development. But Bhakaria has reliable rains and is able to feed its people using factory farming methods.

"But, Australians, who have experienced famine, reject industrial development and high density living because they were not able to obtain food in a drought and there was not enough water and energy for electricity production or for much industry or transport of supplies. Consequently, they have been reluctant to take on more mouths to feed

and have been keeping the number of guest workers and immigrants to a minimum."

Abajoe wanted to finish off with discussion questions. If he could get people's attention to Australia's population problem without being too alarmist, the conference could be led to accept T One's policy of voluntary population control. Malthus, around 1800, had shown how demand for food would inevitably exceed supply but T One's Government was refuting this by population control that was 'voluntary'. He would have to be careful how he explained this: few people would accept the Government telling them how many kids they could have.

He had always been interested in ideas about Australia's ultimate population. Australia was almost down to zero growth. Reduced demand for material goods and services had been offset by a binge in purchasing personality and group-role development programmes.

People were buying experiences and technologies to develop exquisite and unique personalities esteemed within their diverse communities. For example, an Aborigine might follow tradition as one of a kangaroo tribe and learn their beliefs, didgeridoo music, dance and song, staying in costume and in role permanently. A person of European descent might train to become a conversation 'cat': cool, composed and soliciting those with resources. Creating experiences for these 'characters' to enjoy kept many people employed. Everyone had become their own work of art, with help from expert services and exotic technologies.

Because Australia's water and renewable energy resources were limited, the nation had a maxim of 'copulate and perish'. The birth rate was below the replacement level. Immigration had declined to a trickle. The reluctance to take migrants created friction with Bhakaria, where the population was increasing despite the Government's priority of voluntary birth control. If Sudarta were elected, she would allow population growth, material growth, mass markets, resources export and an open-door immigration policy. She would join the SEU and share Australia's resources with Bhakaria.

Abajoe had discussed this with his mother the previous week.

"Share? Why should we share with them?" the Prime Minister told him. "Property ownership is a sovereign right of our culture and also theirs. They don't really expect us to share with them. They think they have the right to come and help themselves."

"What evidence do you have for that?"

"They are demanding we join the SEU!"

"You are on that old yellow peril bandwagon!" said Abajoe. "Bhakarians wouldn't dare come here uninvited."

"They would if they ran out of resources."

"They should be able to get them from us without invading," he said in his soft, giving voice. "I believe in neighbourly sharing."

"Hmph! I know sharing is in your genes, but the reason it is rare and recessive is because it has a low survival value. If a person shares their resources, they don't survive. It's that simple."

"Not true. That is how our people survived droughts, by collaborating with kin. Collaboration is a survival strategy that has worked, through collectives. Humans have entered a new age of collectivity," he said smiling, as if it was self-evident.

"Collectivity? History is full of failed collectives." His mother's voice was sceptical, hard-edged.

"Unless we share, we may not survive. We could share our mineral resources with people, who would help us with food in a drought," he reasoned.

"It wouldn't work because people are inherently selfish. They wouldn't give us food when we need it."

"Indigenous people are not selfish…Why are you smiling like that? I'm serious."

"You're so like Arnhem, your great-grandfather. He was brought up in the tradition of always sharing with your kinfolk. With those beliefs, it was difficult for him to make it to the top in a dog-eat-dog world of national politics. He overcame racial barriers to sharing and brought the segregated races together in a collective. Then, under his leadership, Indigenous Australians chose to forego being top of the heap. Arnhem brought our peoples together as a united nation."

"He was a great man. Our family should take the lead again, in sharing with Bhakaria."

"What have they got that we want a share in?"

"Food, when we are in drought."

She thought for a moment.

"You may be right. Perhaps we should trade minerals for food. Can you bring me a policy proposal I can take to the Party?"

Abajoe was delighted. Their study group had discussed it and had a proposal ready. Now he needed the right words to end his speech. He dictated a closing paragraph into the memory of his communicator.

"Australia is out of step with her neighbours' free immigration policies. But if the flood gates were opened, would Australia be swamped? Would Australian culture survive? Would it create a racial schism preventing unity? To prevent famine, should we barter our minerals with the people next door, for food in an emergency? Or should we allow them in to help themselves?

"Those are some of the questions we need to address during this conference."

'There, that should nail it,' he thought. It would give participants plenty to talk about. He would like to have included a further question: 'Would Bhakaria be able to slow down their population growth as their resources ran out or would they obtain them from Australia?' He wasn't sure humans had ever voluntarily reduced demand as they reached the bottom of the resources barrel. With petroleum, they hadn't until after the collapse in world supply. Would hardship teach people to anticipate scarcity and moderate demand, even when costs were held down? Perhaps they would have as little anticipation of starvation now as before the famines.

He could test this with rossits. The role of environmental factors in controlling their reproduction might be similar to humans. Rossits raised in cages on pellets had artificially low costs of obtaining food. With abundant food, they could populate rapidly, reaching sexual maturity five months after conception.

He needed an answer to these questions: 'Will the rossits slow down their breeding and keep their numbers steady if I keep the food supply steady? Or will they suffer a famine cycle of starvation and death followed by overpopulating reproduction? Would any famine-averting learning take place?'

When he proposed the experiment to Paula, at first she was against it.

"How many can a pair breed to?" asked Paula.

"Under ideal conditions, one doe produces 7800 adults after a year and after two years more than 3,000,000,000."

"That's unbelievable!" said Paula. "What are these ideal conditions?"

"Plenty of food and space, with no disease or deaths, with an average of five female kits per kindle of 10, every 46 days."

"But humans control their own fertility," she objected, "with abstinence, withdrawal, hormones, prophylactics or abortions."

"So can rossits," he replied. "Rossits have possums' sixth sense of food availability. When conditions are bad they absorb foetuses, eject their babies from the pouch or cannibalise their kindle. These are three natural strategies, whereas humans have only artificial methods."

"There's also celibacy."

"That's unnatural."

"Ha-ha. It's a cruel experiment," she told him. "You could have rossits dying like flies from thirst or hunger. I really do not want to have anything to do with it. Isn't there any other way of doing an investigation? Why do you have to use rossits?"

"I can't do a controlled experiment on humans. Imagine the outcry if government food aid was withheld from a district, simply to see what would happen to population numbers. I could use mice or rats but they build up to plague proportions and migrate. I am more interested in capacity for voluntary population control. Rossits stay in their territories, like possums."

"But rossits aren't like humans. They're dumber."

"At talking, yes. But in self-control to avoid adversity, humans may be just as dumb. Take obesity. It can kill you but people are fatter than ever. Did you ever see an obese animal in the wild?"

"But rossits aren't wild. Domestication may have lost them their self-control. They reproduce irresponsibly."

"We are finding out whether self-control of reproduction is acquired and can adjust with the environment. If we get evidence, which refutes that reproduction is automatic in rossits, then if we assume that humans have at least as much self-control, we will be refuting that human sex is automatic. But without that evidence, human reproduction is out of couples' control."

"But setting up rossits to suffer droughts and famines is cruel."

"We need to study reproduction in a controlled setting. The conditions are those they could encounter in nature. Nature is hard but it is not cruel by intent. We will euthanize individuals that are in pain and the animals will have the same standards of care that are normal in ethical scientific experiments."

"Except that we will be deliberately creating hardship."

"Only if they would be bringing it on themselves by reproducing... We are studying reproduction under hardship. We can't get away from it."

"How will you limit their pain?"

"We will monitor loss of appetite, weight loss, dishevelled appearance, withdrawn behaviour and response to handler. If three or more of these are unsatisfactory, they will be euthanized."

"Okay," said Paula. "I don't like it but I can see how this data could be useful."

"So, we'll do it?"

"Okay."

They applied to Meannjin's Animal Representatives Committee. Although the rossit representative objected to their use at first, Abajoe showed that the conditions would simulate conditions in the wild to understand their reproduction. Rossits were the most suitable variant species. He obtained a committee majority approval for use of up to 5000 rossits per year.

He and Paula set up the experiment with a buck and a doe in each of two pens. The large pen was a lounge room and the other a bedroom with one quarter the area. There was a wall between them. He labelled the lounge 'Australia'. It would get green feed and one 20kg sack of pellets per week. The bedroom was 'Bhakaria', with a quarter of the area. It would get ten times more green stuff and ten sacks of pellets per week because of the ten times higher human population. Daily food quantities would be randomised in Australia but held constant in Bhakaria, reflecting the effects of the different climates. The rossits would be able to breed freely. Numbers and biomasses of the two populations were to be the dependent variables monitored.

"It isn't a perfect model of the situation," Abajoe admitted. "But it has the major factors."

"I wonder what we'll find out," Paula said.

"We may find that cognition and voluntary control of reproduction is more important than geobiology and innate sex drives," Abajoe mused.

"In which pen?"

"Maybe both."

"What if it shows Australia has too many people already?"

"We would need population control."

"That's unpopular. Who would take it on?"

"Someone with vision."

"Someone prepared for a fight."

"Someone with enough support."

"Someone like me," he groaned. "Would I have to do it?"

"Yes."

"Why?"

"Because you're a Yabra," said his sister. "It's your duty to your country."

He sighed. "I suppose it is. Okay. I'll do it. But hopefully it won't be necessary."

CHAPTER 2

Abajoe

66You did good to make me different but why did you have to make me
so different?" Abajoe complained to his parents when he was six. "I
want to share but Paula keeps things for herself. She takes my stuff and
won't share hers. My friends are the same. Can't you make me a brother
or a sister like me to share everything with?"

But he remained an only natural child, a freak. A human with an
allele for sharing is rarely found in a primate male and this behaviour is
extremely unusual. Marko and T One had known he would be different
from his genome report at birth. He was missing the allele for the
'territorial imperative'. It was linked to resources aggression, male
domination and reproductive advantage. It had been replaced by a
recessive gene for mutualism, carried by females but expressed in about
one in 200 male Indigenous Australians. It was extremely rare in other
races.

Abajoe had a pedigree for sharing. Selfishness is only partly
dominant and both of his parents and grandparents displayed unusually
generous sharing characteristics. His grandmother, Zelta, had fostered
development of kin relationships and sharing when she was Prime
Minister and now, as an Elder, continued to promote them. His father,
Marko, like most of his ancestry, was predisposed to accept sharing
arrangements, even with strangers. When his relationship with his first
wife ended, he had asked a dating service to find him a sharing person.
Only one profile they supplied met that criterion: T One's. She wanted
communal living and spiritual union. When she became pregnant, they
expected their child would be a sharer but they were surprised by how
extreme he was.

He willingly allowed other children to use his toys. It was his no-
strings-attached 'hosting' of borrowers that distinguished him. It was not
like conditional Crucian charity. Indigenous people welcome kin to use
their resources in a self-effacing manner. Abajoe went further and sought
out opportunities to make his resources freely available to support others.
It contrasted with the other races' material selfishness.

Whereas he shared generously, every person who took from him
realised that he or she was the recipient of a loan and not a gift. He could

not have given it anyway, for he was the custodian and his stewardship demanded that it be returned when its use for the original purpose had ended.

His sharing was an unusual attribute. When new resources or territory were on offer, his gentle negotiation to share them with all those interested was quite distinct from others' greedy territory acquisition. Instead of competing with other children in the obtaining of resources, Abajoe allowed others to use his, while vehemently holding his territory and resources in trust for those in need and for future generations.

He swapped his expensive clothes with poor children. He helped several children with money for their schooling. He tutored disabled children, when they were unsuccessful in their studies at school. On weekends, he gave his time to various community projects, even before attending to his own chores. He lived for others. His extraordinary adolescent behaviour kept his parents busy answering questions about him.

People asked, "Why is he so generous? What's in it for him?"

"He doesn't have the normal male territory and material acquisition characteristic," Marko explained, "you know, the one that causes so much trouble. But it's not lack of aggression that makes him different, there are plenty of passive kids. No, it's his generosity towards people he hardly knows. Most people will pool their resources with their sexual mate and, to a degree, with their kin. But they don't offer help to strangers the way he does. He cares about people, all people."

His parents were watching Abajoe, 14, cart racing on a slope. He heard them talking with the father of his friend, Peter.

"Abajoe's very sharing compared with Peter," said the father. "It's usually thought of as male to grab at possessions, isn't it? Is Abajoe more of a female do you think?"

He knew that sexuality was regarded as a spectrum rather than different sides of a coin.

"No," answered T One, "females are just as interested in territory acquisition as males. They tend to be more subtle, less physical. Abajoe's geneplex isn't gender-linked. It's true that there are more females than males without territoriality, like Mother Teresa was. But most people are territorial, unfortunately. It causes competition instead of collaboration and wastes community capital."

He raced Peter and won. Then they swapped carts.

"Abajoe wants to share his resources and skills with all people…like reports of Jesus in the Bible," said Marko. "It's very unusual – a recessive trait."

They raced again and Peter won this time. He let him keep using his cart.

"He seems to be possessed by a need to share," Peter's father said. "When someone behaves like he's possessed, the next question is, who or what is he possessed by?"

"Ask him."

"I will." Peter's father called to him. "Do you believe in God, Abajoe?"

"Maybe. Actually I am agnostic," he answered softly.

"So who do you serve?"

"No one; just myself."

"It seems like you do things for others, not for yourself."

"No. I do them for myself."

"But how do you benefit?"

"It pleases me to help others when I can, that's all. I'm not a do-gooder. When I help others, it is good for me."

"It seems to be ingrained," Peter's father said. "He just has a reflex for a limited type of altruism, giving to others when he can afford to, sharing when he has plenty. Do you think he inherited it?"

"There's no history of it in my family for at least ten generations," said Transcending One. "I've had a DNA search done. It's the sort of thing that word is passed down about. My half of his genes could carry a mutation."

"I know how I'm a carrier," Marko told them. "Mungipingu, my great-grandfather, was famed for his spirit of community and I heard that he was like his mother."

"Indigenous persons?" asked the friend.

Marko nodded. "They were elders. They both sacrificed their lives fighting racial discrimination. They fought for equal rights for people of all races, rich and poor alike…"

"It's not about equal rights," Marko interrupted her. "That's white fella talk, same as looking out for yourself. What I mean is, moving over, sharing what you have. Like my grandfather, Arnhem, did when he gave away the indigenous position at the top of the pecking order.[*]

(* See by the same author 'The Top Is In The Middle', a planned publication).

He didn't have to: he knew that the pecking order was unfair to Browns, the third arrivals. We indigenous people didn't want first peck at everything, even though it did our self-esteem the world of good. It wasn't fair to Browns and the others. So Arnhem did something about it that cost us: he got rid of the pecking order. Everyone was equal. It was the right thing to do. Abajoe is like him, a sharer."

"Sharing can go too far. We have to look after our own first," said Peter's father.

"Abajoe does that," replied Marko. "He only shares what he can do without."

"Let's hope that one day when he's Prime Minister, he won't give away the farm."

"He couldn't do that even if he wanted to. Indigenous people hold the land in trust for future generations. He can only share how the land is used, for example, between the members of a commune."

"Nomadic peoples often share," said T One, the Prime Minister. "It makes for efficient living. Now with scarcity of water, food, energy and materials, it is once again highly valued. Abajoe's sharing approach is making him popular already."

"The girls won't leave him alone. He'll have a busy sex life," Marko laughed.

T One frowned. "Promiscuity and polygamy are not genetic. They're acquired, as well you know. Nor are they efficient reproduction units in a peaceful society. You are not to teach him any of your dirty tricks," she warned. Marko, with his good looks and top job, had cut a swathe through the ranks of Australian femininity before finding T One.

"Chip off the old block," he laughed, "willing to share it around."

Abajoe's interest in sharing was an extreme case of the new mutualism that had displaced individual material achievement. Materialism had reached its high water mark 50 years earlier and had now declined. Material possession no longer brought esteem, and in some countries, it was criminal. It was not used for selecting a reproduction partner. For most people, possessing and consuming were the antithesis of minimizing use of resources, shrinking one's carbon footprint and committing to spiritualism.

A person's benign influence on others now counted for more than wealth or income. Because he made sure others were taking care of his loans and respecting his territories, Abajoe's spiritual domain increased.

Grateful borrowers often returned their loan with gifts. He used them for the benefit of others. Like a library with most of its books out on loan, he had an important place in the community.

Abajoe lived in a commune with the Jurilpa people. Their territory was the former suburb of Westbury, South Meannjin and Gravely Park. They were descendants of the Wagarra tribe that lived there before European invasion. The most prominent family was Abajoe's, the famous Yabras. Jurilpa people were loyal Middle Way Party supporters. They supplied bodyguards to protect the Prime Minister at home and guarded her when she was away. Most indigenous people supported the Middle Way Party but Jurilpa territory was adjacent to the Lota people to the north, who were not kin. They supported the Progress Party and its plans to return to materialism.

"The rejection of materialism came slowly," Marko had lectured the young Abajoe, Paula and their companions in a lesson on the age of technology. "It started three centuries ago, with planned obsolescence due to shoddy materials and careless design. Suppliers stopped doing maintenance. Components were designed to fail after a short time. When one component failed, the whole unit had to be replaced. They stopped making replacements for previous models so the whole unit would have to be replaced. Replacement models were designed so they could not be replaced by any other brand. Eventually products were updated solely to make sales without competition. Suppliers had usurped their customers' choice of products and services. Is there a problem with that?"

"Yes," replied Abajoe. "The technology would become expensive and dysfunctional."

"Correct," Marko replied. "It was a rip-off. In some cases, it was already dysfunctional, because suppliers' advertisements carried subliminal messaging that exploited customers. It went too far when suppliers rapaciously misled the public with dishonest performance information, trapping the unwary into buying products that were useless. Then people rejected all but essential products, turning away from manufacturers. As they owned less, there was more sharing within communes. Industry withered away, until only products for communal sharing were produced."

During famines, it had been everyone for themselves. Afterwards, people were distrustful of each other, were reluctant to lend their meagre resources and gave a weak effort to community projects. Under T One's leadership, the population embarked on living in communes. Community was gradually restored. Physiques, health and longevity improved and people could expect to live to 130.

Materialism declined further. People learned to do without products and services that had once been available. The Governments of Zelta and T One encouraged material austerity and meditation to guide people's lives. It was an extension of the indigenous dreaming culture that enabled development of objective languages, observation and analysis. It was an empirical oral science. They had learned to evaluate technologies for their contribution to survival and sustenance of cultural traditions. Consequently, people had little interest in scientific experimentation, except where the scientific conclusion would converge with sustaining the environment.

Commune people enjoyed rich social lives. A family usually meditated together once a day. Each of them concentrated on a physical sensation or a mantra to the exclusion of all else. Meditation nurtured the mind by mental processes like those used to grow plants: preparing the soil, planting seeds, weeding, nurturing and harvesting a crop of ideas, insights and enlightenment. People pursued enlightenment through religion or meditation in communes of kindred spirits united to support each other.

Nevertheless, there were residues of materialism, competition and selfishness that prevented commune life from transcending earthly concerns. Abajoe's reputation for sharing was like a breath of fresh air and he excited interest and inspired communes to new heights of spiritualism, when he was invited as a youth leader to speak to groups at communes.

When he was 17, Abajoe had invited his parents to one of his weekly soccer games in the junior competition. His team were his MWP friends, calling themselves 'Middle Way'. This week, they were playing the Epicureans, a commune that grew specialty foods, such as coffee and spices and traded them for staples.

Abajoe loped backwards and forwards with the play; tall, medium-build and dark. His jet-black hair bounced a little with his tireless, springy step. His face was oval, with a high forehead widening down to a straight flat nose of medium length above a broad mouth and triangular jaw. His restless, blue-grey eyes were set wide below bushy eyebrows, with high cheekbones. Overall, it was a handsome determined face, observant, thoughtful and communicative.

"Yes!" Abajoe commanded John, his best mate, playing on the wing, from his position as striker. He was in front of the goal. His pass rushed towards him in slow play at chest height, too low for his head and too high for his boot. He could hear the grass ripping as a defender behind him tried to get to the ball past him and he instinctively blocked him. He found himself in trial and error land, a place with which his 17 years was familiar. 'I haven't had one like this before,' he thought. 'So I can try anything. If I stay cool, I can work it out. What's best for the team?' The ball had nearly reached him.

"C'mon Ab," his mother yelled support from the sideline, caring more that he should acquit himself well than about his team winning. Abajoe knew he had his parents' approval whatever he did, because he had their respect. He had his own space. He could do what he wanted.

He considered running forward, catching the ball by softening his abdomen, dropping it to his feet, dribbling it past a defender and blasting it into the net. There was a small chance of getting through and scoring, but it would be greedy of him because there was a better passing option. His forwards were covered by markers but John had started a run towards the goal. Now John was marked and covered by a back-pedalling defender. He couldn't pass to him. Another alternative was booting the ball high to drop in front of the goal and sprinting in for a header. There was a fair chance of scoring.

The ball reached him, coming hard for his belly.

Most players would have gone for the shot, keeping the ball as long as possible to show their skills, while the chances of getting through disappeared as defenders arrived. But Abajoe's play was best for the team. He booted it up and over the goalmouth and tore in. It was generous to the other forwards, but risky. John was there to head the ball but a defender pushed him and a penalty was whistled. Abajoe took the shot, feinted right as he ran in, putting the goalie on the wrong foot and hammering it left in a long arc past the wall of bodies into the top of the net.

John, Paula and the others ran in to hug him.

The players' and crowd's attention was riveted on him as he jogged lithely back to the centre, as if the game and spectators existed only for him to demonstrate his prowess. His body had the conformity and musculature of an Olympian middle distance runner. They watched his every move and his every move had intense grace. They knew he was gifted and the only question was in what sphere he would choose to be first amongst equals. Would he follow his family's tradition and go into politics or become a professional sportsman?

Abajoe was used to being looked at and liked it. His confidence effervesced in bursts of creativity that raised his awareness, focused his concentration and lifted his performance. He knew instinctively that it wouldn't get any better than this, even if he became a star. As he got older, he would get smarter, but never again would he be so smart at being 17 years old. He couldn't do all the things older people could do. Nor could they do the things only a person of 17 could do. The great thing about his age was that it was different to being 16. He would never be like this again and he loved it. No age was any better than any other was; everyone was a person and counted equally.

Non-indigenous children in peer groups demanded distinctive attention for their egos but indigenous adolescents were more modest. Abajoe gave his attention to other people's ideas rather than pursuing self-promotion. But he always got attention and knew that he was special. Growing up in the Yabra family, the subtext was that one day, he would be Prime Minister.

A leader's popularity can divide a team, with as many players jealous of them as are loyal. However, Abajoe's success was the team's success and every player backed him to the hilt. Each player knew that Abajoe was counting on him or her to give his or her very best. As Captain his attention would be on them as much as on himself. Each knew that if they let the team down, then Abajoe would take it up with them at the first opportunity.

When the Epicureans scored, he talked with the player who had let the scorer through. He walked back with him from the goal.

"You would normally have stopped that, mate," he spoke gently and kindly. "Got something on your mind?"

"My mother's ill. I was worrying."

"I'm sorry," Abajoe put his arm around his shoulder. "I know you'll do everything you can for her. Let me know if I can help or if you need any money. Do you want off?"

"Nah, I'll be okay."

"We don't want you just okay. We want your best. I think you should go to her. You won't lose your place on the team, I promise."

"Thanks, mate. I'll owe you. You'll get my best ever."

"I know."

Abajoe beckoned a substitute to come on and the player ran off the field.

At half time, they were in front but his parents had to meet someone and left. Their pleasure in watching him was great. During the game, he had never sought glory for himself, only for his team. It was a behaviour that Yabra leaders had espoused in freeing the nation from corruption. There was no limit to his unselfishness. He always looked for a mutual solution. The genetic fluke, that had endowed him with group concern alone, kept thrusting him into the limelight. There could be no limit to his political ambitions but he didn't have any for himself.

From an early age, Abajoe seemed destined for greatness in the service of a great cause. People equated him to Jesus, Gandhi and Mandela. He seemed inspired but he had no affiliation. They knew that when he did take up a cause, he would become a famous leader. It was strange how much people believed in this boy after only a brief encounter.

T One overheard a conversation between two parents as they left a theatre, where his followers had performed a play written by Abajoe.

"That was amazing. Have you met him?"

"Yes."

"Did you see his eyes, when he looked at you?"

"He knew me, as if he had come across me before. But he hasn't... not that I know of. When he talked with me, it was as his friend. He confided in me and asked me questions that he couldn't have asked if he hadn't known me before."

"Maybe he has great insight...or special powers."

"Spooky!"

"No. I trusted him implicitly. I wanted him to...this sounds stupid...I wanted him to be in charge... It sounds stupid, he's so young. There's something wonderful about him."

"Wow...and after you talked for only a few minutes."

"He's a phenomenon all right!"

"Our Lani thinks he's wonderful...very mature."

"He passed the voting test when he was only 13."

"Well, if he's going to be a leader, he's started in the right family."

"He doesn't seem like a politician. He's more like a spiritual leader."

"A statesman? A prophet?"

"Maybe. We'll see."

Abajoe knew he was different. He wanted to use his gifts to help people. When his companions started calling him 'Messiah', he read about Jesus' life and death and the prophecies of a second coming in the Bible. He could find no signs that his existence was spiritual but coincidences happened to him with such frequency that he felt he must be under the influence of some higher power. He began to treat his team as 'disciples' and his game plans became prophecies.

"You shall keep the ball from the enemy and deliver it from above unto him or her, who is without the goal mouth."

At first, the players were amused and humoured him.

"Behold, Cruc has risen and come amongst us. Speak to us of soccer, O Holy One!"

He taught them the ethics and morality of the game with inspirational parables.

"Once there was a man, who was rich and well-respected but he had the misfortune to lose all his money on an unlucky investment. He was bankrupt. Some of his friends said, "I don't know what his mistake is, but it might be catching!" They deserted him. However, one stuck by him and lent him money. He went to gamble it at the racetrack and his friend said, "Why are you spending it this way?"

"Why not?" he replied. "I am finished."

"No," he replied. "This is only a temporary setback. Use the money to pay off someone and ask him for a job. If he is unable, go to another. You can make your own good luck. You deserve some but the horses will lose it for you."

"So, he did what his friend told him and within a few years he had paid him back twofold and recovered his position. What you must remember is that when someone on our team is having a bad day and wants to go off, do not desert him or her. Be sure to feed them good ball so they can get some success and recover their confidence. Then they will do the same for you. You have to look after each other and share your good luck with their bad luck until it is mended."

Abajoe's stories were taken seriously by his disciples and he began speaking to groups about teamwork and his political ideas wherever he went. His messianic posture became full-time and his companions' raillery was transformed into respect. He was their leader and they followed him in good times and in bad.

"Let's go!" he called out to his team as they ran back for the kick off. As they got older, players tended to care about the group more but they became less adventurous, refraining from trying new things that could draw criticism if they failed. Yet all players had to take risks to gain opportunities.

"Shoot," he yelled when a player was about to pass the ball, instead of trying a shot, because he could be accused of being greedy if he missed. But Abajoe encouraged cerebration rather than caution.

"Shooting is a lottery; you have to be in it to win it. The risks have to be weighed and the right balance found in every situation."

Indigenous persons were the best team players. Most whites played for themselves first and the team second – they tried for self-attention, rather than helping each other put the ball in the net. While a non-indigenous person was jousting with a defender, an indigenous person would have taken the ball through an opening and be looking for support. On most teams, he would look in vain because the man who made the break usually was too selfish to pass until too late and running in support was a mug's game. But Abajoe's soccer team was different: under his influence, players passed the ball to the player, who had the best opportunity.

Few teams supported each other as much as Abajoe's players did. Other players tried to make their position play look good, failing to exploit opportunities that required them to step out of position. Their players competed for prima donna status and winning came third after avoiding mistakes. But Abajoe had them play the game like chess. He started moves for the whole team to finish. They vied to take his passes because he opened up scoring opportunities. He varied his own role continually and their opponents learned to use several players to cover him, leaving openings for his team mates. Abajoe was after a team win, above all else.

They won this game 5–1. Afterwards, there were high spirits in the changing room. They carried Abajoe shoulder high into the shower and soaked him. He didn't mind – they were just showing that he was theirs rather than the way it had seemed on the field, that they were his. Laughing he wrung out his jersey.

If individuals like Abajoe would multiply, mankind's future would lie in devolved communities. Individuals would have the commitment of African hunting dogs, running a wildebeest to exhaustion, each taking his turn in the pursuit, each with special skills in overpowering the victim, working together and sharing equally in the kill.

How different such a human community would be from those of the industrial era when, like leopards, the raising of the young has been entrusted to a solo female's hunting prowess and good fortune, while males form a coalition to defend her territory. If either fail, the young perish or their development is stunted. Abajoe's type could lead to less precarious, more social working and living.

"See you at the Harlequin," he told his team, naming a local club as he carried his wet clothes out the door. "The drugs are on me."

"Let's go," was the reply and they left, walking there as a mob, the males calling out to females along the road to join them. Abajoe walked with Paula and John, talking about how the others in their team had played, considering changes for their next game.

He didn't always go to the club with his team. Resisting age-peer pressure, he socialized widely with people of different ages. He sought out other ethnicities and religious groups and took part in music, song and dance in a spirit of peacefulness.

"What are you hanging out with them for?" a team mate asked him once, when he had attended a Yamen festival. "It's all mumbo jumbo with them."

"You don't know their language. I'm finding out about them, their history and what they want. They're good people."

"So long as you remember who your friends are."

The soccer team sometimes clashed with other teams verbally and even physically in rough play. Abajoe acknowledged differences, sought inclusivity and defused conflict. His objective perspective was valued and he increasingly found himself thrust into a leadership role.

Besides his sport, Abajoe, at age 17, was in a political group with his disciples and others, where his idealism and commitment led their activism. His activism taught him grassroots politics and to practice the skills he saw his parents and their associates using.

Abajoe had learned to campaign by accompanying his parents. Now he practiced the more partisan skills required to attract the attention of the media. While his age peers were learning to string together an argument, he would be organizing a protest rally or a petition. While they were learning how to compose a persuasive speech, he would be persuading national conferences to adopt his policy proposals. While his contemporaries were studying constitutional powers, he would be generating political power, playing hard and fast for a win. Activism, the way he played it, was like soccer, requiring a captain on the field.

He developed his political skills and created a network of support, with his friends and disciples going with him everywhere. On and off the field, in the clubhouse or in a local restaurant, he gained and kept loyalty. At 17, he was an influential leader of the nation's youth, with an extensive network of supporters.

When they got to the Harlequin, Abajoe opened a slate with the pharmacist. He was well known there. His largesse extended off the field too. The team were used to him paying for their food and drugs. He had a lot more money than they did, because his parents were in top-paying jobs. He liked to share his good fortune with them.

"Thank your mother for all this shit," said John, trying to talk through the echo only he could hear from his drug. John, who was also indigenous, was his key supporter within their political group. They stood side by side, relaxing, watching the holographs of aliens mingling with the group.

"I'll tell her what you said," Abajoe replied evenly. He wasn't doing any drugs himself, saying that he wanted to meditate later. He had bought a neuro drink to boost his learning from the game. He occasionally did use drugs, like the others, for novel social experiences.

"You had better say 'drugs' not 'shit'. Don't want to upset the PM. She was a scientist wasn't she? Scientists call a spade a spade."

"She still is, part-time."

"How come? Who's PM the rest of the time?"

"My father. He's deputy."

"Why isn't she full-time?"

"She believes that the PM has to balance the work with ordinary concerns, to keep her job in proportion. She says the last thing we need is a megalomaniac in charge. Two days a week, she has a welfare job with Meannjin City Council. She finds out about people who are sick, old or poor. Then, as PM, she can deal with any national welfare issues."

John's curiosity was satisfied. "Well, thank her for the drugs. It's a good job someone earns some money. Part-time leadership is rather indigenous," he mused. "We bring in elders with different skills as needed, with the hierarchy depending on the issue and the experience around. For example, we would have one government for welfare and another for war."

"It makes sense," Abajo replied. "I wonder if there will be a..."

They were interrupted when someone came up and asked Abajoe for a student loan. Whereas some people saved their money and others wasted it, Abajoe lent the money given to him. He was not a soft touch. He gave it out wisely, to help those in need. Although very well off, Abajoe required that when others borrowed from him, they acknowledge the ancestral rights of the Yabras, operating as the Middle Way Party.

"I can loan you the money but it is to be repaid to the Middle Way Party when you have obtained a job. If you can't repay it then you must do voluntary work to that value with the Party. I will pass full details of the loan to Central Office."

"What type of voluntary work?"

"It could be care of aged people, or labouring on construction of a dam or paddy. Would you have any problems with that?"

"No. I'll repay the money next year when I get a job."

"Then I'll credit your account tomorrow."

"Thanks very much, Abajoe."

Most Australians spent their time socializing, doing a minimum of work to support their lifestyle. Most used drugs to escape, but he meditated. Abajoe valued practical experiences more than formal education and became a voluntary worker, developing skills in problem solving and in educating others. His studies focused mainly on science, using programmed learning materials. He stood in the shoes of the discoverers of physics, chemistry, biology and earth science. From his father, he learned about technology and the philosophy of science, and developed expertise in water and energy supply. From his mother, he learned the behavioural sciences. They discussed problems that they came across in their work and related these to possible experiments. This led him to his own investigations. He had learned to experiment in horticulture and animal husbandry from his development of the family businesses in hydroponics, poultry and rossits.

"What's your overall goal, Ab?" Paula sidled up to him, rehearsing him. She had asked him this before.

Abajoe didn't hesitate.

"To make Australia and the world a safer place to live," he said, handing her his drink for a swig. They always shared together. He looked her over.

When Paula walked by, heads turned. She was fair-skinned, blonde, slender, supple and poised like a cheetah. Her presence was magnetic and women looked at the clothes she had on, while men took them off in their minds. He liked the tilt of her nose, her mischievous grin, her creamy skin, dressed in green, so different to his dark looks.

"You look great," he said, taking his drink back from her.

Paula, his adopted sister, had grown up with him. They lived next door and he worked, studied, played soccer and was politically active with her. She was in love with him. He occasionally had friendly sex with her but kept it in a separate compartment, like brushing his teeth, so their intimacy could never become a passion. He could always rely on her for anything. He never really focused on her as a person, who had feelings for him that could be damaged.

He allowed her to think that, eventually, their relationship could become exclusive, because it seemed to be a possibility. He liked her more than any female he had ever known. He had let her think that when he had sown his wild oats, his passion and commitment would be hers. He usually had sex with others and told her he wasn't ready to commit. Devoted and loyal, she suffered his affairs in smouldering silence.

He knew she was hurting but she knew him too well. She had the fatal flaw of knowing who he was. He liked women who didn't recognise him from the news. He tried to hide the fame of his family from them. He liked to score women in his own right, rather than as an icon.

"I want to be wanted for what I am, not who I am," he told her. "When they find out who I am, it's all over."

"It's not your family that's the attraction for me," she told him, "it's you. We would be good together."

"You are very important to me, but at the moment I want to be free."

"Are you looking for a better woman?"

"No. You know I think you're terrific. I don't know. I'm just looking around."

"Doing a survey, are you? Well don't expect me to wait for you."

He couldn't imagine being without her. They did everything together. She was goalkeeper on the soccer team. Tall and agile, she played the position colourfully. She often clowned around, mirroring the team's mood, keeping them in hysterics as she imitated an opponent's walk or distracted a shooter with a bizarre posture or mime. But when they were losing, she absorbed the team's self-criticism.

"I carry the can for everyone's mistakes," she said, resigned. "You get the glory, I get the derogatory."

"You're my anchor woman, Paula!" said Abajoe. "I know I can count on you."

"Yes, and it's not fair," she muttered, blinded by tears, booting the ball as hard as she could.

It was her choice to make sacrifices for him, he told himself. He was completely honest with her and, if he was indecisive, then that was the way it was. He felt too young and inexperienced to make a commitment, but he would be a loyal friend to her. Didn't Jesus keep his women at arm's length?

"Why?" asked Paula, wide-eyed, taking the drink and sipping playfully.

"Why what?" he said, coming out of his reverie.

"Why do you want to make Australia and the world a safer place to live?"

He thought for a moment.

"Our family has suffered from drought...you lost your parents... my stepbrother died...he hadn't even been born. We have to be friends with our neighbours, so they will help us if it happens again."

"Bhakaria?" She passed the drink back. They always shared everything.

"I haven't yet worked out about Bhakaria," he said.

Paula liked to recount histories. "That's what Australians have been saying for 300 years. Once, a long time ago, our Government started to embrace the Bhakarian culture, with language immersion in schools, exchanges of students, immigrant access to land and minerals and the beginnings of trade. However, the disparity in conditions between the two nations caused so much unrest that the flames of mutual development were quickly extinguished.

"Australia laid herself bare when they came here to help in the Great Famine, but since then we have gone our separate ways," she continued. "Mum still keeps relations with Bhakaria centralised through her President. It's a cool relationship...no real intercourse, if you can imagine that..."

Abajoe smiled. Paula's humour tended to be raunchy.

"School students these days learn nothing of their huge neighbour's language or culture, and immigration from Bhakaria has been mostly illegal. So what do you think we can do about that? Would we want to stir the pot?" She took the drink again.

"We should support each other," said Abajoe, "and value diversity."

Paula was doubtful. "Give them a share of our resources?"

"That's an oxymoron. Giving isn't sharing."

"Well, barter...minerals for food."

"It's all we can do. They are more developed than us and their civil society is, if anything, more advanced."

"Ours fell apart in the Great Famine. But we're getting there..."

"They are having trouble with poverty and social welfare due to epidemics and an ageing population."

"How can we support them?" asked Paula, taking the drink from him.

"Maybe we can take some of their emigrants...I don't know."

"But you are against immigration!"

Abajoe winced. That was putting it too bluntly. He wanted to share the riches of his homeland with deserving refugees but they could only be identified with case-by-case investigation.

"I am against an open door policy. If we let them come freely, so many would come, our culture could be threatened."

"That's a false dilemma. Can't we let some come?"

"Only a very few. It really is a dilemma. If we let many come, it could get out of control. It could create pressure that worsens relations with Bhakaria."

"It was the reverse during the Great Famine, when Bhakaria would only let a few of us in."

"I've an idea," said Paula, passing the drink back. "In the rossits' experiment, why don't we make a hole through the wall between the two pens and fit it with a grill. Then we can monitor their attempts to get through."

"Like boat people trying to cross the border."

"Or an invasion force."

"Great idea," he said. "How about another hole from each pen into the passageway, blocked with a grill, to see if they are trying to escape to anywhere-will-do?"

"Suppose there is pressure to accept immigrants from hardship in either nation. Under what conditions might Australia let Bhakarians in?"

"We could let in people who are a burden to them, from poor areas."

"Yes; and old people," said Paula, "but we wouldn't want them either. They might not let young people go. Those, who they keep from emigrating, are young, skilled people. They are needed in Bhakaria to support the aging population."

"But there isn't always enough work there..."

"If we let in guest workers...we need workers for the mines..."

"Who would send home money..."

"And when they go home, they would understand our situation with droughts," Paula enthused. "We would be helping Bhakaria overcome overcrowding and poverty..."

"And they would dissuade their people from colonising us again," Abajoe said grimly, referring to Bhakaria's sending of settlers to Australia 15 years earlier.

"And supply them with minerals..."

"And they could supply us with food in a drought."

"We're in a drought now aren't we?"

"There's always a drought here somewhere," he said, putting the empty glass on the bar. "We haven't got much time. Let's get going. We can nut out a paper to let in guest workers to the conference. Then tomorrow we can organise a rally."

The two circulated through the group saying their goodbyes and left together, hand in hand.

CHAPTER 3

Family Fare Tower

Abajoe pedalled his cyclo around the puddles to the local shops to buy groceries and poultry and rossit feed. The rain could only be a respite from the drought. The shops still had most foods but stocks were running low. He and Paula grew most of the food for the three generations of their family, but bought rice, spices, sugar, flour, kangaroo meat, fish, vegetable oil, fruit and for a treat, chocolate and snow cream. For animal feed, they bought cereals and meat by-products in season. They were expensive and would cost more than this week's sales from their gardens, taking half his earnings from the 'Family Fare' shows.

He went to the shops every second week, while Paula cleaned the units. The commune's retail outlets in an old shopping mall were about 10 minutes by car away but he set an example of economy and fitness and cycled there in half an hour. They used their electric car, shared with his grandparents and great-grandparents, for moving groups over longer distances when there was no public transport available.

There was little traffic – mostly cyclos like his, with only an occasional delivery truck. One lane had been dug up and was now used as gardens. Unfortunately, the road surface had deteriorated to potholes; bitumen for repairs was no longer available. Concrete was too expensive, except for major construction work, which was rare. Bitumen to repair the road had been recycled from supermarket car parks and the areas converted to food growing.

In the commune's shops, Abajoe loaded his cyclo directly from the containers of staples. In the animal feed section, he found some freshly harvested, cheap corncobs. They could feed them to their rossits and poultry, supplementing the green feed from the gardens. Most would go as direct feed, but some would be processed through the amino acids synthesiser. He filled half a dozen sacks, all the cyclo could carry, and pedalled to the checkout.

He was well known to the people there, not just from 'Family Fare' and his political campaigning, but from his whole life of involvement with the local community. The commune's market was where he communicated with his 'balangay'. The balangay had once been boat builders, who would go on a voyage together and they were the basic unit of his political organisation. These were his people, who looked out for him and who did their best for him within the Kurilpa Commune. He looked after their interests when he could. People crowded around to talk with him and it took him several hours to get away.

"When is the Middle Way Party going to encourage more industry?" a shopper asked him. "We need more goods and more jobs."

"What goods do we need?"

"What we used to have. Tools and household appliances. Clothes and shoes. Medicines and healthcare products. Cleaning products and paints. Electrical generators and cars. I could go on and on."

"I agree with you about tools but isn't life easier without the others, without having to earn to buy them?"

"I like to have a job and hard work to do. I don't like growing food by myself and I want to earn money and buy food."

"But you can do that now."

"No. There aren't any vacant jobs out where I live and they pay next to nothing. I'm a robot servicer, but there isn't any work."

"Could you move to a place where industry is starting up?"

"Competition for jobs is fierce and they're all sewn up by the locals. We should get factories to come here."

Abajoe thanked him and suggested he should propose a tool-making project to their local commune. He would get other people's ideas on developing industry and there could be a Party policy initiative. He would contact him and inform him what had been decided.

People told him their concerns and these contacts were a great asset to him in judging which of the Party's policies were most popular. For each petitioner, he wrote in a notebook the actions he had undertaken and when to follow up with them.

The near-deserted city was under the overall control of Meannjin South Community Council. The roads, factories and shopping malls were mostly empty. The state government had withered long ago and the peripatetic national government had devolved most of its functions to local government. Office towers, where a generation before national and state bureaucrats had controlled the city's industrial economy, now stood empty and crumbling. The local communes controlled the little commerce remaining. Jurilpa Commune operated from a handful of large shops at ground level in an old shopping mall. Shops, that had once supplied dreams implanted by manufacturers, now stood empty. The people had become independent and spiritual: they now had their own dreams.

Abajoe finished his week's shopping. With his cyclo heavily laden, he pushed it up hills and it took him an hour to get home. As he pedalled towards Family Fare Tower along the main thoroughfare, he looked up at it. The upper storeys glinted with solar panels, their shiny black faces upturned to the sun. Abajoe thought how beautiful The Tower looked. An efficient system, like The Tower's, had its own special beauty for him because he knew about energy technology. He thought back to a recent 'Family Fare' show, in which he had described The Tower's energy system, to show viewers how a family could make their home self-sufficient.

The show had opened with a close-up of Abajoe's well-known face, with their familiar 20-storey building behind. He had spoken to the camera.

"Today I'm going to show you our energy system. My family came to live in this empty tower after the first famine. There was a solar system already installed. We have kept it going and improved it to convert the sun's energy arriving at The Tower into enough energy for our family's requirements. We also export into the commune grid. The grid distributes electricity and stores it by recycling water into a hydro dam."

Shot of the poles of the grid marching away beside the deserted boulevard and the commune's pumped storage dam.

"We knew we couldn't obtain all the energy in the radiation from the sun because there would be some left in our waste that is too low in energy to be extracted. We try to minimise waste energy. Here are our energy wastes.

"About 90% of the sun's energy reflects from shiny surfaces."

Shots of glare from the shiny surfaces of the solar panels and glass outer walls.

"Of the 10% the building captures, more than 80% is re-radiated from hot, dark surfaces."

Shots of black solar panels and dark surfaces in full sun.

"Of the 2% going to energy converters, only about 25% is converted to electricity: the remaining heat is taken away by the panel coolant.

Some goes to hot water taps and the rest warms the garden rooms to get winter growth."

Shots of pipes leaving panels, a steamy shower and a room filled with hydroponic vegetables.

"The remaining 0.5% useful solar energy heats thermocouples. When two dissimilar metals that are touching each other are heated, electricity is generated and flows through them around a circuit. The problem is to get the sun's heat arriving in an instant of time in two dimensions absorbed and converted efficiently, requiring three dimensions. A design is needed like breathing, where oxygen entering the lungs branches out into smaller and smaller passages until it reaches tiny spherical rooms called alveoli. The walls are capillary tubes where blood flows and dissolves the oxygen."

Diagram of lung vessels.

"The technology for converting solar radiation to electricity is similar."

Comparable diagram of a branching network, leading to thermocouples. The network is a fractal design, with the basic six-sided shape repeated at a smaller and smaller scale.

"The radiation is absorbed by black polyethylene liquid alloy, which has a high heat capacity. It heats up and flows into and through a network leading to capillaries with thermocouples wound around them. The current generated is transformed to a high voltage for use and export."

Micro photo of capillary unit encased in glass and stacked in a panel.

"This technology is tried and tested. These panels were installed when there were 60 families living here 40 years ago. With only four of us in residence, with our food growing, The Tower exports electricity to the commune, sufficient for many families."

Shot of Abajoe with The Tower's coronet of solar panels facing the sun behind him.

"Solar technology has advanced and now self-sufficiency is within reach of most households. The cost, if you are prepared to assemble the components yourself, is surprisingly cheap. Your commune will provide help. The sun delivers a huge amount of free energy and the challenge is to make the most of it."

Fade to credits.

He had arrived at The Tower. He felt a surge of affection for this place, where he had lived all his life, and learned his energy and water technology skills. He pushed the heavily laden cyclo up the front ramp, through a deciduous forest in the shade of the building. As it was summer, the leaves cooled the air flowing into the conditioning system. In winter, the sun penetrated the bare branches and heated the air being circulated through the part of the building they used. He walked around to the fire escape door at the rear of the building and under the canopy of a tiny rainforest. The evergreen leaves shaded and cooled by transpiration, the air flowing past into the electrical system. With satisfaction, he heard the voltage rectifier in the basement vibrating the leaves of rows of bushes over the air ducts. Paula must be running the washing machine, he thought, drawing power from the batteries in the basement that ran the hungry studio equipment and made recording at night possible.

Despite the panels and batteries, the commune couldn't supply enough power for the lift, and there was a regulation preventing its use. He could run it from a generator but manure and plant wastes barely provided enough biogas for pumping and cooking. He would have to sweat the shopping up the stairs.

The air inside was fairly cool on his skin, as he carried sacks of corn through to the poultry barns on the ground floor. By the time he had lugged boxes of groceries up to the first floor and bags of pellets up to the rossits on the fourth, the perspiration dripped from his brow. He peeled off his shirt. He peeked at the rossits in the pens of the experiment. Both does had kindled and their pouches were bulging with pink fingerlings. He guessed the population in each pen had leapt from two to about 12. Pleased, he went down to tell Paula.

"Cold drink?" she asked. She was in her cleaning apron, hands on hips, openly admiring his glistening muscles.

She brought him a glass of cold water and he gulped it down. She seemed different in her apron, homely and domesticated, instead of her usual free, wilful self. It triggered memories from his culture's past and he played with the idea of her as his woman. His pulse quickened and his member stirred. He made a plan.

When they went into the freezer room with the meats, the sudden chill made them draw in breaths. It was run by solar panels on the roof and delivered most cooling on the hottest days. It was thickly insulated to stay below zero overnight and during cloudy weather. It also stored frozen vegetables between harvest and consumption in the winter months, when fresh vegetables were scarce.

When Paula was bent over a cabinet packing away his purchases, he put his arms around her from behind and cupped her breasts through the apron.

She started and laughed, then turned to face him. They kissed, at first gently, then ravenously. He untied her apron and then released her sarong, letting it fall as he pulled down her panties and she undid his sarong. She shivered as his cold hands held her buttocks. Their bodies sought each other's warmth, convulsing with ecstasy, as they stood gyrating in the cloudy, cold air between the shelves of food containers. Waiting for each other, they together reached a shuddering climax. Soon after, their bodies unlocked and steamed as they parted.

They kissed perfunctorily and Paula, naked, put on her apron and went back to packing the cabinet, hurrying against the cold, humming a popular tune. Whistling the melody, Abajoe got dressed and went outside for his weekly check of the water system. His plan with Paula had worked wonderfully but now things had become more complicated. Perhaps she was the one. Did she expect some sort of commitment from him? He knew he should think about it but it was easier to think about the water system. He would think about their relationship later.

He clapped his hands to scare away a duck. The building's three-level underground car park was filled with water up to the first level, which was kept dry for the batteries and water processing plant. Below, carp splashed noisily between the columns. It held water harvested from the roof and surface drains, topped up with treated grey water. The smell was muddy. Every five years, they drained it and dug out the sediment to build up soil in the gardens.

His thoughts followed the flow through his water treatment system. Water from the basement was pumped up five floors to the top hydroponic garden, from where it journeyed down through terraces within each floor, then down to the next floor and so on. At the end, the remaining water, aerated and filtered by the roots it had passed between, was used in the flats for showers and washing. Finally, it was used for flushing wastes to the biogas generator, also in the underground car park.

The building had recently been connected to the water company's supply, although it could only pump for a few hours each day due to the drought and water restrictions. The connection had made life much easier. Before, they had carried top-up water from a creek, dammed by the river embankment three kilometres away. Images of the Prime Minister's family carrying water with buckets and yokes had inspired the nation's families to self-sufficiency in water supply.

Abajoe had an illegal system for recycling water. His pride was a cascade of old baths, where water for drinking trickled through a bed of living sponges, which fed on the bacteria that had decomposed the organic solids in the dirty water. Large molecules of phosphates and other salts, which built up during recycling, were taken out by a nanofilter. The cleaned water for drinking, cooking and hygiene was irradiated for supply to the flats and animals. Several neighbours came daily with containers to purchase drinking water. His defiance of the law against recycling was no secret.

He knew it was illegal for anyone to recycle because pathogens could build up in untreated water. An epidemic had recently been traced to a home-built system. Any overflow from gardens had to be collected and processed by the council's water recycling company who treated it, mixed it with pure water and held it in storage with water plants and fish for one year. The council had a majority of Yamen councillors and they imposed the Yamen purification and diet laws. Drinking of effluents was not permitted, even though his processing had produced pure water.

Many people viewed the council's regulation as overkill but they complied, grudgingly, bearing the extra expense and repurchasing their water at a high price. However, Abajoe continued to recycle defiantly, processing his grey water safely. He hadn't dared to show the system on 'Family Fare', even though he would have liked to. He would keep quiet about it. He did not want to challenge the council. If he went public, T One would have a conflict of interest, that the Yamens in opposition would be keen to exploit: they almost certainly knew and were keeping it up their sleeve.

T One's Government couldn't change the racial make-up of the council, but she could require the council to allow domestic recycling. So far, although she was sympathetic, she had not done so. Consequently, Abajoe had felt protected. Home water recyclers in several communes were following his lead in defying the Meannjin Council. It only seemed a matter of time before the council would make an example of him. He wanted T One to intervene and allow domestic recycling under strict control. But she wouldn't do it.

"Use of local water resources is a matter for the councils," she told him.

"Recycling of drinking water is scientific," he replied. "The non-drinking of effluents is nonsense. All water is an effluent from previous uses. The only issue is the quality and that can be controlled. It is not for councils to be able to prevent recycling because of superstition."

"Then you must show this scientifically. When you have the evidence, the council will have to change or get voted out. You must be patient."

"I'm not so sure. The Yamens are in a majority. There could be conflict."

CHAPTER 4

Flashback to Independence & Floods

"Good evening, Australia," T One had said. Abajoe, Paula and T One were watching an old doco from his mother's library, about her leadership during the Independence Referendum of 2223. She had been a striking, middle-aged woman with frizzy, raven-black hair, wearing an urban camouflage suit. In the background, soldiers lounged beside a military vehicle. She was speaking with authority and urgency to a camera interviewer with a national audience.

"Over there are Bhakarian troops. If tomorrow's referendum succeeds, they will go home. We, in the Middle Way Party, want that. They were brought in by the Progress Party, when it seized power, while our Government was busy obtaining food during the Great Famine three years ago. Now they are overstaying their welcome. After they have gone, there will be a national election and democracy will be restored after three years under the dictator Sudarta."

"Most of you already know me. My name is Transcending One Yabra or T One for short. I am the Leader of the Middle Way Party. If I am elected to represent Meannjin South and our Party forms a Government, I will be your Prime Minister. Come with me now on a virtual tour of Meannjin. We will begin in the suburb of Jurilpa."

The camera showed a tower block and zoomed in on a ground floor balcony, where she stood beside a dark-skinned man of medium build, also wearing camouflage. Two small children stood in front of them, one a dark-haired boy and the other a girl of about the same age with fair hair.

"This is my home in a disused apartment building, where I live with my family. My husband Marko is a water resources engineer and running in Meannjin North. He would be my Deputy. These are our children Paula and Abajoe. They are running everywhere," she said laughing.

"In the apartments above ours, Marko grows vegetables for our family to eat."

The camera showed lush green plants growing under lights in the rooms of several residential apartments.

"The plants grow by hydroponics. Water supply has been a major problem for us, as it has been for many of you. When it rains, we fill the swimming pool and underground car park. Due to the energy shortage since fossil fuels were banned, there isn't enough electricity to pump water up to the gardens. When there is a drought, we have to buy water but there is not enough biogas for the truck to bring water from the reservoir. So, we all give a hand, or rather a shoulder, in carrying water."

Shot of Marko and T One with yokes carrying containers beside road.

"We hope to get connected soon to the water main."

"Now let's have a look inside our unit."

In what was once a bedroom, presiding over a bank of monitors is an intricately carved and gilded wooden chair with a high back and a seat in red velvet.

"Here is the studio where Zelta, my husband Marko's mother, used to take part in our virtual parliament as Prime Minister."

She sat down in the chair. Facing from the front and sides are three cameras on fixed stands and another on a robot arm. She spoke formally, using a remote control to vary the camera shots.

"I hope to become your new Prime Minister. Now that food is once again plentiful, Meannjin is getting back on its feet. But there is no reversal of the exodus from our cities. After the Coal Wars, industry began to recover, but it collapsed again from drought. Hunger drove out most of the surviving city population. The refugees fled to places where there was still enough rainfall to keep water in storages, in the coastal hinterland and in the north. There, they are growing their own food using irrigation. People have gathered in communes and divided up the land into farms of about a hectare.

"Famine is no stranger to Australia. Here in Jurilpa, the Wagarra people have come and gone with the rains for 50,000 years. They led a nomadic existence because the food supply varied locally, depending on irregular rains. They even migrated to the far north, to Bhakaria's islands, when food could not be had on the mainland. Their most important survival strategy was to share territory and resources with their kin: those tribes who always shared with them.

"Before Europeans arrived, the population of Australia was fairly stable, with around half a million people. Indigenous technologies assisted hunting and gathering. When European settlers arrived, they brought technologies that suited conditions in their homelands. They tried to create European conditions by clearing forests and planting monocultures. In the 400 years that followed, the food supply was increased artificially and the population grew 100 fold to 50 million. However, the soil, water, flora and fauna ran down. When the foreign technologies were no longer supported by cheap energy and petrochemicals, the land failed to support the large population.

"After record droughts, there were famines in 2190 and 2206. Deaths were around one million each time. Then catastrophe struck us. Three years ago, when drought had already emptied food stores, epidemic plant diseases left our food crops rotting in the fields. Fifteen million Australians, 30% percent of our population, died."

The camera showed photographs of the diseased plants and a holocaust of emaciated figures wandering the roadsides, hospital corridors blocked by rows of diseased patients, skeletal people dying on dusty, bare allotments and heaps of dead bodies.

"Suspended animation emporia were full and whole families took their own lives, leaving tissue to regenerate clones after the drought. Unfortunately bandits took the energy used to run the coolers and they died."

The photos ended and the camera went back to T One in front of the soldiers.

"Now, we are the survivors."

There was film of an angular, dark-skinned woman with white hair inspecting an almost empty reservoir.

"Five years ago our Prime Minister was Zelta, Marko's mother. Like the two previous Prime Ministers, she was a Yabra Elder, 80 years old. Her father and grandfather each held office for about 40 years."

"Yabra elders have provided Prime Ministers for the past 150 years. They have been the elected national leaders of the many diverse indigenous tribes, who are custodians of all Australian lands. Whereas Caucasians have multiplied 100 times from the time when they first outnumbered Aborigines, indigenous people have only grown five fold. Now there are two and a half million, but they are only five percent of the population. Nevertheless a Yabra has always been the leading Elder of the ruling Middle Way Party. They have been elected to leadership for their wise reconciliation of differences between Australia's racial and religious groups and for their experienced stewardship of land, water, energy and mineral resources.

"In 2220, Zelta's Government was attempting to share out fairly what little food and water remained. It was the worst drought ever but Zelta's Government was blamed for too few water storages."

There was a movie clip of an Aboriginal Elder, dignified, running the gauntlet of an unkempt and angry crowd. Then there were pictures of looting and burning of buildings.

"The Government lost control and the country was terrorised by outlaws. The Opposition Leader, Helen Sudarta, accepted Bhakaria's offer to send troops to restore law and order. With their backing, she deposed Zelta's Government and installed a new Government. But when the rains came and the Great Famine ended, the Bhakarians did not go home. Australia became a Yamen state, like Bhakaria, and the Middle Way Party was banned. Since then Bhakaria has ruled Australia as a colony.

Soldiers had moved up to the camera and were listening. One of them tried to put his hand over the lens. The camera rocked in a scuffle. T One continued talking.

"There, my bodyguards have got the upper hand for the moment, but more Bhakarians will soon be here in force. They have tried to stop our independence movement and have done nothing to repair infrastructure damaged during the Great Famine, or to secure our future.

"Australia is divided along sectarian lines, between on one side the Yamen colonial power and its settlers, and on the other the traditional population of indigenous people and the descendants of European immigrants.

"Now the Regional Government, the South East Union, has forced Sudarta to lift the ban on the Middle Way Party and ordered a referendum. But, as you have seen, the Bhakarians are trying to block our campaign for independence. The SEU has sent observers to ensure the referendum is conducted fairly. Independence is a vital step we need to recover from the Great Famine."

The camera showed a convoy of troop carriers arriving and soldiers disgorging. The sequence was cut to T One dressed in a sarong, with field workers tending horticultural allotments behind.

"Here in Jurilpa, which is a commune in a former Meannjin suburb. The old freeway has been dug up and people now use it to grow vegetables in allotments."

A corridor of verdant gardens was bordered by mounds of concrete rubble. The camera showed people demolishing houses and carrying away building materials. In another shot, gangs of workers were recycling used building materials to construct a large communal facility at the centre of a group of houses.

"Jurilpa Commune Centre is used by the people, who live in the surrounding houses."

A team of residents is preparing food in a large well-equipped kitchen. Others are setting the long tables in a dining hall for about 100 people. Children are kicking a soccer ball around outside in a green space, with players of all ages, girls as well as boys.

"The commune people share the kitchen, refrigerator, generator, batteries, tractor, biogas generator, sports facilities, library, gardening, care of the aged and disabled, with joint parenting and education of their children. There is a commune bus and an electric car. The tasks of growing food, cooking, washing, gardening and child supervision are rostered. Many hands make light work, each according to his or her ability.

"It is a new age of social endeavour with great public works, such as constructing more rice paddies. All these adults are rostered to help build them."

Rice paddies, lush with growth, and gangs of workers building earthworks for new terraces.

A photograph of a large family in front of a rambling house.

"Not all people want to live in a commune. Here are a family of 10 people, who own an entire street. They work all the gardens together as a small farm and share an electric car. The empty houses provide a supply of spare parts and materials. Nearby is common land with the ruins of matchbox houses, where herdsmen now graze kangaroos. Most people are engaged in subsistence activities, first providing for their own needs, then selling any excess.

The camera panned across an open green space, dotted by ruins, with mobs of kangaroos feeding.

"Australia has broken ranks with the industrialised nations and is leading a growing number of countries with its non-material, transcendental lifestyle. People are self-sufficient for the essentials of life. There are few jobs. Most people prefer instead to spend their time with their families, tend their gardens, socialise within a commune of others having similar beliefs and meditating in the open air. Each commune decides for itself the value of creating jobs. Many people prefer to create their own work rather than depend on unfulfilling jobs that can disappear overnight. We must never return to the days, when commuters lived in isolation and sublimated their loneliness into over-consumption, paid for by working in a dull job. Such jobs are only able to provide a vestige of the socialisation that people want. In the past, industrial jobs were disguised as a mutualism between workers and capitalists, when in fact workers' lives were little more than slavery.

"Now self-sufficiency is their aim."

Cut to the family harvesting potatoes by hand, with parents digging, children picking up, youths carrying and elders sorting. There is talk and playfulness.

"Now we go to the centre of old Meannjin city."

Panorama of a flooded city centre from the top of a high building. The camera switched to T One, standing on an embankment in front of a cultural centre, with a flooded city behind her and water at her feet.

"The rise in sea level has burst through the embankments. Here the water is lapping the ground floor of the old cultural centre, which has been adapted to become Jurilpa Aquatic Centre."

Shots inside flooded auditoriums.

"The theatres have become swimming and diving pools and there is a water harvesting storage in the car park below."

Shots in the museum of animated models.

"These exhibits show where we've come from. Here is an exhibit of Meannjin, dominated by road traffic, with major public investment in freeways, bridges and tunnels. These were disused when petroleum production ceased. Here is an exhibit of isolated living at the height of materialism when families had their own robots and cheap energy to perform almost every domestic chore, freeing family members to exercise on machines. Here is an exhibit of high-energy living, when electricity was so cheap that people lived and worked in artificial environments and in locations with difficult access, built and maintained at huge energy cost, such as rotating jungle-filled offices, atop a skyscraper, beside an excavated lake with whitewater sports. Here is an exhibit showing the industries that disappeared, when power stations were shut down to prevent pollution from their waste."

Return to T One, standing on an embankment, with the flooded city behind her.

"The centre of Meannjin has been flooded for the past four years. It does not seem reversible and we have been getting used to the disaster.

"We'll tour the city centre in a gondola."

She stepped into a gondola, which set off between the buildings. Close-up of her and her Party plying along the flooded mall.

"City life goes on here, with overhead walkways and waterside restaurants.

"The middle floors of most buildings are still occupied. The upper floors are without electricity for lifts. Our gondola is taking us down Marta Street to Brahiminy Place. Now we're returning up Oodgeroo Street to Albert Holt Bridge."

View of T One with a forest of masts behind her. Close-up of ships moored side by side.

"Here is the tidal harbour from Albert Holt Bridge down to Crossing Point, crowded with sailing vessels. Ships leave daily for all points of the compass. The ships are catamarans with sails made from sheets of solar cells. To allow them to come upriver with their masts, six bridges have been cut. Material from demolished bridges and roads has been used to wall up under the riverside freeway to exclude the tidal waters from the city centre."

The camera showed the pillars that held up the freeway, filled in with a wall made from the concrete rubble of the overpass.

"The harbour is the passenger depot for international travel and import of goods. You can hear the sailors' shouts, and see and smell goods being unloaded from foreign parts, such as fruit, coffee, cotton and cocoa leaves. They are too irrigation dependent to be grown in arid Australia. Local ships bring back staples such as rice, graize and preans from the paddies in the north.

Gantry cranes swing containers over the embankment to waiting barges.

T One and her Party went aboard a riverboat.

"We are going downriver with the outgoing tide, through a winding canyon of levee banks, like a bobsleigh down its luge."

Views of the river within high embankments, which widen out to coastal sea walls. Then wide shots of island jetties, focusing in on a welcoming party gathered to meet the boat.

"I am on my way for a campaign visit to the islands of the bay at the river mouth. They are all that remains of the string of sand islands that have been washed away by ocean waves."

Receding jetties and waving group of island people.

"I have had a busy and successful day on the Quandamooka Bay Islands and now we are returning to Meannjin with the incoming tide."

View of the city over the top of the levees, with tributaries pooling into lakes behind the river walls. The camera panned an empty river estuary.

"Down here, near the mouth of the river, flooding has submerged the airport, oil refineries and fertiliser plants. They became obsolete when petroleum and natural gas production ceased. Now the submerged structures are used for fish farming."

Beside the embankment, overhead on the roof of a tower block is a wind turbine slowly turning.

"This wind turbine is one of fifty that pump out water from behind the levee banks. It will be years before the water is pumped dry from the whole flood plain of the river.

"The sea broke through when, during the Great Famine, a storm surge breached the unattended levees. Emergency workers, who could have prevented the erosion with sandbags, had left their posts to search for food."

Shots of water pouring through a breach in the embankment.

"There is a rumour that Bhakarian troops secretly dug away part of the embankment so that it would fail, shut down our businesses and create openings for theirs to take over.

"Our boat is a steamer. Tickets include a tax on emissions, which is collected for mitigation of flooding. Meannjin is waiting to receive funding for repairs to the embankment from the world-funding agency. Flooding in several other countries is a more serious threat and higher in priority. So far, Jurilpa's attempts have failed to mend the wall."

Cut to a hive of activity at a wall of sandbags, with a dam of metal piles being driven in from both sides.

"We do not want the Bhakarians here. They want material growth, whereas Australians want spiritual growth. Our people have transcended from material competition and have united to solve population growth and prevent further famines. We want the Bhakarians to go home and I hope you will vote for this tomorrow. Vote against the Bhakarians. This is not a vote for the Middle Way Party because, if the referendum succeeds, there will be an election and you will be able to vote for any Party.

"The way forward is to encourage and support a diversity of lifestyles in communes emerging across Australia. The Middle Way Party will bring you ecumenical, spiritual leadership to unite our nation. We stand for small central government. The role of our national government should merely be to protect our borders and allocate land, water, energy and other resources fairly. We will seek a national consensus on population growth and reduce immigration to a trickle.

"By tomorrow, you must decide whether you want to remain a colony of Bhakaria with a puppet government, or independence. The colonial powers of Britain and Eurany, who forced their way in to get our resources, have been sent packing. Independence movements like ours have succeeded in sending home Bhakaria from East Timor, the USA from Iraq, Britain from Ireland, Britain from India, the Romans from Britain. Even where the colonists have created a civil society, eventually they have had to go. Without the Romans, Britain may not have had the infrastructure for their own empire. But Bhakaria has little to offer us and they must go.

"Think carefully before you decide to allow them to stay: will they allow you to be yourself or are they using us for their own purposes? Do you want to be ind...?"

She was interrupted by soldiers, who surrounded her and the picture wobbled, then went dark.

The next day, Australians voted for Bhakaria to withdraw, with a narrow majority. In the national election that followed, the Middle Way Party won Government and T One became Prime Minister.

CHAPTER 5

Meditation

Abajoe found T One in the grandstand in one of the team boxes, where players had used to sit between running on and off the football arena. She was in her third term as PM and her tiny national government mostly ran itself the way she wanted.

She was lying back on a bench, holding on her abdomen a two-handled water pitcher in orange clay, shiny with a clear glaze. She often retreated here with a work of art to focus her thoughts, the way others used a religious icon in their prayers. She had closed her eyes and her body was relaxed, breathing deeply and slowly.

He turned to go but she heard him and came out of her reverie.

"Hi, Abajoe." She yawned and sat up, rubbing her eyes, as if half-awakened from a blissful dream.

"Sorry, Mum," his voice was hushed. "I'll come back later."

"No, stay, I've finished," she smiled serenely. "What do you think?" She held the pitcher towards him.

He took it from her, holding it carefully by the handles.

He studied it, taking his time. The pitcher was in the shape of a Rubenesque woman, with rounded bosoms, wide hips and bulbous buttocks, imposed on a pear-shaped pot, while still soft from the wheel. A slender neck flared out for pouring through a chin-shaped spout, narrowing gracefully below to fine shoulders with generous breasts pushing out. Slim handles jutted out like arms from the shoulders of the vessel, with elbows akimbo, the hands resting on the ledge of hips. Below, rotund buttocks curved smoothly down into fulsome thighs, truncated at the knees to form a flat base.

"Pretty sexy," he said, sitting down on the bench in front. He let his hand slide down over the shape, feeling the curves. "It's beautiful," he enthused. He turned it over in silence for several minutes, enjoying the way his mind excluded all else and engaged with the artist's creation. Then he drew in his breath sharply and spoke in awe. "The artist has seen the outside of the female body as a hollow container."

"Is that not how you see it?" asked T One.

"No. I look for the physique of a middle distance runner, light and strong, a fine-boned skeleton that is a system of efficient machines, built for endurance, solid, with muscular curves. I have never seen a female like this, as a hollow receptacle for another to fill."

"Who would do that?"

"Her lover, her foetus or herself, with milk for her baby," said Abajoe.

"Trust a man to see her like that!" T One observed, smiling at him.

She lay back and closed her eyes. There was absolute quiet on the balcony except for birds in the distance. Abajoe continued to look at the pitcher, holding it at different angles. Presently he talked quietly, as if to himself, building each thought up from the last. "A lover could want to hold her and control her positions...with her curves fitting into and around his own. He could hold her and fill her...her body could hold his member. He would know her by this outer shape...a different kind of beauty...without skeleton and sinews within...empty, waiting and fragile. That is what the artist must have realised. It is erotic art and transcends a woman's singularity...she belongs to the desires of the people who depend upon her!" He turned and looked across at T One. "That's how I see her. What do you think?"

"I also looked at this." She showed him her communicator, with a still-life painting of the same woman outlined on the clay of a plain pitcher, rather than being moulded into it, as in the sculpture. "Picasso produced hundreds of these paintings, always with two apples placed at the entry to the neck, as if their protagonist, a penis, was engaged inside a vagina. His cubist insight was to transform the 2D sketch on the pitcher into a 3D uterus, waiting to be filled, with fallopian tubes as handles."

"Wow," said Abajoe, holding the pitcher at arm's length. "That's amazing. He had a fertile imagination!"

"Not just imagination. He had eight wives and lovers and fathered four children, the last of them when he was 68. He appears to have practiced what he painted."

"So you contemplated that...?"

"It gave me an insight...the woman is young and her uterus is probably unused. Its potential dominates her being. But for me, my uterus has fulfilled its role...and delivered...you. Now I have started menopause...I need another concept of my body."

"Oh, I see. I'm sorry...is that what I should say?"

"Don't be sorry. It is nature, a new phase of life. My body is still to be used by Marko, but no longer as a container...now we enjoy each other's body as an instrument of fulfilment. These days, the effects are in my head. I have been thinking about how my head relates to my body." She stared sightlessly as she recalled an hour of meditation. "I have found that my body's purpose is to support my brain. I can't get fulfilment from Marko and transcend unless my brain gets what it needs, blood, nutrients and oxygen, without the distraction of ailments. I need a healthy body so I can disembody my thoughts and achieve inner peace..." Her explanation trailed off into silence, as if she was listening to her body.

Abajoe waited. He reclined on a bench, breathing deeply and evenly as he looked at the pitcher. Several minutes later T One looked at him again.

"That's where I reached this time," she said, "contemplating regular exercise to get all of my organs operating efficiently and in harmony. Until I am fit, my body will lack beauty and fulfilment."

"So, will your beauty shine for Marko?" he asked, grinning.

"Yes...such as it is...he will have a new image of me...and it has to shine for me too."

"So, where did you end up?"

"I must get fit."

"Your meditating today could make so much difference to your life," he enthused. "This pitcher is wonderful. Now that having more than one child is anti-social, women who have had a child need to find a new purpose, like you have."

T One laughed. "My purpose has always been to follow the family tradition of national stewardship and leadership. I thought yours might be the same. But what has changed is the meaning of my body for my purpose."

"I have a separate and higher mission...I have to share my good fortune...my understanding, influence and resources...not my body...with less advantaged people or...I lose my self-respect. When I am selfish, I hate myself. My sharing tells me how well I am leading my life...it allows me to be happy."

"What about your body...?"

"I have to use my body with integrity...or it's the same problem, selfishness."

"How are you doing?"

"Not so well," he admitted regretfully, lying back on a bench and looking up at the sky. In his relations with females, Abajoe had always been casual, resisting even Paula's attempts to monopolize his attention. He had ongoing relationships with half a dozen women, who had caught his interest. He had some older and younger partners, not restricting himself to age peers alone, like non-indigenous persons often did.

"Sometimes my sharing with others hurts females...they are so territorial...it threatens their independence...injures their pride. They resent me...reject my mission. Then I want to be partnered by a woman, who shares in my mission and keeps me going. But the pitcher has shown me a new perspective on a female's purposes and there doesn't seem to be much room for compromise."

"You can be sustained without a partner," T One replied quietly. "Religious people believe an outside force acts on their lives. Do you ever think there is something controlling yours?"

"I know you don't. But yes, lately I have been noticing coincidences ...but there is no pattern I can find."

"Are the coincidences malevolent or benign?"

"Benign...perhaps I am blind to the negatives because I am optimistic..."

"Is that not a pattern? Something could be helping you... Do you feel you are being steered in a particular direction?"

"Yes, the feeling is often strong."

"What direction?"

"My mission...but it is probably wishful thinking. If there is interference, it is random. Probably I just remember the things that go right. My brain is just trying to discover a pattern for the positive outcomes."

"Does it change your behaviour?"

"Yes...sometimes there seems to be a pattern vindicating my mission. Then I have to stop myself playing prophet...messiah." He stopped and laughed. "It is becoming a delusion of grandeur."

T One smiled. "You are certainly different. Do you think you could be inspired by a higher power?"

"In my more sober moments, like now, I know that if there is an outside force, its influence on me is random...and unwelcome...almost schizophrenic. I need the steady support of a partner."

"Have you anyone in mind?"

"It's like two raindrops on a pane of glass. They may run the same way for a while, fast and purposeful. Then they may move apart and run different ways, slow and halting. I can't tell if they will join up again..." He stopped talking and contemplated the pitcher, as if it held a secret.

"Is it Paula?" T One asked.

He nodded.

"Have you been quarrelling?"

"Yes...about commitment ..."

"You don't want to?"

"She is...marching to a different tune."

T One laughed. "Your tunes are quite different. I doubt you will find any girl, who is crazy about your ideas about sharing. Perhaps you will have to commit to her ideas first, then later you will be able to get her to join in with you."

"It is leaving too much to chance."

"She is a beautiful person the way she is. Does she still work with you most of the day?"

He nodded again.

"Her work should have beauty for you," T One said quietly. "Is she well-organised?"

He nodded. "Wonderfully – much better than me..."

"Do you find her well-balanced?"

"She's amazing. You know she is. I rely on her judgement all the time." He handed her the pitcher. "I admire her so much. Do you think it is possible to get close to beauty, or does it always have to stay at arm's length?"

She smiled. "You are asking if you can have your cake and eat it. Beauty is not hollow like this," she said, looking at the pitcher. "Beauty is not an outside impression to be admired from a distance. True beauty is when you admire the inner person and learn to share ideals and even a mission...it motivates true intimacy. It takes time."

Abajoe lifted his eyes and pursed his mouth. "We have had time...all our lives, but still..." He stopped. He didn't want to say anything critical that could get back to Paula. It was his longest chat with his mother for weeks. Although he talked with her every day, it was usually about politics or social arrangements.

"I believe that to find a partner, you will have to compromise your mission," T One told him.

It was a hazard of any chat with his mother that it would finish on a moral note. As usual, she had brought his ideas down to earth. He felt a surge of resentment but caught himself and turned it into a positive.

"You have done a great job in getting the people to meditate."

"Thank you. I have tried to switch their aspirations from material things to spiritual goals."

"That is my aim too," he said, "but my meditation is sometimes mistaken for indigenous dreaming...I like to do that, but I also want to contemplate real things, which give my life firmness of direction. When I meditate, I try to bring them into unity with my eternal true nature or cosmic consciousness."

"Me too," said T One, stretching lazily. "This morning was so exquisite. I explored every sensation, every thought. I contemplated the ultimate purpose of my body for what seemed like hours, until my thoughts merged with the cosmos."

"Do you think spiritualism will continue to grow?" he asked her. "Or has it grown because you cannot get material things anymore? If things become available, won't people turn back to materialism?"

"No, because people's motivation has changed. Once bitten, twice shy. Private possession has become antisocial. I doubt that the chicken of industry will ever lay another egg of materialism in Australia. I think spiritualism will take over people's lives," said T One, gazing out across the arena. "More and more people are meditating to find their ultimate purpose. Most people have moved to a commune with a simple lifestyle they like. A few communes have gone back to capitalism, some are dedicated to an art or craft, many follow an organised religion or philosophy and one has existential anarchy. Most people live as communists with spiritual goals. There has been a spiritual awakening."

"There are some pretty ugly communes," Abajoe grimaced.

"A book doesn't have to be balanced, but a library should be," replied T One, rolling onto her side. "If a commune is abhorrent, its council will have to deal with it or it won't be re-elected."

"Some communes will revert to materialism," Abajoe argued. "Their consumption will be in everyone's face."

"I agree," she said with the afternoon sun warming her back. "It will happen. There will still be rich and poor suburbs. But everyone remembers that materialism failed us and led to the Great Famine. Material consumption has become, for most people, a necessity that enables transcendence, rather than a goal in itself. Most people want to support their transcendence with a simple material lifestyle, rather than through wealth and possessions."

Abajoe sat forward. "The new upper class are the time-rich. They have time for their families, their neighbours and for meditation."

"People need opportunities for aesthetic experiences, self-actualisation and transcendence," said T One.

"More importantly, meditation will put food on the table, by preventing another famine. Individuals will share meanings and be able to rationalise contributing to communal works, such as the huge earthworks for paddy fields."

"The parable of the loaves and the fishes...is that it?" she asked.

"Exactly. A miracle of community." Abajoe leaned back and clasped his hands behind his head confidently. "That's how the pyramids were built...by shared meaning. However, Australians are not into monotheism and national projects any more. The commune has replaced the corporation as the basic affiliation. Corporations will no longer be around to promote individuality, competition and private dreams of selfishness through subliminal advertising. Essential wants will be decided by the commune."

T One looked at the pitcher. "Has the artist used sex to subliminally advertise a water jar?"

Abajoe laughed. "That's different. The sex is not advertising a jar. It is a sexy work of art."

"Quite sublime."

T One's eyes came back from meditating the pitcher and switched to him.

She put the pitcher to one side.

"Wouldn't it be great if we had more time for meditating like this? What can we do to lead Australians towards a more spiritual life?"

"Set an example... Show that the important things in life are not material...through more science."

"Wouldn't less materialism mean less science, not more?"

"No... Material cares can be entrusted to the scientific method."

"What is it with you and science?" asked T One. "If it's so needed, why aren't we using it more already?"

"It tells the truth," said Abajoe, "and the truth does not enable our leaders to grab credit. They are too untruthful, greedy and impatient to rely on science."

"I hope you aren't meaning me!" T One protested. "Our spiritual leaders won't acknowledge that science tells the truth. It is not in their interest to do so. They accept it as a mere tool that is useful sometimes."

"Only practicing scientists are committed to the 'objectivity' concept that they call 'truth'," T One told him, "because practitioners are on higher ground in any discussion of objectivity, and so scientific truth is exclusive and ordinary people have no process through which to contest it. The principle of peer review by independent experts is not sufficient to convince most people. Spiritual leaders whip up fears of a conspiracy of scientists and the media amplify it."

"And sometimes they are right...there have been occasions, when well-meaning scientists have misled people," said Abajoe.

"Exactly...because scientists are usually marginalised, when they get a little power they let it go to their heads and they lose their objectivity. That was what happened way back, when global warming was first realised."

"Yeah, they caused a panic. After that, no one believed anything they said. Now people have started trusting them again," said T One. "They are ready to let more science into their lives."

Abajoe spoke with passion. "What we need is a national vision with goals, which can be reached through science without being sidetracked by our system of adversarial politics. Politicians will raise a spectre of evil to gain kudos from delivering us from it. Real problems are better solved by science, so long as they are not distracted by politicians manipulating them, as they did with global warming."

T One thought for a minute. "I agree. Could you and your group look into how science can move into the driving seat? We could bring it in at the next election."

Abajoe and Paula, together with several others of the MWP's youth under Marko's guidance, including John, Peter and Thomas, sometimes investigated issues for the Middle Way Party. They were observers at Party meetings and held study sessions to thrash out policy recommendations.

"Okay," Abajoe said, smiling. "We'll see what we can come up with." It was a task close to his heart, for these days his meditation often led him to the science of an issue.

CHAPTER 6

Professionalism

He found the PM in her studio, talking with colleagues, on the bank of monitors as they waited in the virtual parliament for a debate to begin.

"Morning, Mum," he said. "What's the motion?"

"Professionals should have unlimited responsibility. It's an old chestnut and we have always lost in the past. We are trying to put through a law to make doctors, architects, lawyers, engineers and others responsible for all foreseeable consequences of their work. You should be for it, because it encourages professionals to work in scientific teams."

"That would be terrific...instead of each doing their own thing separately and blaming the others when things go wrong! But why is a national law necessary? Surely each local council could decide this for their own situation?"

"I agree, but the councils have not been able to resolve it. The issue is dividing local communities and they have asked us to provide leadership. So we are having a national debate."

The Chairperson announced the start of the debate. "Order. Would the Affirmative's Proposer commence for the motion that 'Professionals Should Have Unlimited Responsibility'."

T One began her speech.

"Madame Chairperson, Honourable Members of this House, the motion 'Professionals Should Have Unlimited Responsibility' will be affirmed by our team as the bridge to a new and better society. We will show that clients need professional responsibility to protect them. In addition, professional responsibility has to be unlimited to draw them into setting appropriate community goals and achieving them.

"A professional is a member of a vocation founded upon specialised educational training, who is required to adhere to strict ethical and moral regulations. Responsibility is legal liability for the consequences of both action and inaction. It is not subject to caveat emptor, the usual dictum of exchange, when the supplier's responsibility is unlimited.

"Traditionally, many professionals have combined private liability with public responsibility. Once they have earned enough to sustain their practices, they have volunteered their efforts and resources altruistically to those in the community, who are unable to pay. They have encouraged governments to accept responsibility for care of disabled people and sharing of living places, jobs, possessions and childcare. They have used their expertise to prioritise shortfalls from government goals."

Abajoe listened, admiring T One's oratorical skills. Her arguments transcended the poverty and grubbiness of the people's everyday experience with the promise of a sublime spiritual future. The monitors showed screen after screen of Members of Parliament intent on her argument.

"But society degenerated before the Great Famine and professionals became instruments of government policy. They no longer earned enough for volunteering. They had lost their objectivity and freedom to prescribe treatments. They also declined responsibility for the final effects of the treatments prescribed by the Government. With the increase in longevity, few old people were able to fade away usefully in the bosom of their families."

The public gallery was motionless and absolutely quiet. It was the crowded dining hall of a commune near Warringa, randomly chosen from all the communes across Australia. Other communes were watching but could not be heard.

"Professionals took the Government's side. They gave out all sorts of placebos to clients, instead of solving their deep-seated problems. The Government would only pay to get them well enough to return to competing for possessions, turning up for unfulfilling jobs to finance them and paying their taxes. Physical, social and monetary problems kept people busy.

"Until recently, local government regarded people as isolated individuals to be enraptured by the ritual conflicts of religion, politics, football and foreign wars. Residual emotional needs were harnessed by advertisers' images that associated desires for belonging, the esteem of others, and self-actualisation with acquiring possessions such as a fashionable type of home, car, spa, holiday, or some other object of conspicuous consumption. The focus was on individuals and families, as

isolated tax-paying, working and consuming unit. The popular credo has been 'consumo ergo sum'.

"The things they wanted were sometimes met by free markets, but usually markets were ruthlessly exploited by monopolies and oligarchies. Rather than achieving the freedom the markets are supposed to deliver, their purchases of computers, communicators, robots and other technologies locked buyers into complex financial and technological relationships. The suppliers, acting in concert, denied them their needs and robbed them of their savings and self-confidence. The result was impoverishment, frustration and compliance. Local governments, because they depended on retailers and their puppet media to be re-elected, turned a blind eye to corporate rapaciousness.

"The media cultivated fear of economic disaster. Professionals did little to debunk people's worries. Growth, the leaders agreed, was the sinecure. Population growth was wanted to sustain house prices. Jobs needed to be secure to repay borrowing and an annual increase was needed to meet the rising cost of services. When they got their increase and house prices increased, many voters accepted that their local government has been instrumental in saving them, and elected the politicians cultivated by the media. Professionals often supported the media's imagery or let it go unchallenged, because the media and local government were their main employers."

There was a shout, "Cowards!"

"Professionals' work can only be evaluated by their peers. They have allowed the emergence of technologies, some of questionable value, as panaceas for illness. The new technologies they peddle are often pie-in-the-sky or controversial and are able to clash with traditional values, for example, selective memory enhancement. Wise introduction of new and controversial technologies is purported to be left to responsible professional associations and ethics committees, but in reality these have been bastions of greed, where pseudo-professionals have pursued their sponsors' interests.

"Previous governments before the Great Famine allowed the professions to police their own members' excesses and they have merely addressed ethical concerns and left societal problems for politicians to dabble in. In short, the professions have kept citizens on treadmills of exploitation, abandoning the professional holistic care of their clients."

A shout, "Greedy bastards!"

"Now the pendulum of responsibility is swinging back," T One continued. "Professionals today are assuming responsibility for their clients' wider needs."

Call from the gallery, "About time too!"

"They are refusing any longer to be dispensing agents for local governments' quick fixes. They are declining to follow the old pattern of treating the elderly by keeping them in their isolated homes until they succumb to loneliness, depression and illness. They are refusing to mitigate symptoms of people with diseases induced by the despair of inadequate community care by prescribing drugs, android implants, experiential drugs, virtual living simulators and beds in palliative care wards.

"Professionals today are seeking government funding for self-sufficient groups and for team working. The professions have recently become more responsible and look for ways to interpret government programmes with more consideration for their clients' interest. Led by professionals, aged care is changing from a compulsory societal burden staffed by health workers, to imaginative voluntarism. From their own resources volunteers provide meals, wheels, deals, spaces, places and faces. They are tailoring preventive solutions that remedy underlying wants for comfort, esteem, belonging, affection, love and caring in the general community"

Applause in the public gallery.

"This is a return to the true professionalism sworn by followers of the medic Hippocrates, who extolled the virtue of serving the clients' interests without regard for the practitioner's own reward. In many other contexts, the term 'professional' is a euphemistic deceit, derived from the Greek word hypocrite, meaning actor. They are mercenaries, who mimic tribal allegiances and champion their sides to glory.

"The new professionalism is ousting materialism and greed and promoting spiritual happiness. True professionals genuinely represent, interpret and even act as surrogates for their clients. It recognises that quality living depends on their active participation in communal groups of family, friends and fellow believers, who are the person's kindred."

Enthusiastic applause and excited talk in the public gallery. Abajoe checked with some other communes and they were all applauding at this point.

"Under the new regimen, professionals are engaged in altruistic communality rather than selfish competition. Both competition and communality have their strengths and weaknesses. However, Australia has cultural and geographic variations, nomadism and sharing, which prevent true competition between suppliers and the emergence of free markets. However, true communality with only local goals has not been tried, until now. I predict that it will be fairer, more efficient and implemental throughout the dispersed population of Australia.

"Communities, where kindred groups eat, work, play, meditate and pray together, are being led by professionals. The professionals work in their own time, to plan and manage construction of dining halls, schools and gardens, where people can share. They can share appliances such as refrigerators, farming equipment and vehicles. They can share work for the commune. They can share jobs outside. Older people will have opportunities to enjoy multi-age communal living, where they can contribute their experience to younger people, who in return will support them and provide them with a more dignified end.

"Communality depends on a fractal pattern of professional self-altruism at the levels of individual, commune, council, nation and global. At every level, professionals will lead in the retreat from materialism into diverse meditative and aesthetic living that will bring greater fulfilment and greater happiness.

"Professionals have realised that their allegiances should be to their clients. They should seed and propagate self-altruism and refuse to implement government plans that draw clients away from communality.

"Thank you."

She sat back. There was strong applause, whoops and shouts of approval from the gallery. One every screen, the member became engaged in animated discussion.

"Order," called the Chairperson, after several minutes.

The Opposition Proposer outlined their case, that professionals could only consider knock-on effects, as far as their corporate responsibility went. It was up to the client to consider further effects.

"As ye sow, so shall ye reap," T One mused quietly, so only Abajoe could hear. "Zelta made the mistake of growing a crop of so-called professionals, who merely implemented government treatments without a thought for ultimate results. We paid a very high price – with stronger public leadership, the worst of the Great Famine might never have happened. If only we could turn the clock back."

T One's attention went back to the debate. Her Government's Seconder was arguing for professionalism with a broad view of the client's interests, as in the Hippocratic Oath's *'primum non nocere'*, meaning 'First, Do No Harm'. It recognised that human acts with good intentions may have unwanted consequences and sometimes the cure is worse than the sickness. Medical students have as their first principle 'non-maleficence'. This means that, given an existing problem, it may be better to do nothing than to do something that risks causing more harm than good. The speaker concluded that the practitioner should consider all the risks, not just direct consequences.

"Well said," whispered T One. "Now let's see if they can argue against that."

They listened to the Opposition's Seconder, who rebutted the 'Do No Harm' argument by putting up a straw man with technological complexity and infinitely long chains of cause and effect, saying that if the principle was strictly applied, professional treatments would grind to a halt. She concluded that unlimited responsibility was impractical and professionals should be guided by traditions of reasonable care.

"Hmph!" said T One. "Just as well we saw that one coming."

As planned, their Concluder rebutted that, in this case, *'reductio ad extremis'* was *'eductio ad absurdum'*. Arguing from the extreme of an infinite chain of responsibility was absurd. If a treatment would have infinite repercussions, it should not be undertaken. Responsibility should have the same boundary as the professional's authority so he or she would be responsible for sins of both commission and omission. Any less was unreasonable.

Then she reiterated their side's position and dismissed the negative's case.

The studio monitors were turning on as Members of Parliament, who had been away, connected for the vote. The Opposition's Concluder was on his feet, reasserting the impracticalities of a professional's total responsibility for the clients' wellbeing, when there were other professionals separately involved. He attempted to rebut the Proposer's argument that professionals must work in teams to meet clients' holistic needs, providing evidence of clients that preferred to deal with each professional separately. He argued that professionals could not take full responsibility, even if they wanted to.

"That's the post hoc fallacy," said T One. "Most members will recognise it as nonsense. The negative side has assumed that the client has to take responsibility because professionals can't. Of course, they can, they just don't want to. If professionals had to, the client could leave it up to them. Clients don't have the skills to investigate effects of professionals' treatments: this should be done by the professionals themselves."

"The negative side have offered nothing but deceit," said Abajoe.

The debate had finished and members were voting. The tally showed an even split but support for the motion was gaining. T One entered her vote on her communicator, with an iris scan before and after, as required for security.

The late voting was heavily in favour of the Government and the result was: For: 103, Against: 56.

"Congratulations, Mum," said Abajoe.

"Thank you," said T One. "At last we are getting some common sense out of people. Law will require professional responsibility. The legislation can go through immediately. It's going to mean a big change in how professionals do business."

"Here beginneth self-altruism," muttered Abajoe.

CHAPTER 7

Vision

After the debate, T One turned to Abajoe. "Now, did you want to see me about something?"

'This is it,' thought Abajoe, 'my chance to make a difference to the future of Australia.' He felt humbled by the difficult task of fairly representing the range of opinions in their group. The rest of them had wanted teamwork as their arch vision of Australian life but Peter had dissented, wanting individual incentives.

"People are selfish," Peter had said. "They will only participate in teams for their own, greedy ends."

"No," said Abajoe. "People are motivated by belonging to a group and by the esteem of others. When they have these, then they may strive for individual achievement. Teamwork is basic." But Peter had not been persuaded and had remained doubtful, as he often had in the past.

Abajoe knew T One would want definite answers and he would have to present their views as if they were unanimous. Now Abajoe was at the stadium to report their findings to T One.

"You wanted us to propose national goals for the Party. Well, we have come up with...one."

"Only one?"

"Only one so far...we are still working on it but we thought one was most important to get started."

"Well, what is it?"

"Teamwork. We think the Party's top priority should be getting people to work together in teams. There isn't much teamwork now... available jobs are lonely and unsupported. Australians are steering clear of employment because it's not much fun. Unless the work is satisfying, the projects won't succeed, even if it is important to the commune. Teamwork requires sharing but people don't know how to share fairly."

"Science can decide how to share fairly. Sharing through science should be our national goal. It will bring fulfilment and lead to a more spiritual lifestyle."

T One swung her chair to give him all her attention.

"Sharing through science," she repeated. "It could be a goal...sharing between who?"

"People involved."

"Like between workers and managers...?"

"Yes, and owners..."

"...and customers?"

"Yes, and suppliers..."

"...and creditors and debtors?"

"Their interests can be represented by the owners and managers. Sharing would be between the others. They should all be in it together."

"Even more than they already are, when they elect the top manager and his team?"

Abajoe knew that a cornerstone of the Party, since it first came to government 134 years earlier, had been election of top managers by employees, owners and customers. Then the method of sharing had been by voting. Now they had moved on and should use science. He was excited by his own words because his special gift was sharing and now he had the opportunity to get his nation's people to adapt by taking on this mind set. Too bad that Peter didn't want it – he was too much an individual, reluctant to join groups. It wasn't an ego trip, he told himself, because mutual sharing was a logical development in a species, in which sociality was evolving. But the sociality he wanted was limited.

"I don't want to be a worker bee, one of hundreds all the same in a colony," he said.

"I agree. Who wants to be infertile?" T One said.

"If only people had the territory and freedom of polar bears," he replied.

"Polar bears aren't very social," she objected.

"Nor are humans," he said.

"They gather together to share their resources, sometimes."

"So why can't we? People have so-called shares but there is no sharing. It is everyone for him or herself."

"So what can we do?" asked T One.

"We need a fairer way of sharing," he said. "Our democracy can choose team leadership, but it does little to empower ordinary individuals. We want employees to have more involvement than just voting for their managers. We think everybody in the group should give and take together. They would all share in profits...and they would all put in to cover losses..."

"Equally?"

"No...there would be different types and amounts of contribution."

"And this would be measured by science?"

"Yes."

"How will it work that will be different from what we do at present?" asked T One.

"We propose that no profession or skill shall have a standard pay rate," Abajoe said. "Each person makes a unique contribution. A person, who has undergone long training at their own expense, could be highly valued if their work requires that training. The stakeholders in every work group shall evaluate each person's contributions on its merits."

"Hmm. It could be time-consuming." T One sounded doubtful. "Do you think there will be much change?"

"Time spent evaluating a person's contribution will be very worthwhile. Call it planning if you like," Abajoe enthused. T One was always in favour of more planning. "We need to give all employees the incentive to strive shoulder to shoulder with the givers instead of having their potential overlooked and being relegated to being a taker. During a typical year, a group uses only a few of the skills that its employees have. It is the givers, who supply the skills the group wants to use, who contribute most. However, strong contributors often go unrecognised and are insufficiently rewarded. Others are often seen as takers, who contribute little, are consciously kept in reserve or are redundant. They may be regarded as overpaid and their motivation left to fester. We will require organisations to empower all stakeholders with opportunities for them to contribute valuably."

"How would value be assessed?"

"By their contribution under the financial forecast."

"Would that include equity? Are you proposing that employees and other stakeholders should share in the ownership?"

"No. That would be putting all of their eggs in the same basket. If the business failed, workers could lose their jobs and their savings at the same time. That's too much. There must be owners to provide a safety net, to carry the risk of extreme losses."

"So how would your financial sharing work?"

"It would depend on the contribution an individual has made most recently."

"And how will that be decided?"

"By considering the effects of each one of the stakeholders: employees, customers and owners."

"I see. You want to value the contribution of each to the enterprise?"

"Yes."

"Would an employee's contribution be valued by comparing with nobody doing that job or someone else doing it well or badly?"

"Neither. The alternative would be the best reassignment of employees to cover that position. If an employee would be difficult to replace by reassignment and they had contributed strongly to the enterprise's goal achievement, he or she would be eligible for a large share of any bonus."

"So would the greatest contributors get most rewards?"

"Yes."

"Wouldn't that be the manager?"

"Reassignment of the team manager would be considered, as for other employees. Stakeholders together would decide that everyone's contribution is rewarded fairly."

T One stretched.

Abajoe looked into the distance. "If we can make it work, it would be fantastic."

T One mused "Hmm...sharing through science...it might work. Where does science come into it? Why is it necessary?"

"To provide objectivity. Sharing is delicate, a matter of trust, justification and agreement. Science can quantify contributions. This cannot be left to the blunt instrument of politics, where value would depend on how many friends the different stakeholders can muster. Politics, by its very nature, is divisive and corrupt, with conflicts of interest that would distort sharing into a negotiated settlement rather than an ongoing culture of teamwork. Science can show what people are doing and what the consequences are for others, by methods that are reproducible. Its method is above corruption."

"Who will do the science evaluation? Won't they be got at?"

"Stakeholders shall prepare a joint scientific report. The group will see that bias is eliminated, even where subjective values have to be brought in. Sharing will be fair, by measuring causes and effects scientifically. Science shall only turn to politics to make decisions, when there is no other way."

His mind raced through the evidence of his similarity to Jesus...his iconoclasm and his disciples. Was he the prophet forecast as the Second Coming in the Bible? They could be explained by his privileged upbringing and his mutant genes. He didn't even believe in God. Perhaps the takeover of science meant the end of the Biblical World. Sometimes, when he spoke, the ideas came into his head from nowhere, as if he was a mouthpiece for a higher power. He knew T One was listening but he knew he would have to be more persuasive when he presented these ideas to the MWP, so he wouldn't sound like a zealot. When he had first become involved with the MWP youth group, some of them had made fun of his earnestness. "Thus spake the prophet Abajoe!" they teased after his first speech. "His father art in Science!" He tried to present his ideas more conventionally than in the impassioned torrent of ideas, which poured out when an insight moved him to speak.

'Hmmm...' T One pondered.

"The teamwork Australian people need is like that in a pack of African hunting dogs. There is a feeding order, or hierarchy, at the kill. It is a hierarchy of their contributions to the chase. Those who get to eat first have risked everything and survived to play a key role in the kill. Human groups value risk taking too, as well as other contributions, such as education of young players. The different contributions shall be decided by science."

Abajoe paused. Would T One accept the analogy? Human life in the communes wasn't much like a temporary encampment of hunting dogs on the savannah. Nevertheless, it was the hunting, like human work in groups, that the analogy explained.

"Very often there isn't a kill to share," said T One.

"Hunger has to be shared, maybe equally, or perhaps certain individuals shall carry the blame. We know it is radical but Australians will not go back to work until there is more accountable leadership and less loneliness and scapegoating. Teamworking has an accountable leader, social fun and acceptance of personal limitations. An employee's contribution in a sample of events can be measured."

"As we heard in the debate, it is possible to consider the effects a professional has. However, the contribution of a support worker is more diffuse and I'm not so sure science can decide. For example, take a dental receptionist. Her work can set clients at ease and manage a queue of people with appointments. If she fails, the availability of clients may dwindle and the dentist will lack work. How can you compare the contributions of, say, a dentist and a dental receptionist?"

"Whereas the dentist may have spent many years learning to operate a drill, the receptionist may have spent years learning to deliver to the dentist a continuous supply of patients, who most need drilling. Their contributions could be equal and they could share equally in rewards."

"What if an employee's share is so decreased that they would leave?"

"If the cost of replacing them would be great, then the stakeholders shall look for a replacement, who would accept a fair share."

"So rewards are ultimately controlled by supply and demand for those skills? Like at present?"

"No. Evaluation shall be of a particular person's actual contribution in a position on a team. The traditional value of a generic type of employee is irrelevant."

"Will teamwork increase?"

"Yeah, professionals will want to work in teams. First-contact specialists will want to share their expertise with one or more treatment specialists they refer people to, and each case will have teamwork. Rewards will be shared."

T One chose her words carefully. "I think the Party will like your ideas, because people know from sport and Party work how fulfilling it can be to have a valued position on a team. Teamwork thrives where a group's purpose is well established but for some groups, the goals can change as roles are refilled and redefined, and individual opportunism can take over. Where the predominant culture is change, and teams are shifting and unstable, sharing is difficult. People look to the Government to provide stability by setting conditions for the types of development they can look at."

Abajoe gazed out the window, his mind searching for insight. Their group had discussed what could be the goals of development and had concluded that the future should be an adventure, without national goals. But he accepted T One's argument for development to be guided by the Government. He knew he must defer to T One's experience on this issue.

"We had trouble with development policy," he admitted, slipping into the role of acolyte. "It seemed to be a matter of strategic choice, of where councils want to go."

"Not at all. For mutual benefit and to prevent competition, councils should all be going to the same place," the Prime Minister told him. "Did you know that the Party has already put forward its vision for Australia's future – the types of industrial activity, which will receive government support."

"Do you mean minerals development?"

"No, more than that. I got the Party to agree on a strategy at the last conference. I had them consider three alternatives. One – continue running Australia down; two – return to a full industrial economy; and three – export to import. Do you remember what they decided?"

"Export to import," said Abajoe. "Using money from overseas minerals' sales to import goods."

"Good! And why was that decided?" continued T One, testing his recall.

"Australia had been run down long enough. People were missing things they regarded as essential and they were hurting."

"That's right. So why didn't we go for full-blown industrial development?" T One was an admirer of Socrates, who asked questions that challenged his interlocutor to take an opposing point of view.

This was an issue Abajoe had investigated with a scientific survey, and he answered with confidence.

"People are prepared to work to obtain a few essentials, but not for most factory products," he pronounced.

His voice was too loud, he realised. Prophets did not make generalities like these, which could be refuted. Attitudes could change. Behaviour could be different. He lowered his voice. "People are used to going without. They would lose their independent lifestyles. Most don't want full-time jobs. The population is too spread out and transport is too difficult for many people to be included in industrial development. Full-blown industrial development wouldn't work."

"Correct," T One agreed. "So the only alternative is to buy the stuff, hence we will export to pay for imports."

Abajoe spoke urgently as another insight kicked in.

"Export earnings must not be frittered away on luxuries. We have to convert depleting mineral resources into something to replace them, something to enable Australia to continue producing essentials when the minerals run out. We should invest in food production infrastructure, such as paddies and water storages, so we don't need food from overseas. We should invest in resources for maintaining health and developing education. The Australian people must develop independence."

"Must? Who says?"

"We do, our group. It's logical. It is..."

It was his own creed. He rejected the materialism and hedonism of the past. Nor was he content to live in his imagination. Rather, he used science to guide minimal materialism.

"It's a young person's perspective," said T One. "What about other things people want, such as washing machines and communicators?"

Again, the group had investigated the alternatives and Abajoe was ready with their conclusions. "We think that technologies of convenience, like washing machines, should be commune facilities and purchased from commune earnings. Communicators are private and needed to participate in local and national government. Everyone should have one to achieve national goals of cohesion and harmony. Their purchase could be subsidised from resources revenue."

"So you have a vision of the national Government using up some of its export earnings to unite Australia?"

"Yes," Abajoe confirmed. "We have to promote the sharing and science ideas. It will take time for councils to understand. But our elders, Zelta and Hugo, support them."

"It will be a huge change. We have over three years to the next election to do the groundwork. Is it enough?"

Her question surprised him, as she was such a last-minute person.

"It depends when we get underway. We need to debate it within the Party and get the councils committed."

"If we start now, there's time," T One replied. "These goals of yours are great but they are radical. They are abstract ideas and not easy to sell. Some professional people, who enjoy traditional privileges, could regard sharing them as heresy and support Sudarta against us. The MWP must persuade them to accept the rewarding of contributions as just. We need a high-energy campaign and must get started right away to educate voters about the need to use science to determine rewards. I'll propose the vision of teamwork and ask cabinet to launch an internal debate."

Abajoe felt an adrenalin rush of success. Their ideas were set to become a reality.

When he told the others, they were elated and congratulated him because they said the insights had mostly been his. Again, he wondered in trepidation if he, Abajoe, was a prophet. If so, was it a coincidence that his message of sharing was the other side of the coin from Jesus' message of loving? Sharing gave loving a practical edge. Had some higher power cast him to re-live Jesus' life with a new message? He was repelled by the brutality Jesus suffered and tried to push the analogy away but he couldn't. 'I am so steeped in Crucianity, even though I don't believe in God, that suffering for others has a fatal lure,' he thought. Then he gave himself a reprieve: 'Unlike Jesus, I have science to justify my actions. I can't imagine any context where townspeople would demand the ultimate sacrifice for attacking their lack of sharing and lack of science.'

Abajoe was impatient to have the new national goal applied. He wrote to the man, who had spoken to him at his commune's retail outlet about developing local industry, telling him of the Government's policy of export-import and the reasons for that. Few jobs requiring his skills were expected from industrial development at Jurilpa. He suggested that he contact the mines at Mount Argus, where there might be an opportunity to contribute to a team that serviced robots.

Then he remembered that the Government was allowing the mines to recruit workers from Bhakaria. They were being allowed in as guest workers as immigration had ceased. It was a policy that made him feel uneasy. He tried to imagine how Australia was regarded by her closest neighbour, Bhakaria.

CHAPTER 8

Citra

Abajoe kept a thick diary of his thoughts to generate ideas for the MWP youth group and for his motivational speaking and writing as a leader. In his studies he had learned all the hard facts about Bhakaria, but the souls of its inhabitants were only dimly understood by his teachers and consequently by him. He needed to understand conditions and attitudes in neighbouring Bhakaria accurately but did not know any ordinary Bhakarians to whom he could talk. Therefore, he imagined a Bhakarian, whose life he could discover by research, so that eventually she could become a virtual sounding board for his ideas about relations between Australia and Bhakaria. He made up a girl, a few years younger, attractive and interesting. The name he gave her in his writings was Citra, meaning 'image' in Bhakarian.

He wrote, 'Citra has cocoa-brown skin, long, thick, black hair, an oval face. As a young girl, she has learned to defer to older people, to be modest and draw her identity from her family group and local community.

'When you meet her, you feel from the warmth of her smile that you are in an extraordinary presence. Her clear, green eyes sparkle with vitality and engagement that welcomes you to her world, as if she has been waiting to meet you, to realise a personal mission.

'Citra lives at Pedang, a country village 400 kms from the capital, Gataka, on the island of Gatra, the largest island in the Bhakarian archipelago. Beyond Gatra, a string of islands sweeps past Jengara to Mitor and Lakua, which is near the vast Australian continent.

'Pedang is on the border of the Rabat National Park, with its active volcano. The shanty houses of the village are huddled around an ancient banyan tree. The people regard banyans as sacred, believing them to be the first tree on earth. This one's gnarled branches hold the village 'kul kul', a wooden gong used to sound danger, telling of a death or summoning a meeting of the 'Kelompok' or village community. Under its spreading branches, the people gathered to play cards and gossip until dawn, or for village feasts. The villagers are gregarious, doing everything in pairs or groups. There is a platform of bamboo, where they can sleep safely in the group. Some people spend more time at the Kelompok than they do at home.

'Each person has an equal say in the running of the village, in the work of repairing roads, bridges and irrigation canals, the upkeep of the temple and in preparation for celebrations. They can take equal part in the ricefields' association, in the local dance group or in the gamelan band supporters' group.

'Citra lives with her parents, a brother and a sister in the poorest part of Pedang, furthest from the banyan. The family's rented home is one of a row of makeshift structures standing shoulder to shoulder in the village. It has two rooms with dirt floors. There is a living area and a sleeping area.

'Citra is renowned for singing the Kitab, the Yamen holy book, with a voice of extraordinary beauty. Pedang girls are modest and she hides her talent, except when she is called upon to entertain her elders and sing the sacred verses at services held in the 'Gereja', the holy temple. Then her soaring, pure voice wrings out the congregation's emotions like a wet sponge and fills the worshippers with purity and grace. She has a holy and serene presence. People come from the villages around and even from the city to hear her and see her, so she will heal them of their troubles. She is quietly confident about her talents and radiates a peacefulness that uplifts everyone.

'When people look at her in awe and ask "How can you be this way?" she answers simply with lowered eyes. "It is God's will." "Praise be to Yahm," they reply'.

In Abajoe's imagination, Citra's family is on the borderline of poverty. Their income is about median – above the abrupt destitution of the incomeless poor half of the villagers, but below the wide income range of the other half, who subsist on their own farmlets, or have regular earnings or wealth.

'Citra's father is a propertyless, casual labourer. Paddy agriculture has provided him with employment on most days in the past. However, employers are subdividing their land to provide plots for their children, who work these small plots themselves. Labouring work is becoming hard to get.

'They are surrounded by poverty, but they have their own space and live respectably, better off than the homeless beggar families, who roam the village, slowly starving. When they become too weak to forage, they stay at the village dump, where they eventually die. Citra's parents sometimes give to beggars but like most villagers, they only have enough for members of their extended family. They are trying to save to escape from the grinding poverty.

'The family grow about half their food in their small backyard. There are cabbages, choy, sweet potato, melons and pawpaw. Plants grow vigorously all the year. The tropical climate is hot and dry in winter and very hot and humid in early summer, until the monsoonal rains start. Then the rain buckets down every afternoon and the temperature falls.

'In a pen with a hutch are rabbits, with genes engineered for heat resistance. Citra looks after them. They eat garden and kitchen wastes. To supplement these, she gathers grass from the roadside in their neighbourhood.

'Citra is a doer and she has learned many survival skills as a child, such as the best ways to harvest grass seeds and make them into cakes, which are their staple diet. Gathering the seed is a group activity with other children from the village. Now she has left school, she leads the children on foraging expeditions. On the way back, she stops and gossips with the mothers.

'She is acutely aware that they lack a home of their own. If her father's labours do not bring in enough money for the rent, they will be evicted, as were her grandparents on both sides of her family when her parents were children. Her mother and father lived on the streets, until her grandparents succumbed to epidemics, leaving their small children to fend for themselves.

'It is her father's dream to rent enough land to live off and eventually buy. The whole family makes sacrifices to save for a place of their own. Further education of the children is rated a low priority by parents, who never attended school after puberty.

'Like the weather, the life Citra leads is traditional and predictable. She has only a few small possessions and is dependent on her father for financial support. Property belongs to males. The daughters of well-off fathers go to university but Citra's family cannot afford it.

'Citra's ambitions are different: she wants to become a holy 'kudim' or priestess. She attended school until she reached puberty and it rated her of exceptionally high intelligence. Since then, her parents have kept her at home, because the school fees are high. Her days pass in helping with chores, playing with other teenagers and going to occasional education classes at the Kelompok. They usually play basketball and through her play she has learned how to deal with aggression: to downplay conflict and give the other person 'face', uplifting the other's power in defeat, avoiding humiliation, from which lasting enmity could spring'.

Abajoe paused in his writing. Giving the vanquished 'face' contrasted with the finality of conflict and competition in Australia, where there was more space for schisms between people and within groups. Australians were more individualistic. It was a problem in building active communes. Although her family did not talk about their emotions, they supported each other through touch and affection, for example, when taking away a hurt. Immigrants from Bhakaria could show Australians how to build supportive communities.

'The family lives by Yamen precepts. Citra prays at home at dawn, noon, afternoon, sunset and at night. The Kudim's loudspeaker calls the villagers to prayer. "Yahm ust hebat, Yahm ust hebat." God is great. Yahm is great. "Dalam nama Yahm dewa kebanyakan simpati dan memaafkan, mekari!" In the name of Yahm, the God most understanding and forgiving, come hither.

'Heeding the call, men walk purposefully to the gereja. The Kudim excuses women, as they are preparing food or caring for babies but Citra goes with the children for instruction. On Sundays, she paints her face with the traditional rias, or make-up, whitening it to a mask to hide her expression and beauty from strangers.

'She participates in Yamen festivities and fasts during Waktu Puasa each year. Until now, religious ideas have meant little but the Kudim's discourses on Yamism have set her imagination alight. He was a learned interpreter of the prophet Numan and her holy exegesis in the Kitab. The teachings are about an ideal world and Citra is hungry for knowledge of the real world.

'Fearfully, she has exchanged a few words with pale-skinned tourists from Australia, another world. She is interested in the images of their world, which she sees in the news and documentaries. She is able to compare that way of life with her own. She is deeply suspicious of people, who do not live the Yamen way of life and she regards them as untrustworthy. Her Kudim has recently returned from a study visit to Australia and his stories about a Yamen revolution there and the possibility that it could become a Yamen state in the future enthrals her'.

Abajoe paused in his narrative because he knew little about Yamism and would have to do some research. Yamism's origins were complex, derived within the past 200 years from the traditional Gatra religions: Janduism and Dubbhism. He traced the origins of Yamism on secular Gatra island. Essentially, Yamism was a blend of the other religions, but with prescribed living standards, an evangelical mission and libertarian attitudes towards opposition.

Thus, Abajoe imagined Citra's childhood to be dominated by the religious traditions of Kitab beliefs and Yamen morality. She was being led into the future by a worldly-wise Kudim, who excited her interest in the outside world, especially Australia. He would find out about Yamism so that, when he eventually confronted Citra with his ideas, he would be sensitive to her world.

'She is unaware that the poverty in Pedang causes a tense existentialism, a preoccupation with the present and disinterest in the distant future. Although Citra enjoys the belonging and acceptance she gets from their close-knit community, many people are striving to save enough to leave the village. She has no earnings but is devoted to her religion and singing. She wants to become famous and rich so she can help the suffering poor.

'Sometimes she dreams of emigrating to Australia, that rich country of opportunity. If asked why people there have so much and she has so little, she would shrug, believing it was chance or fate. When asked would she really leave her family, Citra would hesitate, then answer shyly, "I would go home one day with money to help them, or bring them to where I was, or send money'."

Abajoe's creation, this girl interlocutor, had now become real in his mind. She had a magnetic attraction for him and he had a warm protective feeling towards her. She was very beautiful, talented, naive and innocent. He wanted to create for Citra and her people a less vulnerable, healthier, less hungry future.

CHAPTER 9

Biological Controls on Population

Four months later, Abajoe showed the progress of his and Paula's experiment with rossits to T One. The does from the first generation were pregnant to the buck from the other pen, to prevent inbreeding. Their brothers spent their time fighting for territory and losing to the two original bucks, which were much heavier. The two original does were heavily pregnant for the third time, with the second kindle two months old and weaned. There were 22 in the Australian pen and 23 in the Bhakarian one.

The six pregnant does in the Bhakarian pen had thrived with a regular food supply. He lifted one up and his fingers pushed aside the intestine in her bulging belly to count the foetuses.

"Thirteen," he said, "the same as last week. Let's see what difference last week's famine in Australia has made." The six mature does in the Australian pen had starved the previous week, as the food supply had delivered famine conditions. However, food arrived by chance before any had to be euthanized. He picked one up and probed her lean abdomen with his fingers, until he could feel the knobs of foetuses in a row along the backbone.

"She only has five now," he told T One. "There were 11 last week but the others shrank away and disappeared over a couple of days. I guess her body must have fed on them to grow the remaining five."

"It's an impressive response to hunger," T One remarked. "What's the overall idea again?"

"We need an answer to this question: Will the rossits slow down their breeding and keep their numbers steady if we stick to one sack of pellets per week? Or will they suffer a famine cycle of population explosion, then death, then profligate sex again?"

He explained to her the feeding arrangements, with Australia getting random amounts, whereas Bhakaria received a steady quantity.

"I see. There's plenty of food in the Australian pen now," said T One.

"They'll kindle in about 10 days and until then they'll have a hearty appetite," replied Abajoe.

"I guess if they go hungry again, their kindle will be small in size."

"Some of them, not all probably. The does may eat the runts when they're born."

"It seems extreme. Will it be relevant to humans?"

"In the Great Famine we had abortion, infanticide and child cannibalism."

"Oh really? This experiment is horrific!"

"Which is the better way to find out: a small experiment or the reality of another national disaster?"

"An experiment of course, provided it's relevant. Your model seems to have the main ingredients of our situation."

"Thanks. We're hoping for some useful results."

CHAPTER 10

Citra in a Dense Population

'Pedang people were accustomed to disease and death, they didn't realise it was due to overcrowding.' Abajoe paused, trying to find words to explain the situation he had observed in news stories he had accessed using his communicator. 'When there was illness locally,' he continued, 'and the Government told them to boil their water, to cook their food and to wash their hands, they complied, assuming that there was a new strain of a disease. No one told them that endemic disease had reached epidemic proportions through the multiplicity of their contacts with each other, the pollution of water, ground and air and through build-up of the disease in vector organisms such as mosquitoes and pigs.

'Bhakarian cities are densely populated and suffer wave after wave of viral epidemics. At first, the death rate had been lower than in the countryside because the cities had better medical services. However, the crowded city conditions overloaded people's immune systems and diseases spread rampantly there.

'When disease struck, people tried to flee but there was nowhere to go. Legal emigration meant queuing for several years and then being lucky enough to have the right qualifications. Illegal entry to Australia by boat had become more difficult as fuel became hard to get and ordinary Australians ceased to co-operate. When Bhakaria had an epidemic, Australia had turned her back.

'When her younger sister, Nyoman, was struck down with coughing fits, Citra prayed to Yahm to make her better. The little girl lapsed into a coma. When her mother counted her savings to call a doctor she could not afford it. Citra found a diagnostic programme on her communicator and told it her sister's symptom of coughing bouts, sweating and blood-flecked sputum. It diagnosed sporangoid fever. Cases were reported every year, sometimes in epidemics that killed hundreds. A mucus slime mould was attacking nasal, bronchial and lung tissue, particularly in the young and the old. Treatment required an antibiotic and she hurried to the pharmacy. The pharmacist called a nurse, who kindly came back with her and injected an antibiotic, but it was too late. Nyoman died a few hours later'.

Citra and her family's loss deeply moved Abajoe. He could have let Citra accept it as bad karma but he wanted to improve their situation and prevent such cruel loss of innocent lives. He had Citra assuage her grief by investigating the infection. Her communicator revealed the following information.

'Morphology: The mould feeds on epithelial cells of rotting fruit and the moist lining of animal respiratory systems. It lives in symbiosis with the plasmodium fruit fly, which acts as a vector in epidemics, as follows. The fly feeds on the plasmodium in rotting fruit and carries its spores to other fruit and into the air. When the spores are inhaled, they germinate as amoeboid cells, which unite and then divide repeatedly to form a plasmodium feeding on the victim, who succumbs to secondary infections, such as bronchitis, leading to pneumonia. The symptoms are coughing, fever, asphyxiation and death.

'Epidemiology: The mould is endemic and epidemics initiate in poor, unhygienic and crowded conditions. It spreads where there is a population density high enough to sustain swarms of fruit flies. There is no treatment and no vaccine. Prevention is to keep the fly population down below threshold density by removing rotten fruit.

'History: Both the plasmodium and the fly are biological warfare weapons that escaped from Australian trials in 2170 during the Coal Wars. No outbreaks have ever occurred in Australia, but in 2220 an epidemic began in Bhakaria at a camp of refugees from the Great Famine in Australia, resulting in 15,700,000 deaths. All Bhakarian cities were evacuated to the country until the disease subsided. Further outbreaks have occurred in Bhakaria, in densely populated parts'.

'When she had finished reading Citra was angry. 'Damn those Australians and their biological weapons,' she thought. 'They made a horrible disease and let it loose killing 16 million Bhakarians. Perhaps that was the idea'.'

When Abajoe had written this, he wondered if he had exaggerated Citra's antipathy. There was no love lost between the two nations. The Bhakarians had stood by while Eurany invaded Australia, as had the other countries in CPEC, the coal exporters' cartel. Then in the Great Famine, Bhakaria had helped as a good neighbour, letting in refugees from Australia. The export of sporangoid fever to Bhakaria at that time had been an accident. Alternatively, it could have been carelessness. However, it was resented, and when Australia turned its back on them after the famine, most Bhakarians felt aggrieved. He thought Citra would have a jaundiced view of Australia and tried to write this down.

'She reviewed what she knew of Australia. It was an inhospitable territory, with a small population living in cities around the edges, like Norway, except larger in area and with rich deposits of minerals not yet developed. We had answered their call for help during a famine, accepting refugees and sending a peacekeeping force. But, afterwards, when the country was still in ruins, Australians voted to send our troops home. Australian people are selfish and thankless. Their country was in a mess and they seemed to have turned their back on normal, decent living and to be subsisting in cults. There were several million of our settlers living in Yamen communes. But we have given the Australian Government the cold shoulder ever since they went their own way, just as we did with the island, Mitor.

'Australians seemed to lurch from one famine to the next. Perhaps that is because they have droughts and floods in a random pattern. El Nino events occurred due to the cold ocean off the coast of Allende, heating up every seven years or so as dry winds blew across Australia and eastwards across the Pacific, resulting in drought along their East Coast.

'There are rice paddies in the north founded by our Jandus from Hani. However, half of the population is of European origins, adapted to temperate conditions and cannot live in the tropics because of the heat. Australia's dryness means that little food can be grown. Kangaroos abound in the wild and provide much of the nation's meat supply. The vast centre is dry and eroded flat, without mountains to generate rain or gorges to build good dams. Consequently, irrigation is limited and most crops grow after rain. Because rains are irregular, Australians have had to abandon intensive farming methods and adopt opportunistic subsistence methods. People grow their own food, living in the country with large gardens for crops and food animals.

'Citra read that in Australia, cases of sporangoid fever were rare because there were too few fruit fly vectors in the low-density population. She realised that Pedang was densely populated. She recalled there had been epidemics of several diseases in the last few years. Disease was endemic and every year, during the monsoons, the hospitals filled to overflowing. In contrast, life in Australia was healthy, with a much higher life expectancy.

''If my family had been living in Australia, my sister would still be alive,' she thought. 'I would like to live there, if they would let me in. However, I could only go for three years as a guest worker. Australians are selfish with their living space and mineral resources, keeping them unused and refusing entry even to refugees.'

'She reflected for a moment. 'I feel sorry for Australians. They suffer harsh conditions in isolation. Without interaction with others and spiritual guidance, their long lives must be barren and meaningless.'

'However, Citra sadly realised that by comparison, life in Pedang was precarious. Premature death was commonplace and the only way for families to survive was to have many children, who would scatter so that some would survive. Large families created overcrowding and poverty and the disease cycle repeated endlessly. When landowners died, their wills divided property between their many children and living units became tiny. Citra's destiny was to be married to a farmer with an insecure living from a tiny farm, with the slavery of having many children, many of whom would die from malnutrition and disease, with the survivors living in utmost poverty. She despaired and looked for a way out.

'Her future seemed bleak. To escape, she embraced the teachings of Yamism, so she would have an idyllic afterlife in heaven, so sublime after the harsh life she knew. She learned the holy rules of diet, hygiene, meditation and evangelism that brought order to the chaos of poverty. Although reality was unremittingly grim, there was the satisfaction of living a good life, which Yahm would reward in the hereafter. This was a justification for sticking to a traditional lifestyle that had lasted 1000 years, foregoing the instant gratification of a modern, western lifestyle that could lead her to hell. Yet sometimes, as when her sister had died, she doubted that hell could be any worse than Pedang.

'If Citra had misgivings about her religion, she did not show it. When she read the mysteries of the Kitab, listened to the explanations of the Kudim and prayed dutifully for the salvation of her family and herself, the burden of her life seemed lighter. As she became older, she began to understand the words she recited from the Kitab, reflected on the possible meanings, and checked them with other uses of the same words. There were layer upon layer of meanings and each reading was rich with new associations.

'She became devoutly religious. She was certain that Yahm was watching over her and his presence in all things made her life less hard. He alone understood why he had taken her sister from them. There was more to it than science could explain.

'Citra sensed that an opportunity to fulfil her mission would come and she would need to travel. She had studied English at school and now, as an autodidact, continued using programmes on her communicator and practicing it with the Crucian missionary living in the village. She quickly developed knowledge of world history and science theories but her experience was limited to Pedang'.

CHAPTER 11

Jandu Coalition

"There, if it rains again you'll be laughing."

Abajoe loaded his gardening tools and farewelled the old man. He had tilled his garden and planted it with seed vegetables. People of his age commonly did voluntary work. He also gave away most of his earnings from 'Family Fare' to help those in need.

T One continued to follow the progress of the experiments with rossits. On her visits to The Tower, she would ask for an update on results. So far, the rossits in both the Australian and Bhakarian pens were breeding up to equilibrium and now, after eight months, the pens held about 50 in Australia and 70 in Bhakaria. There had been a severe drought in Australia, with many euthanized deaths, but when chance delivered food, breeding had resumed with larger litters. It was too early to tell if breeding had slowed in either pen in response to learning about the limitations of food and territory.

On one of her visits, Transcending One, as Party Leader, asked Abajoe and his friends to review the policy on membership of the regional body, the SEU, for their platform at the election later that year. They accepted the task with alacrity and divided the task between them: Abajoe would look into the political implications; John would investigate what SEU control would mean; and Paula would find out how it would affect Australia's mineral resource ownership.

Abajoe was taking every opportunity to learn about Australian politics. When Divine Muller, Head of the Jandu religion in Australia, came for a meeting with T One, she asked him to do some research for the meeting.

The MWP had brought the Jandus to Australia after the Great Famine. Marko had wanted to increase food-growing capacity through paddy agriculture and the Government brought Jandus from Bhakaria. They had experience in building paddies and irrigation systems and took a leadership role, developing them at communes on the floodplain of the Burkedin River. The Jandu deity, Dubba, controlled relations between all living things and the festivals of the Jandu calendar co-ordinated the irrigation and cultivation of the communes' lands. The scheme was very successful and had been expanded to other northern rivers. Commune members converted to Janduism and the number of Jandus had grown rapidly.

His conclusion was that they had become a significant voting influence. Abajoe was interested to see T One's dealing with them as a practical case of the MWP's ecumenical leadership.

"There is enough of them that we will just have to meet Muller's demands, won't we?"

"Why? He'll just be asking us to curb Yamen growth," T One said. "I can't see how I can do what he wants. Jandu support is important to us and they have sent in a detailed report on Yamen discrimination. If I pick on the Yamens, we'll not only lose swinging voters, but many supporters, who want to assimilate them. The meeting could be a disaster."

"What if the Jandus opt to run a candidate of their own?" asked Abajoe.

In the last election three years earlier, the MWP had 52% and the Yamens 40%. MWP support from Jandus had been 10%.

T One shook her head. "They'll only go their own way if we won't support them. There aren't enough of them to confront the Yamens directly. They'll hide behind us if they can."

Abajoe asked if he could attend the meeting.

"It seems like a crucial meeting," he said. "I would like to see what happens. Can I be there if I stay out of the way?"

"Okay. I don't want you to say anything unless I get pinned down; then you can rescue me!"

The meeting took place at her stadium office later that week.

The Divine had come from Flinders City in the south, on a tour of his northern parishes. He arrived by electrotaxi from their Meannjin temple, where he had officiated at services the previous day.

Muller was of indeterminate age, bald with a full, grey beard. He wore a white robe wrapped loosely about him and fastened at the shoulder, like a toga. Two assistants, similarly dressed, accompanied him. One carried a communicator.

T One and Abajoe met the party at the tunnel exit, where football players had once run onto the playing field. T One was wearing a sarong and Abajoe a data poncho, which would relate the discussion to their's and the Jandus' previous involvement with the various topics, and display strategic conclusions covertly for his perusal.

They showed the visitors the view over the horticultural allotments that now occupied the arena. Then they took the party under the stand, to a meeting room, where they had coffee and relaxants. After small talk, the visitors took one side of the table and T One and Abajoe the other.

"Thank you for seeing us," said the Divine. He spoke quietly, gently, the irises of his luminous eyes dark green. "We are concerned about the rise of Yamism and where it will end up."

He paused, waiting for T One to speak, but she declined. Instead, she tilted her head and eyed him quizzically, waiting.

He continued. "Our concern is whether your Government will ensure freedom of religion. Already the Yamens have a majority in some communes and are imposing their hygiene and dietary customs on everyone. They are discriminating against our followers. Local councils are turning a blind eye. Are you going to do anything about it?"

Abajoe knew the Divine's concern. In Bhakaria, the Yamen majority had persecuted Jandus. They had fled to Hani Island, where a Jandu majority emerged in a polarised nation. They feared the rise of Yamism in Australia could have a similar result, so they sided with the MWP in opposing Sudarta's Yamen-aligned Progress Party. The ecumenical MWP had embraced Jandu concerns and acted to prevent racial discrimination. They valued a multicultural community with a minimum of enforced assimilation.

T One leaned forward. "If the Yamen dietary customs are unscientific, they will be stopped. If the existing laws are too lax, we will tighten them up. Our Government protects the religious freedom of all Australians. If the laws against religious discrimination are being broken in a commune, we will direct the local council to enforce them, by whatever means are necessary."

Abajoe poured relaxant tea into fine china bowls. He passed them out while the conversation continued.

The Divine steepled his fingers. "The laws concern physical access to public places but it is access to goods and resources where they are discriminating against us. The communes won't allow the selling of chicken meat. It is a traditional food of ours. We normally eat…"

"It is up to the communes to decide what foods are made available," said T One, sipping her tea. "Other foods can be acquired from outside."

"Exporters are distant and difficult for our people to get to. The Government should allow all basic foods to be produced locally or imported by communes."

T One sighed. "I'm sorry that it's hurting you, but local governments aren't empowered to dictate a commune's culture. In any case, the plurality you want contradicts the minimalism that local governments are seeking. Communes are encouraged to develop predominant cultures with a simple selection of foods and a minimum of material requirements. Yamen communities are entitled to specialise." T One paused and sipped again. "The Government has to be fair...in several communes Jandu is a majority, isn't that right?"

"Yes, in about a handful."

She spoke slowly and quietly. "Where you Jandus have a majority, do you provide support for the dietary and hygiene customs of the Yamen minority?" Her eyes searched his face.

"No...That is different. It's..." he stopped, trapped by his double standards.

Abajoe could understand the Divine's predicament. Jandus lived together to share their cultural traditions and religious worship and in opposition to Yamen hegemony. Their resistance to Yamen growth was passive, whereas Yamens were assertive in resisting Jandu growth. It was the conflict of a bear with a bull.

"How is it different?" T One encouraged him to continue. When he did not she said summarily, "It's simply a case of majority rule. It is the same in Kurilpa with water recycling. We are a minority and have to acquiesce."

The Divine, flushed with anger and jaw clenched, put his hands flat on the table, getting ready to stand up. His eyes squinted with the narrowness of his vision. "Look," he said gruffly, "if you won't support us, why should we vote for you?"

Abajoe's heart sank. The Jandus wanted favours for votes. Unless they made them an attractive concession, they would quit the Party. They would probably put up candidates of their own. 'How can we keep their support?' he thought.

T One spoke firmly. "The MWP guarantees you your religious freedom and access to basic foods. No one can impose unscientific customs on you. But if they..."

The Divine was indignant. His voice was raised. "The way they treat their children...denying them their rights...is that 'unscientific'? No...their customs are a matter of belief rather than of science. Their schools are abhorrent...the way they separate girls and boys."

"The Yamens favour gender separation. There is some scientific support for it to improve students' performances. If a Jandu minority cannot accept the ruling morality, when it is within the law, then members may have to move to a new home outside the commune. They can go to a Jandu commune, where they will be part of the majority culture."

Muller's words came in a hot torrent. "Your science is biased against us! Separating boys from girls does not provide a rounded education! How can it be an improvement in education? Do your performances include understanding of the opposite sex? Do they include harmony in relationships? I think not. And all you have to offer is that we can move? Bah! It's not good enough!"

He had put them between the devil and the deep blue sea, thought Abajoe. If T One ordered the scientific evaluation to be redone, it would provoke the Opposition and become a major election issue when there was little they could gain. On the other hand, if they ignored the Divine's complaint, they could lose his support.

T One thought for a long moment.

Then she replied "I don't think you fully understand our position. Let's go back a step. The MWP is committed to democracy and multicultural diversity."

"That says...nothing," he spat out the word, '...about stopping the ill treatment of religious minorities like ours!"

"We have anti-discrimination laws," T One said, leaning back, as if that should be the end of the matter.

But the monk shook his head vigorously, in despair. "They don't cover our problem. We are being subjected to Yamen customs that interfere with our lifestyle."

T One seemed to count to ten before replying. 'If you can produce evidence that the communes' regulations are wrong, the council will support you in having them changed. If they do not, then you can take their behaviour to your national representative for action. Can you see that we have one system of law for all, based on science?"

"Yes...but it is unjust!" he slammed his fist on the table. "Yamism shouldn't be able to drive us from our homes!"

There seems to be no way of meeting his demands, thought Abajoe. He expected Muller to tell them to go to hell at any moment. T One's quiet voice interrupted his thoughts. She spoke calmly, soothingly.

"Yamen culture varies from one commune to another. You are concerned because, in Flinders, it has been evangelical, intolerant of minorities and aggressive when challenged. It is, after all, a militant religion, based on the philosophical and moral imperatives of a warlord prophet, Numan. Her god, Yahm, inspired her to carve a fiefdom with the sword from the chaos at a crossroads, where different cultures overlapped in the Middle East. She conquered city-states and imposed her moral laws. Whereas prophets of other religions taught transcendent passivity and forgiveness of oppressors, Numan taught opposition and vengeance in their struggle for survival. She told them how to live, love and oppose their enemies in the Kitab, a book that structures the lives of Yamens. As long as its adherents are law-abiding, we have to accept their takeover of communes such as yours."

"Our fear is Yamens' high birth rate and aggressive evangelism. They encourage the having of children and because their families are closely knit, they survive famines better than the rest of us. Their numbers are growing very fast."

"When they are more secure and have grown to a majority, their expansion will slow down," T One reassured him. "At the same time, they will become less deviant, respectful of the Government and more tolerant of minorities. You will recall that your own religion, Janduism, had extremism and large families in the early days. Today, you still keep your religion's essential lifestyle, but your people are assimilated and conform to the two children policy. Yamen communities are newer, with extremist elements. Many have suffered from other cultures' prejudices and from famine. They have not forgotten that our Government did not stop prejudice against them during the famines and there was genocide in some provinces. Now they are alienated from the Government. They won't follow our guidelines for treatment of minorities."

"They'll vote for Sudarta, every last one of them!" said the Divine vehemently. "The MWP is in trouble! We have been thinking about running Jandu candidates but that would conflict with our desire for assimilation in material and economic matters. We have a long history of voting for the MWP but now our people are beginning to suffer and our leaders only want to be in a coalition with you if you will protect us from Yamen fundamentalism."

"I know you are in a difficult situation and I am proposing to move the seat of national Government to Flinders City, where, if we win, we can oppose extremism and work out a solution. But that's as far as I can go, today."

The cleric was quiet, then whispered with his companion.

"That is an excellent proposal," he said.

There followed some agreeable discussion of other issues. No one mentioned immigration, a hot potato. Then the visitors prepared to leave. Before going, the Divine took T One aside.

"It looks as though we could support the MWP in the election," Muller said.

T One offered her hand but he did not take it.

"It depends on the other issues. We'll let you know as soon as we can."

T One had been skilful in steering the negotiations away from coalition. There was not enough common interest and it was the last thing she wanted.

Abajoe had learned that where there are racial differences, an arbitrator has to spend a lot of time explaining how a system would be fair to everyone and would prevent racial discrimination. He wanted a role, where he could facilitate more sharing.

Abajoe felt relieved but he wondered about Jandu concern for other issues. The Jandu vote could make all the difference between success and defeat. Fear of Yamen hegemony connected them strongly to the Jandus. The MWP's policy for dealing with the Yamens would have Jandu support unless something went wrong, such as religious violence.

He looked at the sky. Although it was cloudy, there was no more rain and the old man's seedlings he had planted would die. However, his voluntary work had not been a waste of time because his time with him had included him in the community. Although securing water and food supplies were the top priority, building a caring community was of equal importance because it would decide how to share them.

CHAPTER 12

Rossits and Population Controls

Abajoe had started to keep rossits four years before. A genetic engineering company had given T One two pairs of this new animal during an official visit. They had designed it for meat production in backyards. She was developing the 'Family Fare' self-sufficiency idea and asked her son to find out their potential.

At first, he worked the does hard. Although a doe need only be empty for a few hours, he soon learned to allow a couple of weeks for recovery from kindling before mating her again. The strain of nurturing foetuses and simultaneously producing milk would pull the doe down to skin and bones, even when she was well fed. Then she would reabsorb some of the foetuses and produce a small litter. However, with a short break between pregnancies, a doe could average a dozen kits eight times per year. The youngsters reached sexual maturity in four months. In a year, one breeding pair could produce 250 does and 250 bucks. After only a few months, they could provide a regular supply of meat for several families.

When coccidiosis first struck the rossits, he had been shocked. He had thought their engineering, with possum digestive systems, would make them immune to the endemic disease that had slain his purebred rabbits. He had bought new bucks from other rossit keepers to diversify the genotype, but the disease had mutated from the rabbit disease. It struck the healthiest, bringing them to a painful death within a day. This virulent disease was a single-celled parasite, which disrupted intestinal function. It produced a bloody, watery diarrhoea. The pathogen attacked the lining of the intestine and rapidly spread along it, killing the rossit. He countered with disinfection of the rooms and medicated feeds, but to no avail. The endemic disease ran out of control through the units, decimating his warren overnight.

More had died in the crowded pens and he had realised the disease was caused by overcrowding. When there were too many rossits in a pen, healthy movement was inhibited. An epidemic resulted when the transmission density threshold for that disease had been exceeded. If the environment was unpleasant, their nervous systems inactivated the immune system, equivalent to suicide.

After six outbreaks and various experiments he realised that the disease was always present. He studied the resilient wild rabbit and found that the best antidote was the green feed that they enjoyed between outbreaks of myxomatosis and calicivirus, which did their cruel work in the crowded sets and warrens during rabbit plagues. Abajoe concluded that high densities in rossits, as in rabbits, was not sustainable. He provided more space per rossit and more green feed.

Nevertheless, the rossits were a success, producing more and better quality meat than rabbits. Paula and his breeding programme maintained a steady population of around 2000, housed spaciously in eight residential units on two floors of The Tower. With sufficient feeding of vegetable waste, they could keep coccidiosis under control. The rossits provided enough meat for the four generations of their family, with sometimes extra, which they gave away to poor families.

On one of her regular visits to The Tower, Abajoe showed T One the set up of the rossits experiment.

"What are you trying to show?" asked T One. "Australians breed like rossits and then die from disease or famine or get culled in a war?"

"The opposite. Our experiment will show whether rossits will limit their population under Australia's extreme conditions. Our hypothesis is that the Australian people have learned to control its population by individual choice."

"It doesn't seem likely," said T One. "After a famine, people always go at it like polecats. Then there's a baby boom, which sets up the next famine. Malthus in 1800 assumed that man had two hungers: food and sex. He said neither could ever be quelled or controlled."

"Maybe the boom is to replace those that died," Abajoe replied. "Then they will halt the population explosion. Malthus was very unscientific. There was a lot of evidence that births vary up or down depending on conditions, even though in those days, birth control technology was not available. Nowadays most pregnancies are voluntarily controlled."

"Correct. When danger looms, people often have more babies, so some will survive. Like a cactus, which will flower before it dies in a drought? At other times, reproduction is limited by conditions... Oh, excuse me." She took a call and talked for several minutes.

"I'm sorry about that. There has been a border incident...a fishing boat with illegal immigrants from Bhakaria. We have sent them back...so why not use human statistics instead of doing this experiment with rossits?"

"I have tried to. However, there are too many possible contemporary causes, such as economic conditions and migration, to be able to see whether the population is being unconsciously capped at some level. That is why I need the rossits. I need a controlled experiment."

"That's interesting. But why are you modelling Bhakaria? What have you found so far?"

"It's too early to say. In the Australian pen, there has been a famine already and we had to euthanize about 30 youngsters, but they have bred back rapidly. There are now about 60."

"What's been happening in the Bhakarian pen?"

"There's about twice that number. There has been plenty of food so far and they're all large and it's beginning to get crowded. The pregnant does seem to be carrying fewer foetuses now."

"Is that what you were looking for?"

"It may just be coincidence."

"Anyway, you'll discover the effect of less space."

"Or more regular food."

"Or illegal immigration!"

"Haha! No, they can't change pens. That would make it too difficult to find the pattern with food and space...it could take a couple of years for a stable pattern to emerge."

"I'll be very interested to see what you come up with."

"One trial may not be enough. We may have to repeat it and find how climate differences affect the outcome."

"You could build a mathematical model and test it by matching your results."

"Yes," said Abajoe. "But we would need more data to validate it. Effects of disease are complex and difficult to predict. You need as many backcasting years as you have forecasting years. It stands to reason."

"So it is with population predictions – until you stumble on an equilibrium with the environment that has existed for long enough and can verify that it will continue to exist. That's what we're looking for."

"It's worth a try."

CHAPTER 13

Staying out of the SEU

Abajoe was talking with his mother in her office at the stadium when she received a call. Abajoe listened as she talked with him.

"Hello, T One, this is Robert Chan."

He was President of the South East Union, the regional economic community.

"How are you, T One? The reason I'm calling is to persuade you to join us. We'll help to get Australia back on its feet."

"We are back on our feet, thank you. Maybe you would like to see us running around consuming more but that's not what our people want. They are lying back and enjoying their self-sufficiency."

"That may be enough for the moment but they'll soon want the higher quality life that the rest of us are enjoying."

"Some of your people benefit at the expense of others. We've not forgotten the SEU's racial inequalities."

He knew T One was referring to the time when, 235 years ago, Australia had been a member of the SEU and indigenous persons had first access to land and resources, because they were first to arrive. Australia could only end racial segregation by leaving the SEU. Abajoe's great great grandparents, Arnhem and Marta, had achieved Australia's peaceful withdrawal only seconds before an Australian terrorist, Natalee, Arnhem's sister, would have detonated a huge bomb under the full SEU Parliament. Arnhem had stopped her and they went on to win the debate, ending racial segregation in Australia.

Although the confrontation with the SEU had been many years before, most Australians regarded the SEU with contempt because it had maintained its system of segregation. The system, which granted privileges to races in order of arrival, contradicted Australians' most cherished value of individual equality.

Abajoe considered how two geographically neighbouring groups of people could have such different attitudes to race? Was it Australia's harsh climate that was the leveller, or their nation's low population density, that enabled her people to value each other without racial prejudice? Or was it the clash, between the world's great religions in crowded SEU countries that had created competition, which they tried to limit by segregation?

His mind rejoined the conversation between T One and Chan.

"It is Australia that has racial disharmony," said Chan. "Our system works very well. However, we would allow you to opt out of our system because of your climate. We would not impose segregation on you again. There would be major benefits for you from joining. For example, you would get support in a drought. You wouldn't have to worry about another famine."

"What type of support?"

"There are many features, for example, relief supplies. We explain it in our policy document. I will send it to you."

"We'll look at it," said T One. "Thank you for your invitation to join. We'll consider your proposal and get back to you."

After some small talk, she ended the connection. She turned to Abajoe.

"Over my dead body we will join! We have nothing in common with the SEU nations. They would only exploit us for their own benefit. However, many Australians don't understand that and we need to educate them by raising the possibility of joining as an issue. Would you and your friends like to look into this, to come up with a response to the SEU's invitation?"

"I'd love to. I think we all would; but I'll ask the others and get back to you."

The others accepted the task with alacrity and they divided the task between them: Abajoe would look into the political implications; John would investigate what SEU control would mean; and Paula would find out how it would affect Australia's mineral resource ownership.

They met to discuss their approach at the Jurilpa Commune's Scenarium. The hemispherical projection chamber created moods for meetings, parties, weddings and social events. Paula and John were there but Peter was at home, ill with a predatory, commercial virus manufactured overseas. Its developers had marketed an expensive antidote. Peter had bought it with money borrowed from Abajoe and was recovering.

Abajoe had made the booking and selected the scene. Their meeting simulated an Aboriginal restaurant on top of Uluru. They could see each other's outline, as they reclined in huge armchairs made of boulders filled with soft cushions. The surrounding rocks disappeared over the edge, with tawny desert below to the horizon. The roof dome was a black sky studded with stars, with the only other light coming from a glowing image of the Milky Way and flashes of green auroras above the south celestial pole.

They ate together before the meeting. The food was filleted goanna, a large lizard, with yams, saltbush seed bread and leaves from Alexandra Palms. Although Abajoe and John were Aborigines and Paula had been brought up with them, their ancestors' fare was a novelty.

Paula swallowed and told them "The goanna tastes a bit strange...like eagle...I suppose because it lives on small animals like lizards too. It brings me closer to this land and our past. It makes me feel at home here rather than just seeing it from the outside."

"Like you belong here?"

"Yes. It's a good feeling."

After that, they ate in silence, with the food and surroundings filling their thoughts.

When they had finished eating, Abajoe started the discussion. "We are here to consider whether Australia should go it alone or join the SEU. I chose this scene for our meeting because I believe Australia should evolve from diversity, rather than kowtow to edicts from the Seutosa Parliament. Our land is so large and varied that we should leave government of most things to local communities. However, the matter of the structure of the Government itself should be considered nationally."

"Do you think people want to be that organised?"

"Enough do. People want a nation and that means cohesion. Make no mistake, our nation is at a crossroads. Our civilisation may pass away, but the consequences of our words tonight will not pass away. The MWP has to make a choice, so when people vote they will get either our Australia, or the SEU's. If we win, the structure we want will determine the quality and quantity of life throughout our land, as communities wax and wane, until a new idea of what Australia is...what it can be... replaces it. If we lose, people will remember our ideas as a counterpoint to the SEU's melody, however untuneful it is.

"Then we have an easy task," said John. "Most people can't be bothered to work out whether or not we should join the SEU. They want rational leadership. All we need do is provide a reason for not joining and a snappy slogan."

"I think the onus is on the Progress Party to promote advantages of us joining, such as centralisation, and larger markets. Then we shoot down those reasons," said Paula.

"We don't need Big Brother SEU. Central authoritarian control is appropriate where sudden changes in the environment have to be responded to by the group as a whole," said Abajoe, "such as conducting a war or relief of a widespread natural disaster. However, Australians are used to adapting quickly to local conditions. Central authority will take control away from Australia and obstruct local initiative."

"We are not looking to export manufactured goods to SEU markets and we don't need central control."

"More than that, Australians are a proud people, who want self-determination..."

"...borne of bloody-mindedness rather than success!" John laughed.

"We are not unsuccessful," Paula bristled. "We have not done too badly...our spiritual lifestyle is the envy of the world!"

"It has come from suffering, in the Coal Wars and famines. Serious stuff-ups if you ask me."

"There's nothing to be gained from laying blame for the past. The point is, how would being in the SEU avert future problems?"

"The SEU helped T One get rid of the Bhakarian Army after The Great Famine," said John.

"They didn't do it to help us," denied Abajoe. "The SEU is the regional policeman. Its intervention had more to do with stopping a Bhakarian challenge to its authority than with protecting non-member Australia. The SEU may give us as much protection if we don't join as if we do, so long as we let them get our minerals."

"Might not the SEU invade us?" asked Paula.

"There is an old Greek proverb, 'Prosperity is never friendless'," Abajoe replied. "The rest of the world wouldn't let them...if we sell to them as well, that is."

"Going back, it is not the MWP's role...our role is to look for advantages of joining," said John. "If they are not apparent, they don't exist. For example, what evidence is there that they would actually help us avert a famine?"

"None. They did nothing last time."

"Exactly," said John. "We need to focus on the disadvantages."

"The main disadvantage," said Abajoe "is free movement of migrants between the countries of the SEU. A wave of immigration from SEU countries could result."

"How sure are you of that?" asked Paula. "The yellow peril theory was dead and buried long ago."

"There have been large migrations within the SEU. Australia is inferred to be a popular migrant destination from the high volume of attempted illegal entry."

"How will that affect us if we join?"

"Politically, it would be disastrous for the MWP," said Abajoe. "Socially, it could cause the dilution and even disappearance of traditional Australian culture. Australia's capacity to assimilate immigrants is limited. Yamen acculturation could be offset by rapid Yamen population growth. If the immigrant population grew too fast, it could reach a tipping point, where Yamen culture displaces traditional Australian culture."

"Apart from beer swilling and football, what aspects of Australian culture would be threatened?" asked Paula.

"Our 'have-a-go mentality'," said John. "The battling spirit of rugged independence."

"Aren't these characteristics admired in the world's other pioneering communities generally, rather than being exclusively Australian?" asked Abajoe.

"But Australia is so large and conditions here so harsh that our pioneering has been and continues to be at an extreme. Perhaps our battlers are the toughest?"

"Could be. Our culture also harks back to our convicts, with a disdain for hierarchical authority, suspicion of the ruling class' motives, cutting down of tall poppies, supporting the underdog, rejection of arcane viewpoints, distrust of theories and preference for terse, ineloquent communication."

"These are cultural cannons that may be taken up by immigrants. But there are more important features of Australian culture that may not survive. We could lose..." she counted on her fingers, "...English language, Dreamtime, Crucian religions, Crucmas, Easter, Invasion Day, cricket, rugby, elected managers, communes, local parliaments, scientific management, evolutionary causality, presumption of innocence, independence of the judiciary, water and land rights, freedom of expression, gender equality and perhaps..."

John interrupted. "What about our oral traditions, our stories, our songs, our literature, our movies, our theatre and so on. These could all be forgotten. Traditional Australian communities will break down."

"It is a terrible prospect," said Abajoe. "Most of our supporters will strongly oppose it – the Jandus especially would prefer living under Australian culture than under Yamism and they would be against joining the SEU if this could lead to a Yamen state."

"The other alternative is some form of Apartheid..."

"Don't even mention it," said Abajoe. "The MWP has come from there. The SEU forced on us their caste system. However, we did not like it...not even indigenous people who were on top...it was so arbitrary and cruel...so we quit the SEU. There is no way we will set up a colour bar to exclude the Yamens. We have to win their support."

As his words jostled and echoed in the blackness, Abajoe heard himself talking about Yamism as a defined religion, rather than as a threatening force. He realised that he was finally free of the deeply ingrained prejudices he had held against Yamens until that moment. It was a profound realisation, one of James Joyce's epiphanies. He had come to respect Yamens. Their religion was powerful and they knew about prejudice and fought it, an eye for an eye. Abajoe admired the Yamen spirit and religious cohesion. Adherents were law-abiding citizens and merged well with Australian culture. Yamen communes displayed independence, help to others, and were an asset to Australia. Traditions of diet, whatever we may think about how misguided they are, and their hygiene and prayer, gave their lives structure and they seemed to have fewer social problems. Nevertheless, for him as a scientist, some Yamen traditions seemed harmful. He wondered if familiarity would diminish them. It was unfortunate that a Yamen majority could control local councils, but that was the essence of devolution.

"The politics of the situation are difficult," Abajoe concluded. "What we need is a system of government based on ecumenism. Science will be the best co-ordinator..."

"But people think science is a religion," John interrupted him.

"You are right...that is a problem. We will have to show them that a scientific opinion has the possibility of being denied by objective evidence, not like the infallibility claimed by every religion. Scientists are tentative gentle people, without the self-righteous pig-headedness of religious leaders.”

“They won’t accept that science is neutral.”

“They have a point...science certainly is not neutral,” Abajoe replied. “Neither does it interpolate between religions or offer a least common denominator like most ecumenism. It is very heavily weighted in favour of a morality justified by objective arguments, in other words, wide agreement.”

“I’m convinced; it is the way to go. Therefore, what’s next...setting it up? How can we establish it?” asked Paula.

“What I think we need is apolitical...scientific...hearings...or... tribunals...” He broke off, thinking.

John’s findings about the results of SEU control had a more confident conclusion. He said the SEU would replace Australia’s devolved subsistence economy with centrally-planned urban industries. Australians would be cast as workers and consumers rather than meditators. Although the less ascetic members of the community were uncomfortable with a spiritual lifestyle and would welcome the change, the spiritual heartland of the MWP would find the new conditions abhorrent. Australia’s Yamens, however, were able to combine spiritual values with consumerism and would welcome SEU control. Jandus deplored consumerism and would be against joining the SEU.

Paula had investigated the mineral situation if Australia joined the SEU. She stood up and pointed in a northern direction towards the SEU’s Headquarters in distant Seutosa.

“The SEU wants to own Australia’s minerals,” she said scathingly. “Because we are not aligned, they do not have as much security of supply as they would like. They want to integrate vertically by bringing Australia into the SEU fold.”

“That sums it up well,” Abajoe said. “Our strategy has been to export minerals to Bhakaria at market prices. We used to use the revenue to buy our essential imports from them. The arrangement was the envy of their neighbours but they rested on their laurels. Now it is cheaper for them to buy from SEU countries because our minerals cost them more. They resent our prices, harking back to the time when they were occupying us as a colonial power and exploiting Australia’s minerals for a pittance.

Yamen voters would be happy if Australia showed preference to Bhakaria. This might bring some Yamen votes to the MWP."

"The Jandus and other small religions won't have a bar of the SEU and they will vote for us to stay out," Paula said.

"They could go the other way because of other issues..."

"Yes, that is a worry," Abajoe concurred. "We need a way to make their SEU position into the decider."

John unhooked his legs from over the arm of his boulder chair and sat forward. "Could we tap anti-Yamen sentiment by investigating the lack of scientific merit of Yamen hygiene and diet laws that they are imposing on others? The Jandus will like that!"

"True, but we would lose at least as many Yamen voters."

Paula said, "Nice try, John. But do you agree we recommend that our main plank should be remaining independent from the SEU? I feel very confident that Australians will want to stay out. Don't you?"

Abajoe felt that this was an historic moment and wanted to mark the founding of their election platform with some fine words, announcing their core beliefs. He thought of his studies of Crucianity and tried to recall how Jesus had announced his core beliefs. There was the Sermon on the Mount, with its blessing of various groups and assignment of their rewards. On a whim he stood on the top of the highest rock with his arms spread wide and his palms towards them. When he spoke, his voice resounded with strength and conviction.

"Happier will be those who seek independence, for the centre shall not tell them what to do."

John and Paula laughed and clapped.

"Happier will they be that want to belong to a strong local community, for the centre shall not weaken it."

They clapped again and after each of his edicts that followed.

"Happier will be those that seek to preserve their cultural traditions, for they shall not be displaced by foreign cultures.

"Happier will be those who want spiritual transcendence, for there will be freedom from the distraction of consumerism.

"Happier will be those who hunger and thirst after security of their food and water resources for these will be under local control.

"Happier will be those who fear our mineral resources will be stolen by invaders for we will sell them to those who would protect us.

"Rejoice that we have this choice, for when there is no choice, there is no happiness.

"Today we can choose, but unless we do choose, the choice will disappear and our happiness will be gone.

"For the happiness of Australia, choose to stay out of the SEU. Amen."

Abajoe jumped down from the rock as Paula and John whooped and yelled their agreement.

He had felt drawn to the Bible by something. His recurring idea was that his leadership would mirror the exploits of earlier prophets and statesmen, using success to breed success. In detail, it seemed to conflict with his science because he accepted the poverty of historicism. However, it was a new strategy overall. Reversion to earlier forms was intrinsic to evolution and so his urge to parody the past was vindicated.

The three of them agreed that the Party should oppose joining the SEU. A reason that could not be stated was that SEU membership would threaten Janduism in Australia. If Jandus could bring their relatives, Yamens too would also come in even higher numbers. Yamism would become the majority culture.

"Do we want to whip up fear of a Yamen takeover?" asked Paula. "Do we want to polarise the nation? No, the MWP is a multicultural party. We should embrace the Yamen people's concerns and enlarge our voter base."

"I agree," said Abajoe. "We are a non-discriminatory party. We need to attract the Yamen vote and I believe we can attract people, who have formerly voted against us, who would prefer an ecumenical Government rather than a Yamen Government."

"Are there such voters?" asked John sceptically.

"Yes, lots," said Abajo. "If we can get a new profile across that attracts the people who have been disaffected from the MWP's marathon incumbency. But the challenge is to win Yamen voters."

"How are we going to do that?"

"Well, first we need to get their attention with something they like. A snappy slogan, like 'Australia Is Not SEUtable'."

"Hey, I like that. Then we need a paragraph to explain why not."

"We need to scratch their itch, when we have worked out what it is. I am working on it."

CHAPTER 14

Citra becomes a Yamen Acolyte

Abajoe closed his eyes and imagined the wraithlike Citra had discovered Yamism the way his Aboriginality had been revealed to him, through his family and through the teaching of elders. He began writing that captured the essence of Yamism emanating from the sea of humanity that washed against Australia's northern shores.

'Citra had never left her village, Pedang, in Bhakaria. Her understanding of the outside world came largely from the teachings of Yamism. As she recited the Kitab, prayed and listened to the preaching of the Kudim, she became absorbed in the religion, even though she understood little of the text and needed an interpreter. Her father would read to the family from the Kitab in the evenings at home, explaining where he could. The stories captured her heart.

'One night, when she was 13, she had gone outside and looked up at the glowing splendour of the stars in their swarms. 'How small am I?' she thought. 'I will never ripple the universe. But I want to make a difference here on earth by living my life according to the words of our prophet, Numan, recorded in the Kitab. I will be an exemplary follower of Yamism in everything I do. I will give my life to helping my people escape poverty, overcrowding and disease. I vow this, before God, who made these stars.'

'From that day, her demeanour radiated a serenity that attracted attention wherever she went. She was fulfilling a sacred mission. It occupied her every moment.

'As she became older, she began to create meanings from the Kitab for herself, because some of the stories were just fine-sounding words, foreign to her experiences. However, Citra was curious and checked the associations she discovered. She would ask the Kudim, or borrow a communicator from the gereja (temple) and research the meanings, recording them in a notebook. Her understanding grew, and with it her dedication to Yamism.

'Her scholarship so impressed the Kudim that, when she was 15, he sponsored her to attend a school for Yamen youths interested in training to become Kudims. It would be the first time she would leave the village and she was filled with excitement as she waited out the weeks to her departure. Eventually, the day arrived and her proud family went with her to the station to see her off. She was accompanied by a gereja official for the journey to the school in Hanuso City.

'What a journey that was! They travelled by steam train, burning wood, in a huffing and puffing cloud of smoke, echoing across silent tree-cloaked valleys, yelling with speed through cuttings, zigzagging backwards and forwards up steep escarpments, with wheels spinning wildly and hammering insanely in flurries of reciprocation.

'They shared a sleeping compartment and she soon slept to the rhythmical rocking of the carriage and to the snickety-snack of the wheels below. Several jolts and squeals of shunting awoke her, the glowing signal lamps swooping past outside. By the time she was used to it, the sun was climbing and she had only a couple of hours of rest before breakfast. It came delivered in a package from a vending machine. She savoured the novel foods as she looked out on the orderly patchwork of paddy fields, where buffalo ploughed in the mud, as they had for centuries.

'Then the hovels, slums and painted boulevards of the capital arrived, with impatient crowds at level crossings. Citra was amazed that there were so many people, so varied in appearance and so different from folk in her village. In some places, there was more poverty than she had ever seen: desolate wastelands with people, who watched the passing of the train without hope of ever going anywhere else. These, too, were her people, whose lives she had vowed to improve. There were tall, grassy embankments, where urchins played chicken on the track, dodging aside at the last minute as they rattled past. Then they plunged underground and stayed down in the darkness, hurtling at breakneck speed into pools of platform light, rouletting through rocking switchyards, they jolted on and on.

'At last, wheezing and hissing, they ground to a door-slamming halt. Citra and her guide asked the way and then rode tandem in a cyclo to the magnificent, central gereja for Gatra Island, next to the university, where the Yamen orientation school would be held. She would stay in a residential hall for a month during the students' summer vacation.

'When Citra arrived, she joined the others at prayer in the gereja. Thirty trousered rear ends jutted above prostrated heads, shoulders and arms. She knelt on the intricately patterned carpet and thanked Yahm for her safe journey. When they sat up, a few curious glances came her way.

There seemed to be an equal number of boys and girls. Yamism was an advanced religion that did not distinguish male and female roles. Her guide squeezed her arm and was gone. Then the Kudim, raised on a small platform at the front, welcomed them and addressed them. Sunbeams streamed through the stained glass windows, depicting scenes from the life of the prophet. His voice resonated, exalting in melodic pronunciation of the holy words. He said the purpose of the school was to prepare them to become full-time students of Yamism the following year at their college next door.

'Then he spoke to them about the sacred purpose of Yamism and Citra flung open the gates of her heart. She closed her eyes and her prayers echoed in the silences of her soul. She had been alone and now God was with her. His wind filled her sails and she strained for the vessel of her being to set forth across the vast sea of life. Now, she cast off her moorings and her body shuddered as she got underway, guided by the compass of her dreams. As the voice of the Kudim rose and fell, she surged down the waves.

'After prayers, still resonating with inner navigation, she carried her things to the residence and up to a room with two beds. She put her belongings on the one closest to the window. The door burst open and in bounded a boisterous girl, laughing noisily.

'"Hey, I'm Rachael. I guess we're roommates." She threw herself on the other bed.

'"Hi, Rachael. I'm Citra," she offered her hand. "I'm pleased to meet you."

'Rachael took her hand briefly. "We are going to have the coolest time!"

'She said it as though she was familiar with a wide range of illicit activities. They talked about their families and where they lived. Citra felt naïve beside her. She had never met a city girl of her own age before and she wondered what she had been missing out on. She had never stayed away from home for more than a one-night sleepover with a friend and she had little experience with boys. In the village, she had spent her life with females. She had rarely spoken with her father and younger brother, as tradition decreed that they eat together in silence.

'Rachael seemed to know about boys. She was like a magnet with them. During services, the two girls sat in the back row and Rachael held hands with the boy beside her. The boys competed to sit next to her.

They were deterred by Citra's devout aura and left her alone. But one was smitten by her beauty and sat close beside her. They talked shyly and became more and more involved with each other.

'Citra had never held a boy's hand affectionately before and she was amazed at the sensations and emotions that a hand could convey. The tedium of the lectures was enriched by hidden handholding, secret smiles, feverish fingers, gentle groping, whispered endearments and calculated kisses. The hand and lips were far more articulate than their shy owners with their few blurted words. Their minds could not concentrate on the prayers and, instead of studying, they talked.

'She thought what they were doing was probably wrong because it was so enjoyable. Rachael wasn't worried about it. Citra did not know for sure that she was not living up to her vow of obedience to Yamism. She did not know exactly where the Kitab forbade her explorations. Rachael said what they were doing was harmless and encouraged her.

'In the residence, they got to know the boys at recreational activities. Then the boys visited them in their room. Citra knew she was getting into deep water but Rachael reassured her it was allowed.

'"What's wrong with kissing boys?" Rachael laughed at her.

'"It might lead to sex!" said Citra. "I'm too young for that."

'"Not if you don't let it. I know when to say 'Stop'."

'Citra deduced from the noises coming from the other end of the dark room that Rachael's idea of when to say stop did not exclude heavy petting. What Rachael allowed a boy to do in one session, Citra was expected to allow in the next. Rachael changed boys several times. Citra realised that Rachael was out of control but it was already too late to stop.

'One of the other girls complained about them to the Course Administrator and he caught them with boys in their room. He applied the new Yamen ethic that treated both males and females equally. Both the boys and the girls received a formal warning. Citra was acutely embarrassed and stopped seeing her young man. He was devastated but she was firm. She distanced herself from Rachael, who continued undeterred.

'"C'mon, Citra. We won't get caught again. We'll go to the boys' rooms."

'"No, Rachael. I'm out of this."

'A few days later, Rachael was caught in a boy's room and sent home. The Administrator said he would report the girls' behaviour to their sponsors. Citra protested her innocence but he would not discuss it. Rachael was laughing defiantly when she said goodbye to Citra.

'"You can have it, this fucking course! It is for weirdos. I wouldn't be a Kudim for quids. All that praying. Staying celibate is unnatural. I'm going to get my fair share of sex and no one's going to stop me!"

'When she had gone, Citra felt relieved. It was as if a temporary madness had been cured. When she considered her experiences with the boy, she felt sex was messy, earthy, male-centred, demeaning and animal-driven by a low instinct. She had higher ambitions. She thought she would never again allow sex to become an important part of her life. It was overrated. She wanted to be a celibate Kudim, spiritually wed to Yahm, following her sworn mission. She hoped that her mistake under Rachael's influence would be overlooked if she devoted herself to her studies.

'Over the following month, Citra learned as she had never learned before. There seemed no limit to the complexity of their religion and she revelled in it. There was a routine of sleeping and eating in the girls' dormitory, attending classes and praying, their day revolving around prayers every three hours. During prayers, she reflected on what she had learned during lectures and marvelled at the rich tapestry of her religion. There was a full schedule of lecture and study in the evenings. She learned about the history of the prophet, the meaning of his teachings and their modern application. There were the deeds of saints and the origins of legends to puzzle over. Above all, there was the melodic recital of the Kitab to practice. The Kudim knew of her Kitab singing fame and invited her to perform at a broadcast service. It was what she enjoyed most: stretching the virtuosity of her voice as she incanted the holy words, holding in rapture the national audience.

'Citra was unusually mature and developed a critical perspective of her religion. Through all her training, her mission was kept soaring on the thermal of the Kudim's concern for hunger, poverty and overcrowding, that she had vowed to alleviate. There were a million ways her religion supported her mission and reaffirmed its importance. However, Citra became aware that the teachings merely acknowledged these difficulties and accepted them, doing nothing to keep her mission aloft.

'Worse, there were basic ideas in the Kitab that contributed to hunger, poverty and overcrowding. They were like a downdraft working against her mission. To overcome the overpopulation problem, she could see that couples, who wanted a child, should logically consider whether the community could afford an extra user of space, food, water and resources. However, Yamism required that couples should have children if they could afford it. Such action would worsen the hunger, poverty and overcrowding she was trying to overcome. Hardly believing this was possible, she suspended judgement and investigated these teachings until she was quite sure. Then she realised that her religion embraced only part of her mission.

'She agonised about her loyalties to her mission, or to Yamism. It was a question of whether she should accept all Yamism as an end, or merely that part that was a means to her mission. She had to choose between them but she didn't know how. Her knowledge of Yamism was incomplete and she hoped, desperately, that further training would reveal to her a solution to this dilemma. She never wanted children herself and knew other young women, who felt the same. Perhaps if she deserted Yahm in this, Yahm would desert her at her time of need?

'Despite her reservations, she loved the religious training and floated happily on the stream of prayer and enculturation until it was time to return home to her family, which came all too soon. If she could have stayed, she would have, for Yamism had taken over her life. Now she might have to face the music of her indiscretion. Would her devotion to her studies after Rachael left be sufficient to bring redemption?'

CHAPTER 15

Rossits and Voluntarism

Paula and Abajoe were showing John and Peter the rossit experiment. The Bhakarian pen was crowded with a variety of individuals of different sizes and condition.

"The population varies around 450," Paula told them, "even though there's plenty of food. The number has been kept down by wave after wave of disease."

Next door, in the larger Australian pen, there were only 50.

"There have been three severe famines," Paula said.

A few individuals in both pens were thin and dishevelled.

"Those are disease and famine victims," Abajoe explained. "We may have to euthanize them, unless they continue to get better."

"I think we have enough data to stop here," Paula told Abajoe. "It has been running for two years. We should repeat the experiment to validate the results."

He agreed.

"There is a lot to discuss," he said. "Let's have a round table on the results and see what we can tease out."

They went downstairs to his flat. Paula gave an overview of the data in tables on the view-wall, showing the record of how the population had varied in each pen.

"If there are patterns, they are complex," said John. "I can't see the wood for the trees."

Abajoe and Paula explained their interpretation of the data and, after a lengthy discussion, they all agreed.

"Where to from here?" John asked.

"What we need next is a human population model for Australia that matches our history," Abajoe said. "We can construct it using the rossit results and local councils would use it to predict local population numbers, considering the possibility of famine. It's a real possibility with this drought."

In Meannjin, the summer rains had failed after a dry year. There was still water in storages but use was severely restricted.

"No matter how bad it gets, councils won't bring in population control," said Paula.

"Then we have to include death by starvation or thirst," said Abajoe. "There could be voluntary control within a social group…the ages and genders of those, who die from starvation and diseases, have to be considered."

There was silence as they considered this.

"Voluntarism assumes the rossits decided which individuals should die first," Paula suggested. "How can we know that? There is a danger of anthropomorphism in attributing to rossits a human psychology – their thinking may be quite different from ours."

"I think the reverse is more likely," said Abajo. "I think that we would behave like rossits."

"Why so? How is a rossit model relevant to humans?" asked John.

"Under the duress of famine, humans may revert to the mammalian brain."

"Do you have any evidence of that?" asked John, sceptical.

"Yes, anecdotal," replied Abajoe. "We noticed that rossits seem to interact like humans in a famine. If we simulate a famine situation, we can check… Are you willing to take part in a little experiment?"

"Uh-oh! I'm not going to starve," said Peter. "Is that the idea?"

"No, but I do want you to think like a hungry rossit. My hypothesis is that lower mammals lack our memory. Rossits have much smaller frontal memory lobes, a reduced hippocampus and lower memory retrieval ability.

"We can simulate human thinking by temporarily putting a tourniquet on the human parts of the brain, the mid-cortex, with a drug that will temporarily prune it back to a rossit-like structure. The mid-cortex would be reduced, shedding human language and analytical abilities. We can see how we would behave when starved."

"How will this help?" asked Peter.

"For our human population model, we need to predict how humans will share food when it is scarce."

"So, I am going to be dumbed-down," said John, "and put in a food-sharing situation when I'm hungry?"

"Exactly. Thanks for co-operating," Abajoe got up to go. "Now, I want you to fast until we meet here tomorrow. We will have a camera recording us. Okay?"

"I'm starving!" said John, when they had all arrived in Abajoe's flat the next day and were sitting at the kitchen table. "Fasting has brought me to a halt. I can only think about getting food. I hope it is going to be worth it!"

"Here, swallow this." Abajoe handed each of them a small capsule and put one in his own mouth. He drank from a glass of water. "Get ready to have a rossit's brain."

"A starved brain," said Paula. "An atrophied..."

"I can't..." John's mouth moved but he made no sound.

There was silence. The drug had blocked that part of the brain they used for speech.

Abajoe lost awareness of what happened next and could only remember it afterwards. He recalled noticing each of the others as if for the first time. Paula was extraordinarily beautiful. She went to the food cabinet and they all followed her. It was empty, except for a small bowl with a dozen vegetable nougats. She took it out and ate one. She held it towards Abajoe. John and Peter reached out but Abajoe took the bowl before they could grab any and ate several. He offered it to Paula. The two of them ate the lot. Peter and John got nothing and turned to searching through the cupboards in vain. Abajoe and Paula sat together on the settee and went to sleep.

When they woke up, John and Peter were hunched in their chairs.

"H...hello. Can you t...talk?" Abajoe asked.

"Hello," said Paula. "Yes, I can. What happened?"

John and Peter stirred and stared at her, uncomprehending.

"I'm not sure," said Abajoe. "Let's wait for these two to come out of it; then we'll watch the movie. Let's get something to eat."

They went next door to his grandparents' unit. There were several plates of sandwiches.

"Good ol' Gran and Gramps," said Paula. "They've saved my life."

They carried the food back to Abajoe's unit and shared the sandwiches with the others. John and Peter began stuffing them into their mouths two at a time.

"Those were great sandwiches," said Peter, when he was full. "Why aren't you two hungry?"

Then they watched the camera recordings on the monitors in the studio. They saw Abajoe and Paula eat all the nougats, as John and Peter watched.

"Hey! You greedy pair!" said John. "You didn't give us any – I thought you believed in sharing?"

"We let them," said Peter. "Perhaps because it was Abajoe's territory."

John shook his head. "It was gallantry. Paula was female – does and kindles first."

"What about Abajoe?"

"He was her buck, her chosen male. We deferred. She must survive and reproduce at all costs. We wanted them to survive and accepted that we lower-ranking bucks should starve."

"It seems logical," said Abajoe. "That's how I see it."

"Thanks, you guys," said Paula.

"Now, let's see what we have learned about who would get most food in a famine. What would happen if there were 10 rossits in a pen, but there was only enough food for two of them?" Abajoe asked.

"The healthiest male and female would survive," Paula replied.

"Why?" asked Peter.

"The others would stop eating," replied John.

Peter held up a hand. "But what if the food was only enough for one?"

"A pregnant female would get the lion's share."

"What if there wasn't one?"

"One would breed, like a cactus flowering in a drought," said Abajoe.

"Why would the others sacrifice themselves?" asked Paula. "Is reproduction the ultimate value?"

"So rossits will continue."

"But the life would be so hard," said Peter. "Why would they want it to continue?"

"They hope life will get better," said Abajoe.

"What is 'hope'?"

"They are optimistic it will get better," said Abajoe.

"Why?"

"Optimism is decreed by survival of the species, which is the ultimate value, don't you think? Nature selects optimistic individuals; pessimism weakens the immune system. Pessimists don't survive."

"Pessimism could reduce adult numbers quickly then?" John proposed.

"Yes, and cleanly. If there is a turnaround in conditions, the dying wouldn't be physically damaged. Immune system failure bears no scars." Abajoe replied. "They would go back into the pool of hopefuls... believers...in survival."

"But the age and gender of deaths would depend on the pecking order," said Paula. "What you have predicted actually happened with the rossits. Sharing of scarce food had a pecking order, with pregnant does first, then the alpha physical male, followed by mature females and last of all, young males."

"Our pecking is academic combat. Perhaps physical prowess is less important than intelligence for the alpha male?" asked John. He had a tendency to intellectualise even simple matters.

"Alpha females can do their own thinking," said Paula. "These days, the male pecking order is resourcefulness."

"Shit!" said Peter. He had recently left his wife and children in their family home, taking nothing but an obligation to support them. "What about sceptics?" he asked hopefully.

"A sceptic has a personal disposition toward doubt or incredulity of facts, persons, or institutions," Paula told him. "A sceptic is best equipped to provide an alternative viewpoint to help guide pregnant females in the difficult decisions she must make under adverse conditions. If there is food for two, the female will choose a sceptical, resourceful male."

"That lets you off the hook then, Abajoe," said Peter. "You have resources, but you are not much of a sceptic."

"Oh, I don't know..." quipped Abajoe.

They laughed.

Abajoe became serious. "I doubt that humans have a common pecking order for sharing food – this would depend on each family's different beliefs. The female in a famine has to consider pregnancy controls, such as abortion..." He paused, remembering that he would have had an older half-brother if Marko's first wife hadn't aborted in a famine.

"Then how can we predict?" asked John.

"The rossit data gives us an average," said Abajoe.

"Yes. Rossits keep their numbers down by cannibalising infants, ejecting kindle from the pouch and absorbing foetuses."

"In a famine, perhaps we have less control?"

"Humans have contraception, abortion, febrile euthanasia and infanticide. There's not much difference."

"Could the population be controlled earlier in the life cycle...as an aversion to ovulation?"

"Humans have the pill, but many do not use it..." said Abajoe knowledgeably.

"...especially when they are desperate," said Paula looking at Abajoe. "A responsible female needs security before allowing herself to become fertile."

"Rossits may be able to control ovulation," said Abajoe, changing the subject. "That is what our experiment will find out. When we run the data through a regression analysis, it will tell us any causes...and how confident they are."

"Whether lower fertility is associated with crowding ..."

"Can we use the rossit model to predict human behaviour, including starvation?"

"Yes. We verified that in our simulation. We can have some confidence in predicting the survival of the different age groups and genders."

"What about disease?"

"We found that disease strikes the starving and pessimistic when the population is dense, particularly the very old and very young. There were few epidemics in the Australian pen but they were common in the Bhakarian one. Families frequently lost members to disease."

'Then population numbers are subject to complex controls," said John. "Are we going to be able to learn anything?"

"Yes...how much of the control is anticipative rather than reactive...how early the rossits begin to deal with the situation of scarce food supply."

"Whether they recognise a pattern?"

"Yes, they seemed to, but we don't know how they learned. Their response could have been due to an association between sexual activity and starvation. Alternatively, their response could be that reproduction was restrained by reinforcement, with the reward of less competition for food. Or even that they had cognitive awareness that the quality of life was enhanced when reproduction had been limited. Whatever their learning process, the boom and bust mentality was present but inhibited to a degree.

"As Malthus noticed," said Abajoe, "famine does not seem to deter the zest for sexual activity. It may even increase it, like those cacti I mentioned that flower just before drought kills them. Neither rossits' nor humans' starvation experience may feed forward into avoiding further famine."

The discussion continued for some time. By analysing the rossit population data, Abajoe, Paula and their friends proposed human population dynamics for variable water and food supplies, including famines. Over the following weeks, they built a population model and explored possible futures for Australia.

When they presented their findings to the MWP's Population Committee, the representatives found the range of possibilities interesting but no one wanted to plump for any particular future because of their policy of local diversity. However, they agreed that the consequences of population numbers were of concern and should be co-ordinated nationally.

In one of few national initiatives, T One decentralised the population model to co-ordinate councils and their infrastructure development. The 149 councils had to input their population numbers and water, energy and food plans for co-ordination. In assiduously avoiding prescriptive central planning and allowing the councils to respond in their own way to the drought, she was in a cat-and-mouse game with the Opposition, who wanted no government planning at all. She was finding it difficult to play the cat because she could not prevent people rejecting the restrictive population controls that some councils had introduced, by deserting the MWP and voting for the Progress Party.

Nevertheless, all but a few councils provided their information and began co-ordinating with the other councils.

"I think you have done a good job on population," said T One. "Central co-ordination is necessary to avoid further famine."

"When you co-ordinate, you will be planning. Central planning is in direct opposition with our goal of diversity by devolution," said Abajoe. "We can't have both."

"There is a way," said T One. "Would you and your chums work out the minimum subscription to national goals that councils need to make under devolution. Don't say 'nothing at all', because that is what Zelta tried. It did not work and some people still haven't forgotten. There have to be some national goals to prevent another famine. Period."

"They blamed her for the famine. It was unfair, trying to put 15 million deaths on her conscience. How is she these days? I haven't seen her for a while"

"Your grandmother is fine, and Hugo too. She will be 100 in April. They have reached the average lifespan but they look like going on to 140. They still do flamenco together and get lots of bookings."

"Perhaps the national plan could be a dance," suggested Abajoe. "The 149 local representatives could be choreographed to the music of flamenco, representing the weather. The Murray-Darling could be a progressive square dance..."

"...they would each try everyone's position along the catchment," T One laughed.

"...and dance with every other council representative."

"...in all types of weather."

"Let's do it!" said Abajoe. "What do you think?"

"It will have to be virtual," said T One. "We could never get all together. I'm not sure that a virtual river square dance would be much fun, even if Zelta and Hugo were performing." She reflected for a moment. "Perhaps your population model might be better."

"Better? It's the best! For the people!" Abajoe said proudly.

"I'm glad to hear it," T One smiled. "But we will have to see if that's what the councils want," she cautioned. "It's one thing to have a population model with all the bells and whistles. It's another to have a model that every local council will trust and benefit from enough to input accurate data. It will be a big job finding out, for their territory, the number of people and their ages, water supplies, energy sources, weather forecasts and food availability. These models fall down when people enter rubbish. Rubbish in, rubbish out."

"You are right," said Abajoe. "It has been tried before and didn't work. This time it will be different, you'll see. The councils will learn to love it – because the way they are will be okay with us. It's only their neighbours they have to get on with. They will be okay with that."

T One thought for a moment, then asked, "Would you be okay with a diverse...I mean really diverse...neighbouring council?"

Abajoe didn't hesitate. "So long as they stayed legal...why not?"

"Because some people will be scared," said T One. "Our idea of devolution has to be sold to people, who want their council to be kept under control."

"Our model will do that."

"It won't be easy to convince them. Could you look into the advantages of devolution we can tell them?"

"Easy. Our case will piss it in."

"Don't forget the minimum subscription to national goals!"

CHAPTER 16

Commune and Council

Far below, a boy was driving a dust cloud of goats across the drought-red ground between The Tower and the nearest house. Except for a table and chairs, the room in The Tower they went to was empty. Breathing hard after climbing up the fire stairs, they sat down. Paula set her communicator to beam on the wall her title 'The Case For Keeping Australia Devolved', and underneath a map with the locations of the 149 council territories.

Abajoe introduced her seminar. "Paula has been trying to find out how Australia should be controlled by studying nervous systems in natural organisms."

She talked to headings she put on the wall. The first was 'What has to be centralised?'

"Australians work for individual survival," she told them. "A family's decisions on where and when to have babies and plant food crops does not involve central government. Although these actions affect mutual interest and the community, central planning is not required."

Peter grimaced and interrupted. "Central planning could prevent a regional imbalance of food crops."

"True, but individuals can do the analysis for themselves," replied Abajoe. "The minimum is that everyone has to record their crop type and its area. If there is going to be a glut, farmers can see this and plant something else."

Paula's next heading was 'Is centralisation needed for fair sharing?'

"What if water storage is needed but the local council can't afford it?" she asked. "Should a central planning authority tax all the councils to pay for it?"

"Why shouldn't a council get its own funding?" asked Paula. "If they can't, people will have to move somewhere else that does have water. They are part of the whole organism. Each part adjusts to the others. There needn't be a control centre or brain."

"Bullshit," smirked Peter. "Every organism has to have a brain." He sat back confidently, with his hands behind his head. His biopsychology studies had inferred that groups of living individuals generally needed a nerve centre or brain to provide leadership.

Paula eyed him coldly. "Your rudeness is exceeded only by your ignorance. A tree doesn't have a brain and it gets along very nicely," she said quietly.

"Your argument is not helped by a personal attack, Paula," declared John. "Peter cannot help being ignorant. Anyway, Australia is not at all like a tree. Councils are not like leaves with constant tasks they can do independently. Trees do not move or change position much, but councils have to deal with changes and emergencies. For that, you need a central brain for experienced support and leadership. Is there anything that moves quickly, which doesn't have a brain?"

"Peter," said John immediately, taking Paula's side, as he always did. They all knew he was besotted with her.

They all laughed.

"You're just envious of my reflexes, John," Peter protested. "I only think when I have to; instead of worrying about all the things I don't understand, like you."

"You just shoot from the hip," said John. "Mostly you miss the point..."

"Good point, John. You are right, reflexes don't require a brain. They are controlled by local nerve tissue giving simple responses quickly. Do we have to have a central brain for, say, co-ordinating movement? Let's have a look at some animals that don't."

Paula interrupted, ploughing on with her presentation.

She put up the heading 'Is centralisation needed for co-ordination?'

She told them that some simple animals did not have a central brain. Sea anemones, jellyfish, and hydra were animals that moved, but there was no brain, only a net of nerves. Their tentacle waving and swimming actions were co-ordinated by sympathetic cell action rather than by a brain.

She made a few keystrokes on the hand control, and then coral and reef life surrounded them. The camera zoomed in on a large, five-armed starfish that moved busily towards the camera, as it sifted through debris using its rows of many tube feet, which worked busily under each arm to find plankton on the sea floor. She told them that like a human organisation, a starfish was a congregation of cells that obtained its food by appropriate responses to the materials it encountered. It made good sense to have a central digestive system, but it did not have a 'front' or 'back' end. It didn't decide every movement of each tube foot in its brain

– it didn't have a brain. There was a nerve ring around the mouth, with branches to each arm, but the ring did not do any kind of processing of information. To detect light, there was an eyespot at the tip of each arm. Starfish were not cephalized, meaning that there was no concentration of functions at a head, as there is in vertebrates.

"Councils can work together, co-ordinating like a starfish with 149 arms." He paused for them to visualise the image, as they watched a diver turn a starfish over and it invert itself by turning the tentacles on one side underneath and curling those on the other side up and over.

He told them how the five different radial nerves must co-ordinate, if the starfish is going anywhere. The theory is that some sensory information is shared between the different arms and that the arms can inhibit each other – that is, one arm can take charge of the whole starfish for a time. The arm in front of the starfish co-ordinates movement. When trying to locate an odour, the arm that senses the odour most intensely seems to be the one that takes charge, directing movement in its own direction.

"From these analogies, I conclude that the equivalent of a starfish's nerve ring can co-ordinate Australia's councils. The best-qualified council will take the lead and they will all co-ordinate with each other. Central planning is not needed." She turned off the communicator beam.

"I don't agree," said Peter hotly. "Australia is less like a starfish and more like an octopus, with its large eyes. We need central vision to sense dangers and opportunities. There are so many councils, that co-ordination cannot be on trust, but needs to be imposed from above. The nation is so large and diverse, Australians want to be centrally governed!"

"There can't be central vision when the action is so far away!" Abajoe explained patiently. He was used to reassuring Peter, who was inclined to panic. "Reflexes have local detectors, so electrons won't have to hurdle synapses all the way to and from a central brain, arriving back with a response that is too late. The tentacles of large, centralised organisations lash around out of effective control, like the old Soviet Union. We tried having a brain in Canberra but it was too ivory tower and slow to respond. Devolution like a starfish is necessary for the nation to hold together as one."

"They threw the baby out with the bath water," Peter protested. "Canberra worked well enough most of the time."

"Canberra let the famines happen," said Paula. "Wasn't that enough for you?"

"I don't agree," said Peter. "There must be central planning."

They discussed it and none of the others supported having a fixed centre but Peter stubbornly stuck to his guns.

"You are saying that co-ordination should be around a ring of 149 councils," he summarised Paula's proposal. "But the strength of the ring or chain is no more than that of the weakest link. A council that delays, refuses and misinforms could wreak havoc. A higher control, or centre, is needed."

"You are assuming that a dissenting council can be brought into line better by a superordinate authority than it would by its neighbours," Abajoe interjected. "Studies of hunting dogs and hyenas contradict that. If an individual doesn't pull its weight, it doesn't get a share in the kill. There doesn't have to be a single, fixed boss. There is more evidence against it than for it!"

Peter was silent for a moment.

"But..." he began.

"Peter, your brains are in your dick," joked John. They all knew that Peter had fathered several children and left his partner with them, while he had pursued an intellectual life and become a follower of Abajoe.

Upset by losing his argument, Peter hesitated. "John, your brains are in your ass and you talk shit," Peter spat the words at him. "A centre is needed for a quick response that considers the national interest."

"Situations like that hardly ever occur if there is no one at the centre causing trouble, like you," replied John.

"Okay, you two, devolution is an argument," Abajoe placated them. "Let's get the Prime Minister's viewpoint." He called T One at her office.

"Good morning," she greeted them from the view-wall. "What can I do for the pipe dreams department?"

"We're considering how far devolution can go. We wanted to get your ideas."

"Okay, but it's a difficult issue and I have a meeting to go to now. Briefly, the MWP has always devolved project decisions that depend on local conditions. Renewable energy projects have had to be fully funded locally. Since independence, we have had a central policy of a moratorium on industrial development. Communes have developed food production, such as paddy fields, on the river floodplains in the north. The national government brought in the Jandu paddy experts but after that we let the communes get on with it."

"What's to make the councils follow a national approach on industrial development?" asked Peter. "Would you send in the Army?"

"Don't be ridiculous," laughed T One. "We don't have a standing Army, only reservists."

"How are councils punished if they don't conform?"

"We withhold their share of money from taxes on mineral exports."

"But policing that must take an army of bureaucrats."

"Only a few. Conformity is voluntary. The money is handed out to those, who follow national guidelines for industrial development."

"Such as...what?"

"We are just framing the guidelines for industrial growth, population, water and energy. If you would suggest what minimal national guidance is needed for the councils to adopt a common approach, it would be a great help. Now, I have to go. Bye."

T One disconnected.

Abajoe put his feet up on a table. "We have a population change and co-ordination model from our rossits study but we have to work out how to get councils to use it. Let's start by asking what have been the Party's population and water policies in the past?"

Peter objected to this approach. "The Party's governance of these stretches back 140 years. If we consider all the policies about population and water and their implications, we could be here for days. We just need to consider the problems that would arise if Sudarta is elected."

"Sudarta is our biggest obstacle to stopping famine," Abajoe said. He opened a window. A bird alighted on the sill and they all watched it. The bird population had been slow to recover from local extinction during the Great Famine, when starving people had trapped and eaten them all. It ate a spider, trapped in its web in the corner of the glass.

"Meannjin Council isn't typical," said John.

Yamens had recently taken over the council.

"It is one of the nation's more politically unstable and inward-looking councils," Peter complained.

There he goes again, thought Abajoe. Peter has become negative, reactionary. Maybe he has problems with his new partner – he never mentions him. Yet, I like him because he has deep insight into human nature and always has a different point of view in conversations.

"If Meannjin Council isn't up to the job, it will be corrected at the next council election, when they will lose their seats," Abajoe rebutted.

"The council will impose Yamen fundamentalism. Elections will be rigged," said Peter.

"There is no reason to believe that," said Abajoe. "Yamens are as law-abiding as anyone else. The bigger picture is that there will be more room for diversity and racial tolerance than ever. The council will want to conform to most things. I wish you would not prophesy doom! It could be self-fulfilling. If we leaders don't expect good behaviour, then no one will!" His voice had become impatient.

Peter tried to back-pedal. "But I have just been trying to warn you that you have enemies in high places, who will try to stop you. I accept your argument and support devolution."

Abajoe looked at Peter grimly. "Trying is the operative word, Peter. I wish I could count on you without always having to argue to get you on my side. It is like having one of the Opposition in our midst. I am beginning to think they have planted you as an agent. That's the second time this week you have set yourself against me. I have always supported you."

They all stared at Peter.

He went red from ear to ear and shook his head vigorously. "No...I thought I was helping!" he mumbled.

"The next time will be your last," Abajoe told him ominously, "whether the cock crows thrice or not."

Just then, there was a squealing furore in the passage outside, startling them. They went out into the passage. A long-bodied, sleek, short-furred animal, like a weasel, held a struggling rat in its jaws. As they watched fascinated, it shifted its grip and bit into its neck. The rat stopped moving. Then the killer began eating its prey delicately, oblivious to their presence.

"Is that your mongoose?" John asked Abajoe.

"Yes. He does a good job at keeping the rats down in the rossit and poultry units."

They went back inside and sat down.

"That's what happens to rats," said John looking at Peter.

"Get fucked," said Peter.

Abajoe glared at John. "Leave it, John. Now, what does a good policy for population and water look like?"

"Jurilpa Commune!" Paula told them excitedly. "Our population and water plans really work. We have been pioneers. The community allows in skilled immigrants to maintain the population when the birth rate falls. We have water supplies for a 500-year drought, which we share with neighbours. Most communes are still stuck on land reform and haven't got around to providing common facilities. We are streets ahead of the rest of Australia."

"But Jurilpa has indigenous control," said John. "Why should our methods work for communes of Caucasians, Yamens, and Jandus and...weird sects?"

Abajoe sat up and spoke quietly of his people with pride in his voice. "Our methods are scientific. The Jurilpa people are descendants of the Yagarra people, who lived here before European invasion. The pre-eminent family is the Yabras, and Jurilpa people are loyal Middle Way Party supporters. The Party's methods of bringing the different tribes together have withstood the test of time in this harsh environment."

The MWP was led by Aborigines, who gave authority to relevant experience and eschewed egalitarian concepts of voting and representation.

"We don't send representatives to the triennial corroboree at the Nubya Mountains: everyone goes. Resolution of community issues is led by elders. They are responsible for continuing the tribal traditions that evolved over 50,000 years. They have solutions for misdemeanours, nuptial infidelity, theft and disrespect. There are procedures for obtaining marriage partners outside the tribe, sharing scarce resources and for defending territory against invaders."

"What about industrial development? Do Aborigines have experience with technologies then?" asked Peter.

"Aboriginal groups only slowly developed material technologies, although hunting methods were complex and evolved quickly. Due to the harsh conditions and the nomadic lifestyle, artefacts had to be low in weight or they were left behind. Also, peaceful solutions to disputes with neighbours were preferred and heavy weapons were not as highly valued as in other civilisations.

"When Europeans arrived, the number of Aborigines was around 500,000 and in equilibrium with food and water resources. Over the next

200 years, the invaders applied unsustainable technologies, tree-felling, imported animals, monocultures, fertilisers and herbicides. The population grew to 50 million but the stock of soil nutrients and ecological diversity ran down. When it was realised the technologies were harmful, they were scrapped and the population has been declining ever since. It could be that we are returning to conditions that existed before the European invasion."

"Well said, Abajoe our Elder!" Peter applauded. "In most of Australia, through the MWP, indigenous methods have been gaining control for a long time. But now control of Meannjin Council has been taken over by the Yamens. Are we going to accept their leadership?"

"Why not?" said John. "They were elected fairly. Devolution leads to diversity. Having to put up with leadership by a different culture for a few years is a small price to pay for self-determination. Anyway, they will not be able to have much effect on our lifestyle here in Jurilpa Commune. If they bring immigrants in, they will first have to have land, water and energy for them."

"I agree," said Abajoe. "Shall we have councils like Meannjin controlling population numbers, or Yamens hardly controlling them, or shall we have no control at all?"

"I say to you that the heart of government shall be the 149 local councils across Australia. Each shall administer about 250,000 people. Each council shall decide the issues, such as population and water, by sharing and by science. There will be scientific and logical consideration of the facts. That will be the common language. The central government should initially provide population and water models to aggregate the quantities and co-ordinate the councils. We can define councils' role as using our model and we will enforce it with all the weight of a national consensus from a referendum."

"That would be decentralisation like an octopus, not devolution like the starfish," Paula objected. She wanted pure devolution. Her face was a mask.

"No...don't worry, Paula," said Abajoe kindly. "If we had de-centralisation, it would retain ultimate power at the centre. Under our devolution plan, councils have the responsibility and the authority to take decisions. The councils will consult with each other and decide. When the science of an issue is indifferent and the people are divided, they can debate it in the local council's parliament. Our national government will, at most, provide only initial guidelines."

They decided to present their vision of the councils' role to the Party for discussion.

"We can expect opposition from development interests and unions, who are accustomed to dealing with central government, but they will be outnumbered and we won't compromise or make deals with them," said Paula. "Devolution will create a new Australia."

"Congratulations, folks. I think we've spring-cleaned the Party," Abajoe chortled, excited that he and his friends would be able to influence the moribund Middle Way Party.

He had particularly enjoyed working with Paula. It seemed only recently that he had teased her for thinking too much and not talking enough. Now she seemed full of ideas that complemented his. He felt very close to her, and her wonderful intelligence and beauty resonated in his head. He recalled his mother's advice to get on her wavelength and wondered if it was time he made a commitment to her. However, something was still missing and he continued to look around. His dalliances with other women were causing her to lose patience and he wondered how long before she would begin to hate him. Perhaps it was already too late.

"Thanks, guys. That was a terrific meeting."

Abajoe followed them out and closed the door. There was a damp patch on the floor, where the rat had been and beside it a fragment of liver with the gall bladder.

"Humans' morality with food is less fastidious," said Paula, as Abajoe picked up the offal in a plastic bag. "We will eat just about anything if we're hungry enough..."

"...even our own kind," said Abajoe.

"It doesn't bear thinking about," she replied.

"It's in our model," he said, "to match the rossit data. It has been quite common in the famines. Leaving it out would be playing God."

"That hasn't stopped you so far, " said Paula.

"That was unkind."

"If the hat fits, wear it."

CHAPTER 17

Abajoe The Guru

Abajoe was a brilliant scientist, whose solutions to land, ecology, energy, water and mineral resource problems benefitted ordinary people. He acquired technical knowledge in a wide area at a young age because he was an autodidact and learned constantly, supported by the expertise accessible to the nation's leading family. He became Australia's most famous scientific and technological guru, consulted by the Government and industry leaders.

For several years, he had initiated investigations that brought many new technological 'miracles'.

In Meannjin, the current drought made food and water supply problems his first priority. He invented a solar still for families to produce pure water from salty and contaminated water using only sunlight energy. The still, which could be bought cheaply, was a toroid, shaped like an inner tube of a tractor tyre, made of rigid, carbon fibre, with a transparent cover curved around half of the outside, and a sheet metal cover around the remainder. It was aligned with the sun's transit from east to west, and from dawn to dusk the transparent cover let in solar radiation. It heated an inner surface of black, heat-absorbent tiles onto which impure water dripped. This evaporated and the vapour was swept by air convecting up the eastern side and around. When the saturated air passed through the shaded cooler half, water condensed on the black metal, ran down and was collected. The salts and other impurities left on the tiles were removed periodically.

A unit could provide all the drinking water requirements of a family of six. The Yabra Water Wheel design was available patent-free and a manufacturer made and supplied it to all parts of the nation.

"How did you discover the design?" interviewers asked him.

"It was 1% inspiration and 99% perspiration," he answered. "We made a series of prototypes of different shapes until we hit on this one. The key was to find a heat-absorbent, non-conductive material that would stay hot enough to evaporate a lot of water. Our search ended with ceramic tiles of beryllium silicide, formerly used in space vehicles."

"How long did it take to develop?"

"Three years of experimentation. It was a labour of love. I especially like energy problems."

"Which do you prefer, science or politics?"

"Science," Abajoe replied without hesitation. "People should only resort to politics when science isn't available...either politics or religion."

He created several widely used water technologies. Many families wanted to live on a hectare or two but lacked a reliable source of water for growing garden foods. His design used eucalyptus trees cleared from the building site to construct a rectangular pole house. The ground floor was set high and underneath was completely taken up by a water bladder, made from home-welded polyethylene, that filled with rainfall from the roof. Its position under the living space protected it from sharp objects, abrasion and from deterioration in sunlight. The stored water kept the house warm in winter and cool in summer. With the house on a high site, it could irrigate the garden by gravity. Many users recycled and treated grey water to fill the bladder and it became known as a 'Yabra Kidney House'. Abajoe made the design freely available and it was taken up by a kit-manufacturer, who supplied it throughout Australia.

As Abajoe's fame spread, scientists brought problems to him. Together they would discuss ideas and design tests, that the researcher would then carry out. His advice was always wanted because he allowed free access to his information and ideas.

Abajoe was asked to assist in rainmaking in drought-stricken districts. Cloud seeding with silver iodide had been successful but it was too expensive. He obtained a supply of deuterium oxide, known as 'heavy water', by extraction from sea water and ejected it upwards through nozzles as high-pressure deuterium oxide steam. The heat induced air thermals to billow up, carrying the vapour through clouds, then releasing it to cool and condense, falling back as a mist, seeding raindrops and creating rain without harmful pollution. This method was used worldwide and 'Yabra Heavy Rain' technology was exported.

To feed people in droughts, he advised researchers on modifications to food plants that would retain moisture under arid conditions. They developed plants that would remove water from the air by knocking in characteristics of cacti, enabling them to grow without rainfall or irrigation. Abajoe advertised these varieties on 'Family Fare' and made them available to nurseries free of charge.

Abajoe noticed that crop plants, which lacked leaves to shade the soil, were most affected by droughts. Leaf growth required nitrogen absorption by the roots and in poor soils this was lacking, except in species that grew root nodules, such as legumes, for example, lucerne. Geneticists knocked the genes for nodule growth into a wide range of grains and vegetables. Lands that had been dustbowls in droughts were transformed to produce leafy, green crops.

People marvelled at Abajoe's creativity but he shrugged it off. "I just connect the researchers with the problem. You should admire their skill and persistence – that is what has made these miracles happen."

Australians could also obtain food from the sea. He showed how waste heat in sea water from thermal power plants could grow algae for crayfish to feed on. The crustaceans would be eaten. Alternatively, plankton could be grown and processed into biofertiliser to grow pineapples on poor land, for alcohol fuel production.

The scarcity of fuels created problems in agriculture and fishing. When he was a young teenager, he had a holiday on a trawler and showed how the rundown of fisheries could be prevented by training young dolphins to round up fish for the nets. At first, there were few dolphins because dolphins moderate their breeding to sustain fish stocks. When the fishery had recovered, many young dolphins were available to bring in bumper harvests. The cycle repeated, with dolphins stabilising the fishery.

In agriculture, he recruited various species to the tasks formerly done by machinery. He developed headsets that trained cattle to weed and manure row crops. With similar training methods, pigs tilled the ground by snout and unearthed potatoes. Dogs shepherded and mustered sheep by remote control. Horses, without riders, drove cattle. Pigeons cleaned weed seeds from grains and sized them. Sheep defleeced themselves when camera-trained to rub their way along a line of shearing heads.

Abajoe established a reputation for creating scientific theories from the ecological insights forged by his indigenous forefathers in the cauldron of survival over many millennia. He pioneered research into firestick farming techniques that created and maintained kangaroo pastures. He led investigations of Aboriginal uses of bush foods and medicines. He helped communes that reconstructed Aboriginal lifestyles. Most prominently, he brought the Aboriginal respect for the advice of elders into public policy making.

As the nation's pre-eminent technological guru, Abajoe became a legendary figure, called on to investigate problems in the national arena. Despite his scientific orientation, he was ecumenical and respected individuals' values and religious traditions. He was widely respected and politicians learned to seek his approval before making technological decisions.

He was a fierce critic of the shoddy science that had held back the solving of societal problems in the past. He was writing a book, called 'The New Science' that called for a new scientific endeavour. Science would command politics, rather than serve self-seeking politicians, as it had in the past.

CHAPTER 18

Water Policy

The drought had worsened. Although the long-term average was 980 mm per year, very little rain had fallen at Meannjin for the past three years. This year, 2240, the wet season from October to March had failed to provide more than a few millimetres.

Inland, the situation was critical. Rivers with town weirs had dried up and the water table in wells had lowered below the reach of pumps. The land had turned brown and kangaroos ate the green pick that grew after bushfires. Graziers had felled bushes and trees for their cattle and sheep to eat. Where there was no water, they shot the livestock that had not died, as food for feral pigs that they could hunt.

In The Tower, Abajoe and Paula turned off the sun lamps and water pumps and harvested vegetables from the hydroponic gardens. All they could hear was the trickle of water, as it drained from the root clumps and ran down, through the maze of nutrient troughs, and poured into the recycle tank on the floor below. They picked eggplants, corn and long beans for themselves, for their grandparents and great-grandmother living in the same building and for their parents at the stadium. They grew most dietary requirements but they bought items such as rice and tea with the revenue from selling their surplus.

Besides modelling self-sufficiency for 'Family Fare' shows, the two laboured in the gardens for a few hours every day for their well-being. Their parents had taught them to love gardening. Marko, Abajoe's father of Aboriginal descent, valued the land and nature above all else. T One had taught all their family to transcend through physical work.

When they had gathered enough produce, they left their laden baskets on the landing and began the weekly garden maintenance. Together they cleared dead maize stems and clumps of roots. Growing plants and animals in buildings had the advantage of excluding the heat of direct solar radiation that would cause evaporation. They achieved ideal growing conditions in humid, sealed rooms. They recycled transpired water by circulating humid air through a condenser. They controlled growing conditions in the hydroponics rooms to give high yields. Under these conditions, indoor hydroponics was more water-efficient than field irrigation. Every drop of run-off from irrigation was collected and recycled, despite the Meannjin Government's ban on recycling, to prevent diseases. Abajoe had contested the ban and gained the enmity of the council. He had to be careful, as he knew they would like to make an example of him.

As they worked, they talked, continuing their discussion of the MWP's water policy. "Australia will always have undeveloped minerals, because we have an imbalance," said Abajoe. "Plenty of minerals but not much water."

"We are likely to be invaded for our minerals, don't you think?" Paula said.

"Bhakaria may defend us. Or perhaps the SEU," Abajoe replied. "They won't want their supplies cut off."

"If the invader would supply them, they might not care. Colonial powers have invaded undeveloped countries for their undeveloped resources before. It was the basis of the British in India and in Australia, the French in Vietnam, the Americans in Iraq and Eurany, when they tried to grab our coal. It has happened to us twice before."

"But Australia was already developed when Eurany invaded..."

"Not by Eurany's standards – there were vast unused coal resources here that they wanted."

"Foreigners don't understand why our minerals are undeveloped. They think we are slack – globally irresponsible – a pushover for invasion. Our diplomats should have been telling the world about our water problems, not pumping up our resources of minerals. I don't know what Winston can have been thinking about."

"I'll ask him later. There has probably been a change of perspective. In those days, growth was all the go."

Then Abajoe switched on the trough-cleaning robot. It hummed and hissed as it worked its way through the maze, washing root bundles and surfaces to prevent pathogen build up.

Abajoe checked that the nutrient dispensing magazine was full and that the mixer robot was maintaining the concentrations correctly.

Then both of them tended the plants, pinching back unwanted shoots in raspberries and excess flowers on tomato plants.

"Water is the key to Australia's minerals," continued Paula. "They use it for dust control, separation, chemical processes, waste transport, rehabilitation, miners' homes and for the mining town."

"Where there is a huge amount of mineral in the ground, the resource being exported is our precious water."

"Export needs to be sustainable, without subtracting water that could be stored to prevent famine."

"Shutting down of a mine is too late once a drought has hit," said Abajoe. "It should be shut down permanently or changed over to dry methods now if the water supply cannot be sustained. The ore can be treated overseas where there is plenty of water. We don't have enough water for a large minerals export industry."

Meannjin City's reservoirs were empty. Storages inside the flood banks along the tidal reaches of the rivers were dry. Water supply companies were pumping low quality water from underground, but this was insufficient for pumped delivery, and a consumer's rationed quantity had to be collected from a pumping station and carried to their home.

There was a ban on baths and showers. Watering of garden plants was allowed once a week. Washing machines could have only half a load per week per person. The ban on recycling had been lifted to allow grey water to be used in toilets.

Paula asked, "How much of our water should be allocated to the minerals industry, how much for food production and how much for domestic use? Where should the balance lie, remembering the fifteen million people who died in the Great Famine?"

"I don't know," said Abajoe. "Let's ask Marko...a water consultant ought to know."

Abajoe set up his communicator as a projector. A few seconds later Marko's image, sitting at his desk, was on the garden room wall. As Deputy Prime Minister, he stood in for T One on matters of state but he preferred a technical role and had gladly deferred to his wife for the top position. She was a people person, whereas he enjoyed analysing problems and preparing plans.

"Hi, Dad. We are looking at our water policy and we wondered if you could help us with a question. How much water should be kept for domestic use and how much allocated to irrigation and minerals?"

"Gidday, you two. Good question right now because there is not enough for all three. It is a matter of arbitrary opinion rather than absolute truths. I believe we should reserve water for essential domestic needs and essential food growing to meet 100-year drought conditions."

Since Abajoe had become the nation's expert on ecology and food growing, he had asked his father's advice less and less. He was jealous of his father's long experience, but he was better known than Marko, who stayed out of the limelight. He could feel the tension between them in this overlapping area but he couldn't help testing Marko's expertise to find out the evidence on which he based his opinions.

"Why a 100-year drought?" he asked his father. "Why not 1000 years?"

As they talked with Marko, Abajoe and Paula thinned out lettuce seedlings, transferring the stronger plantlets to plant holders, with their roots dangling into a trough. They would put the other seedlings, left to strengthen in the seed-raising mix, into water next time.

"You can't store water indefinitely. It will evaporate or leak away. Yearly evaporation from a reservoir can lower the surface by about one metre per year. Of 100 megalitres put into a surface storage now, only 20 megalitres may be left after 10 years. So you have to save five times your requirement. For 100 years time, you could have to store 50 times your consumption, and for 200 years, 100 times. This is obviously too expensive, even if you can do it. Dams holding water on the surface would take up too much valuable land and would silt up over that period of time. However, if you can store water underground, in an aquifer sealed to prevent it running away, you don't need to store as much."

He paused. "Okay so far?"

"I don't get it. Would you have to maintain a minimum of sufficient water in storage for a 200-year event at any time?"

"Yes, that's right. Just topping up the evaporation loss each year would be demanding with consumption taken first, especially in dry years. But you couldn't count on that. Most of the water harvested in that year would be taken before to supply shorter term needs, such as lesser droughts."

As they listened and questioned Marko, they were spreading roots over aeration spheres and adjusting stem holders, to keep the plants upright.

"So it's a matter of affording huge storages?"

"Exactly. But there are few natural water storage sites deep enough for evaporation to be replenished. There is a little storage in voids left by surface mining. Fortunately, the cost of storing water underground for a

100-year drought using polysilicate solutions is affordable. But for 1000 years, it would be too expensive."

"Perhaps a 200-year drought would be more realistic? That would have prevented the Great Famine. There would have been enough water for essential needs."

Irritated by his son's challenge of his judgement, Marko spoke briskly. "It depends on how you define essential needs. My view is that there is a hierarchy of water supply priorities. Electricity generation by combustion uses too much water for cooling and has to be shut down. The remaining grid electricity supply has priority consumers, such as safety systems, medical consumers, ambulances, public water pumps and water trucks to take water to people, who live too far from pumping stations to be able to carry water. Air conditioners have to be banned, even in public buildings. Communication systems, vehicle battery charging and lifts have to be restricted to public users in daylight hours. Public systems at night and private users have to fend for themselves. With these restrictions, planning for a drought of once in 100 years' severity will be sufficient."

Abajoe stood up, where Marko could clearly see him.

"You have omitted essential food growing!" he challenged. "That has to be a top priority for both water and electricity."

"I left it out because it's a can of worms. What do you propose?" Marko deferred to his son's expertise.

Abajoe told him the sequence of disappearance of foods from the commune store during the current drought. When water for irrigation had stopped, green vegetables first became expensive and then unavailable. Fruit ceased to be sold soon after. Root crops, like potatoes, continued for some time, but with the high demand, they soon went too. Meat was cheap, and people ate more and more as herds were slaughtered, including valuable dairy cattle. Grain stores provided the flour for bread, cereals and pasta. But diets lacked vitamins and health problems were appearing, including lowered resistance to epidemic diseases.

Importation of fresh foods from SEU countries was not possible because sailing ships were too slow. Few steamers were available and their deliveries only reached the northern port vicinities.

He summarised, "Our idea is to sustain a survival diet of grain, legumes and leafy vegetables, grown in home gardens, irrigated by treated grey water, topped up when necessary from public supplies."

"So we would have to be vegetarians?" objected Marko.

"Not necessarily," said Paula, straightening up from preparing seed trays with a mixture of sand and sludge from the biogas generator. "The storing of nutrients 'on the hoof' is a viable strategy. Animals would consume plants, such as native grasses, when there is a glut and the meat can be harvested in a drought."

"Wouldn't it be more efficient if the basic foods were grown on farms?" asked Marko.

"No. This would require more energy and more water. Besides, the physical exercise of gardening will help maintain physical wellness. Commercial food is needed for people, who, for one reason or another, do not grow their own food and are not supplied by neighbours."

Marko, on the wall, leaned forward to conclude his advice. "Okay, you seem to have a good handle on the essential water for food. You wanted to know about irrigation and minerals. Any remaining water should be available for selected industries, for example irrigation, electricity generation for the grid and for minerals' production. Growing of non-essential and high-water consumption products, where we have no special advantage, should be banned. For example, dairy products, cotton and rice should cease to be grown. Users can get supplies from places with abundant water."

Abajoe agreed. "What about beef?" he said.

"Lot-fed beef uses a large amount of water for growing cattle feed, drinking water, washing down yards and in abattoirs. It is less effective than kangaroo meat in return of protein from water resources."

"The meat is less nutritious too."

"I suppose we should stop lot-fed beef to use the water for kangaroo meat and minerals?"

"Yes; it makes sense."

"I'm not sure it is up to us to decide who can use water for what, as if the water belongs to the nation."

"Who does it belong to then?"

"I think catchment owners have shares in the area and the rainfall there."

"Would that take away people's rights to be connected to a water supply and have water delivered to them mostly at community expense?"

"No. Catchment owners would sell their water to the community water authority."

"It would increase the value of high-country land."

"Well, so be it. Water resources should be sold to the highest bidder, not grabbed by cities."

"This is a radical change. For a start, mountain country has been regarded as valueless, except for national parks. Now those wilderness tracts would bring a high income."

"If there is no governance of water allocation, mining projects could buy up all the water. Gold mining, for example, can use a lot of water."

"Gold is useless. It can be left in the ground unless dry processing technology is adopted."

"Mines sometimes have their own catchments, so they are independent. In other places, where minerals command a good return on water purchased, minerals could outbid the community."

Paula had filled several seed trays with seed raising mixture and sowed carrots, fennel and eggplants.

"So how can droughts and famines be averted?"

"The community would have to buy and store enough water for everyone for a 200-year drought. Because there may not be sufficient natural water resources, in some places supplies to mines and industry may have to be stopped."

"So minerals' revenue may cease, just at the time when it is needed to avert famine by buying food from overseas!"

"It means that our credit must be good with our neighbours."

"Good relations with neighbours keeps cropping up," said Abajoe. "Thanks for your help, Dad. One last question. How much can the population grow if we rationalise water supply the way you suggest?"

"That's a hell of a question. I calculate the population must stop growing to safeguard against even a 100-year drought. There could be a little immigration. To handle a 200-year drought, the population will definitely have to shrink because there won't be enough water to fill storages even if we build them."

Abajoe was glad that Marko was on their side. His evaluation of situations was always thorough and accurate. His mother called him her 'secret weapon'.

"Thanks, Dad."

"See you two this evening."

"Bye."

Marko's image disappeared.

Paula said, "Our job is done. That seems like a complete famine policy."

"I agree...but it's only the bare bones."

"What do you mean?"

"Well, people need to be prepared to grow their own food and to limit water to essential uses in a drought. We have to adapt Marko's national water model so councils can put their own numbers on water quantities and restrict use."

"There are domestic restrictions in force now."

Their own water had to be brought several kilometres from the water company reservoir by truck or yoke and cans. Abajoe was the water carrier in 'Family Fare' shows, encouraging self-sufficiency. Indoor hydroponics conserved water. Eventually, a reticulated supply had been connected, but this was currently shut down because of the drought. The swimming pool and underground garage were empty and he and Paula carried water to their home. Paula walked with a jar on her head, whereas he used cans suspended from a yoke across his shoulders. The elders cooked, washed and cleaned for them.

"But irrigators, cattle lots, mineral processors and industries are continuing to help themselves to water. If we go for a 200-year event, they're in trouble. Zero growth is one thing. Reduced consumption is another..." Abajoe was lost in thought.

Zero water resources consumption growth was unsustainable now that they were demanding ever-higher certainty of supply. Natural water storages had all been taken and water had become a finite resource. The bogeyman of zero resources growth that had been dispelled, when the economy had switched from producing material goods to human services of care, education and personal development, had returned to haunt planners, who contemplated population growth. Low water consumption primary industries, like quarrying, poultry farming and marine fisheries, would be selected for growth.

His brilliance at planning had already enlightened Australia's dealings on the international stage. He had developed for T One a simulation experience, based on optimal assignment, to orient international leaders to Australia's situation, which he called 'The Game'. Each leader would play a different nation and choose goals. Many chose growth and development. Moves involved capturing markets, chance availability of energy, water and minerals, with international trading of resources. Leaders who played 'Australia' and chose growth always became bogged down in drought and famine and unable to sustain even its low population density. On the other hand, 'Australia' had a surfeit of unexploited minerals available for trading. 'The Game' helped visitors understand Australian interests and exempt her Government from full participation in the global economy.

He removed the trough-cleaning robot and emptied out the sludge into a toilet.

Abajoe knew there was a crisis of confidence in their Party and in T One's leadership. She had not been able to famine-proof the nation and the MWP Government's hold on national leadership had become precarious. The Yamen population was growing and looked to Sudarta for leadership. In contrast, the Middle Way Party's voter support was falling and it was doubtful that they would be re-elected.

"Shrinking the population is going to make us unpopular," said Paula. "But that's the price of affirming our responsibility. People will see we are doing the right thing."

"When pigs can fly," said Abajoe.

He thought to himself, 'Paula has great skills and means well, but she shouldn't support me when I'm on weak ground. She is devoted to me, when she should be critical.'

"Most of Australia won't accept shrinkage," he continued. "We will have to go for zero growth. In the famine areas, the population is already shrunk but even they won't have the courage to plan for a 200-year drought. They're still getting over the Great Famine," said Abajoe. "They still blame us...it was 20 years ago. They think we have an account to settle. It's time there was closure. Until we do, they are existing, not living. They have little resilience and don't accept responsibility to prepare for the worst. If there is another famine, they will be the first victims."

"Well, it was the Government's fault...the MWP...us..." admitted Paula.

She cleaned the fluorescent tube of a sun lamp with a cloth.

"We should require councils to provide water for at least a 100-year drought."

"Will they do what we ask?"

"Yes, I think so...we need to show we're sorry we didn't insist last time...because they will have to make difficult water allocation decisions. Many irrigators will have to shut down. The councils will want us to back them up.”

“Can we keep the spectre of famine before them...?”

“...how last time we allowed an uncontrolled water feast...that ended in disaster? I think so.”

“We can announce a new national approach, devolution.”

“If we say we’re sorry, they will know who to blame and then they will ask ‘what has changed?’ When we tell them ‘devolution’, they will think we have obfuscated the problem. They want a rich and powerful central government that stores water and food and distributes it fairly, without the poverty and corruption of their local government. We could lose votes. The ‘devolution’ message can’t be sent ex cathedra...we have to show councils how to restore voters’ trust in their planning to prevent famine.” Abajoe thought for a few moments. “How do you feel like going out west on a tour for two or three months?”

“On your annual jaunt?” asked Paula. “I thought only you and Marko go?”

“He can’t come. He’s doing the water model. I’ll be organising it this year.”

“Are you going to change it?”

“No, not much,” Abajoe replied. “It works pretty well as it is.”

“We have an election in 12 months.”

“It will take all of that to get people to prefer devolution and vote for us again,” he said.

“How?”

“Reconciliation. It’s about the people who are alienated, the famine victims,” Abajoe told Paula. “We have to heal the hurt lingering from the Great Famine. It is about starting people trusting the Government again ...so they will co-operate on water...we counsel the hurt people...”

“Counselling hurt people...I’d like to do that...okay, I’ll go with you,” said Paula.

“Great!” he said.

Abajoe knew that she would expect to have him all to herself. He was not ready yet to make a commitment to Paula, but her presence on the tour would inhibit his usual womanising. Single women would be coming, hoping for precisely that outcome. He was fond of Paula and while he would not be disloyal, their relationship wasn’t yet exclusive. Or would this be a test whether it would become that way?

"Our role is most effective if we operate alone," he told her. "We can travel out there together but we will split up to work in different districts. We need to get our whole gang to go. We can advertise it to the Party."

"Okay," Paula was disappointed that she wouldn't be staying with him, but agreed. "I'll spread the word. We'll set it up as the major event kicking off our campaign."

They switched on the pumps and waited until water flowed steadily through the channels, adjusting the flow with clip-in weirs. Solar electricity for circulation was available in daytime but the pumped storage reservoirs had dried up and load shedding occurred after dark. They used electricity from their batteries when it was left over from essential uses.

The two of them stood side by side, watching the water fill and flow.

"This is a microcosm of Australia," said Abajoe. "All growth has its roots in water."

"If the water is used up, everything will die."

"People want to be careful with water supply and water use, but they don't know how."

"They need leadership," said Paula.

"Guidance." said Abajo. "Councils should aim for no population growth and a 100-year drought for domestic supply…bugger the other users…they have to have their own supply plan."

"Unless by some miracle, there would be enough for everyone!"

"No, that would be a contradiction. In a famine, there is never enough for everyone."

"What if urine can be made into water and recycled?"

"Are you taking the piss?"

They both laughed.

CHAPTER 19

Runaway

‘ When Citra returned from Hanuso gereja’, Abajoe wrote, ‘her home had seemed smaller, meaner and dirtier than she remembered. Only her rabbits were more beautiful and she picked up the doe and cuddled her. While she had been away, she had kindled, producing five offspring, all the old doe could raise on peelings from the kitchen, vegetable waste from the garden and grass from the roadside.

‘Her mother’s greeting had been perfunctory and she had known something was wrong. When her father came home, he told her the village Kudim had received a call from Hanuso gereja about her behaviour and he wanted to see her. Her heart sank. She was in trouble.

‘She waited for several hours at the gereja before the Kudim had time to see her.

‘“I am very disappointed, Citra,” he told her. “You had the possibility of a bright future as a Yamen leader but you have shown you are not to be trusted.”

‘“I’m truly sorry, Father, I don’t know what came over me,” she said weeping. “I promise it won’t happen again.”

‘“It’s too late, Citra. You were warned and knew that what you were doing was wrong. You have shown that you are most interested in worldly love. That should be your future...you can serve God as a loving mother of children. No, I will not help you to go to the university. I will talk with your father about your future.” The Kudim turned his back on her, leaving her sobbing, rejected by the man who had taught her so much and meant everything to her. She was angry that the Kudim was so narrow-minded about her harmless experimentation with a boy and overlooked her subsequent devotion. He was punishing her because she was female, when he would have overlooked the same transgression in a male.

‘Later that day her father had berated her and told her that he, contrasting with her selfishness, would do his duty. He would try to find her a husband as soon as possible, before rumours of her indiscretion got around.

‘His plan meant that he would arrange a marriage in which her say would be minimal. He would give a dowry to her husband. The luxury or its absence in her marriage was partly up to her. The more she helped her father, the larger would be her dowry and the wealthier would be her husband. If her husband were wealthy, he would have several wives and servants to share the work of running the home. If he were poor, she would have a gruelling life of unending work.

'But Citra did not want any husband because none would support her religious ambitions. Wives were for having children. Acquisition of land and resources was most girls' strongest ambition but it was not for her.

'Citra's serenity was shattered. In her mind, she had already become a Kudim but now her plans were in ruins. She regretted allowing herself to be influenced by the wilful Rachael. She could not eat or sleep. Her parents tried to console her but she withdrew from her whole family. She performed her chores mechanically and at other times hid behind her rias, searching the Kitab for guidance.

''What am I going to do now?' she thought. 'To become a Kudim, I must go to university for four years. But no one will pay for me to go.'

'Her parents wouldn't pay to keep her at school and she didn't return. After puberty, girls were regarded as women and usually were kept in the home, only emerging with their faces hidden by rias.

'One day, a year later, her father called her to him and said he had found a man, who would accept her as his second wife. It had been a difficult search because local gossip had exaggerated her downfall. She knew of him already as a neighbour – he was 20 years older than her – a tenant farmer. He was not wealthy but with enough to have one wife already. He was prepared to overlook her indiscretion as a childish prank rather than as wantonness. She would be married to him and live in his small house in the village.

'"No!" she screamed.

'Her father slapped her across the face, leaving her ear ringing. "Shut up, you selfish bitch. You will do this to please your mother and me. He is a kind and respectable man and you will grow to like him. He will give you strong, healthy children."

'"I don't want him! I don't want children!"

'"Silence, you fool. It has been decided."

'Despite Citra's protests, they arranged a marriage. To Citra it was the end of her dreams to become a Yamin scholar and fulfil her mission to help her people escape poverty, overcrowding and disease. Instead, she had become a liability, to be offset by a dowry. But she was already dedicated to God's service and she had no desire for a lover. Her duty would be to have children, as many as they could afford. She knew from her mother the backbreaking slavery of continuous childraising. As the day of the betrothal neared, she was filled with dread.

'Disaster struck when a feral cat broke into the hutch and killed three of her young rabbits. Citra was heartbroken and buried the bodies in the corner of the vegetable garden. She knew the rabbits would kindle again within a month and that this time there would be a larger litter because of the lower probability of survival. There would be lower foetal re-absorption. It was an involuntary response.

'She knew that in Pedang, the human birth rate increased after natural disasters. Hani was beset by floods, cyclonic winds, tsunamis, earthquakes and volcanic eruptions. One disaster seemed to follow another, with death a frequent visitor. A woman's duty was to get pregnant and replace those killed. A bride's duty was to have enough babies to survive inevitable disasters and replace her great-grandparents. Citra shuddered at the prospect and she was filled with dread at the thought of the impending marriage arranged for her.

'There was nothing she wanted from the marriage arranged. She met with her future husband at her house, wearing a sarong and her face concealed by rias. He came wearing a peasant's smock, clean and neatly ironed. She tried to imagine his first wife getting his clothes ready for this meeting. He smelled of soap.

'"Why do you need another wife?" she asked him, her eyes on his. "Is your first wife unwell?"

'He didn't hold her stare. His eyes looked over her shoulder, as though his words had dignity but not the truth. "She is well but she is lonely for a woman's company. We both are looking forward to your coming. I have seen your face and heard you sing," he replied. "I want my house to be filled with your singing and our children."

'"What are your plans for the future?"

'He was puzzled, then resentful. "Plans? My plan is to work hard and trust in God."

'She wasn't impressed. His future went as far as acquiring her but no further. She wondered if she meant anything more to him than a status symbol.

'She asked him about his prospects but he said he was content to work his fields. Her mission, to help Bhakarian people escape poverty, overcrowding and disease, was hopeless.

'When he was gone, she brooded darkly. "He offers no hope of freedom," she told her mother.

'"You had your chance," her mother told her, "and you blew it. Soon you will be married and will forget all your nonsense about solving the problems of the world. You will buckle down to having children, who will look after you in your old age."

'"I don't want any children," Citra protested. "I want to be free to do what I want."

'"Nonsense. It is your duty to God. No one is free here."

'She met with her intended man once a week with a chaperone for a year but she developed no affection for him. He was bovine, without imagination, only interested in farming'.

Abajoe paused in his writing, thinking 'Citra will soon come into my life. We will meet and she will let me know what she thinks of my ideas. At this very moment, I can imagine what she is doing.'

He continued writing his narrative.

'It is about a week before the wedding when Citra's life abruptly changes.

'Her eyes are red-rimmed from crying as she waits until her mother goes out to the market. When she leaves, she stops preparing food for the feast. She pulls a bag out from under her bed and finishes packing her few things.

'She put on her gereja clothes and rias. She would be safest as a devout Yamen. She packed in an old suitcase her best clothes – one of each type of garment. Then there were spare shoes, her hairbrush, toothbrush and make-up. She put her Kitab in her handbag without bending it and squeezed in some pieces of fruit. She prayed to Yahm to understand why she was going and not to be angry with her. She had no future here. She wanted to serve him so much but not as the wife of that farmer. If she went to the city, she would have a chance and a chance was all she wanted. She closed her eyes and prayed to Yahm to help her!

'She scribbled a note to her mother saying she was going to the city to live and that she would always love her family and pray for them. She put some food for the journey in a woven bag. The garden gate let her out into the lane behind the house. She took a backstreet so she would not run into her mother. Walking casually so as not to attract attention, she left the neighbourhood and ran to the railway station. The daily train to Hanuso was due shortly and she tried to calm herself by reading the Kitab, but the words were a blur. She kept imagining her father running to stop her.

'Then the train arrived. As it pulled away, she sighed with relief and looked out of the window at the receding village. She felt happiness for the first time in months and her serenity returned. At Hanuso, she bought a ticket to Gataka, the national capital, with money she had stolen from her mother's purse. It was money to pay the musicians at her wedding.

'She learned later that her father had pursued her on the next train. He expected she would seek work in Hanuso near the railway station and he searched local hotels, returning home worried and saddened late that night. When there was no news from her after a week, he informed her betrothed that she had gone. The wedding was abandoned and the dowry of four cows returned to him.

'Citra was thrilled as the train broke free from the tortuous gorges of the west coast to rush through the central plains towards the capital. As they picked up speed, she left behind the cloying certainties of her former life and marvelled, then trembled, at her freedom.

'What would Gataka be like? How would she look for work and a place to live? Did she have enough money until she could find a job? The questions kept popping up, becoming more insistent as the train neared Gataka.

'She looked from the train window and tried to imagine living there, alone in the sea of humanity that surrounded the train in every town. What would it be like to push through a crowd of complete strangers, so unlike Pedang where she knew everyone? Would she be robbed? Would the food stalls overcharge her? Would she be able to afford a room? Would every job be filled?

'She had eaten the fruit and was hungry. She made her first purchase of a pie and leaned out of the window to pay a vendor. The food seemed expensive, but it was good.

'The country they passed through was farmland with occasional rocky outcrops. Rice was being grown under irrigation from water harvesting ponds beside upland rivers. The water flowed by gravity across terraces that cascaded in steps down the hillsides. Then it was channelled to the next cascade of paddies and so on. Citra had seen paddy culture before but never on such a large scale.

'Night fell and she curled up on the seat to sleep. She was awoken several hours later, when police entered the far end of the carriage and worked towards her, scanning every passenger's identity card with their monitor. Taking her things, she retreated away from them to the back of the train. Through the glass doors, she could see them getting closer and closer. When they had almost reached her, the train stopped at a station, and she got out and walked along to the front of the train, where she hid in a toilet until the police got off. She found an empty double seat and slept.

'The next day, the train passed through dry, rocky country with herds of goats.

'Their arrival at Gataka was heralded by passing dozens of railway stations, where commune factories and workers' smallholdings radiated outwards. The factories became larger and the plots smaller, until the green ceased and there were just industrial conurbations with adjoining dormitory buildings. As they slowed, the city centre became a forest of tower blocks around commuter stations, each overhung and dark.

'Finally they came to a screeching, door-slamming halt and she walked out from the station. The crowds amazed her. She had not realised there were so many people in the world. She felt out of place, as if people could tell she did not belong there. She tried to keep out of people's way and was surprised when they stepped aside for her. At first she looked for a face she knew, then for a friendly face, but saw none. She looked for any sign of acknowledgement to relieve her aloneness, but she lowered her gaze when men looked back at her.

'She was used to poverty in Pedang and beggars who came to the door, but she was unprepared for the beggars who accosted her and pestered her, sensing her uncertainty. The beggars frightened her. There were many sitting behind begging bowls alongside the street, wearing rags, with hollow faces and glazed, sick eyes. She couldn't meet their gaze. One was a girl of her own age, as far as she could tell. Her empty eyes stared at her, appealing. Citra gave her a coin, enough to buy a pie. As she went to put her purse away, an urchin snatched it and ran into the crowd.

'Citra was shocked and lurched to the side of the road, blinded with tears. She had no money. She could live for a couple of days without food or shelter but she needed a job urgently or she would have to join the beggars. Her fear swelled in her and she almost vomited. Leaning against a wall, she prayed to Yahm to help her. Gaining strength, she continued her trek into the city. She asked about a job at several cafes, but the managers just shook their heads.

'"We have nothing for you, sorry. All our positions are filled."

'Then she reached the entertainment district and her misgivings fled. Here were shows with her favourite stars live. Citra stood and watched outside the glittering entrances, hoping for a glimpse of a favourite performer. She was caught up in their make-believe worlds and, for a while, she forgot about the precariousness of her position. She was distracted by the foreign sights and sounds and thrilled with the excitement of her adventure.

'Citra's elation on arriving in the capital turned to dismay when she realised that it was impossible to find work without experience. She searched the restaurant area for a job but there were others ahead of her and there were no positions available. She became desperate and a restaurant manager sent her, with two other young women who had arrived from the country, to a man called Dundas. As they went there, Citra recognised they were entering a sleazy area but she was so naïve she didn't recognise it as the red light district. Dundas, pompous and middle-aged, said he would lead them to a place where they could stay. They followed him through narrow streets with brightly lit doorways bellowing music, where muscular men in uniforms enticed passers by with offers of free striptease and cheap sex.

'Hungry, she followed behind the other girls thinking 'My God, how I hate this place. There is no food I can afford, nowhere I can hide away. My only hope is Dundas. He might look after me, though he does not seem kind. He will want something, sex or work. I hope it is work. He is ugly. He looks at me in my sarong with fascination as though I am a religious emblem to desecrate. My mother warned me never to go with strange men but now I am following him with the others through the backstreets. There are starving people in doorways, begging us as we pass, although we have nothing. He has promised us some food. One of the girls has told me he is a pimp of whores. I do not know exactly what that means. I know that a whore is a fallen woman who sells her sex. I have never been with a man and am not sure what having sex requires a woman to do, unless it is what female dogs do. Perhaps it might be a passive role and not too unpleasant. If this pimp man can get me food and a place, then I might do sex with a man, a kind man who is gentle with me, the way those boys were at Segura. I have never known a truly evil man. I have known men who are stupid and others who are too full of themselves to consider others, but the ones I have known would not deliberately hurt me. I will trust in God to continue to protect me from such men, if they really exist.'

'Now, they entered a house and a tough looking woman inspected them. She asked her if she was pregnant and felt her stomach, held her breast, wiped her rias off one cheek to check her skin, lifted her sarong to look at her legs and opened her mouth to see her teeth.

'"Over there," she said, pointing, and two of them were separated from the others. She talked with the pimp man, he looked at her as if he wanted her, then he took the others away. The two girls followed the woman to a kitchen, where she fed them noodles in a thin vegetable soup. It was delicious. They asked her what was to become of them but the woman ignored their questions. They followed her to tiny rooms with iron beds and stinking mattresses, where she locked them in separately, saying she would return in the evening.

'Citra lay on the bed. There was a cheap, red carpet from the doorway to the bed, worn down to the pale backing. There was no window in the room but there was light from a grille over the door. As the light faded, the pink walls changed to brown. It dawned on her that the woman was a house madam and she was in a brothel, much larger and more grandiose than the one in the poorest quarter of Pedang and forbidden to Yamen men, although it was said some went there secretly. She was in desperate straits but she had her mission – no one could take that away from her. God would protect her. Comforted by that thought, she slept'.

Abajoe stowed the microphone he dictated his writing with in his communicator and put it in his bag to take to Thornton, where he hoped he would have time to continue the Citra story. It was getting close now to where she would be able to respond as an adult Bhakarian to his immigration ideas.

CHAPTER 20

Reconciliation Tour

Here in the interior, the people were getting desperate for food, due to the drought. Their convoy passed dry dams and bare garden plots. He swerved to avoid children foraging along the side of the road for seeds of grass and old man saltbush to grind into flour for bread. There would be beggars at Dalford, where they would stop to get recharged batteries. He would buy them food, if there was any to be had.

He kept his distance from their escort of electrobikes to stay out of their dust clouds. He looked in the rearview mirror. There were four vehicles following him, shiny with painted solar cells over every surface, their narrow bodies cutting through the wind on rows of inline wheels that glided over the potholes. These were the latest vehicles for country travel, rugged to survive the bitumen-less concrete-less roads. They could cruise for four hours and then replace their batteries at a way station. The hum of the motors had been insulated and it was so quiet that he could hear the Party's flags crackle in the wind on the outriders' bikes.

He looked at the ammeter. Half full. They only generated enough from the solar cells for a fraction of their cruising needs, and batteries of rechargeable lithium cells provided the rest.

"How far to Dalford?" he asked Paula beside him.

Paula consulted the satellite navigation system. "One hour, 25 minutes."

"I'm hungry," said Abajoe.

"You are always hungry," said Paula smiling with her cat-that-ate-the-cream look that he found hard to resist.

Abajoe looked in the mirror. Paula was right, he did look hungry: lean and angular. His eyes were hollow, with clear whites and blue irises. He knew she wanted him and he wanted her but it would have to wait until they returned. Behind them were 30 volunteers, including 11 of his most loyal followers, his disciples, who were giving up a month of their time to work hard for no pay. They would be working separately in scattered communities and there would be few opportunities to socialise. The rewards would be in alleviating sadness and angst that still lingered from the Great Famine. Abajoe had inspired them to volunteer for the humanitarian work.

The Middle Way Party reconciliation mission was an annual event started by Marko, his father, the year after the Great Famine was over, 16 years before. Abajoe had gone with them for the past five years. This was his first year as leader of the group. It was the largest group ever and there was an atmosphere of scarcely suppressed excitement. The majority were females. He hoped his counselling aims, rather than his charisma, had attracted them. Humans were contemptible the way they surrendered their judgement to charismatic, apocryphal, self-adulatory leadership. He had found that leaders, who lacked real leadership skills, often had an affected bravura that was the disguise of the villain, who was a confidence trickster. His father called it the 'Hitler Syndrome'.

Abajoe's leadership style was that of a playing-coach of a national sporting team, bent on acquitting itself honourably in international competition. His self-effacing presence was uncanny and mesmeric in its objectivity and attracted a cult-like following of hardheaded realists. They trusted his judgment because they knew and approved the processes he used. He didn't need to self-present dramatically to gain attention because he had the skills in spades and could show others his hand. His leadership was transparent. He hoped that this was the objective basis of his power to lead them.

They looked at the huddled homesteads dotting the dry plains. Most Australians lived on hectare lots on the dry savannah. The open woodlands along the east coast, which they had passed through earlier, had better climate and vegetation, but smaller living blocks. The city people had gone to where they could grow food. Here, many homes were no more than humpies, made from old sheets of iron, torn from buildings no longer used. A few homes were burrows dug into the ground to escape from heat, cold and the incessant wind. There were green splashes of crops amidst the bare earth. There were oxen and horses slowly ploughing and pulling drays. Women and children carried water from slowly turning windpumps. Other windpumps were stationary. The communes had deepened those in use, probably by subscription.

"They're doing it tough out here…" he said.

"The MWP has let it happen again!" replied Paula.

"It's not as bad as living in the city. There is no food in the shops."

"No; most city folk are helpless. At least, here, they have a way of getting food: grow it."

"City gangs steal anything of value. It is frightening. Here, there is hardship too, but more dignity."

"Country folk don't thieve unless they're starving because they can't get away from pursuers. Only the police have cars."

"I feel guilty riding in a car when these people struggle on foot."

"Don't. It gives them something to look up to, something to aim for."

"I can't believe you said that."

"We are on government business that can't be done without cars. When we get to Thornton, I'll loan this vehicle to the community leaders, to use for the time we're there. It's all we can do."

"This reconciliation is pretty important, hey?"

"Yes. We are rescuing people who are disabled by injustice. It doesn't get much more important than that."

At Dalford they joined the queue at the battery replacement machine. Recharge would take too long and it was solar electricity and would be expensive. The replacements had been recharged from the local grid at off-peak times. Beggars went along the line of vehicles. Abajoe bought food from the shop and gave each one a piece of fruit or a bread roll.

When they had installed the fresh batteries, they gathered in the cafeteria. There was the usual group of 12 he had selected as his disciples. He had travelled with them many times before on MWP campaigns. The others were novices. Sitting in one group with the tables pulled together and Abajoe at the centre, they lunched on stew, potatoes and cabbage. When he talked, he included everyone.

"Who's going where?" someone asked, as he ate.

"I can't tell you yet, not until I've talked to Ellen at Thornton."

Ellen was the community leader, who would be hosting their first week of the tour.

"Will we be in pairs, like last year?" another asked.

"No."

There was a disappointed groan.

"Pairs don't get as good results. Communities don't embrace us as well as they do singles. You won't be entirely on your own, as I aim to visit each of you for a day and you can always give me a call if you need support. People are more likely to open up to you if you are alone."

'If I am celibate, it will be best for the group,' thought Abajoe. 'It would be fun to pair off. I would go for the dark, attractive one, Rachel, but Paula would sulk and the others would be jealous and it would interfere with our work. This way, I will get to know most of them and I can wait for sex until we return to Meannjin. I am attracted to Paula, but not enough. I would like to have sex with her but I really must stop encouraging her crush on me. Or I might be attracted to one of these others. Sex will have to wait until we return to the city.'

Sex would have been a distraction. This was no holiday. They would be dealing with horrific cases of theft, violence, torture, rape, murder and barbarisms. He indoctrinated them in the counselling methods that Marko had developed.

While he was talking, the restaurant staff stopped work to listen.

His method of reconciliation, he told them, was first to identify victims, perpetrators and leaders at the time of the incident. There was a new wrinkle this year of more emphasis on the scientific evidence: they would be backed up by a forensic investigation team in Meannjin, who would investigate samples, photos and records. They could even come out and do an exhumation. Guilty persons had to be found and persuaded to admit their crimes in formal statements. Then the counsellor would convey to the victims the perpetrators' expressions of sorrow and desires for reconciliation. They would negotiate any necessary retribution. Finally, they would schedule monitoring to check that retribution had been made.

Other customers, who had been eating, turned to listen.

"An amnesty would be enough, wouldn't it," interrupted Jake, one of the disciples. "What is the point in settling old scores, with an eye for an eye? People need to be forgiven. It will be enough for people, who wronged others, to admit their crimes and be exonerated. There should be no need for charges to be laid."

Abajoe shook his head. "Sorry, Jake, I know you mean well but that approach doesn't work because it doesn't include the aggrieved parties. The only people, who can forgive, are the victims and that's why we have a reconciliation process. The perpetrators can confess, as you suggest, but their victims have to accept their confession. Do you understand now, Jake?"

Everyone looked at Jake and he shrugged and studied his fingernails. "Okay, whatever," he said. Abajoe wondered why he was there if he didn't want to do reconciliation. He seemed to be challenging his leadership and he wondered if he could count on his loyalty. He suspected that one or more of the group was a spy for Sudarta because she was upstaging him with such regularity that he could no longer put it down to coincidence. She had access to the innermost workings of the MWP and Jake seemed to be the most likely culprit, operating behind a smokescreen of dissent. But until he had proof, there was little he could do. If he kept major strategic decisions from Jake, he would also have to keep them from the disciples. Their loyalty was built on his confidence in each of them and to abandon that was unthinkable.

To succeed, he told them, they needed to be scientific. They had to let the evidence determine whether a crime had been committed, rather than listen to speculation and stir up emotions.

"I don't get it. What has reconciliation got to do with the Middle Way Party?" one of the volunteers asked.

The crowd groaned in disbelief. Evidently, not all of them knew what had happened 20 years previously in the area to which they were going. Abajoe stood up where everyone could see and hear him.

"The Great Famine ruined many lives, and some are still alienated from society and blame the Government, our Middle Way Government," he said sadly. "The Government let them down badly... Now the local council wants their support for population control and water allocation to prevent another famine. The MWP would like to regain their votes or at least stop them voting against us. So our job is to bring them justice."

Several customers had come in and they stood at the back, listening. Abajoe sat on a table, where people could see him better.

"So we can acknowledge that the MWP should have done more?"

Peter had asked the question on all their minds.

"Yes...it was our fault...by omission. We should have controlled water and immigration better."

"Is that our purpose, to deliver that message?"

"Yes...but our main purpose is to bring justice against law-breakers through reconciliation! People have to behave within the law, even in a bad situation. If they vote for us, we will plan to prevent a bad situation becoming a disaster."

"Yes. I see now."

There was a crowd of people listening as Abajoe answered a call on his communicator. He turned on the speaker and they could all hear. It was a call from the 'Family Fare' multimedia show, who wanted an interview with him for an 'on-the-road' segment. They wanted a piece to remind the audience to prepare against famine by self-sufficiency. It was arranged for when they would arrive in Dalford.

T One called to wish them well on their mission. The room hushed as he explained to the Prime Minister how forensic science could help reconcile famine victims.

"We will take samples of tissue from bodies we exhume and get positive identification from genomic records."

"Terrific...how and when they died will help nail the murderers."

"We will also use one of the new memory reading units. If we can get a brain in good condition, we can read out the person's information just before death, with images of the perpetrator. It can take the guesswork out of prosecution."

"Fabulous. Will there be time to get the results and take action?" asked T One.

"We'll set the ball rolling for community leaders to take over."

"Yes, the leaders need a helping hand," T One agreed. "Communities are still divided from the Great Famine. Your great-grandmother told me that after the Coal Wars, the Party had to win people's support again. Although we had won the war, people blamed the Government for getting into it in the first place. They had to present the Party in a new light and they did it on the stump, the way you are about to try."

"We're doing more than that," said Paula. "The forensic work is making individuals responsible for their actions. This is personal empowerment and reduces the need for political representation and the corruption that has always gone with it."

"Good," said T One. "Your investigations bring a paradigm shift towards total devolution. I support it in all but one aspect, how it explains the past. I don't see the necessity to go back and find fault with our ancestors. I recall that Zelta and Hugo did all they could to avert famine," she protested. "Politics has held this nation together through some hard times. Since the Great Famine, my Government has given Australians a meditative lifestyle that is the envy of the world. Yet science cannot measure the benefits of meditation. We don't need your investigations to undo all the progress we have made."

Abajoe agreed and chatted briefly with the Prime Minister about other matters, until they finished the call.

"Got your orders from the old lady?" asked Peter, laughing.

Abajoe didn't laugh. "I value my mother's experience."

"Will you run for Party Leader against your mother?"

There was absolute silence.

"No," Abajoe was firm. "She has said she may step down soon. I would then apply for nomination in her electorate."

"What about the Prime Ministership?"

"She would go in time for a new Prime Minister to lead us into the election."

"Would you go for PM too?" said Peter.

"Perhaps...it would depend on how much support I have within the Party."

One of the others said, "But you would be new to Parliament. You aren't even in the Cabinet yet. Do you think you can handle it?"

"From living with family members doing these positions, I know the job backwards. But I would do it in my own way."

"How would your way be different?" asked Thomas, another of the disciples.

Abajoe's gaze rested on the questioner. When Abajoe talked to a person or a group, they knew they had his full attention. He looked at them on their level, as to an equal, persuading without being dominating. He looked steadily straight into their eyes, from under his arched eyebrows, without blinking. His eyes never flicked away, even for an instant. The blue eyes, with large wine-dark liquid pupils, focused on the receiver's eyes, as close to their brain as he could get. They became the sole object in his vision. He was intent on making a powerful entry into their life, like a hunting cat. He was intent that they would give him their fullest attention and follow his advice. His intensity was overpowering, almost intimidating.

"If I were PM, I would bring New Science into our politics. As Paula, John, Peter and most of you others know, our group has supplied the Middle Way Party with a contemporary morality that has displaced the historic traditions of religion, law, ethics, politics, economics and psychology. It has come from our belief in New Science. New Science does not support materialism or elitism like its precursor, and it is sceptical about the benefits of technologies. It is revolutionary in its implications. Already changes are flowing through from the Party. I would take up the banner and bring these changes through to every corner of society.”

They listened, spellbound, and he continued.

“Another example would be control of advertising. Each advertisement would be required to display a rating of the scientific content and a label declaring any emotions appealed to subliminally, for example; sex or violence or elitism.”

“Don’t we have that already?” asked Peter.

Abajoe shook his head. “No. T One has stopped the worst excesses but we want it stated boldly on every type of advertising image in every medium,” he replied.

“Some people like to see sex and violence. Ads entertain.”

“Yes, they do,” Abajoe crossed his legs. “But people don’t like finding out they’re being misled. Ads are to con people and advertisers have to lift their game. It is the same with public policy; people will no longer accept wishy-washy methods for the allocation of public funds to certain groups and projects. I would have New Science provide the dominant philosophy and methodology of public policy making. Science precepts, not politics, law, or economic arts, would decide public policy.”

“What difference will that make?” someone asked.

Abajoe uncrossed his legs and leaned forward. “A big difference. Much of government expenditure in the past has benefited the middle class at the expense of working people. The bias has been hidden by subjective decision methods. We will make a major change: New Science will decide public policy and it will be devolved to include the wants of all the people. Consequently, parliamentary debates will be conducted to support or refute hypotheses that belong to the people, not the exclusive province of politicians, lawyers or even scientists. This means that governance will aggregate the work of 149 local parliaments. Whereas science was once arcane, for the benefit of sponsoring organisations, I would make it the evaluative tool used by communities to approve development. I would have a structure that could fuse New Science with democratic and historical traditions. Public policy will be based on scientific decisions that consider people’s values and acknowledge the values applied in decisions that have gone before.”

“Good on yer, Ab!” someone said. “That would be terrific. I reckon all of us here want science to rule, not politics.”

"I agree. It is a radical, cultural shift. I am sorry but we'll have to stop there. We're on a schedule and we have to get to Thornton. Before we go, there are some things to discuss with our reconciliation team and we need to be alone for that, so I'll say goodbye for now to you locals. We'll be back! If anyone wants to see me about anything, there may be a few minutes before we leave."

The Dalford people left, heartened by the promise of a government that would be more open and fair. When they were alone, Abajoe addressed the volunteers.

"You are the missionaries of New Science. I hope you are as excited as I am at the prospect of four weeks ahead. It will be a renaissance, a paradigm shift.

"Some will be healed by time passing, some by your attention, some by your observation, some by unburdening themselves, some by being told the pain will lessen, some by an anaesthetic, some by a placebo, some by justice, some by reparations, some by vengeance, some by being punished for past misdoing. I don't expect miracles, but you have the power to heal. Let's see how much healing you can do."

The meeting finished. They stayed chatting until the batteries were charged and the convoy set off again. As they rode along, Paula used the radio to start them singing in all the vehicles. They did some popular songs, traditional work songs, such as 'Gonna Jump Down, Turnaround, Pick A Bale O' Cotton' and songs of retribution, such as 'John Brown's Body Lies A Mouldering In His Grave'. The hours soon passed.

It was getting dark when they arrived in Thornton. They pulled up at the road services depot and stood in a semicircle under a flood light as Abajoe oriented them. Local people appeared and stood watching and listening. By the time Ellen, a Community Elder, joined them with leaders from surrounding villages, there was a crowd of over 100. The leaders varied in age from 20 to 70. They had come in electric cars belonging to their villages. Ellen gave each of the visitors a slip of paper with their leader's name.

"Ellen, and village leaders, thank you for coming to meet us. I am Abajoe Yabra and I have with me the women and men who have volunteered to try and help Thornton people obtain justice for any illegal events that occurred hereabouts during the Great Famine. We're all members of the Middle Way Party but our business is not politics – it is reconciliation. Our volunteers will be following the same process as in past years, which they will explain. Now over to Ellen, who has been working hard to make arrangements for our stay."

A middle-aged woman, holding a clipboard, began speaking quietly to the group. People moved up around her to hear.

"Thanks, Abajoe. I expect you are all tired from the long trip so I'll be brief. I recognise some of you from last year but Abajoe tells me six of you are novices. Thank you for coming to work with our village leaders. This year we have another group, from different communes in Thornton area. They'll bring you to meet people for whom the hurt of the Great Famine isn't yet over, who are living in the past. It would be easy for us to regard these people as flawed, but they are not. They are still suffering from the traumas they experienced. You people cannot imagine the horrific conditions here 20 years ago. More than half the population starved to death in some villages. Hunger, dehydration and thirst led to violence, torture, rape and murder. These words overlie unimaginable pain, desperation and powerlessness.

"Everyone here is pleased that so many of you could come. We value your visits because you help the troubled people in our community to make peace with the past and move on into the present. They have been alienated and are full of doubt, self-reproach and hostility. Your visits open up new avenues for our leaders to help them.

"I have given Abajoe a list of names of commune leaders for each of you to contact. I wish you every success."

Abajoe shook her hand.

"Thank you, Ellen, we'll do our best. Our aim is to rescue individuals, families or even whole neighbourhoods. You will not be working alone here because I stand right behind you, as an advocate of New Science and as a reconciliator. When people question your role, as they will do, you can be proud of the Middle Way Party's experience. You will keep a distance from the people and not get drawn into their disputes, even when their causes seem just. Then they may become suspicious of us, as if we are a cult seeking an exclusive destiny. Nothing could be further from the truth. The MWP is not a cult. Cults believe that their members have a special destiny, apart from the world, whereas we have a constitution, anyone can join us and there is transparent election of Party Leaders. We contest national elections and if you can reconcile people, they participate in the next election and vote for our team's anti-famine policies, so much the better."

Abajoe ended the briefing. "Now," he said, "find your local leader and go with him or her. Find people still troubled by the Great Famine and earn their confidence. It is a difficult task, requiring patience and empathy. I look forward to hearing your daily progress reports.

"I'll see you soon."

The group milled around, as each of them met their contact. He stayed with Paula, until she met her host, then he hugged her as she left. The pairs dispersed to the vehicles and drove away into the night.

CHAPTER 21

Rape

Ellen fed Abajoe a delicious shepherd's pie made with emu meat and sweet potato. Then there were pink prickly pear fruits with ice cream. As they ate, they made plans for the next day. She showed Abajoe to his room and he sat at the desk and told the next chapter of Citra's story into the voice-to-text system before turning in.

'When it was quite dark,' he enunciated carefully, 'a key turned in the lock and the house madam came in. Citra awoke and stood up, taller in her mantle, her serenity shining in her eyes.

"Did you get some rest?" she asked kindly, sitting on the bed.

'Citra sat down beside her.

"A little, thank you. I want to leave now and find a permanent place to stay."

"Are you a virgin?"

'Startled by the question, Citra blushed and her eyes moistened, "Yes, of course."

"To stay alive here, you must learn to make men happy. You know what I mean?"

"No, I..."

"There is a man here now, who will teach you what men like. You must do everything he says. Do you understand?"

'Citra's face became fearful and she started to weep. "Please let me..."

"It's too late for that," the woman hissed. "You owe me for this room. Pay me now."

'I've no money."

"Then you must earn some.'

'The house madam went out and returned with the pimp, who had brought her there, dressed in a suit and tie. He smiled at her cruelly.

"Hello, my Yamin sweetheart! I've been looking forward to this!"

"This man will pay you if you please him."

"No! Don't go!"

'But the madam left.

"It's Citra, isn't it?" he said, taking off his jacket. "Behind that grease paint and mantle you are a good looker, aren't you...and pure, like a nun, Madam reckons. Well, let's get your gear off."

'Citra tried to get away from him, weeping.

"Help me off with your clothes," he growled, trying to lift her mantle over her head. She was terrified and pulled back, sobbing. Her mantle tore.

"I like you," he said, ripping it off. "You've got a cute ass."

'He began lifting up her sarong and she held her arms by her sides, stopping him.

"Come on," he spoke sharply. "Clients will like your gear but you have to take it off when they want."

'He held her wrists in one large hand and tried to drag the sarong up over her shoulders. She screamed, terrified.

"Quiet, or I'll hit you!" he warned.

'She screamed again.

'He punched her in the stomach, taking her breath away. He reached for the sarong and she spat in his face.

'He took a knife from his pocket, wrapped his arm around her neck and held the knife to her throat.

"I'll slash your face," he said, and she knew he would. She let him take off the sarong and she stood there, shivering in panties and bra, with her arms across her chest, feeling naked. He started to unclip the bra but she moved away and he swore and ripped it open and pulled it away from her. Then he tore off her panties. Her fear made her vomit a little into her mouth and she was coughing.

'Then he put the knife back in his pocket and grabbed her in a bear hug, pushing her down on the bed, lying on top of her. It was a totally new feeling of oppression. The boy at the gereja had lain alongside her and touched her gently. The pimp was heavy and she could hardly breathe. She heard herself scream, but he put his hand over her mouth and she bit him as hard as she could. He swore, took off his tie and stuffed it in her mouth. She couldn't get enough air. With her breath constricted through her nose, she panicked and struggled with all her strength to get her arms free. His grip on her wrists was vice-like. She almost passed out and her strength faded. He dragged her wrist across her body in one hand and locked her other arm under his arm, freeing one of his arms and hands.

'She had watched her buck rabbit forcing himself on her doe, the same day after she had kindled. He held her down with his heavy body on top of her and sank his teeth into a loose fold of skin behind her neck. Then he tried to enter her and she evaded him by turning her opening away. But he would bite her and hold her with his claws until she yielded. He entered her and turned his pelvis into her for maximum penetration, thrust once, then fell away to the side.

'It felt much worse than she had imagined. Citra was paralysed by a searing pain as something tore the entrance to her most secret place, the opening she had never seen, nor felt. Then an unthinkable foreign object pushed roughly into tenderness that had never been touched before. Fearful, she panicked, involuntarily twisting her hips wildly, but the thing stayed in. Its owner grunted with pleasure and thrust deeply several times, ramming her whole body back, jamming her head against the bedhead. Then he groaned, shuddered and lay still.

'Her panic was replaced by a numbing fear. The unthinkable had happened, she was now the kind of fallen woman she despised. What would the brute do next? She lay under him, her body cold and hurt, scarcely able to breathe, wanting to die.

'He fell asleep on top of her. When he was snoring noisily, like the sawing of wood, Citra wriggled an arm free and pulled the tie from her mouth. She gasped on air that smelled of mouldy carpets. The coldness of his seed was pooling beneath her. She beseeched Yahm that she would not become pregnant. She asked Yahm's forgiveness for her sinning with the boys at the gereja school, for that was the only error she could think of that could have brought this terrible retribution.

'When she listened to his breathing, her hearing was fuzzy in the hurt ear that he had hit.

'She lay still, lest she should wake him but twice he woke up with a snort and raped her again. She became more and more exhausted. Her weak struggles stimulated him and he forced her into other positions. Eventually she was passive.

"Come on, try to stop me! It turns me on," he challenged.

'In pain, and thinking she was going to die, Citra began to hallucinate that it was all a dream and that she would wake up, safely in her bed at home. Later, she woke, sobbing uncontrollably.

'The pimp switched on the light and made her swallow a pill.

"This will cheer you up," he said.

'Her mind was instantly seized by a world of distorted sensations and extreme pleasure. She was feeling his hands on her breasts and laughing. Then he raped her again and she was aware of how sore she was and all the smells of that room. Wanting him to finish, she helped him.

'When she was compliant, he pushed her head down into his lap.

"Suck me off, Yamin girl. Then that will be the end of your training. You have a good body, quite enjoyable. From now on, men will pay you. You'll get a hundred thousand a trick, more if they're rich, or want something special."

'It was a lot of money. In Pedang, you could live for a month on a hundred thousand.

"Aren't you lucky? Remember, I get seventy five cents in every seu."

'She was so tired, she could hardly stay awake but the smell and taste of his member made her gag.

"Come on! What's the problem?" Dundas protested. "I thought you liked me."

'Suddenly her spirit rebelled and she bit him as hard as she could, continuing the bite when he screamed and pulled away, tearing sideways with her canines and sawing her incisors through living flesh. Her mouth filled with warmth and the iron taste of blood. Then he punched her in the other ear and his cries went fuzzy on that side too. The punch hurt and her jaw unclamped from the shock.

"You mad bitch, you'll die for this," was his muffled howl of agony when he turned on the light. His member was almost severed. He opened the door and screamed for help. Girls came running and crowded around, peering into the room and laughing when they found out what had happened.

"The bastard had it coming!" she heard a girl call out to her through her damaged hearing. "Thank you from all of us!"

'The madam arranged for someone to take him to hospital.

'Citra was dressing as fast as she could. In the mirror, her eye was black. The woman grabbed her hair. "You had better be very sorry you did this," she spat.

'Citra picked up her bag and made for the door.

"Not so fast." The woman held her arm, hurting her. "You owe me for this room."

'Citra pulled her arm away and shrugged. "I've no money."

"Why did you do it?" she asked.

'Citra's smile was brief. "For myself."

"You can't afford that. He'll find you and kill you."

'She stood aside and Citra ran away into the gloom. Passers-by stared at her, surprised to see a woman with her rias smeared and a torn mantle, running desperately, her shoes echoing through the dark streets. She fled past homeless people from the country keeping a vigil over their meagre possessions in dark doorways, past brightly lit night clubs spewing drunken clientele onto the early morning streets, past markets, where gardeners from distant suburbs displayed produce they had carried all night, by yoke and pannier, past handcarts cooking breakfasts of noodles and coffee.'

Abajoe stopped dictating and shut down his communicator. He slept, dreaming of Citra fleeing from Dundas' retribution. Next morning, he awoke early, as he usually did. He continued telling his story, incorporating what he could remember from his dream.

'When Citra reached a shopping mall,' he dictated, 'she couldn't see anyone in pursuit and slowed to a walk. It was prosperous with shops for rich people and it seemed safer there, with security cameras following her progress.

'Besides the hurt in her ears, a new body pain added to the bruising from Dundas's punch, a midriff sear of hypoglycaemia from lack of sugar in her blood. She had to eat soon or she would collapse. She was exhausted. Then she had an idea. If she could get work, she could buy food.

'Citra angled across the mall, past beggars and buskers, down the escalator into the cavernous Food Hall of subterranean Stope City. A million people lived below ground, in caves in the walls of huge chambers, left where gold ore had been hollowed out by robots and conveyed to the surface for processing. The roads, bridges and buildings of the city above had been constructed from concrete made from the spent ore.

'She could hear twitters of an artificial bird as she went past an artificial tree. The underground inhabitants worked, rested and recreated underground in comfortable temperatures away from the scorching sun. They lived there in a giant, social co-operative, like termites, doing community work voluntarily and sharing equipment and facilities. Anarchic beggars were not welcome down there. It was a separate city, without the selfishness of life at the surface. There were factories owned by their workers. Individuals competed in groups rather than in isolation.

'She found the City's Administration Office and asked a robot if they had any work.

"Do you live in the stopes or above-ground?" it asked.

"I am from Pedang," she answered.

'The robot nodded. Folk from small towns were used to working in a close-knit community.

"What work have you done?" it asked.

"I couldn't get a job there. Jobs stay in families," she replied. "But I worked at home, cooking and cleaning and caring for my mother's kids."

"We'll see what we have for you. Would you please step into testing booth number three, over there?"

'Citra took tests for several different jobs. There was training of a robot to serve cold drinks, conditioning it with the feedback it sought to progress its training: human approval or disapproval.

'It was the first time she had shaped a robot's movements and they were rather jerky. The feedback she received was critical: "You did most of it well but it slammed down drinks over-confidently rather than presenting the drinks smoothly, with a hesitant and courteous flourish."

'Then there was a more intelligent robot that had to learn how to sell clothes by flattering the customer. She tried to train it by imitating her, as she subtly cajoled the client into buying. All she taught it was to recognise when the length was right and there were no bulges, creases or folds. Then it said "That fits you so well! It shows your figure beautifully!" But Citra had little experience as a buyer of clothes from a store and couldn't imagine a repertoire of sycophantic patter that the robot could copy.

'Finally she was tested for training a robot for a check-out station, to detect various types of fraud when customers exited, by logical reasoning.

'Firstly, greet the customer and scan the irises of their eyes to establish identity. Verify this in small chat while their general credit status is being checked, politely searching for all the unpaid-for goods in their possession, reading the product codes, calculating the total and applying to debit it from their account. Then as it goes through, you can continue with chat or you can say "Good. Would you like me to gift wrap them for you, with our compliments?" She modelled each step, explaining its instigation, purpose and possible outcomes, for the robot to adopt. However, she wasn't able to create logical consequences for every eventuality, such as customers who, at the last minute, decided not to take an item.

'Afterwards, the human resources robot told her what she already knew. "We like your calm manner but we need a trainer with more experience. We're sorry, we don't have anything that would suit you just now. Get more experience of job routines in retail and come back. Try again in a couple of weeks."

'Citra lurched away, blinded by tears. She sat and cried. Soon she stood up and asked around the hall. There was nothing.'

Abajoe paused the recorder while he considered how to continue. He decided that Citra would, above all, be fearing Dundas' revenge. He unpaused and continued.

'Just then, she noticed a man at the other side of the food court glancing across at her and speaking into his communicator. Grey shirt, middle-aged, balding, potbellied, dark glasses. Fear momentarily paralysed her. She had to escape. Summoning her courage, she got up and walked quickly to the escalator and out into the mall. She saw his reflection in a shop window, following her. She trotted down the next escalator, pushing past people, ducked into a tunnel, took several side passageways and then, with an effort, turned to face the way she had come. The white-tiled tunnel walls were silent. She waited, hearing her own breathing, her bladder tightening uncomfortably and having to cross her legs. The pain became unbearable and she walked quickly, following signs to a toileting unit and dashed in.

'When she came out, he was there again, in the distance, pretending to look the other way. She had to stay where there were people. She dived into a footwear shop and looked at boots. The assistant brought some for her to try on. He walked past outside, glancing in. She tried on a different pair but the assistant saw her trembling and was suspicious and wouldn't bring out any more for her to try, clearly wanting her to leave. She fetched a boot from the display and tried that. The assistant asked her to leave.

'Citra walked along to a food shop. She asked a service robot for the manager and when she came, Citra pleaded with her for work, any work. But she didn't have any. Citra's cool exterior melted and she wept, the tears rolling down her rias.

"What's the matter?" asked the manager, who was a motherly Yamen.

"I'm hungry," Citra sniffed. "I don't have any money."

"Never mind, we'll feed you, love."

'She heaped a plate with leftovers. Citra thanked her. When she turned around, she saw the man was sitting at the far corner of the empty food tables.

"That man over there is following me," she told the manager, looking across at him. "Who do you think he is?"

'The manager shrugged.

'The man, aware of their scrutiny, stood up and left.

'A half an hour later, feeling much better, she left the Food Hall. The man was gone but Citra remained vigilant. Her injuring of Dundas could have consequences, by way of severe retribution, at any time.

'She walked through several tourist markets to a public park, where she sat on a bench. She was unwashed, smelly, tired and hungry. All she had was her bag with her clothes.

'She fell asleep.

'From a great distance a voice penetrated her troubled dreams.

"Hello, Miss. Wake up. Hello, hello!"

'She opened her eyes. The absence of shadows told her it was noon — she must have slept for several hours. A street urchin's face was peering at her.

"You want a place to stay? I will take you!"

'He led her to a Yamen gereja, where there was a kitchen serving a line of derelicts with soup and bread. The boy pointed to the man serving out the food.

"Him, good man, he will help you," he said and left her there.

'Although she was no longer hungry, she lined up. The people shuffling forwards in the queue were thin and quiet like shadows, apart from a few with coughs. When she reached the front, she saw that the man serving was a Kudim with black robe and a white collar. He was friendly, a foreigner.

"What happened to you?" he asked, observing her black eye and dishevelled robe.

'She was too ashamed to tell him about Dundas. She told him she had run away from an arranged marriage. She didn't tell him where she came from, in case he contacted her family.

"You can clean up over there," he said, pointing to a toilet cubicle with a basin. Using a blouse from her bag as a flannel, she washed off, as well as she could, the dried blood and semen. The smell of Dundas lingered in her nostrils.

"Can you tell me where I can get a job?" she asked the Kudim.

'He shook his head. "It's impossible here. Your best bet is to go home."

"No, I can't go back!"

"Then you'll have to go somewhere where they need workers. You could get a job in Australia. I know because I'm from over there. Would you consider going to Australia? The Government is offering assisted passages if you're prepared to work in a mine."

"Would it pay well?"

"Very well. Operators get about one million seus a month and you can save most of it. That's enough in a year to buy an electrocar or put a deposit on a house. You would earn enough to be able to live well."

"Can you send money home?"

"Yes. There are no restrictions."

"Can you leave when you want to?"

"You have to stay two years. You cannot stay more than five. Then they will send you home. But you could bring back enough to set you up in a small business here. Interested?"

'Citra wanted to go as soon as possible, before Dundas found her. The Kudim said he would take her to apply for a working visa the next day. He gave her the address of a women's refuge. She found the place a few streets away, a large house amidst comfortable, private dwellings. She was welcomed into a crowded community of scared women. She told her story to a Teutonic manageress, who found her a bed in a shared room. The previous occupant had mysteriously disappeared. The major topic of conversation was what could have happened to her. Then they asked Citra her story. They were still asking her questions when she fell asleep and they put her into bed.

'When she awoke, she was rested. Several of the women there had been raped. The talk was of how they hated sex and men. Later, when she was alone, she reflected on what had happened to her. It had been so terrible, that if Yahm did exist, there was no reason to worship him. The loss of her belief in her religion filled her with loneliness and grieving but she still had her mission, stronger than ever, but it seemed harder to achieve now, without a God beside her.'

With Citra in transition to a new life, Abajoe halted his telling of her story. His plan was that soon she would meet him. Ellen called him to breakfast. He had a busy day ahead.

CHAPTER 22

Reconciling Cannibalism

"That's her, over there, poor thing. Her name is Jenny Craig. She's waiting to talk with you," said Ellen, looking towards a woman sitting alone at a picnic table amid the sand and dead flowerbeds of Thornton's Civic Park. She wore the kind of smock commonly worn by Australian women of European ancestry for social outings, in a flowered pattern.

"Someone local attacked her during the Great Famine and is still living here, but she won't tell me who." Ellen continued. "She wants justice but doesn't trust the police. I tried to get her to talk with you last year but she wouldn't. She said it hurts too much but that's all I could get her to say. Then yesterday, she came up to me and said she wanted to talk with particularly you, alone, when you arrived. She must trust you."

"Where's she from?"

"Gularaba. It's a tiny village about an hour from here. She has come on the bus."

"Do you know what happened?"

"No, except that she had a husband and three children and she lost them all. She says local people attacked them."

"Did she go to the police?"

"Yes. Years ago, when she came back to Thornton from the city after the Great Famine. Like most people, the Great Famine drove her away. But she didn't have enough evidence and the police couldn't do anything."

"Okay, I'd like to meet with her."

"C'mon, I'll introduce you."

As they walked across, Abajoe thought that this might be difficult if she was as traumatised as Ellen had indicated.

"Jenny, this is Abajoe Yabra."

"I know. I've seen you in the news."

"Hello, Jenny. Did I meet you last year?"

"Yes, briefly. But not alone."

"Well, now you can talk confidentially," said Ellen. "I'll leave you two together."

"Thank you, Ellen."

She left them together.

Abajoe sat beside Jenny at the picnic table. She would know of his reputation for curing mental illnesses and emotional problems as well as physical conditions. He needed her trust.

"Jenny, my role is to obtain your testimony of what happened to you and your family and who were the perpetrators and leaders. I will try to get guilty persons to admit their crimes. If there is sufficient evidence, then I will support you in requesting the police to lay charges. You will be able to convey your feelings to your attackers and I would seek retribution, and finally reconciliation, so that you can lay this matter to rest and move on with your life. Is it okay if we proceed like that?"

"Yes...I suppose. I have never told anyone."

"Why is that?"

"I am...ashamed..."

She hung her head.

"I expect you did the best you could...was it a difficult situation?"

She nodded and wept.

"I will make sure your testimony is kept confidential..." Abajoe said.

"I don't want Ellen to know!"

Abajoe looked at her steadily.

"You can trust Ellen. We have worked on several confidential cases together. She will keep it to herself."

"And the police?" Jenny objected. "I don't want them to know."

He decided not to argue with her.

"Well, if we decide to go that way, they'll need evidence. But they won't need to know everything."

"I don't trust the police..."

"Why don't we leave that for now and come back to it if we need to. There may be no need to go to the police."

"There should be...the murderers are walking scot-free around Gularaba!"

"That must be terrible for you. Tell me about it..."

Her face was pained. "I have nightmares. I wake up screaming."

"Can you remember the nightmares?"

"They are taking my children..."

"How does that make you feel?"

"I am angry. I never feel easy, comfortable...I am scared all the time...like this is a dangerous place. Sometimes, I think I am imagining things. At other times, I am sure they happened."

"It sounds like post-traumatic stress disorder. Have you had any treatment?"

"No. I keep myself to myself."

A magpie flew up onto the table and begged.

She spoke to it. "There, there. Are your babies starving?" She turned to Abajoe. "Life here is hard," she said and wept.

"When was the worst time?"

"It was in 2219, September I think. The drought was far worse than now…it had gone on and on for years. We had homegrown vegetables, preans and graize. We carried water to grow them. Then graize, our only carbohydrate, was hit by a virus from overseas and preans suddenly blackened and withered…they said it was a mutated fungus.

"There wasn't enough water to grow anything else. We lived on meat from our animals and hunting for some time. Then bores, springs and melon holes dried up. We had to buy our food and we sold everything we had to get money. The Government promised food from overseas but none got through to us – it must have been stolen on the way from the port. Thousands of starving people were walking along the railway lines to the coast. They came through Thornton, dying beside the track. When trains came inland with food, the guards let them help themselves, leaving nothing for us.

"Families, who had sold their blankets, huddled together for warmth in their empty houses. Every tree was cut down to make fires. Those who had been evicted searched for disused buildings, culverts and caves or dragged together waste materials to make shelters. In daylight, the adults and older children, those who had enough strength to walk, scoured the countryside for nuts, berries, shoots, leaves, weeds, bark, scraps of food, anything that could be eaten.

"Corpses had their faces and mouths stained green from eating grass and nettles, even though the human digestive system is not able to breakdown raw plant cellulose the way grazing animals do. They were unable to extract much nutrition from them…they merely filled their empty bellies to stop the hunger pains.

"There were bodies by the roadsides. People died mostly at home and were dragged out by the survivors to the roadside, hoping the body might be taken away and buried, because they were too weak to dig a grave."

She broke off. Tears coursed down Abajoe's face. He had heard about the terrible conditions before, during previous counselling, but they still wrung out his emotions, leaving him labile.

"Let me help you," said Abajoe, sniffing. "At the start of the Great Famine, most well-to-do families fled overseas," he recalled from previous visits in this area. "More people died from the diseases that struck them in their weakened state than died from hunger alone. The coastal areas were more prone to dysentery and cholera than the drier inland. Theft of fruit and failure of vegetable crops resulted in scurvy, pellagra and other vitamin deficiency diseases. Lack of nutrition caused immune systems to become weak and there was an increase in onset and fatality of diseases such as smallpox, measles and tuberculosis. Vaccine resistant strains resulted in infections of epidemic proportions. Did you lose your family to disease?" he asked.

She shook her head. "No. Those who stayed here and secured food supplies became targets for bands of criminals who lived by invading property and stealing. Civil order deteriorated. Theft and rape were common. Of the three acts listed by Freud as strictly prohibited: homicide, incest and cannibalism, the first two were widely practiced. Cannibalism was suspected as the last resort of more than a few, but attributed to dingoes. Men were behaving like wild animals, predators," Jenny sobbed.

He put his arm around her as she fought for breath, unable to talk. After a few minutes, she sat up and turned to face him.

"One night, we were in our house, starving, when there was hammering at the door.

"'Who is it?' my husband called.

"'Just open up,' a rough voice called.

"There were bandits in the village. We had heard they were going from house to house, robbing people of what little food they had.

"'What do you want?' my husband called though the closed and barred door.

"'Food,' came the reply.

"'We don't have any,' he said, loading his gun. 'Go away, I've got a gun.'

"Then, there was a volley of shots and the door splintered. My husband slumped to the ground, bleeding. I couldn't do anything. He died in my arms.

"They hammered again. 'Come on, woman, let us in.'

"I called, 'Just a minute,' I was petrified. My children were whimpering. I hushed them, hoping the bandits would go away. It was quiet, eerie, in the empty living room. Every stick of furniture had been sold to buy food or burned. The vinyl on the floor was faded around the patches where items had stood. It was so cold, my breath steamed in the light from a candle. I blew it out.

"I picked up the baby. My four-year-old son clung to my left leg and my two-year-old sat on my foot with her legs around my ankle.

"Trembling, I finished loading the heavy gun the way my husband had shown me. My mind was overshadowed by the screams we had heard earlier in the week, when the bandits had raped a village woman and stolen her children."

"Did anyone know who the bandits were or where they came from?"

"We thought they came from Kaldara, the next village.

"Without warning, there were heavy blows on the door. 'Open up,' the same voice demanded. 'We won't harm ye!'

"I didn't believe him. Those animals were capable of anything. The Great Famine was so severe that villagers had been keeping food from their weaker children, and when their bodies disappeared, no one asked how they had been disposed of. No one said anything. The awfulness was bad enough, without talking about it. We supposed that putting the abandoned children out of their misery and eating their bodies had seemed reasonable to some people, although I would have stopped them if I could."

"It must have been terrible," Abajoe agreed. It was better, in his opinion, that people should die from starvation rather than eat from corpses. Death, whenever and however it came, should be dignified. Cannibalism lacked dignity. Murder of children for food was the most heinous crime of all. But he was aware that he had never faced starving to death. It was nature's way of recycling nutrients in a carnivore unable to abort its offspring as easily as the marsupials. The further up the food chain an animal was, the more precipitous was the effect of famine lower down. Predators could pass from glut to starvation within a very short time, creating conditions when cannibalism could emerge.

"I pointed the gun at the door with one hand, like this." She held an imaginary gun at waist level. "My baby was on my other hip, here, like this. I doubted if I would be able to hit them if they came in a rush. There was pounding at the door with some sort of battering ram and then the lock burst and the door swung open against the wall. I had a glimpse of them silhouetted against the grey sky. I fired and kept firing until I ran out of ammunition. A body fell forwards and lay groaning in the doorway as I reloaded. Then they came back and dragged it away. I heard a shot. They must have killed the injured one."

"Did you recognise any of them?"

"Their faces were masked with scarves. When they were dragging away the injured man, one's mask slipped down and I could see his shrunken face and the sores around his mouth from starvation. He came to live in Gularaba after the Great Famine, I knew it was him. I heard his voice through the door.

"I dropped the gun and tried to get away with the three children. I was weak. Two was all I could carry and I was heartbroken. I kissed the two-year-old and left her behind. She reached out to me, crying, as I fled out of the back door carrying the other two."

Abajoe felt his throat tighten and he wanted to cry for what Jenny had suffered. He understood why she was still reliving it, 21 years after the event.

A flock of galahs swerved on to the lawn in front of them and bobbed around picking at seeds. They were hungry but the place of each one was respected.

She continued her story. "When we reached the railway, we walked in a group with others who were starving. We stayed together for protection, travelling in the warmth of daylight, not stopping until we reached the city. I eventually found a safe place, an empty room high up the fire escape of a tower block. I searched the streets for food. The only water I could find was in an open drain. After a couple of weeks, my kids caught a fever and were dead within 24 hours.

"There had been five of us at home in Gularaba but now I was alone. I was overcome by grief. I drifted around, for...I don't know how long...until the rains came. Then I came back here to the house. My two-year-old was gone and no one knew anything." She broke off, sobbing.

She buried her face in his shoulder and he hugged her.

Without warning, the galahs launched themselves into the air and were gone. He knew that they wouldn't harbour one who had killed within the group, whatever the circumstances. It would have been ejected to live as an outcast. The group was not a resource to be exploited for individual survival. Here, a crime had been committed and the perpetrators had to be brought to justice. It couldn't be overlooked any longer.

When they separated, Abajoe vowed to do everything in his power to help find the daughter she had left behind.

"Perhaps another family or even a bandit family took her in. They wouldn't be talking about it to you. If you like, I'll make some enquiries."

Then he talked with her about the identity of her attackers and the one who now lived in Gularaba.

"Have you confronted him?"

"The police went to him but he denied it."

Abajoe said he would question him. She gave him directions how to get there, thanked him profusely and they parted. He had raised her hopes and her demeanour had changed. She seemed hopeful and more outward looking.

Abajoe went with a policewoman to the man's home the next evening. They were met by his wife, who went to get him. He was about 50, partly bald, with a beard.

"What's this about?" he demanded.

The policewoman introduced Abajoe.

"We would like to ask you some questions about what happened in the Great Famine. Could we meet with you first and then with your wife?"

When they were alone with him, the policewoman asked, "How did your family fare in the Great Famine?"

"We all survived, but only just."

"Were you living here?"

"No…in Kaldara, up the road."

"Is it true that men from Kaldara raided other villages for food."

"No. Who told you that?"

"You were seen in Gularaba."

"Whoever says that is a liar. That Craig woman is nuts. I feel sorry for her…"

"Several people saw you there."

"They must have mistaken me for someone else."

This line of questioning was getting him nowhere. Abajoe tried a different tack. "What did you eat in the Great Famine?"

"Whatever we could find."

"Is it true that you ate from human bodies?"

His face flushed red and he stood up. "How dare you!"

"Sit down and answer the question," said the policewoman.

He sat down, his fists clenched and his arms folded.

"Of course not."

"Did you know anyone who did?"

"No."

"But it was common knowledge that this was happening in your village!"

"It's the first I've heard of it."

"They say someone stole children to eat," Abajoe said.

His face was a mask. "I don't know what you're talking about."

"But we think you do know. Did you…"

He stood up. "That's enough. I have already told everything to the police. Am I under arrest?"

"No, not yet," said the policewoman. "Sit down. How did you get this house?"

"I bought it, fair and square."

"During the Great Famine?"

"Oh, I don't know…yes," he admitted.

"Where did you get the money?" she asked.

"I sold my old place."

"But this is much larger and newer. Where did you get the extra money?"

"It was cheap. That's bloody obvious. It was the Great Famine. Now, I've been patient but I've had enough of your questions. Leave me alone now!"

He got up and walked away.

The policewoman turned to Abajoe, "They probably sold it to him cheap because they were scared stiff of him!"

"If he paid them, they could have bought food and survived. I wonder what happened to them."

"I checked with the locals," Abajoe told her. "They lived rough, buying food until the money ran out and then they died."

"He could have got the place by extortion. But it's circumstantial and we can't charge him."

Abajoe spent the rest of his few days at Thornton visiting people in Gularaba, who had been present during the Great Famine and interviewing them about the attack, about the identity of the attackers, the whereabouts of the abandoned child and what had happened to the husband's corpse. He arranged for an exhumation and investigation of a mass grave that was used in Gularaba during the Great Famine.

While the forensic work was underway, Abajoe visited several other volunteer counsellors for a day. He met with their local community leaders and stayed overnight. It took all his self control to sleep separately at close quarters with several of the single women, who made him very welcome. When he visited Paula, they went to bed early together and got up late. He felt guilty that he was unfairly raising her expectations of his commitment to her, for he did not intend to settle down in an exclusive relationship with her, or indeed any female, for many years. To spell this out to her again seemed unnecessary. He realised he might be leading her on but he would explain when they returned to the city the following week.

When he returned to Thornton, he found that no two-year-old had been found in the mass grave at Gularaba. A scientist obtained, from the National Database and Jenny's memories, a detailed description of her two-year old child, including her genome. The scientist predicted, from Jenny's and her husband's characteristics at the same age and their genomes, her current appearance now at age 23. She would be fair, like her husband, with a triangular face, a small mouth and broad forehead, like herself. Anna, that was her name, would be distinctive and attractive. He started a search of the National Database for her likeness, first within the local region. There were several promising leads for him to pursue when he returned to Meannjin.

CHAPTER 23

Learned Miracles

A bajoe also applied science to medicine. Although he never commanded a lame man to discard his crutches, as Jesus had done, he inspired sick people to abandon ineffective treatments with dramatic success. He had a reputation for performing miracles.

His prominence in 'Family Fare' and his reputation for solving problems brought people to seek his advice on their health problems. He was a licensed practitioner of medical science, the discipline that had displaced medicine. He took on cases where other doctors had failed and became famous for his 'miraculous' cures.

One day he received a visit from an old man, who was suffering from a metabolic disorder. He had been taking a certain medication for most of his life. Despite the drug, from time to time he had symptoms. Recently his condition had worsened.

"Does the drug make much difference? Have you tested it?" Abajoe asked him.

"No, but I am sure it does me good."

With his doctor's agreement, Abajoe had identical pills made with sugar substituted for the active ingredient and set him a course of medication that alternated between the two types, without telling him that some were placebos. To be ethical, he gave him other pills, containing the active ingredient, to be taken if his condition worsened.

The old man's son, Robert, checked for symptoms every day. At the end of the month, Abajoe analysed his report and wrote the following message.

Dear Erstin and Robert,

I have received your report. The tests have confirmed as I suspected, that the medication has little or no effect. The medication may have been effective earlier but now it seems to make no difference whether Erstin takes the medicine or a look-alike made from sugar. He has taken this placebo for a week, with no worsening of symptoms. It is true that you did have some relief of symptoms during the tests, but you had these just as often when you were on your pills as when you were on sugar. Therefore, it is concluded that you need a different treatment. You can stop taking the pills. However, I would like you to continue with sugar and monitor symptoms daily. A prescription is attached.

    Regards

    Abajoe

Unknown to Erstin and Robert, the 'sugar' medication had the active ingredient as originally. After a month, there was neither relief from nor worsening of symptoms. He concluded that the treatment had only a small effect when he knew he was being treated with it and no effect when he didn't know whether or not he was getting it.

Erstin's treatment was stopped. His health improved. His family were grateful and the story was publicised. Abajoe had achieved the 'miracle' of a cure with an invisible treatment and without needing ongoing treatment.

Many sick people came to him with ailments that conventional treatments had not cured. He changed their medication schedules to tests that alternated a placebo with the active ingredient. To those using braces, crutches, sticks and walkers, he alternated equipment of the same design made of soft materials, such as flexible plastics, that provided reduced support.

"The appliance made from the new materials will be more effective," he said, "if you swap over to it following this schedule."

He did the same with those using hearing aids and strong spectacles, providing dud amplifiers and plain glass lenses, to be used alternately following a schedule.

He found that, in most cases, the placebos were as good as the treatments. By stopping the treatments, there might even be improvement and the way cleared to try for a more effective treatment.

Abajoe appealed to medics' professionalism to get his methods adopted. He spoke to them, saying, "Each treatment is an experiment that must be ended unless there is convincing evidence that it is working. Many people are on treatments that do not work and are no more effective than a placebo. Your professional duty is to perform a double-blind control experiment to discover if the treatment is really more effective than a placebo. In some situations, any treatment at all would help the patient. Such treatments should be without unpleasant side-effects and inexpensive."

Following Abajoe's advice, T One's Government required medical treatment manufacturers to market every product with a look-alike variant, lacking the active ingredient that patients were unable to distinguish. They guided doctors in their use, requiring they test their patients' medications and prostheses routinely. Pharmacists soon reported that medication and appliance sales had been cut to one third.

In a different initiative, Abajoe pioneered holistic diagnosis methods. Sickness was normally diagnosed by investigating each system separately, for example, the digestive system, until a malfunction was found. If the malady was a dysfunctional interaction between two or more systems, for example nerves and digestion, it might never be diagnosed.

Abajoe's medical science was based on comprehensive observation. When a patient was referred to him by baffled medics, Abajoe's assistants fastened instruments throughout the patient's body to monitor every system. When measurements had been made with symptoms present, they measured responses to perturbations, with sampling of tissues and fluids. It could match the symptoms with two or more systems interacting out of phase, for example, nerves, endocrines and digestion. The information was used to calibrate a whole-body model for each patient.

Armed with the model, he could prescribe a biofeedback treatment method that would bring the systems back into balance. For example, the patient could learn anxiety reduction by rewarding its reduction of digestive acidity. The holistic modelling became known as 'Abajoe's Holy Method'.

He became a scientific faith healer and his fame brought miracles. His patients observed their bodies and behaviour carefully and kept detailed records. They looked for chains of causality, patterns of effect and associations. When they tried a treatment, it was singular and under controlled conditions, with monitoring of the whole body for side effects. The rigour he espoused ensured they made progress and were optimistic. This strengthened their immune systems. Always the patient took control and accepted medical advice when necessary. The patient became actively engaged in the challenge of gaining wellness.

Trauma victims came to him with wasted limbs or atrophied mental functions. Some had stopped talking after a brain tumour or stroke. Abajoe motivated them to endeavour to talk again by having them watch, on a brain scanner, how their efforts would grow fibres in another part of the cortex he had targeted for that function. They learned to regrow their ability for speech.

It was the same with sensory and physical disabilities. Abajoe demanded they attempt the injured skill. If their left arm was disabled and in a sling, they were required to change the sling to their right arm and strive to use the left, motivated by watching the fibres grow in a target brain area readied by calibration therapy. It was called the 'Brain Regrowth Feedback Method'.

A man, about to have his legs amputated after a farming accident, sought his help. The case seemed hopeless. Abajoe sent him to scientists, who, on his suggestion, experimented with reconditioning of his immune response to prevent rejection of a specific DNA tissue. He received legs transplanted from the victim of a fatal accident in a first operation of this kind in Australia. It was successful, and he visited Abajoe to show him his fully recovered walking ability with the new limbs, thanking him profusely for this 'miracle'.

Abajoe respected other species and the sanctity of sensate individuals. He abhorred testing of new technologies on animals. If a new technology could not be tested on its customers, on their tissue or on synthetic material, then it could not be tested at all. He was influential in changing medical technology to focus on terminal conditions, where there were human volunteers. Technologies offering only quality of life enhancement and cosmetic effects ceased to be developed.

He encouraged more women to participate in scientific investigation. They had often perceived Old Science as serving the male interests of power, control and efficiency and disempowering females by creating machines and robots, ousting human self-sufficiency and devaluing conception, birthing, nurturing and learning. There was neglect of the sharing, caring and compromising valued more highly by females. New Science would embrace these emphases, attract more female participation and require attention to the concerns of both genders on an equal footing.

The potential of science excited Abajoe. When he spoke to his followers about New Science, he often reminded them of the caution needed in attributing causes that might in fact be effects or associations.

"New Science is sceptical of wishful thinking," he told them. "A responsible person should inquire into the evidence for and against each of the possible causal processes before deciding the causal chain to a problem. Investigators should isolate one change at a time, operating on the problem effect they are measuring, show a strong correlation and identify a temporal antecedence that is plausible, before they can be confident that they know a unique cause. Researchers should have engaged in trying to refute their own hypotheses, rather than gathering supporting data. Scientific reports are to end with a new section, after 'conclusions', called 'refutations'. Whereas an author's supporting data cannot help being biased, his refuting data, honestly reported, might not be so."

Some problems solve themselves, others respond to treatment and many are unsolved. Too often, treatments are assumed to be successful when recovery has been natural. Natural systems are more resilient than inexperienced and biased observers admit. Miraculous recoveries are real and frequent to the sceptical observer.

CHAPTER 24

Rossit Wrap Up

He wrote in his book: *At the heart of New Science lies better public understanding of the methodology of science. The public will be able to distinguish objective observations, falsifiable hypotheses, controlled variables, control experiments and fair tests.*

New Science eliminates other possible causes that could explain results, such as the experimenter's bias. Our 'null' hypothesis requires us to gather data showing that the converse of the behaviour we expect has not occurred.

Tests will be 'blind', without the observers, who assess rossits for euthanizing, knowing which pen they are from. The rossits in both pens will get the same attention and will not therefore be subject to Hawthorne or Stockholm effects. In our experiment, we employed neutral scientific assistants to monitor, assess and determine whether to euthanize animals according to our ethical protocol. Their selection of animals to be euthanized was blind: they didn't know which pen they came from.

Thus, our results do not have the bias of wishful thinking. Besides finding out if the rossits cap or limit their population deliberately, we recorded behaviours that could cause this.

SIMULATION OF AUSTRALIAN AND BHAKARIAN VOLUNTARY POPULATION CONTROL USING ROSSITS by Abajoe Yabra and Paula Yabra.

Aim
We tried to refute the null hypothesis that ultimate rossit population numbers are uncapped, even when randomly occurring famine events kill a large part of the population. In other words, that rossits actively limit their population establishing a carrying capacity. It is to simulate the human carrying capacities of Australia and Bhakaria.

Our Bias
The authors wish to establish, for political purposes, that Australians will naturally learn to cap their population and avoid famine.

Background

In both Australia and Bhakaria, famine or disease have within the past 20 years resulted in significant numbers of premature deaths. Australians have traditionally had two children when they were about 30, each replacing the death of a great-grandparent, who has lived to 136.

In Australia, famines have followed severe droughts or floods in a climate that is unpredictable. There is evidence that Australians, particularly Yamens, have temporarily increased the birth rate to replace children that died in famines.

Bhakarians lived more briefly due to diseases and died at 110. Couples have had a pre-emptive response of a higher birth rate, having their first child at age around 20 and an average of three children, one of whom is likely to die at a young age from disease.

Epidemics begin when a population density threshold has been reached and propagation is multiplied and spread. There is evidence that epidemic diseases like sporangoid fever are increasing and the birth rate has increased as people try to ensure they will have descendants living to look after them in old age.

Populations in both nations are currently increasing at a rate of about 2% per annum from births alone. People are also living longer and in Australia the cessation of industrial activity has resulted in fewer accidents.

The increase in population in Australia and Bhakaria prompts the question of ultimate populations and at what level the populations will be capped by natural processes. Derived from that question is the question of numbers who would immigrate between the two nations if opportunities were present.

Method

Comparative modelling commenced with simulation of conditions in 2237 in both nations, in terms of relative area, population, water and food supplies, with rossits representing humans.

NATION	'AUSTRALIA'	'BHAKARIA'
Position, relative	Adjacent	Adjacent
Area, relative	4	1
POPULATION humans	50	500
Pen area, relative	4	1
Water relative supply, quantity	1	4
delivery	random	constant
storage	4 months	4 months
Food relative supply, quantity	1	4
delivery	random	constant
storage	nil	nil
POPULATION rossits		
2237 quarter 1	2	2
2	12	11
3	51	70
4	46	282
2238 quarter 5	83	514
6	32	447
7	98	464
8	43	459

Rossit population depended on the euthanizing of individuals according to 'blind' monitoring for distress by predetermined criteria.

Results

In 'Bhakaria', which had a larger and regular supply of food and water, the population averaged about ten times the population in 'Australia'. The population was eventually limited by space. When conditions became overcrowded, the does aborted or neglected their young, endemic disease took a high toll and there was fighting. Individuals became physically smaller. Fecundity decreased and eventually the number reaching maturity matched the cull of distressed individuals.

In 'Australia', due to random water and food shortages, a half of all rossit foetuses were reabsorbed, or killed by ejection from the pouch, or when out of the pouch by infanticide. Of the survivors, half died from starvation or disease. There were famines in quarters 3 (0 deaths), 4 (20), 6 (52) and 8 (71).

Analysis

Rossits eventually reduced procreation in 'Australia' to a level supportable under the variable food and water supply conditions. There were three very severe famines, such that more than 50% of the rossits were distressed and had to be culled. Under the stress of famine, endemic disease thrived. The population grew back afterwards but not to such high levels, due to foetal reabsorption and ejection of fingerlings from the pouch. The population continued to cycle but less dramatically, eventually averaging about 40, which was only one tenth of the population in 'Bhakaria'.

Population density of rossits became 45 times higher in 'Bhakaria', similar to humans currently (40 times higher). The simulation showed 'Australia' could support one tenth of the 'Bhakarian' population of rossits on average, similar to the human population that is currently one tenth. However, the 'Australian' population varied significantly between one fifth and one thirtieth due to extremes of food supply variation, with catastrophic numbers of deaths from starvation. Litter sizes were controlled contemporaneously by foetal reabsorption and infanticide. There was evidence that rossits learned to limit their reproduction when the food supply was regular, but where it was variable, each feeding event was a separate determinant of reproduction activities. There was little evidence that rossits remembered past hardship and limited their reproduction, as might humans.

Discussion

Reproduction in the 'Bhakarian' environment was limited by overcrowding and disease, whereas the 'Australian' population was limited by food availability. It related to water supply, which was four times higher and more regular in Bhakaria. In the 'Bhakarian' pen, rossits adapted reproduction to the conditions. It is remarkable that in our experiment, all the rossits in the 'Australian' pen were not euthanized due to starvation. When rossits starve, females eject larger and larger youngsters from their pouches, to die without nourishment. The small amount of food is unequally shared and low status individuals such as the very young and the old were culled first.

Australia's ultimate population, at about a tenth of Bhakaria's, was proportionally about the same as at present, suggesting that the human populations of both Australia and of Bhakaria are already limited by the constraints modelled.

The number of rossits in 'Australia' varied widely, with frequent starvation. Our inference was that in 'Australia' the rossits were unable to anticipate famine due to overpopulation, although there is some evidence that the reproduction of rossits was inhibited in the 'Bhakarian' pen by continuing food scarcity and crowding. The random pattern of food availability in 'Australia' did not deter reproduction. Our starving rossits did not refrain from sexual activity.

Animals, such as bears and squirrels, store fat and food for the lean months of winter ahead. Mating is timed so that the young are born in spring, when there is food. Their assumption that food will become available at a certain time of year is instinctive.

We looked for evidence of rossit learning during the experiment. Cognitive learning has been found in the primates, dolphins, dogs, crows and lagomorphs – rabbits and hares – and in the marsupials, which include possums. They can solve unfamiliar problems, including situations that would lead directly to future problems, such as taking the bait from traps. But the ability to avoid situations with problems in the distant future may have been seen in some of these species, but not so far in rossits. No one has investigated animals' avoidance of future famine situations by population control.

Sexual abstinence has a chain of causes and effects to get to starvation avoidance. We saw no evidence that rossits were able to make associations all the way along a causal chain. However, there was less mating under drought and famine conditions and we hypothesise that abstinence is caused by control from the top of a social hierarchy, or 'pecking order'.

Reproduction opportunities depend on position in the 'pecking order'. The highest status male, who mates with all the females, mates with the highest status females first. They keep the low status males and females from breeding.

They achieve their status when they are young by fighting with tooth and claw. It is trial and error conditioning, with costly errors of judgement. Once achieved, high status has to be maintained. As they get older, combat has a ritual aspect, such as a pushing strength test, so no one gets hurt. The strongest male, who is usually the heaviest, wins. Perhaps when there is a food shortage, he would try to maintain his weight by foregoing copulation and keep the door open for his genes by stopping other males.

Therefore, reproduction may be controlled by the social order to mitigate starvation from drought-induced famine.

We also observed emigration and plague behaviour. Rossits spent little time at the grills between the two pens, except when they were starving, and about the same time at the one opening into the other cage as they did at the one into the passageway. From this we inferred that their interest in a bountiful, adjacent territory was no stronger than their desire to escape starvation in their home territory. In other words, interest in emigration was more strongly motivated by 'push' than by 'pull'.

Future work

Famine can be reduced by storing excess food in times of plenty. In the experiment reported, excess food was wasted but the population effect of storing it needs to be investigated.

Conclusions

Under conditions that simulated droughts in Australia, rossits suffered large numbers of deaths, from famine after famine, without learning to limit their population, except during the immediate gestation cycle, whereas in 'Bhakaria', under constant conditions, the population reached an equilibrium. The grass was always browner, whichever side they were on.

Refutation

Some of our findings refuted the conclusions above. Under ideal conditions, a doe produces about 12 live youngsters per kindle. In the 'Bhakarian' pen, the average eventually became eight and in the 'Australian' pen 10. Fertility was similar but litter sizes were reduced by foetal reabsorption. This is evidence that rossits are able to control their populations. The 'Australian' rossits had a more opportunistic strategy in their nutritionally harsher environment. It is not clear why the 'Australian' rossits adopted such a strategy, unless it was logical that overpopulation was the better pre-emptive response than death by starvation. This could possibly be explained by the prevalence of infant cannibalism as a way of storing nutrients for survival.

Reviewers of New Science invariably denied the relevance of rossit behaviour to human behaviour. Abajoe explained his view that the reproductive behaviour of a species of mammal or marsupial is determined by environment in much the same way as it is for any other species, including humans. It opened up a topic that had been taboo, population control.

Abajoe was interviewed on his views of population control by a national news magazine.

"What have you learned from your experiment with rossits?" the interviewer asked.

"Here in Australia, spring may not bring rains and it is never certain when food will grow. We know that indigenous people in Australia and Canada had an equilibrium before Europeans arrived, although starvation conditions may have been frequent, occasionally requiring extreme solutions for survival, with some evidence of infant cannibalism. However, starvation was unusual and it seems possible that animals with higher mental abilities, such as humans, learn sustainable population equilibrium conditions more quickly, whereas lower animals, such as marsupials, have reproductive adaptations that compensate for their cerebral limitations and enable them to avoid overpopulation."

"Is human reproduction affected by the prospect of overpopulation in the same way as rossits?"

"Like them, we do not recognise overpopulation until it is too late. However, some humans stop breeding during wartime and economic recession, delaying procreation until security returns. There are technologies to control human reproduction. When these are used, sexual activity may be uncontrolled and behavioural control of reproduction, such as abstinence, may atrophy. The deployment of birth control technologies, and their withdrawal, is probably related strongly to partner bonding, health, security of nutrition, shelter, employment, social order and so on. It is a more complex situation than we modelled with rossits. Abstinence was a strategy they used after disaster had struck."

"How should Australians avoid famine?"

"It is essential that the decline in technological production should not reduce availability of fertility control treatments, prophylactics and abortions. Nevertheless, voluntary control may be insufficient to prevent frequent starvation events. Local government should predict future food availability and probabilities of famine so people can volunteer to refrain from reproduction."

"How far into the future should predictions go?"

"It requires more than predictions. Our experiment showed that rossits' strategy was to respond to hunger, after it had arrived, by barbaric usurpation of the rights to life of the young and old, who were denied food and in some cases, cannibalised. This is not acceptable for humans. We need to have a sustainable future by two means. Firstly, we need to have enough water and food resources for the population. Secondly, we need to keep the population at or below that level, if possible, by voluntary control of reproduction. Humans are better able to regulate conception than rossits but after about three months of pregnancy, there is total parental commitment to raising the offspring. Consequently, humans are less able to respond to drought conditions than rossits, who reabsorb foetuses and cannibalise unwanted young. Because of longer lives and high social costs of premature death, humans need to anticipate starvation many years in advance, at least a generation or 30 years. Sustainability needs to be considered for at least a reproductive cycle, or 30 years."

Abajoe's book 'The New Science' was so popular that the Middle Way Party sent him on a national lecture tour. At 24 and already famous in the Yabra tradition, he was the nation's most eligible bachelor. His audiences were mostly women. He hated being a sexual object and thought it would be heavenly to meet a girl who valued him for himself rather than for what he represented.

His ancestry was a heavy burden and he sometimes thought of disappearing into anonymity with his hair dyed and a new identity. How wonderful to begin again, on his own account, without Yabra traditions dictating his every move. But he never got quite as far as packing because he valued his family's good opinion and he knew that they would be devastated if he absconded. He decided the best way he could find more personal space was by achieving leadership.

His lecture tour was a great success. He related New Science to issues of the day. He was able to see earlier causes and multiple causes that uplifted audiences to a higher perspective. Beside his solutions, other leaders' answers seemed facile and trite. They could see only trees but Abajoe saw the forest ecosystem. His ideas addressed the true causes, leaving his listeners spellbound. Everywhere he visited, audiences were packed and full, with others outside listening.

On his return, T One resigned from her seat of Yugambeh, where the Yabras lived, on the southern coast adjacent to Meannjin. Marko was elected by the Party caucus to take over as Prime Minister.

Abajoe was well known in the Yugambeh constituency and was nominated as the Party's candidate for his loyal service to the Party and his public prominence. He threw himself into the campaign. Two months later, in the by-election, he romped home with a large majority.

Marko appointed him Energy and Infrastructure Minister. The member he replaced had less experience of the issues and the Party wanted Abajoe in the cabinet with his wealth of ideas in time to lead the Party into the next election. He was well equipped to step into a national leadership role. As the gifted child of the Prime Minister, born into Australia's ruling dynasty, people took it for granted that he was destined for the highest office.

New Science had become his manifesto.

CHAPTER 25

New Science

On taking office, Abajoe decided the best way to get radical change was to take it to the grass roots rather than declare it ex cathedra. He continued his lecture tour as a programme of ministerial discourses to community leaders around Australia. His first venue was in the local government parliamentary lecture theatre at Warringa.

"Commune leaders, volunteers! Thank you for inviting me here today. I want to explain to you one of the main ideas in the MWP's manifesto, New Science. Afterwards, I will answer questions first from media representatives here at the front, then from members of the audience. I will now read from the first chapter.

"WHY WE WANT SCIENTIFIC TRIBUNALS

"Australians have emerged from hiding in the shadows cast by Darwin's theory of competition for survival. No longer is their inheritance determined in a nature that is red in tooth and claw. We have found out that any differences between our people's genes are small and easily modified to be pretty much the same. There is no major difference between races and there is no need for an arms race. We are learning to foster quality in our own living by developing communality rather than by promoting our individual genes. We are learning self-altruism, the sharing of our spare living space with kindred and the necessity to reduce childbirth to the replacement level when people live longer and longer.

"We need local sustainability. The MWP's solution is to devolve planning to communities, with planning tribunals to approve developments. We will give communality teeth by requiring that developments do not disadvantage anyone, except commercial competitors. Within each commune, developments will be the object of sharing rather than the subject of divisiveness, competition, winning and losing. Who wants that?

"Tribunals will only be empowered to approve change where, after trading and compensation, no one would be worse off. This is an adaptation of the Pareto criterion, which has been kicked around in welfare economic circles since the end of the 19th century. It is an idealistic requirement, that as long as there is anyone who would be

worse off, any stakeholder or member of the general public who would lose, then if their objection is sustained before the tribunal on scientific grounds, a development cannot be approved until a compensation agreement is reached. This will bring a fundamental change to development. Paretian change has so far been consigned to the 'too hard' tray because it could seldom arise from individual self-interest. But now we want a strong sharing ethic.

"There is a new lubricant for bringing stakeholders to a Paretian solution, called 'self-altruism'. It means self-sustaining first, then giving to others. Australians experienced it during the Great Famine. When a person had secured their own survival, they often volunteered to share their surplus with kindred. Now people are giving what they do not need to kindred once again, to prevent another famine.

"Developments that would once have been rejected, such as building paddies for rice cultivation, are now gaining unanimous acceptance through growth in self-altruism and the work of tribunals. Our elders, Zelta and Hugo, are enthusiastic about sharing with kin as it used to be at the centre of life in tribal groups. They also support the tribunal concept, which in many aspects is similar in its mode of working to a counsel of elders that inquires to ascertain who would be worse off from a development.

"The tribunal first acts as a switchboard to connect parties who could swap or trade away disadvantages. For example, job losers could be promised jobs by the redeveloper. Another example, an adjacent business that would suffer from restricted access during construction, could swap premises with another business at a more distant location, if they wanted to be close for the duration of construction, such as a fast-food business that could supply the construction workers.

"Tribunals would quantify shortfalls that objectors would experience from the development and calculate their losses. These could be monetary, or in decibel hours or health consequences and would be shortfalls from community goals that the developer must remedy or compensate.

"Development would be considered for all the changes it could bring, that are not changes, which would be valued in markets. Effects of a change spread outwards, like ripples on a pond, with knock-on effects and reactions that become wider and weaker until the energy of the change is dissipated. The energy of a water splash cannot be destroyed,

only dispersed, reflected and absorbed. To meet the exacting Paretian criterion, an investment splash is aimed to reflect back more than the original amount, after compensation has been absorbed.

"Anyone who still objects can have their claim arbitrated by the tribunal. The tribunal's chief official, the Tribune, will keep a record of the developer's obligations. If the developer is so encumbered to be forced to call it off, there would be an opportunity for voluntary payments by self-altruistic stakeholders, who would be prepared to share their windfall or largesse to compensate objectors. Those who benefit could help those disadvantaged, for example, an owner of a building that would evict tenants, to sell it, could pass on some of his gain to the tenants as they leave.

"Some shortfalls will have been concocted or inflated and the Tribune may accept the developer's scientific evidence that the shortfalls are small or non-existent. If the claimants dispute an approval, the process, but not the content of the tribunal's decision, can be appealed in a national tribunal, where cases with ramifications wider than the council's purview can be considered.

"The process of approving developments would be logical and rational by the methods of science and communality, not by arbitrary authority, nor by politics, nor by disbursement of anticipated project benefits to those who approve it, as bribes. We will have change that leaves no one worse off by a transparent process.

"Tribunals will be an important addition to civil society that will empower and liberate citizens. Our laws now allow strangers to disadvantage you, without legal recourse. Your local tribunal will not allow this to happen, creating security and peace of mind conducive to a meditative life style that requires minimal possessions and only materials needed for self-sustenance. Greedy developers will be answerable to everyone they disadvantage.

"The tribunal system will depend on you. Get your community's goals stated clearly. If you are a professional, able to help in a new development approval process, volunteer your skills, after sustaining your own future. We will need your help in making developers, who would reduce the welfare of the community, compensate losers.

"Thank you."

Abajoe paused for applause.

"Now, are there any questions from the media representatives present here at the front?"

"Does this change mean more state control?" a journalist asked.

"No. Tribunals will be independent and not answerable to local government. They will take over the work of approving developments. The method they will use, science, is not centralised – anyone can have a say. The tribunals will apply scientific scrutiny by transparent and reproducible methods. They will determine compensation of the various stakeholders fairly. Individuals will be empowered, not disempowered as they would be by state control."

"Will tribunals merely enforce community goals on individuals?"

"No. Tribunals will require that a development satisfies individual claimants' legitimate wants and contributes to community goals. The commune is a suitable planning unit, about the size of a city suburb, or half a federal electorate. It will be small enough for everyone to know everyone but big enough to have a power station, water storage and radio station. It would generate its own independent goals, led by professional self-altruism."

"Won't development go to communes offering least compensation?"

"No. Tribunals will be co-ordinated by a national tribunal that will set compensation rates scientifically."

"Will investors' returns decrease and development cease?"

"No. Developments that proceed will be more highly valued and share prices increase. Because some of the profits will be removed and distributed as compensation to a widening group of claimants, investment confidence will be diversified. Gratified former claimants will invest in shares, recycling profits. This is a case of Lenz's Law. 'Any change in status quo prompts an opposing reaction in the responding system'. Derived from chemistry, it explains that when part of the profit is removed and ploughed back, the profitability from an investment will increase."

"Whose side will tribunals be on, the developers' or the claimants'?"

"Neither, they will be a fourth pillar of the constitution, with a mediative function between developers, stakeholders and the community. Tribunals have shouldered the onus formerly on objectors to show why a particular development should not proceed. Their remit is to falsify the hypothesis that the development application is acceptable, by considering claims that it is not."

"Won't fair compensation take so long to negotiate that the developer will 'miss the boat' and pull out?"

"It is expected that the approval process will slow down development at first, until claimants realise that they are stopping development essential for community welfare. People will volunteer to forego compensation by self-altruism."

"Will the tribunals support the interests of isolated claimants or impose the will of the majority?"

"We have all seen the old cottage defiantly preserved in a canyon of high-rise development. What for some people is a commodity, such as land, is for others a precious site, work of art or cultural artefact, having hereditary ownership and stewardship and is not for sale. Tribunals will serve the community in providing a forum where a majority can emerge and make the compensation due known to a minority. With community backing, such as from a plebiscite, an individual would still be able to stop a development."

"How can devolving the Government create a unified nation? Surely a strong central leadership is required!"

"By devolving to local parliaments, judiciaries and tribunals, divisive national government of sectarian Australia will be avoided. The greater the centralisation of power, the greater the dissent and conflict. Conflict is better solved locally than centralised in a national polarisation. The work of tribunals will be unified by the Scientific Method, leading to a stronger nation."

"What will be the overall effect of the tribunals' work?"

"They will profoundly affect the humanitarian quality of developments. Until now, no one has been mandated to investigate and expel harmful technologies such as asbestos fibres, memory implants, text scrolling and atrophic sedentary occupations."

Abajoe then opened up questioning to the audience.

The questions were mainly about how the tribunal system would work. There were several hostile questioners opposed to science and he said that he would deal with that in the next segment when Helen Sudarta would debate the tribunal proposal with him.

At the prearranged time, he spoke to his communicator and the wall of the hall was filled with an image of the Opposition Leader. The debate was being broadcast on National Views.

"Good evening, Helen," he began.

"Good evening, Abajoe, people of Warringa. I have been watching Abajoe's presentation and I must say, his questioners have been very kind to him."

"Yes, Helen, I think at this point I have most people's support for tribunals. Now, you sound as though you are going to be argumentative. Well, off you go."

Sudarta began by attacking the credibility of New Science.

"New Science is idealistic dreaming," she scoffed. *"It has never been tried."*

Abajoe did not rise to her taunt and replied evenly, "Science has had a place in technological decision-making for the past 500 years, Helen. In the past, science has been a tool applied to material problems and ignored cultural meanings. Problems used to be solved by science by referring to the store of scientific understanding and through testing relationships by experiments with observable consequences. Now, science has methods able to include meanings for different stakeholders and work out logical compromises."

Sudarta's reply was derisory. *"Even after including the effects of technology, science is still a narrow endeavour...a small part of human affairs. Most problems of importance do not involve materials or their cultural meanings. In our religion, we solve problems from our store of cultural understanding, through the authority of our leaders."*

"The religions will benefit from the independent power of the tribunals," Abajoe rebutted. "They want their elders to be able to influence development approvals and give special consideration to their followers and their other interests. But that would be contested by the other religions. A fair ecumenical authority is needed. Their creeds may seem to be in conflict with the Scientific Method, as a way of knowing, but tribunals will replace religious conflict with harmony. Tribunals therefore need to take into consideration religious, artistic, psychological, historical and hereditary values, as well as community goals."

Sudarta's tone changed to ridicule. *"Now you want to throw out religion and authority, and expand the role of science to take their place. It can't be done. In most problems, cultural meanings are religious meanings. New Science has no way of taking them into account. Their cultural effects are emotional and can't be impartially observed. When science tries to include these, it imposes its own religious authority in the guise of 'objective' science. Is Abajoe saying that his new scientists will be better judges of cultural meanings than our leaders? Our religion goes back 1000 years, longer than science...a johnny-come-lately. Surely our leaders have more experience?"*

Sudarta leaned back confidently. Abajoe knew that as long as the debate kept to the abstract, Sudarta would be able to carry her assertion that New Science had little to offer. He had to ground the issue in a concrete example, where Sudarta's cultural values could be reduced to reactionary dogma.

He shook his head vigorously. "New Science can replace religion and authority and it certainly should. Consider the problems of our growing population. The Progress Party denies that this is a problem whereas those of us who believe in New Science want to avert another famine by voluntary population control. Your cultural leadership is to assert values that were adopted by your religion when the earth was almost empty of people. Now, when we have over-population, it directs individuals to have children they do not want. Quite clearly, the cultural values you hold so important are nothing more than a device to promulgate your religion as a competitive strategy that ignores the welfare of your followers and attacks the rights of the rest of the community. We will be better off without this so-called culture. New Science is culturally neutral and will work for the whole of the community, not just Yamen extremists."

Sudarta's face was red and she tried to control the anger in her voice.

"We have a right to expand our religion and you have no right to try and impose birth control. You say our leadership is following a competitive strategy but are you not doing the same in advocating population control? We both want more followers. Which is worse, the possibility of famine or to deny people the right to have children? When you preach population control, are you being any less dogmatic than the ancient scriptures? The word of God confirms that individuals have the right to have children. That dogma has stood the test of time. New Science is trying to tamper in cultural matters, of which it has no experience. The people won't accept it. You are setting yourselves against our religion and you will regret it."

Sudarta had not refuted his public responsibility argument and had merely asserted historical precedence. It was weak. Abajoe decided to deliver his knockout blow.

"New Science is not against your religion. We want all Australians to consider which is best: to follow your advice and keep having children as long as they can afford it, or to voluntarily adopt birth control. We want people to accept that God's jurisdiction is spiritual and non-material questions, such as the purpose of our lives. New Science deals with questions of how best to live."

Sensing defeat, Sudarta slid into the defiant posture of a Kudim railing at a non-believer.

"This is blasphemy and if you impose New Science on us, we will begin a holy war against you. Our community lies within our religion and we will not accept being dictated to by outsiders on how to live. We are guided by the Kitab and that will decide how best to live."

It was empty religious dogma. When Abajoe spoke again, it was as the winner.

"People no longer accept authoritarian control by religious leaders. They live in a voluntary society. New Science will empower their participation in the community. They regenerate their own culture by expressing their perceptions and their wants to democratic leaders. This is where population control will be decided. The days of Big Authority and Big Religion are over."

That was the end of the debate. Abajoe had come out against Yamen ideas of community and leadership. He knew that if Sudarta ever gained power, she would mute him, using as much force as it would take.

CHAPTER 26

Philosophical Journey to Mount Argus

‘ Citra stayed overnight at the gereja and the Kudim helped her to find a job in Australia,’ Abajoe wrote. He was impatient for Abajoe to meet with her, as he had planned all along.

‘Normally she would have joined a long queue and had to wait about two years as there were few visas available and strong demand. But the Kudim contacted a mine manager he knew at a place called Mount Argus, who agreed to sponsor her application and a ticket on a sailing ship. She obtained an Australian visa as a guest worker, for the maximum five-year period. The Kudim even paid for a cyclo to take her to the port. His kindness helped restore her trust in males again, but not her faith.

‘“You’ll be okay at Mount Argus,” he said. “There’s a drought and famine further south but the mine has its own water supply and is keeping going.”

‘As the ship began to cast off from the quay, fear gripped her when she realised she might never see her homeland again. She was tempted to run ashore but she had no future there, whereas she was going to well-paid work in Australia. She watched documentaries of Australian life provided by councils that welcomed immigrants. The land was brown and ugly. She felt ill-prepared to survive in such an unforgiving landscape but people seemed to be well off, although some of their ways were alien, such as drinking while watching sport.

‘She recalled her vow under the stars, made years before in faraway Pedang. Emigration seemed to offer her a chance of fulfilling her mission to help her family and countrymen, although she didn’t yet know how. As the ship caught the wind and got underway, she stood in the bows with tears coursing down her cheeks. Her life had been hard but she hoped this would be a turning point.

‘The voyage lasted for two weeks. There was a cyclone, with gusting winds that jerked at the sails, threatening to rip them and they hove to behind Duyfken Island for almost a week. They lay at anchor with the wind whining in the rigging until the swirling vacuum had roared overhead and across the Australian coastline, where it fizzled out.

'Citra found the ship's library. She came across a recent publication, 'The New Science', by Abajoe Yabra, Australian Energy and Infrastructure Minister, translated into Bhakarian. She had heard him speak on the news at home and had liked his ideas about spiritual diversity and diminution of materialism. She browsed through the book and then turned to the final chapter.

'*New Science creates truly new knowledge by rare open-ended induction. There is much closed deduction at the margins of past knowledge following established paradigms. In Karl Popper's terminology, most seekers after knowledge are underbrush clearers in a forest of understanding. They expose the tall trees. They clear glades where a few strong saplings can grow to exploit the light. There is more glory in this than in felling big timber, even if it is dead: The survival of the diverse forest community is at stake. If The New Science has cleared a path to the tall trees of religion and politics, then beware their fall'*.

'The ideas were difficult but she liked the analogy. Perhaps her role could be as an underbrush clearer between the tall trees of Science and Yamism. She wondered if the author would really be as tolerant of Yamism as his writing suggested and whether he had many followers in Australia and throughout the world. She was a seeker of knowledge and this book looked as though it might have some answers. She browsed through some earlier chapters. The proposals for devolution and tribunals especially interested her. She felt that Australia must be a civilised country to have a politician with such ideas. When she had money, she would buy it and study it.

'When the cyclone was over, they screamed along the coast on a broad reach, through the passage inside the Great Barrier Reef to Mirani.

'Citra was thrilled. The freedom of it! She spent her time on deck chatting with her fellow Bhakarians travelling to a new life as guest workers. At night, they seemed to be surfing the Milky Way. She marvelled at the phosphorescence of their wake, a glittering pathway that seemed at the centre of the universe. In the daytime, they trolled fishing lures behind them, catching fighting fish that the ship's cook prepared into delicious sates and curries.

'All too soon, they arrived in Mirani. She was met on the quay by a bearded giant with red hair, a friend of the Australian Kudim, who had helped her.

'"Call me Red," he told her.

'Red gave her a room in his wooden house, built on stumps to be cooled by the breeze. She contacted the Mount Argus mine and they said her employment would be as a robot operator. She accepted and they booked her to go there by train the following Monday.

'She spent several enjoyable days in Mirani, looked after by Red. He took her to a gereja. Despite everything that had happened, she still had an urge to pray and prostrated herself for a few minutes beside Red on the Bhakarian carpet. She had never prayed beside a man before.

'In between visits to tourist sites, she enjoyed his extensive collection of books. He too had 'The New Science', translated into Bhakarian and he lent it to her to read on the train.

'"I don't know why you want to read that book. Abajoe is a godless upstart."

'"I am finding out about politics in Australia."

'"Better that you study Sudarta's writings. The Yabras will be out after the next election, thank goodness. They are our enemy."

'"Then I will study the book to find out their weaknesses in order to overcome them."

'"Then you may take the book. Happy reading!"

'Her seat was near several other Bhakarians and they discussed their impressions of Australia, as they rolled through the parched, scrubby savannah. She read some more of 'The New Science' and found parts of it threatening because science was concerned with material things, whereas she was more interested in the spiritual. She wondered whether it would be possible to remain a true follower of Yamism in Australia.

'She returned to reading the book, interested in the strange ideas.

'"I hope you are enjoying my book," he began, as the train got underway'.

Abajoe paused in his writing. He had reached the culmination of the Citra story, the climax of his relationship with this girl character he had created over the past two years. During her train journey, he would debate with her New Science.

'He imagined them sitting opposite each other on the clattering train, with a table in between. She was dressed as a nun, wearing her rias and mantle.

'"Hello," he said when he sat down.

'She nodded and returned to her book, his book.

'"Do you like it?" he asked, looking at her book, smiling, condescending.

'"Yes..." Then it dawned on her and she closed it to look at his photo on the jacket. "Are you Abajoe Yabra?" she said, awestruck. "Yes, I can see it is you. I like your book very much."

'Although she was physically attractive beneath the uniform of her faith, Abajoe knew there could be nothing between them. She had dedicated her life to Yahm. Even if her uniform was a disguise, she had not yet recovered from the trauma of being raped and could be expected to be hostile to his advances. In any case, he had created her and a sexual relationship with her would be incestuous. He wanted something more, her development as an independent character to test his ideas on and lead him to new insights. It was a new experience for him to sit next to an attractive woman without the possibility of sex but he knew her allure was not for him.

'"There are some parts I don't agree with...because I am a foreigner, I think."

'"Oh. I would like to know what you disagree with."

'"So what is this book to you?" she began respectfully, dignified, within the safety of her religion and with her feelings hidden behind her rias. "I know you wrote it, but why?"

'The question made him smile. He assumed that she had read the sleeve of the book, telling that he was a minister in the national government and famous as a scientist. It would be conceited to remind her that the blurb said he had acquired technical knowledge in a wide area at a young age because he was an autodidact and learned constantly, supported by the expertise accessible to the nation's leading family. Or that he had established a reputation for creating scientific theories from the ecological insights forged by his indigenous forebears in the cauldron of survival over many millennia. He would assume she knew all this. All he would tell her was that it was his manifesto.

'"It is our Bible, or Kitab, except it is more logical."

'"Religions are not always logical," she responded weakly, and then because she could get childish in an argument and wanted to tease him, added, '"The New Science' is like a religion and it isn't completely logical, is it?"

'"It is completely logical," he rebutted, denying her inference.

'"Really," she said. "Everything in it makes good sense, is that the expression?"

'Her tone affronted him, the hubris that her religion alone was allowed to be irrational. He turned to her unruffled, as if to someone who was ignorant about the basic facts of existence. '"The New Science' is completely logical because it is the only book in the world that is the word of a living prophet, who is able to explain every aspect of it." He said it with almost a publisher's zeal, a sales pitch to end all sales pitches.

'"Who is this prophet?" she asked suspiciously.

'"Me." He posed as a person pleased with himself.

'"You?" she was surprised. "Are you the new Jesus or something?" she said, trying not to sound sarcastic.

'"Yes. I am a prophet."

'Her childish stubbornness was growing. "How do you know?" she asked. She stared at him, again, as at an ignoramus. "How do you know you are a prophet?"

'"Because it says so in 'The New Science'," he replied, winking at her.

'Then she knew he was laughing at her own religion. Numan, the Yamin prophet, had authenticated his prophecy in the Kitab. Abajoe had hoisted her religion on its own petard. He was satirising her religion and enjoying it. Instantly, her expression changed, as if she had decided she wanted to shrug off this business; it didn't interest her any more.

'"I don't believe you," she said. "Nor do I believe this book is a work of prophecy."

'"So it is simply a matter of belief," he said gloating. "Could you have been indulging yourself with Yamism?" he laughed.

'She was furious. Holding up his book, she pointed at the back cover.

'"What evidence is there that you, Abajoe, are a prophet inspired by self-sustained altruism, as it says on the jacket here?" demanded Citra.

'Abajoe stared out at the wide, orange expanse of the horizon and answered Citra patiently. "Citra, 'The New Science' can't prove it is inspired by self-altruism but this is what we believe. Our self-altruism benefits others after sustaining ourselves. Their reproductive success is at a cost to us but does not threaten our survival."

'"What's reproduction got to do with it?"

'"In biology, that's the ultimate test of helping others. Promoting their genes."

'"What proof do you have that 'The New Science' actually promotes others' genes?"

'"It's up to other religions to prove 'The New Science' is false, if they…"

'"No!" argued Citra, "You can't put the burden of proof on older belief systems. They've stood the test of time and it is up to 'The New Science' to prove itself. Whereas in most things 'new' is synonymous with 'good', as far as comparing belief systems is concerned, 'new' is 'bad'."

'"Then Yamism, being one of the youngest religions, is so proven."

'Citra paused. Abajoe's eyes watched a line of bottle trees slide along the horizon, miraculously sated in the dry landscape.

'"I disagree," said Citra. "Yamism is every bit as respectable as Crucianity and being younger is not a weakness."

'"Then you are caught in a contradiction," said Abajoe. "That's one to me. The proof of our belief system is its inspiration. In your terms, I am proved to be a prophet by my holy testament 'The New Science'. It was written by the holy prophet, Abajoe, and is therefore an inspired testament."

'"Abajoe, really!" she shook her head. "You have assumed your testament is holy and concluded that it is inspired. That's circular and proves nothing."

'"No, Citra, it does," said Abajoe, "because this is the same method of so-called 'proof' put forward by the other belief systems. If you are right and the beliefs of my followers are false, then you must also reject the beliefs of Crucians and Yamens by the same arguments."

'"Red herring," Citra held up a warning finger. "You are diverting attention away from 'The New Science's' weaknesses by showing that Crucianity and Yamism suffer from the same thing. This is irrelevant to the argument that New Science is false, even if other belief systems are false."

'"They are," Abajoe insisted. "'The New Science' is inspired because it is written precisely as it was revealed to me."

'Citra shook her head again. "Tch, tch, tch. The preservation issue is irrelevant. The real issue is whether your writing was inspired, not whether it has been corrupted."

'"When I became leader of the MWP youth organisation in Australia, racial violence decreased, showing that I am an inspired leader."

'The passing of the train had disturbed a group of kangaroos that hopped inside a fence parallel to the track. One by one, they turned and forced their way over or through the wire away from the train. Their struggles to escape became more panic-stricken as the last few became isolated.

'"The racial violence may have decreased anyway under another leader. It doesn't follow that this showed inspiration, even if it did show statesmanship."

'"If I didn't have my faith in 'The New Science'," he said, "I would have swallowed the SEU's immigration laws hook, line and sinker."

'"It's good that you didn't, but doesn't necessarily mean that your thin end of the wedge leads to inspiration. If we allowed every example of critical reasoning as inspiration, we would have more prophets than worshippers." She sat back smiling. "That's one to me: we're even."

'"To oppose a hegemonic force with faith and logic takes inspiration. New Science has led me to a revelation of the falsity of the SEU's immigration laws." Abajoe was uncomfortable. As an experienced debater, he was more accustomed to ridiculing others' fallacies than defending beliefs of his own.

'"Can one who is inspired judge inspiration?" Citra scoffed. "I think not."

'"That is the fallacy of ad hoc propter hoc. It does not apply if you accept that I have relevant qualifications besides inspiration. It is by the precepts of New Science that I have determined the SEU's immigration laws to be false," Abajoe replied. "The precept of equal rights of all people contradicts the notion of absolute resource territoriality of incumbents. People have faith in New Science's precepts and in its methods. That's two to me."

'Citra was truculent. "Tell us then, Abajoe, in what way people who you lead are faithful. Might it not be a cult? What makes you believe New Science is deserving of the status of a faith?"

'"My followers believe in sharing, whereas a cult believes in a leader. Our ontology is in the first instance the ritual methodology of science we apply for the benefit of others. One of our practices is to explain our belief system to others. Cults are hard to join but we want everyone to come in on this. Cults are difficult to leave but you can leave here at any time. Cults have a leader who has mystical revelations that he uses to control the group. I don't have mystical revelations and I don't control a group. I have scientific insights…they are scientific because they explain my experiences, make useful predictions and can be falsified."

"'You have your standard explanations or arguments," said Citra, "but they just go around in circles. Like all faith mongers or cult leaders, you can't argue a point successfully because you rely on deceits and fallacies."

'Abajoe eyed her coolly. "Your own generalisation is a case of the pot calling the kettle black. Have you always hated faiths?"

"'Am I still beating my husband?" scoffed Citra. "That's a loaded question and it is unacceptable because it begs the premise. I don't hate faiths. But the faith of New Science is circular and is therefore illogical. You wouldn't understand how ridiculous your beliefs seem because you're a New Scientist. Of course you think you are inspired."

"'You aren't doing your side any good by making a personal attack on me!" Abajoe responded evenly.

"'Since you have been unable to demonstrate satisfactorily that 'The New Science' is inspired, it must not be," Citra deduced.

'Abajoe had stopped smiling. Citra was relentless.

'They were in desert country now and a family of emus picked at thin scrubby vegetation, ignoring the train.

"'You can't just bury you head in the sand. If I cannot show that 'The New Science' is inspired, it is not necessarily uninspired. In any case, my prophecies have been fulfilled, demonstrating their inspiration."

"'You can't just count the hits," Citra reminded him. "You have also had some major misses. Like your immigration policy. It is not sustainable. Bhakarians won't continue to accept it. You seem to be fallible like ordinary mortals. We're even again."

"'Immigration isn't decided yet."

"'You'll lose."

"'There are millions of people who think I am inspired."

"'Get off that bandwagon, Abajoe!" Citra laughed. "That doesn't mean you are inspired."

"'Citra, all your arguments could be equally well applied against Crucianity and Yamism, yet they are well-respected. Like them, we have an ideal, not of God but a God-like behaviour, self-sustained altruism or 'self-altruism'. We also have inspired words and our own prophet who creates miracles of technological innovation. Me. Being a New Scientist is a rational dedication of my life rather than the threatening menace you fear."

"'One way you are different is that the New Scientists are commanded to use force to overthrow racial segregation and other forms of racism. Crucians should never use force and Yamens can only use it in defence."

"'What about the Crusades?" said Abajoe. "They were about as forceful as you can get!"

"'The Crusades were uncrucian." Citra was surprised to find herself defending Crucianity. "There is nothing in The Bible about having to use force."

"'I beg to differ. The Bible has many appeals to force, unlike 'The New Science', which has few," said Abajoe. "Force is mandated judiciously, in defence of racial equality. Unscrupulous people have been saying that our belief is that self-altruism recognises a person by their race first and by their actions second, so certain races are condemned, except for those who martyr themselves. In fact 'The New Science' says that self-altruism accepts all races and individuals equally, even if they have been wrongdoers, providing they make amends."

'Citra exploded. "Abajoe, really! You don't think I'm going to fall for that straw man fallacy do you? Who are these 'unscrupulous people'? Perhaps you should save your words for knocking down my arguments rather than your own straw man. Your belief system is not logical. You are caught up in a web of half-truths and downright lies."

"'You haven't come up with any evidence of that!" Abajoe threw his arms wide. "You haven't been able to show that 'The New Science' is not inspired. Therefore, it must be inspired."

"'No, that doesn't follow," said Citra. "You seem to be saying either 'The New Science' is inspired, or it is not."

'The train passed over a wooden bridge across a large, dry gully. Their position seemed quite precarious.

'Abajoe was thoughtful. "That's a false dilemma," he admitted, "between divine inspiration and worldliness. Intermediate positions are possible. Parts of it might not be inspired."

"'So you finally accept that do you?"

"'It may be that there is some soap-boxing, Citra," Abajoe replied. "But New Science is a belief system that teaches intellectual honesty and

214

it is the most potent force for peaceful liberation of oppressed groups and co-operation between rival groups that the world has ever seen. I am proud to be the founding member."

'"It must be hard to be a member," joked Citra. "But you are not such a prick as I thought you would be. You are a tad egocentric, even for a prophet. I'm glad to have had this debate, even if we have to agree to disagree."

'"No harm done," he said smiling. "Standing up for what you believe in is what it's all about."

'That ended their discussion. The train was arriving through the outskirts of Mount Argus and they prepared to get off. From that day on, Abajoe's leadership became more ecumenical and he seemed to strengthen. He became better accepted and he won Yamen voter support in his electorate.

The Middle Way Party, searching for a fresh look in the coming national election, clutched at Abajoe's ideas. New Science became the Party's manifesto.

Abajoe, in his writing, followed Citra at Mount Argus.

'There were many aspects of Australian life that Citra did not understand,' he wrote. 'When she had time from her work at the mine and from learning the language and local customs, she followed Abajoe's political career, as of a powerful acquaintance.

'His arguments had convinced her that Yamism was a bubble of faith in a retrospective report of controversial historical events, whereas New Science had well-tested practices relevant to solving her concerns for the Bhakarian people. She still attended Yamen prayers and social events with them but she no longer believed in Yahm or expected her religious activity to achieve her mission. Instead, she turned to politics and became absorbed in the Australian religion of democracy.

'She met him for dinner from time to time at Mount Argus' only hotel. They would discuss their latest political ideas and how they related to the Bhakaria she had left behind. Gradually she learned Australian politics and argued with Abajoe about the Government's immigration policy.'

Abajoe found her fascinating and longed to meet a real Bhakarian woman like her.

'Citra and the other Bhakarians at the mine felt lonely and rejected in Australia,' he continued. 'Although they were welcome for their work at the mine, the Australian workers and townsfolk opened neither their homes nor their hearts to them at this lonely time and they felt like outsiders. Through her dedication, intelligence, outspokenness and effectiveness as a spokesperson in dealing with employers and the media, Citra became the leader of the thousands of Bhakarian guest workers in Australia.

'Citra realised that the position of guest workers was tenuous under Abajoe's Middle Way Government and she supported the Opposition, who were Yamens and would adopt the SEU's free immigration policy when they won power. But the Middle Way Party might win. She wanted to meet an Australian, who could advance the position of Bhakarian Yamen guest workers with the Yabra Government. She had learned from Abajoe that the Government could be persuaded but it would take a better rhetorician than her to overcome the inertia her questioning of him had revealed'.

CHAPTER 27

Abajoe Becomes PM

The MWP planning model predicted that if the current drought continued, there could be famine in several places in Australia. In the Great Famine, scores of emigrants had evacuated to Bhakaria but now they were expected to be refused entry visas. Abajoe was very concerned.

He mulled the situation over as he sat on the verandah of his unit, plucking feathers from a chicken. He unzipped the small feathers from the bluish body he had killed the day before and hung in the cold room overnight. A light wind stirred the feathers lying around him and a few were swept away.

His rossit experiments had left him with a radical viewpoint on population, that every local council should have sustainable independence. If voluntary birth control did not work, then any council that could not sustain its population in a 200-year drought would have to impose population restrictions. Most Australians did not want any restriction of reproduction, even to reduce population growth. They considered that the number of children one had to be a private matter. Few would condone a government that set guidelines to reduce births below the replacement rate, which would condemn some families to having only one child. There was unanimous support for voluntary control of population numbers even if there was unsustainable growth. Abajoe wanted councils to take responsibility and confront people with the consequences of their reproduction.

Sweeping the feathers into a sack to be sold for insulation or cushioning, he started on the tough wing and tail feathers, plucking them one by one. It was a tough old bird and he soon lost patience. He put the last feathers with the vegetable waste for the biogas generator. With a sharp knife, he cut off the still-feathered wing tips and tail, the head and legs, then drew out the internal organs and put them with the waste for biogas. He turned on a small gas flame and singed the fine hairs. Finally, he washed the carcass inside and out. He wrapped it in a clean towel and knocked on Paula's front door.

"Oh good," she greeted him. "You can help me cook it. Come in."

In her kitchen, Abajoe cut the carcass through the middle while Paula filled a pan with hot water and turned on the gas to boil it. He put the halves in.

"Can you go and get some lemon grass?" she asked.

When he returned, her door was open and he went through to the kitchen. She was chopping onions. With tears streaming down her cheeks, she looked up at him.

"Have you considered that some people won't ever be self-sufficient?" she said. "They will want other people to provide their food."

He got out a chopping board, cut the lemongrass into lengths and smashed it with a hammer.

"A council should be able to look after its own people," he said between blows. "Famine is not acceptable. They must either increase the food supply or reduce the population in their area."

"Is it possible to increase the food supply?" asked Paula as she peeled cloves of garlic.

"A little, in the North but not enough to remove the famine threat if the population keeps growing there."

"What about compulsory reallocation of water to food production?" asked Paula. "Here, slice some of these finely."

She gave him roots of turmeric, ginger and galangal. He bent over the chopping board with a knife.

"There isn't enough support for it. Local councils don't have sufficient authority to enforce it. We don't want to do it centrally."

"Well, what are we going to do?" asked Paula, as she deseeded red chillies.

"This issue can divide the nation," he said, trying to get the yellow stain of the turmeric off his fingers with a wet cloth. "Their commitment to famine avoidance should cause a chain reaction resulting in acceptance of water allocation. However, antipathy to population control is a weak link in the chain. Our planning won't hold. We have to find a way to defuse the simmering hostility against population control."

"What about immigration?"

"That's it!" he said excitedly, chopping the chillies in staccato bursts. "You are brilliant! Any council that cannot sustain its existing population in a 200-year famine must ensure that net migration is either outwards or zero. Only the most deserving refugees should be admitted. I think they'll accept that!"

"I can see how they can stop immigrants coming but how can they make people leave?" she said doubtfully, taking down a gaily coloured, glazed ceramic basin and a light pestle.

"Some will leave voluntarily when they are told they are living on starvation's doorstep. A couple, who want a large family, will be forced to leave when everyone is aware that having more than the replacement rate is going to starve their neighbours."

He put all the chopped ingredients into the basin and began crushing them with the pestle, occasionally making a circular grinding movement.

"It sounds less like a voluntary system and more like state planning!" Paula warned. She opposed the concept of population control.

He paused while she poured in a little oil from a bottle. "There won't be any central rules, just an ethic of voluntarism in holding the population constant. We just have to convince them that local planning for a 200-year drought is sensible."

She added oyster sauce, chicken stock and shrimp paste and he continued lightly crushing and grinding.

"Don't you think planning for a 200-year event is too cautious?" she asked, adding pepper and salt while Abajoe squeezed in juice from the halves of a lime. "Most people let the future look after itself."

He was absorbed in kneading the ingredients. Then he poured the contents of the basin into the pan with the chicken.

"True, people take risks, especially when they are young. If we were a private company growing crops, we would take a risk to make more profit. But the national government is expected to be careful. It is life or death we are regulating."

"You're right," Paula sighed as she used tongs to turn over the chicken halves while they boiled. "We must be strict with the councils. Zelta's Government was lax and 15 million died. A repeat of that is more than I could bear."

They chatted together as the chicken cooked. When it was done, they ate bowls of chicken soup with fresh bread that Paula had baked that morning.

"Delicious," said Abajoe. "I'm going to have another bowl. If there is going to be a famine, then I had better put on as much weight as I can."

"I think it would be better to have given the chicken a reprieve and made vegetable soup," said Paula. "You need to be a lean, mean, fighting machine to stop people stealing our food supply."

"Well, hopefully all the councils will do their sums and we won't have starving people coming to our door."

"Everybody will be saying that."

"Then I would be a damn fool not to!"

When Abajoe presented Marko with their plan for devolving population control to the councils, he was enthusiastic. He asked Abajoe to present the plan to Cabinet later that day. One of them objected to council control, saying, "We could have a neighbour without water resources and persuading their people to move into our area because we do have water. That would stop our people having as many kids as they want."

"Your council would have to allow them in," replied Abajoe patiently.

"Oh, they would," he said. "They want people to fill jobs for their economic growth, even if you do not."

Abajoe was unable to convince him that this was matter for his local council. He needed unanimous Cabinet agreement to proceed to a referendum, to embed the change in the Constitution. Frustrated, he and Paula considered breaking away to form a new political party. However, it would take years to achieve as good a following as they had within the MWP. The old ideas were a hindrance but the Party's ideology was a solid launching pad and Abajoe had sufficient kudos to be taken seriously. Through steady pressure, he believed they would be able to overcome the inertia and force the Party to accept the new political realities brought on by growing competition from the Progress Party.

"New Science is just what we need – a new direction," said a seasoned MWP politician. "It's a very good plan and it can win us the next election."

The MWP decided to seek public support for his proposal and they released it to the media. A journalist who interviewed Abajoe asked, *"When there is not enough water to sustain the community in a 200-year drought, who will decide what use is made of a particular resource, for example, water from a river?"*

"Resources often have disembodied meanings and may be perceived supernaturally. For example, art can give water a special meaning, beyond economic considerations. Perhaps keeping the fountain in the town square going would be of more value to the community than irrigating grass at a dairy farm. There is more to sustainability than benefits of use and costs of resources and wastes."

"Will peoples' values count for anything?"

"People are free to express irrational wants by inflating prices. But tribunals will not prop up private causes from the public purse unless they would achieve community goals. What community goal would be achieved by keeping the fountain going? New Science deals with Paretian change, which will scientifically decide values and meanings at the margin. Changes to be approved would have no one worse off. We won't be going for wholesale redistribution of resources. Even in a famine, a fountain should keep going if someone would be worse off and not able to be compensated by dairy farmers, who would get its water, and by householders, who would get its electricity."

"Will poor people have their wants considered?"

"Poor people will be able to stop changes that disadvantage them, the same as if they were rich. The tribunal will represent their interests to the developer."

"What if their interest is an emotional one?"

"If it achieves community goals and the development would reduce it, then the tribunal will make sure that the developer modifies the proposal or agrees to pay an amount of compensation calculated following a scientific method."

"Yes, but having an emotional goal, such as a feeling of community, would clash with hard-headed science, wouldn't it?"

"No, not with New Science. Subjective criteria will be considered when they are agreed to be important. Science has methods for including them, such as surveys, criterion weighting and evaluation. The methods have to be explicit, robust and reproducible."

"What difference will they make?"

"A huge difference. New Science will replace politics, measuring different groups' wants and bringing them together not by votes but by measurement and logic. There will be communal control of technology, so that technology integrates society rather than fragments it, as it has in the past.

"The days, when planners promoted the idyll of a nuclear family existing in isolated self-contained living units, with all their selfishness and waste, have long gone. Those socially empty boxes resonated with images of materialism and competition. People led empty meaningless lives."

"So individual wants will count for little in future?"

"The opposite. Individual wants count for not much at present but they will do in the future. Until recently, the wants of individuals were shepherded into batches for each generation by an unscrupulous conspiracy of marketers. What are we up to now, Generation M? How presumptuous! New Science spotlights the tendency of producers and governments to control the image making and for consumers to relinquish control. It will enable individuals to be more discriminating and diverse in what they dream. It will help consumers achieve an equitable balance of power with producers and governments, so that choices match real wants, rather than kowtowing to advertising goals and government propaganda."

"What is your vision for the future?"

"The ideas I have been talking about would be considered for adoption as Party policy. Australia is threatened with racism and parochialism. I believe in an ecumenical, multicultural Australia. I am most interested in developing New Science as an alternative to religion. I want people to believe that events in their lives can be better explained by science than by the transcendence of God or His immanence and providence, or by His self-sacrifice, or by the intercession of Ancestors. Instead of individual worship, people should obtain revelation and guidance by participating in community problem-solving meetings.

"I want to enable people to be content with what they now possess and increase their sharing with others, rather than striving to wrest control of resources from people in the community. They do not want a legacy of owning things. In a land beset by scarcity of water, depletion of fossil fuels and inability to sustain production of mineral resources, private possession of large resources is criminal. Resources belong to the community. For me, resources and wealth are constraints on our stewardship rather than goals and I hope I am free of greed so that mutualism and truly interdependent love can flourish."

"Do you see a preponderance of communal living?"

"Yes, most people will spend their time in communes, where they share their living with friends who hold similar beliefs. People in Kurilpa Commune own only a few simple garments and a communicator but they share in a lifetime of togetherness and compassion in serene surroundings.

"Here in this collective, we have a group of heterosexual couples and their children living in polyamory, in comfortable cottages situated around a communal dining and facilities centre, including the group's love room. Many people draw their happiness from merging with a group in every aspect of their lives.

"John Venn, in 1880, represented relations of group members by overlapping circles. For example, one circle may represent the interests of person A, while another circle may represent the interests of person B and another person C. The overlapping area would then represent the set of interests held in common by all three. Individuals in polyamory would have a large area of overlapping interests, including probably their sexuality. There are heterosexual groups as well as sororities, fraternities and asexual groups. Although genetic family living is usual, many commune members live in groups with common interests.

"Polyamory is one example. Monogamy and heterosexuality are passé and child rearing has become controlled by the group. With a shrinking population and genomic measurement, verifying responsibility for a child's parentage is no longer a constraint on sexual interaction. Paradoxically, groups value individuals more than they used to. There is cross-generation sharing of experiences. Young and old benefit from each other, without the stress of artificial peer competition. People of all ages have time to interact for personal fulfilment."

"So you would not aim to restore conditions to those before the famine?"

"Australia today is very different from what it was 20 years ago before the Great Famine. People have given away their possessions, dispersed from the cities, found kindred people to share their lives with, gone to where they grow food, abandoned material living, lost interest in mass entertainment, and sought recreation by meditation or worship. This has been done in thousands of different ways, with a diversity of communes following different beliefs.

"Despite the idyllic lifestyles that people have been creating, Australia could be in dire trouble. If Bhakarian rule continues, with Sudarta in power, they will try to turn the clock back and that is not possible. We predict they would have our birth rate spiralling out of control, with no increase in water and land resources to feed a hungry nation. Life would become precarious. Families that multiply would have their land divided and subdivided and units would become uneconomic. There would be a need for jobs to be created. The placid lifestyles would disappear, as the Bhakarians try to return us to materialism. They would again encourage material imagery, personal greed and commercial competition. Our community spirit, which is solving emerging public problems, will be destroyed."

"Do you aim to be Prime Minister?"

"I want to work for the MWP in whatever capacity my colleagues prefer."

The journalists asked him his views on other topics and he answered quietly and modestly as a group member like any other, but one with a vision. It was his vision that excited them and it became theirs.

As his wisdom in dealing with national and world problems became known, Abajoe's stature steadily increased to legendary proportions. He became the Statesman of the Middle Way Party. He brought far-sighted integrity to planning and he was popular with Party workers, who counted on him for stories that nurtured members' subscriptions.

He travelled extensively to meetings with Party people and learned of their ambitions and concerns. At first, there was a tide of opposition and morale was low but Abajoe presented his policy ideas and left them in no doubt that the Middle Way Party would have a competitive platform under his leadership if he were elected at the Party Conference later that year.

His father added Resources to his ministerial portfolio. The Opposition was critical and vociferous, mounting a concerted character attack to destroy his credibility.

"He wants to give away our resources to other countries for nothing more than promises. He is weak and gullible. He's too gentle to lead Australia and only cares about the poor," Sudarta claimed.

"We don't need a communist megalomaniac," her stooges complained. "Abajoe Yabra is too intellectual. His ideas are impractical dreams."

They argued that the Party was moribund under Yabra control and needed different leadership. Abajoe's ideas were far-fetched and he was too young to attract ethnic voters and unify the nation. Some people were unimpressed by his technological brilliance and vision. They wanted, she said, a leader to resolve ethnic disputes the way T One had, through mediation, rather than by science.

It was a baptism by fire. Abajoe counterattacked with denouncement of Sudarta for her collaboration with Bhakaria in the Great Famine, of her business associates and of the conflict of interest with her private fortune.

Abajoe's technological innovations became part of his legend in the Middle Way Party where he was known as the latest and greatest Yabra. He was the holy man prophesied as the second coming – a gifted spiritual healer with miraculous, scientific powers. The Party became optimistic and prepared vigorously for the election. They denied he was ego driven with inflexible plans and gave examples of his self-effacement, how he operated behind the scenes and devolved the running of the nation to others. Under his leadership, the moribund Party united, renewed itself and moved forward.

At first, the Middle Way Party was in turmoil, as other potential leaders within the Party challenged Abajoe. With his quiet certainty, unequivocal views and faultless decision-making, he quickly became widely respected. He was the hero of the youthful reform wing in adopting radical vote-winning policies. A team of 12 disciples formed around him, meeting regularly.

Paula was one of the 12 and foremost in supporting his leadership. She contributed strongly in policy formulation. Abajoe worked with her closely and they seemed like a devoted couple. Sometimes he was about to commit to her, which was what she wanted, but his mother advised him against it.

"You aren't besotted with her. It would be a marriage of convenience. It wouldn't last."

He admired Paula more each day. She had a particular skill for digesting information and putting it together in new ways, finding alternatives that resolved disagreements within their team. John and Peter were usually with them. John was an opinion giver with a talent for sorting out logical priorities. Peter was their evaluator and critic who kept them on task. Abajoe exerted firm control over this inner group, preventing squabbles from developing. Then there were the other disciples, loyal and hard working, having given up their jobs and families to be with him. Many others found a place to use their unique skills, filling their ranks. Soon Abajoe's team had grown to a size where it had become unassailable and the challengers for the leadership of the Party withdrew.

Marko, as Party Leader, stood above the fray. Although Abajoe talked with him every day, either on government business or on his visits to the stadium's vegetable gardens, he seldom asked him for advice because he valued his independence.

His family connections were valued by older voters but put off some younger voters, who didn't realise that he was independent of his parents.

"He might as well be unrelated," T One said. "He goes his own way and always has. New Science comes from him, not our family, although we're proud of what he stands for and he has our full support."

At the virtual Party Conference later that year, Marko stepped aside from the leadership and Abajoe was elected unanimously as Party Leader and Prime Minister.

While the MWP had been engaged in inward-looking processes, the Progress Party had captured the media's attention. Abajoe's ascendance was seen by government critics as a continuation of the dynastic power that had kept the nation isolated from an economic community with its neighbours for most of the past 150 years. They said Abajoe's manifesto was too late. Benefits from planning tribunals would take time to come through. Many people, especially those who considered themselves disadvantaged by Australia's independence, wanted a change of government. If they were going to win the General Election later that year, Abajoe had to inject new energy into the tired MWP policies.

Abajoe went head-to-head with Sudarta in a joint media interview.

"It's a basic right to have children," Sudarta asserted. "The MWP would take that away and also children's rights to energy and water."

"Nonsense," he replied. "It will be up to the communes to assign land and the water and energy rights that go with it."

"Having to provide for your own children will stop growth in its tracks."

Abajoe replied, "Children will take over from their oldies when they die. With zero population growth, there will be enough energy and water for a 200-year drought."

But Sudarta led Yamen's who wanted to have as many children as they could afford. "Families should be able to grow. They can make do with less land, water and electricity. They would get by. They always have before."

"Yes, but with tragic famines and energy crises," Abajoe reminded her. "Look: if we plan carefully, we can avoid famines."

Sudarta was sceptical. "Planning can't stop famines. They'll still happen. It's nature's way – survival of the fittest."

Abajoe shook his head. He seemed to be the tougher of the two. "You want nature's 'red in tooth and claw' from competition? I want us to rise above that, by not being selfish."

"But people are selfish. They want to be free…"

"…at other people's expense? It's not logical…it doesn't work."

"We'll see." Sudarta seemed to have run out of arguments.

"The majority have no hope of freedom," Abajoe persisted, crushing her argument. "They know it. In some councils they will want to licence the getting of children. They will stop you."

"Only the elite want licensing of reproduction, because they'll be free to buy their licences with favours. The majority will be envious of the free and they'll vote to have the chance to get the same by getting rid of licensing," Sudarta said confidently.

Abajoe countered strongly. "No. The majority will vote for community. They won't accept life as a lottery anymore. They want security."

"They want more than that. They want to have kids, as many as they want. It's in their loins."

Abajoe shook his head. "No it isn't. I have evidence against that. When it comes down to security or loins, they'll choose security."

"It will be loins versus common sense and loins will win. Loins are a basic drive."

"We have shown that in animals, loins are selfish and flawed."

"But loins are what have brought humans to this apex of evolution. They're our tradition…" Sudarta paused as if it was self-evident.

"No, they aren't, not anymore," said Abajoe. "Reproduction isn't sacred, it's scared. It is scared by the responsibility. Nowadays, a baby is caused by planning, not by a casual fuck."

The interview ended there. Abajoe hoped that their policy would be accepted as necessary for the common good. It was a difficult message to get across when so many of the population were still obsessed with perpetuating themselves by having as many children as possible.

CHAPTER 28

Meets Siti on the Stump

After a month at Thornton, Abajoe's convoy drove to Mount Argus mining district, where they would stay two nights before returning the Meannjin. As they arrived, rain began pouring down. All along the East Coast, the drought was broken.

They checked in at the Mount Argus Motel and after dinner went to a community meeting, where they were made welcome and seated on the stage at the front of the hall. The mood was elated due to the rain. Abajoe outlined the MWP's policies and asked if there were any questions. There were several queries about the government's plans to prevent another famine. Then there was a question about immigration. He told them that it would be up to local councils but most would choose to allow a higher birth rate.

"What about guest workers? They have contributed in a big way. They should be able to stay!"

Abajoe shook his head. "I'm sorry. They agreed to go home after five years."

"Racist bastard!" a girl's voice called out. "Let guest workers stay!"

She chanted, "Let guest workers stay!" and the others in her group took up the cry, filling the room with noise.

Abajoe was startled. The girl was in a group of young miners standing near the back. They were olive-skinned, wearing Yamen mantles, probably Bhakarian guest workers. They were disgruntled that they would be unable to settle in Australia.

She looked like someone he knew but he couldn't remember where he had seen her...quite recently.

"Guest workers are allowed to come on the understanding that they will eventually go home," he replied.

"Some of them have worked like slaves and made Australia a heap of tax money. They have earned the right to stay!"

"I understand how it may seem unfair, but when I work with famine victims, I am aware that Australia's population has to be controlled or there could be another famine." He let his commitment ring out in his voice. "We can't guarantee food for extra mouths in a drought and it would be irresponsible to let people stay who we can't take care of. In

229

the Great Famine, immigrants, in some places, were driven out to fend for themselves. They perished. We won't let that happen again. Because we care about them, we won't let them stay!"

"Next you'll be saying this is going to hurt you more than it will hurt us."

"It's true. Being sent home is a blessing in disguise. Immigration to Australia is not like winning a lottery as you are suggesting. Many immigrants have regrets. Moving to a culture that is so different can have serious problems. The dislocation, brought about through migration, can last a lifetime. It affects relations with family members left overseas and it can disrupt cultural connections. It can divide a family when a member wants to repatriate. And it can keep families apart when members are unable to join those who have emigrated. For many people, emigration is less of a panacea than a trap for the unwary. We are not being unkind in preventing it."

"Guest workers aren't like new emigrants – their eyes would be open. They should be able to choose! What right have you to play God and decide people's lives?"

Siti argued with him, insisting that the guest workers had earned the right to choose to stay. He explained his government's commitment to securing each community's supplies of water and food to prevent another famine but the mood of the meeting was behind the protesters.

After the questioning had finished, he got down from the stage and moved over to the group. He confronted the girl. "Excuse me, miss, but I want to explain that our immigration laws are not racist," he said evenly. "We have the same laws for all nationalities and apply them fairly. What evidence of prejudice do you have?"

"The laws are prejudiced against guest workers," the girl said angrily. "They should be treated fairly! Guest workers have a right to be treated like other Australians."

He asked her name. She told him, "Siti."

"I know you are Abajoe. I've heard of you and read your book," she said. "Some good things, but bad too. You are against Yamism, aren't you?"

"No, I respect Yamism. But about the guest workers, Siti, sometimes we have to do things we don't want for the good of all..."

"...and it just happens to be Bhakarian Yamens who get picked on! A likely story!"

"It is not like that," he responded but she had turned away rudely.

He left the meeting early with his entourage and they went to the motel, where they spent the night.

He couldn't stop thinking about her. Siti had a definite presence, as if imbued by the same spirit as Citra. Could Citra be here, pursuing her mission to help Bhakarians through Siti? Siti spoke for the guest workers with authority, a formidable opponent. He wanted to find out her background.

The rain continued overnight. The next day they went on a tour of the mine. The rain had brought most operations to a halt. The staff were available for leisurely tours. They showed him the huge machinery operated by robots.

They stood on the seam floor with the others, watching front-end loaders at work. The air was thick with the bituminous smell of hot coal.

"We have only just started this part of the process," they told him, "so there's mostly manual control. We used to mine the coal and shale altogether and put it through the washery but, due to the drought, we've had to shut it down. We've had to change the mining operation to take out the shale and we're still working out the machinery and techniques before we turn it over to robots."

When he turned around to leave, he saw that Siti, the young woman who had confronted him the previous day, was there. Her coarse overalls emphasised the fineness of her beauty. He went over to her. She turned away as he approached.

"Gidday from yesterday, Siti. No hard feelings I hope. I wondered where you worked. What do you do?"

She spoke neutrally.

"I'm in the office. I'm called a Robot Master. I have to co-ordinate the robots, to make sure they're not getting in each other's way or competing and that they're solving the overall problem efficiently."

"It sounds challenging."

"Yup, it is. I like it."

"Where are you from?"

"Meannjin," she answered, puzzled.

"So you're not a guest worker?"

"Nope. Most of my friends are though. I speak up for them because they're scared that if they criticise the Government, their visas won't be renewed."

"Has that happened?"

"Yes."

She told him that several Bhakarian guest workers, who had been active in campaigning for immigration rights, had not had their visa renewal applications supported by the mine and were made to leave.

"It shouldn't happen," he said. "Let me know if it happens again. I will make sure they get fair treatment."

She spoke with a trace of anger returning to her voice.

"Fair treatment you say! The trouble is you don't know what it's like for guest workers."

"Are you a guest worker?"

"No, I am an Australian, but they are my friends. I want them to like Australia. Do you know that your Government is selling Gunyaba Immigrant Reception Centre in Meannjin, the place that made them feel welcome here? They don't feel welcome anymore!"

"Yes, I know Gunyaba well. It's a lovely old building. However, these days immigrants are welcomed in their sponsoring communes. There isn't any need for an Immigrant Reception Centre in Meannjin."

"But Gunyaba belongs to the people, the immigrants and generations of descendants. It is a symbol of their welcome!"

"It was an empty building and no one had a plan for how to use it. So we are selling it to be converted into homes."

"The guest workers have been staying there when they come to Meannjin. They are very upset about it and many people in the community support them. When they took it to the Planning and Environment Court, your Government called it in and took away their only avenue of protest. Your Government is only listening to the developers. We'll find out if that's true in the election. Guest workers have brought you prosperity but you won't share that prosperity with them."

It was six months until the election.

"No. Guest workers were invited to the party but now they won't go home when the food has run out."

"When the lifeboat is full, you want guest workers to get out so everyone else can be comfortable, even though guest workers have paid full fare with all their work. It's nothing more than racism."

"No; we have to do this for the good of the community."

"Hah. You are preventing a sense of community, creating haves and have-nots."

He paused. "Well, it may be possible to put the development application through the new planning tribunal we are setting up?"

"Will it make any difference?"

"It could reverse the decision to sell it. All stakeholders will have the opportunity to object and receive compensation. A development plan won't be approved until all objections have been dealt with fairly."

"Will guest workers be stakeholders?"

"Oh, yes. They will have the same rights as residents."

"Terrific. Thank you, Abajoe."

"Don't thank me – it may not be possible. But I'll look into it."

She was wearing a sakari, the flowing robe worn by Bhakarians but she spoke fluent Australian, with a drawl, as if she was from Meannjin. She could be from anywhere locally and she had evidently acquired her interest in Bhakarian culture. She was fair, unlike the Bhakarians.

Then he remembered that when he first saw her, he had thought he knew her and wondered why. Suddenly, he recalled the model they had made of the little girl who went missing in the Great Famine at Thornton. He brought out his wallet and searched through until he found it. Siti was very like her. She had her mother's triangular face. It was a beautiful face, with a broad forehead tapering down with classic lines and curves to a narrow chin. His heart leapt with excitement but he couldn't be sure yet. He didn't want to make a mistake.

"Your name is Siti, isn't it? It's Bhakarian; I looked it up. It means 'noble'. Who gave you that name?"

"The Bhakarian nuns at the orphanage, because I wouldn't join in with the other children. They thought I was a snob and giving me that name was their way of jeering at me."

"It's a good name. You do seem superior. Siti what?"

"Iftiqad. It means 'lost' in Yamin."

"Would you be about 19?" he asked.

She frowned, puzzled.

"Yes, in August, why?"

"You are young to be in such a responsible job. How long have you worked here?"

"Three years. I started as an apprentice."

"Do your parents live in Meannjin?"

"They died in the Great Famine."

"I'm sorry. Where?"

"I don't know exactly. At Thornton I think, where I was found. Why are you asking me about this?"

Abajoe drew her aside where they couldn't be overheard.

"I met a woman in Thornton the other day, who lost her three-year-old daughter in the Great Famine. She would be 19 now. You look just like the model we constructed from photos of you as a child, to search for you."

The girl looked down, silent, thinking. Abajoe moved back, allowing her privacy. He knew it must be her and he was thrilled to have found her.

"I'm sorry, it must be painful for you," he said kindly.

Siti looked at her watch. "I have to go..."

"Well Siti Iftiqad, you have a family after all. Your mother's name is Jenny Craig. She will want to see you as soon as..."

"No way! How could she 'lose' me? Abandon me is more like it!" the girl said bitterly.

"Something awful happened to her – but she should tell you herself."

"I don't want to hear it. I don't want you to tell her about me. Anyway, she might not be my mother. It could be a coincidence. Is she Yamin?"

"No, I don't think so."

'Well then. It may not be her. I was found during the Great Famine, brought to the Yamen church building and handed over to their mercy mission, which was evacuating children from stricken areas to the capital. There were 100 of us."

"Perhaps they took children of other religions too."

"The nuns always assumed I was Yamin from birth."

"You could have a DNA test."

"I don't want to. I can't cope with this. Just forget you ever met me."

"Who brought you up?"

"I lived in a Yamen orphanage. It was horrible." Her eyes were moist and her voice wavered. "The school was extremely strict. They beat me almost every day, for no good reason. As soon as I was old enough, I got away and came here."

She wept forlornly. He felt drawn to her, wanting to help her, wanting her to like him. He stopped himself from holding her because he was so attracted to her and because, only yesterday, she had been abusing him. He was very disappointed that she didn't want to contact her mother. Two bitter people would get so much from each other and be able to move on with their lives with each other's support.

"Here, I'll give you your mother's number," he tried again.

Siti shook her head. "I don't want it." Nevertheless, he gave it to her and she took it uncertainly.

"Maybe you will contact her one day. She will call you Anna."

"Anna?"

"That was your name."

Siti shook her head.

"I've got to go."

"Keep in touch with me. If you want work in Meannjin, give my office a call. Leave your name and contacts. I can't do much for your Bhakarian friends at the moment, but things may change. Don't think I don't care, because I do."

Her voice was bitter. "Would you help them to get jobs in Meannjin too?"

"Well, er…"

He hesitated as his mind raced. He could absorb Siti, as an Australian, into his office but placing the Bhakarian miners would be much more difficult, even impossible, without making large sacrifices visible to the media. How could he explain to her his dilemma between self-altruism and pure altruism in just a few words?

"…I think they should apply through the normal channels."

"Just as I thought, racial prejudice…"

She turned her back and walked away. He was angry with her at first, but when he thought about her life, he was sad. Attack was the defence she had learned from being treated badly. It put a dampener on his visit to the mine. Later that morning, at the end of his tour, he asked the Mine Manager whether she was reliable.

"Siti Iftiqad?" he replied. "Oh yes, she's reliable alright, too bloody reliable. In fact, she's quite a character. Sometimes I wonder who's running this mine, her or me. The miners all look to her as their leader and if she wants something, she won't let up until she gets it. She's a natural politician and dangerous to us here. If you can get her out of my hair, I'd be delighted."

Abajoe was fascinated. He realised he had crossed paths with someone who posed a danger to his immigration policy. If he helped her, perhaps she would be less antagonistic. He wondered if he should contact her mother against Siti's wishes but couldn't see any good coming from that. Eventually Siti would contact her, he felt sure. Nevertheless, he wanted to get to know her better.

The next day, on their way out of Mount Argus, they stopped at the mine and he sought her out and found her in her office.

"I would like to be able to help your friends. It may be possible. I'll write to you."

"Okay." She said little, wanting him to go. She gave him her address.

When he got back in the vehicle, Paula said, "Malthus would have understood!"

"What...?" he looked at her disapproving face.

"Your uncontrollable lust after the rain."

"No. She thinks she's an orphan and I want to put her in touch with her mother."

"Very noble, I'm sure," said Paula, not believing him.

It was more than lust, for his ideas about Siti had filled a vacuum. He caught himself imagining Siti was Citra and had a Yamen upbringing in a country village in Bhakaria. Then he would remember Siti's awful reality with a shock. Sadly, there was no point in telling Jenny Craig he had found her daughter. She would have to tell her that herself.

Two months later he received a call from Jenny Craig thanking him for finding Siti, her long lost daughter. Jenny had contacted her and gone to see her. They had spent the afternoon together and she had told her the story of her abandonment. They had both cried and hugged. Then they visited the grave of Siti's two brothers, where she had buried them under rubble on wasteland 15 years earlier. She was going to have them exhumed and buried in a graveyard where they couldn't be disturbed. Also the police were investigating the case against the neighbour she had accused of being present at the murder of her husband. She thanked Abajoe for all his help and she said that now she was able to plan for the future and move on with her life, after being stuck for so long.

Abajoe wrote to Siti.

Family Fare Tower, Meannjin
6 August 2246

Dear Siti
How are you getting on at the mine? I received a call from your mother and you have made her very happy. I hope that your meeting brought you some closure on your painful upbringing so that you can move on into a new and happy era.

I have made inquiries about your Bhakarian friends' predicament and it now seems likely that they will be able to gain citizenship if they work here for 10 years. We have to put it to a plebiscite but I don't foresee any problems, although you'll have to wait until after the election.

It was good meeting you and learning your views. I heard that you are a popular leader. Our Party is looking for people with your ability to become candidates in elections. If you contact Ken Petersen at the mine, he'll let you know when the next Middle Way Party meeting is in your area.

Yours sincerely
Abajoe

A few hours later, he received her reply.

Dear Abajoe
Great news! The Bhakarians are pleased, though 10 years is a long time. Now they'll have hope, even if you win the election! If you announce this publicly, they might even vote for you!

I am interested in going into politics but have too many issues with your Party.

Thank you.
Siti

He wrote back immediately.

He waited for a reply but none came. He called her but she rudely cut the connection. Thwarted, he was angry and then disappointed. It wasn't often that a female he wanted ignored him. He had extended the hand of friendship but she hadn't taken it. He wondered if it would have been different if there had been no issues between them.

Then he thought that she might think she was out of her depth with him and didn't want to encourage him. She was a one-issue activist, a mineworker and not the intellectual he wanted. She predicted he would soon lose interest in her. She was protecting herself against being used and dumped.

Then he realised too late that he had made a mistake in conceding the guest workers would eventually be able to stay. He had done it to flaunt his arbitrary power, to attract her, but he had succeeded only in frightening her. He didn't have authority to make such a promise so far ahead. She must have felt like a mere conquest and didn't trust that his interest in her was genuine.

He would have to wait for another opportunity to get to know her as he had blown this one badly. He was very attracted to her. Although he had only met her briefly, he could tell her ordeal had made her tough and independent minded, with the integrity to deal with him as a person in a balanced relationship rather than exploit his position. The only female he knew like this was Paula but with her, the balance came from their upbringing and he was not sure that it would continue if they came together on their own. He had never known anyone who could stand up to him like Siti and hoped for another opportunity with her with impatience.

CHAPTER 29

Debate wins Siti

The national elections were near and Abajoe's Middle Way Party would be hard-pressed to retain government. People were looking for a change and the Progress Party's plan to rejoin the SEU had caught their interest.

Abajoe proposed that the hustings for the election would be a series of studio virtual debates with Sudarta, the Leader of the Progress Party. Each debate would focus on a different policy topic and be broadcast across the nation. The first was to be on 'welfare'. At first Sudarta didn't want to take part. The Progress Party's reactionary policy-making contrasted unfavourably with the MWP's intellectual vision and bold new plan. However, Abajoe was reported as saying the Progress Party was uncompetitive and his stinging criticisms provoked Sudarta to agree to a debate but they would only commit to one at a time, rather than a series.

The rules of the debate would be opening speeches of five minutes from their Party studios and then follow-up questions from Roberta, their media host.

It was Abajoe's turn to speak first, as winner of the draw. He reviewed his Government's performance before announcing their platform. He spoke confidently, talking about the MWP's policies with the passion of a violin virtuoso about new music he was about to play.

"This five-year period, Australia again made significant progress towards an enlightened society with record low consumption of materials, record low energy use and record high unemployment. We have regulated the free market economy so that suppliers have been restricted to meeting only those customer needs that are genuine. Many factories producing unneeded devices have closed down and many services no longer wanted have ceased as consumers have taken up the challenge of self-sufficiency. Employment has fallen every year, with fewer people spending their days in meaningless drudgery. We helped the unemployed to become self-employed and meet their own food and housing requirements."

Abajoe loved to have an audience and be the centre of attention. His words were often controversial and electrifying.

"We have been able to disperse the economy and reduce energy consumption as transport has slowed down and gained efficiency. But our greatest achievement has been to increase water, food and energy storage provisions to cope with a 100-year drought in almost every local council. The levels of water, food and energy accumulated have almost doubled, so that famine has become almost a thing of the past. Yet if you re-elect us, we propose to increase reserves yet again, to cope with a 200-year drought, guaranteeing our future beyond a once-in-a lifetime disaster.

"Another initiative we propose is to subsidise relocation of families and individuals into low density living with food self-sufficiency. Although our cities are almost empty, there are pockets of population that are not yet independent and we will help them to move to places where they can enjoy the benefits of growing their own food, free from the disease and alienation of city living.

"Medical treatments are now available that will enable individuals to live as long as they can afford and want to. However, many old people are opting for a shorter, more independent lifestyle with better acceptance of death uncompromised by technology. It has become desirable to die naturally, without making demands on family, friends and the community. This trend is making more room for younger lives, and communities are becoming more active and more vibrant.

"Our Government acknowledges the help given by local people to poor families, the aged and individuals in need of help. There has been a growing army of self-altruistic individuals prepared to help others for minimal reward. Their work has been vital in providing needy people with food, housing and education, assisting them to become self-sufficient. The Government is grateful and proposes to continue to foster conditions that have made this possible.

"Again, local communities have provided health and education services largely from voluntary work. Levies on exploitative industries, such as mining, have been retained by local communities. Export taxes have been increased. We propose to increase income taxes on wealthy individuals, enabling improvement in community services to the disadvantaged.

"Communications will continue to be the only nurtured growth area of the technological economy supported by governments. We will continue to provide network leadership so that all Australians can participate in education courses, debates, plebiscites and elections, within local communities and nationally. We propose to upgrade the network over the next five years, applying a means test to help disadvantaged people acquire the new equipment.

"These plans will retain and strengthen our nation's cultural identity. Australia has good relations with the SEU countries but has no need of SEU membership because that would swamp us with immigrants. Our first responsibility is to control our population within our water and food resources, which are sufficient for only the existing population."

Abajoe finished to applause. The Progress Party Leader, Sudarta, was a Yamen descended from Bhakarian immigrants. She attacked Abajoe's policies with vigour, unfazed by his legendary stature. However, the Government had few sins of commission and she was only able to respond to Abajoe's proposals with sins of omission. The Parties' policies were distinguished by their different approaches to participation in the region, with the Progress Party accepting that Australia would become a SEU puppet.

"You have heard how the Prime Minister would increase export taxes on resources industries. We believe these taxes would antagonise our neighbours, who want Australia to participate responsibly in the region and gain their support. We propose to seek membership of the South East Union, the regional economic community, under terms that would bring more revenue than we are currently getting from our resources taxes. This would be distributed to local communities for certain types of industrial development.

"There would be other benefits to SEU membership. We would be defended by all the forces of the SEU instead of by the small Australian Army and Navy. We would receive regional grants from the SEU to develop certain areas. The SEU's tax on economic activity would raise large sums for the Government to administer for the benefit of all Australians."

The Opposition Leader's speech ended with clapping and cheers.

Roberta asked both of them to answer this question.

How would the independence of Australia be affected by joining the SEU?

Abajoe let Sudarta answer first. She replied that they would not sacrifice sovereignty to gain membership of the SEU. Australia would continue with the same culture, the same language and the same currency. What would change would be that there would be larger markets and membership of a powerful club of neighbouring interests. Australians would have freedom to pursue their own way; independence would be gained.

During her answer, Abajoe had at several points shaken his head or expressed surprise. Now he launched his attack.

He said that when someone joined a club they became bound by the rules of the club and had less freedom to pursue independent action. Australia would cease to be governed solely by Australian voters and their representatives. Instead, matters would be decided by the SEU parliament in Singapore. The Australian representatives would have very little influence. Policies could be enacted that Australians didn't want. The SEU would develop industries in Australia that used her cheap resources to make goods for export to the other members. Australians had different interests and it would be best not to rejoin the club in the first place.

Would there be any advantages of SEU membership if there were a drought?

Sudarta's response was brief. Yes, because they were in a club, the other members would help Australians with water and food supplies more than if they stayed outside.

Abajoe shook his head. He said that one of the club's rules was free movement of people and goods from one member country to another. Australia's low density of people would attract people from high-density countries, who would believe they could get more security by emigrating to Australia.

"Migrants would be desperate, not looking decades ahead as they should or remembering the Great Famine two decades ago. All they would think of is that in Australia there is plenty of unoccupied land and buildings standing vacant, whereas at home they can't get a place of their own. Of course they'll come, in their millions. The influx would undermine the drought provisions. If there was a drought, the other member countries' help would not be sufficient to even feed or take back their migrants and Australians would be worse off by joining."

By the time Roberta had received their answers to several more questions, Abajoe was clearly in the lead. He had shown that the Progress Party's SEU policy was risky and that the MWP had on offer a logical response to the threat of further famine, demands for resources from neighbouring countries and interest in cautious industrial growth. The Progress Party seemed to offer a caretaker Government while the SEU took over almost every aspect of Australian life.

Then the adjudicator threw the questioning open to the audience. There were several innocuous questions from faithful Party members on both sides planted in the audience, designed to bolster their candidate. Then there was a penetrating question.

Will history record it as arrogant of Abajoe Yabra to stand in the way of the natural movement of certain people into Australia and the rights of others to have as many children as they can afford? Populations have their limits everywhere, but are seldom limited by one man. If there is to be population control, should it be decided by citizens, when they freely choose a living place and decide when to have children and how many, or by the scaremongering and racial prejudices of political leaders?

Abajoe recognised the hostile questioner as Siti, the lost girl from the mine. She had called him a week ago to thank him for starting the forensic investigation of her father's death. His body had been exhumed at Guralaba. Bullets in his body matched a gun found hidden in the house of the man her mother had accused. He had been charged with murder, along with three others. Her mother had sold up and started a new life at Mount Argus, not far from where Siti lived. She saw her often and they had become close friends.

Now Siti was questioning his Party's right to influence childbearing and migration. She was accusing him of eugenics, an unpopular fascist pursuit of racial purity. Whatever he said, her mud would stick. He admired her intelligence and her beauty. If only he could swing her and her group over to supporting his Party. He replied as persuasively as he could.

"You are correct," he said. "Politicians do not have those rights. But they voted us into office knowing that we would try to stop another famine. Social control of population numbers has been an accepted practice in different species, including humans, in arid lands since time immemorial. Nomadic peoples have exercised rigid birth control and have had customs of withholding group membership from outsiders. The density of populations living in settlements has been regulated by infectious diseases, such as malaria, and the extent of the conurbation by access to resources, especially food. Our first responsibility is to feed our own people and this means keeping out other people. If outsiders' own Governments showed similar responsibility, their people would not want to migrate. Bhakarians should not criticise our Government, for doing for our own people, what their Government is not doing for them."

Siti heard his response impassively, then whispered with a male companion but she didn't follow up his answer.

There were a few more questions and then the debate ended. The adjudicator reminded people that it was for them to conclude the balance of the arguments. Abajoe seemed to have won. Sudarta refused to take part in a further debate when their host invited her.

"The MWP is unable to debate our policies because it only has one idea," she told their host. "They want Australia to continue to shut out the outside world instead of joining in with our neighbours in an exciting new economic community. It is self-evident that they want to live in the past and it is a waste of time debating with them."

"You have lost today and you would lose again," replied Abajoe. "Your policies are the SEU's and they are the least common denominator of members' interests. You would run down our high standard of living. Australians would be worse off. "'

That concluded the broadcast and the studio audience began to disperse. Paula congratulated Abajoe on his performance. Acting on a whim, Abajoe switched to a mobot camera so he could talk with Siti. When her face appeared on his screen amidst a group of Bhakarians, she knew his camera was on her and she wasn't smiling. She screwed up her face when his voice came on her headphones, as if his approach was unwelcome.

"Hi, Siti. Do you always ask difficult questions?"

"Will this take long, only I have someone waiting for me?"

Abajoe felt a strange pang of jealousy. He wondered if she had a male friend waiting. Her curtness was unpleasant for him: it wasn't often that people didn't want his attention.

"Not long. I wanted to hear the rest of your objection. You didn't seem to accept my answer."

"You only seem to care about Australians!" she accused him. "You don't seem to care that other people may not be as fortunate, as if it is their own fault."

"But..." he began.

"No. You don't care about anyone else. You only pretend to have global concerns. You say in your book that the future lies in sharing between haves and have nots but in practice you are not interested in sharing Australia's resources with anyone else."

"That's not true. Last year we gave billions of seus in aid to Bhakaria."

"They had to spend it on Australian resources! You give with one hand and take back with the other. You don't give the kind of aid that gives people what they value most, independence, the opportunity to start a new life."

"You're talking about the guest workers."

"Of course. And their families, who want to join them here."

Abajoe thought for a moment.

"Do you know why we accept guest workers to do that work instead of employing Australians?"

"It costs less?"

"No. It's because our people value that work lowly. We want our people to lead better lives."

"But it's okay for the neighbours to do your crap work."

"Those jobs are better than they would get at home...they're only here for a couple of years."

"You should compensate them for doing your dirty work."

"We cannot let them immigrate..."

"Why not?"

"We would have to provide new resources for them in a drought, resources that we don't have."

She smiled at him for the first time. "There you go! Isn't immigration like birth? You fit them into the slot left when someone dies. You wouldn't have to provide…"

"The immigrants would take away births. Fewer births here would be unpopular. The birth rate is already very low."

She shook her head. "But you are moving to a more spiritual society where births are less essential. You said that yourself. You also said that people were choosing to die younger. There are slots."

"Hmm…I'll have to look into it. I'll let you know if it's possible to accept some…but we won't be able to put it through before the election. As I told you before, we'll give the citizenship after 10 years. I'll announce it after the election."

"Why not before?"

"It could blow up into an issue and lose us votes. But it's a promise and I hope you'll vote for us. It's not true that we won't share with Bhakaria. We are negotiating exchange of your surplus food with us when we are having a drought in return for our medical resources to help bring your epidemics under control. For example, we could develop vaccines that would save thousands of Bhakarians' lives."

"I want to vote for you but it seems like we would be better off under the Progress Party."

"No, they're quite dangerous. You and me…I'm sure we don't have fundamental differences…we want the same things for our families and for our countries. I'd like to persuade you that you will be better off under the MWP…over a drink?"

"Er…okay."

"Over dinner?"

"Maybe. Where?"

"Let's see," he consulted his schedule. "How would you like to go with me to Grove Island next month? On the 18th to 19th."

Paula, who had been listening to this exchange, got up and stood behind him with a hand on his shoulder.

"What is Grove Island?"

"Grove Island is a resort in the Whitsunday passage two hours by steamer from Mirani. It's a tropical island with golden beaches, coral gardens and natural forests."

"You sound like an ad. What are we going to do there?"

"Party dinner in my honour."

"But I'm not in your Party!"

"It doesn't matter. You would be my guest."

"Would I have my own room?" she asked sweetly.

Abajoe wondered fleetingly if her caution was real or whether she was playing hard to get. She would be wondering if Paula would be there.

"Yes, a separate room."

She hesitated. He could tell she was weighing up the certainty that to be the Prime Minister's guest was a once in a lifetime opportunity – it would be good for her campaign, for her political career – against the uncertainty of what it would mean for their friendship. Would she be entertained or exploited?

"I'll be wearing rias make-up. I am a Yamen," she told him, as if this might change his mind.

He smiled, "'Prime Minister escorts Yamen woman'. My PR people will love it. Could you drive up to Mirani and we'll meet at the steamer terminal? I'll let you know when closer to the day."

His answer was satisfactory. Her individuality would be respected.

"Okay," she agreed. "I'll see if I can borrow a car from work."

She noted the date in her diary.

"You will come?"

"I would like to very much, thank you, if I can get away from work. It sounds fun."

"Great. Okay, I'll be in touch the week before. Bye."

"Bye."

They ended the call smiling. If she had a male friend waiting, thought Abajoe, he'd just had sand kicked in his face.

"Your self-altruism just took a dive into selfishness," muttered Paula as she switched off her monitor. "Egoism has got the better of you."

Abajoe was used to Paula's jealous sulks. Since returning from Thornton, Paula had been frustrated in her quest to gain Abajoe's commitment. He had kept their relationship casual and ignored her for weeks at a time as he made other conquests. She busied herself with Party work but she always framed it to get his acknowledgement of her skills and commitment to him. She did not conceal that she had become dependent on him for her happiness. He didn't like the way she clung to him and manipulated his attention. He balked against accepting responsibility for her happiness and told her she had to have an independent life before he would consider making a commitment to her.

Whereas she had no inclination to seek an independent life, he was secretive in his relationships with other women. She recognised in Siti a serious competitor and was consumed with jealousy.

"Are you coming to Grove Island?" he asked her. "I would like you to. We need our whole campaign team there...in recognition of its importance to us in winning the northern electorates."

"No, not if you are chasing Siti. I couldn't stand it."

"Siti could be useful to us, Paula. We need her support."

"I need your support! Don't you think you owe it to me to be loyal?"

"I am not being disloyal and I don't need you as a dependant," he told her.

"But you can depend on me," she replied, "if things go wrong."

"Thank you, Paula. I'm not ungrateful. It's just that I have precious little freedom in this job and monogamy would reduce it to nil."

He was keeping her on a piece of string to see if she would grow strong enough to withstand his neglect. He wanted her on his own terms.

CHAPTER 30

An Evening Together at Grove Island

The steamer terminal served travellers from the Coral Coast, a semi-urban area spread along the coast around Ngaro Beach, sending ships out to the islands of the Northern Reef. When Siti drove in, Abajoe was waiting with his entourage. She waved and parked. Abajoe went over to her. She was wearing a headscarf and beige, embroidered kebaya, hugging her slender body. Her eyes, through the white paint of her rias, seemed mischievous and he wondered what she was thinking.

"Hello, Siti. How are you?" he said.

"Good morning," she said. "Who are all these people?"

"Security people and journalists mostly…and staffers from my office."

"I thought you were a minimalist."

"I am. I'll explain later."

He introduced her to the others as a group, saying she was 'Siti, a friend who is a mining person'. Siti inclined her head. They looked at her as though she was a common upstart. One of them scowled at her. Abajoe introduced her to Paula. She seemed to be with him.

"We're all MWP people," she told Siti. "Are you a supporter?"

"No. I..."

"Then I hope you won't feel left out," Paula interrupted her. "We don't have much time for outsiders." She turned away rudely, leaving Siti alone amongst strangers. She introduced herself to some of the group and they responded in a friendly way to her glamour and humour. Then the group went aboard the steamer. Abajoe and Siti lounged side by side in deck chairs on the foredeck. There wasn't much room left by the other passengers and Paula had to sit on the other side, straining to listen to them, but out of earshot.

"Who is Paula?" she asked Abajoe.

"She's my offsider."

"She's very attractive. Are you having an affair?"

"No, but we're good friends."

"She seems to regard you as her own property."

"Well, I'm not."

"Then why is she glaring at me?"

"She doesn't like me to have female friends."

"She wants you. I suppose you have been encouraging her?"

"No. I would like her to leave me alone but it's difficult because we live next door."

"How come?"

"She's like a sister. My parents adopted her when she was two."

"And you're not having an affair?"

"No. But we sleep together sometimes. It's a casual friendship."

"I think you do care for her more than you think. You seem to be a kind man, not at all like I used to imagine."

"What did you used to imagine?"

"I used to think you were self-centred and a racist. You seemed to assume you knew more than anyone else did and that their opinions didn't count. But you do listen to other people, even those who you don't agree with, like me," she said, smiling.

"You seem to be a pretty good listener yourself."

"Perhaps."

'It's good of you to come to this dinner. You'll meet people who have quite different concerns than your guest workers at the mine."

"Yes, I am looking forward to meeting mine owners and their managers. Their lives will be...more comfortable. I've never been to a resort before and I don't know if I'll like it. I'm used to a simple life..."

"Tell me if you want to leave at any time and I'll bring you back to Mirani."

"Thank you, Abajoe. Why are you smiling?"

Siti, with her head covered and her face hidden by Yamen rias, made him remember with affection his Bhakarian idol Citra, who in his writing had argued with him on the train a few months previously. She had been a guest worker too.

"How are the guest workers?" he asked, not wanting the issue to stand between them any longer and thinking he might compromise.

"As well as can be expected for visitors who are made to feel they have overstayed their welcome. They feel like they don't belong here. Especially with Gunyaba's future in doubt. Have you done anything about that?"

"We have launched our planning tribunals. Your Gunyaba might be eligible to be heard by a tribunal because of its heritage listing."

"Oh, that would be terrific. But would the guest workers be able to make a claim? Gunyaba would come before the Meannjin tribunal, whereas they have to stay at Mount Argus. It is not fair."

"They are fortunate to be here at all. We have stopped other types of immigration."

She turned to face him. "Australia should let more people in!" she asserted. "Don't you care about sharing what you have? You have so much!"

He shook his head. "We don't have enough for them! We care about people having big enough shares to survive. Surely you can see that Australia cannot support more people in a drought," he argued.

"Not more than live here at present?"

"No."

"Including guest workers?"

"No. Not including them. In a bad drought, they would have to go home."

"Surely you need them in a drought, to earn money from minerals to buy food."

"In a severe drought, not even the miners can get food. Mines have to close. The miners would have no way to get food and they would have to return to their home villages and homelands."

"It shouldn't be compulsory to go home. They may not have anyone to return to. If they have worked well here, they should be able to stay if they want to."

Her voice was soft and he fell under her spell. He no longer wanted to win against her. He was captivated by her mouth and wanted to talk with her forever. Her lips were full and moist and moved sensuously. He found it difficult to concentrate on their argument.

The boom swung overhead as the ship changed tack. Siti's deck chair began to slide away and Abajoe grabbed it and pulled it around, his thigh brushing her arm. He could feel the firm softness of her body and smiled at her.

"The Government has responsibility for evacuating people away from famine districts. It is a case of 'last in, first out'. That is fair."

"It is unfair to immigrants who have nowhere to go. To them, it seems like racism."

Abajoe didn't have an answer for this. The discussion closed in Siti's favour. Although they had swapped few words, he realised he had been beaten. He dreaded locking horns again with the immigrant community and Siti in particular. He wanted her to be on his side. Instead of imagining Citra and the Bhakarian guest worker problem remotely, he found himself confronted by it in the form of the very real Siti. He had to take her demands seriously, both because the Yamen opposition had formidable strength and because he found her very attractive. He had never before known a female who was his intellectual and rhetorical equal. His leadership felt threatened and she inspired him to new heights.

"The Meannjin South planning tribunal has been appointed. I will ask that they process the Gunyaba Development Application."

"Wouldn't it be a re-run? Approval has already been given."

"Not at all. This time, the submissions would have to be made on a scientific basis so that the validity of the objections can be assessed and receive compensation."

"The guest workers should be compensated for their rejection."

"If they submit a claim, it will be considered."

"Really? Can their rejection be considered scientifically?"

"I don't see why not. There have been studies of migrant alienation by other developments, such as ethnic housing, that have quantified health and employment repercussions. The selling of Gunyaba can be evaluated too. What the tribunal won't do is hold a plebiscite to find out just how many or how few people give a damn about the plight of the guest workers. That is an ill-informed opinion to which the old political system pandered. The tribunal's work is to decide compensation fairly. Firstly, they will try to find other ways to restore the guest workers' self-respect, such as by building a memorial to their immigration experience, maybe a museum. If none can be found, the developer may be ordered to pay them an agreed amount. The developer may not be able to afford to go ahead."

"I see," said Siti. "That sounds fair. It seems so sensible. Why have we put up with the old system for so long?"

"Governments always wanted as many developments as possible until recently. They wanted growth of the construction industry because they got pay-offs from developers, the votes of the workers and support from local businesses. They didn't care about the people who had their homes flattened, their green space built on and their community culture overrun by outsiders. But all that has changed. Nowadays, if a developer won't pay off genuine objectors, they will be stopped."

"That's excellent," she enthused.

Encouraged by her approval, he continued to chat with her, finding out her likes and dislikes. Then she wanted to know all about his famous family and his young life at The Tower. Her upbringing at the orphanage was in sharp contrast but equally structured. They found they had more in common than they had expected, for both had been hamstrung by rigid expectations and adults who smothered their playfulness.

Abajoe's liking for her increased and she had his full attention. Siti was a year older than him. He found her naivety and lack of cynicism refreshing. She was open-minded on many issues that he was responsible for resolving and he enjoyed explaining his reasoning and being challenged by her arguments. Whereas most of the women he met were from well-off families whose education had been supported by their parents, Siti was an autodidact who funded her studies from her earnings as a mineworker. Her interaction with him was unsophisticated but he found her charming and very intelligent. He found himself agreeing with her often and he knew he had lost his objectivity and didn't care. All he wanted was for this delightful conversation to continue forever.

The shadow of the great genoa sail above see-sawed across their deck chairs. The wind had picked up and the sheets strained and creaked in their cleats.

"Tell me about your being a Yamen. Do you pray regularly?"

"Yes, usually."

"Why?"

"It gives my life a purpose. The nuns taught me to read the Kitab and follow its teachings. It is a way of focusing my life for a higher purpose. Without it, there would be too many possibilities to cope with…"

"Too much freedom?"

"No, you can't have too much. But there would be uncertainty about what to do and how to act. There would be loneliness. Now I am never alone, for Yahm is always with me."

Abajoe wondered if she, like Citra, had a mission to help people. It would be too intrusive to ask.

"Do your political activities serve Yahm?"

"No, I serve Yahm by spreading his words in the Kitab. Politics is different…a way of making a difference for ordinary people," she told him. "I like to represent people…understanding their basic instincts."

"What are the guest workers' basic instincts?"

"They fear that you will send them home. I tell them that is what your Government will do in spite of your promise that they can stay after 10 years, because you haven't announced it yet. On the other hand, the Progress Party has announced they will be able to stay."

"But that's not fair. We've allowed them in and supplied work. They can keep applying for visa extensions. If the Progress Party get in, there will be hundreds competing for their jobs and their pay will be cut."

"We think the Progress Party is more friendly to immigrants. That's what counts."

"It's just a ploy to get votes," Abajoe scoffed. "Sudarta is playing on the immigrants' fears. Is that nice?'

"Is politics nice?"

"You have to treat voters with respect," he said.

"Who says that?"

"We do...the MWP. That's how the Yabras have been in power for so long. People trust us. Sudarta is pulling wool over people's eyes. It may win them the election but people will remember and vote against them next time."

"You are lucky to have your family for advice."

He thought she might be sarcastic, for the MWP had not lost an election for a very long time.

"Sometimes it's a disadvantage – they're not very adventurous."

"Are you adventurous?" asked Siti.

"Sometimes. I like doing things for the first time. Then I get bored."

"I'll remember that – you like change. You will soon get bored with my company then."

He laughed.

"No. You are a learner and always changing. You are a work in progress. I doubt that you would do the same thing twice. You would be more likely to get bored with me."

"You don't seem boring. I've read 'The New Science'. You're so free from greed, so sharing, so spiritual. I think you'll always be an exciting person to be with."

They were interrupted by Paula, who had found space for her chair beside theirs. Abajoe made room for her reluctantly. She started interrogating Siti. The spell was broken.

"What are your political goals, Siti?"

"I want the needs of guest workers represented at the highest level. I want to save Gunyaba. The Progress Party has said they will do this but you never know. They might be no better than the Middle Way Party. You see us as trouble-makers…hey Abajoe?"

"Who have you been dealing with in the Middle Way Party?"

"The local branch. They don't seem really concerned about the guest workers. It doesn't seem likely that the rest of the Party is much concerned either."

"But the local branch decides for the rest of the Party. We don't have layer upon layer of Party officials like the Progress Party. In our Party, we believe in personal representation and you are being listened to at the highest level."

"You haven't supported us."

"We have told you that guest worker policy is under review and to work through your local branch."

"Yes, but I didn't believe you. It's just a delaying tactic."

"Not at all," answered Paula. "If you win local support, you can get what you want."

Siti was sceptical. "We haven't got much information from your local branch and we have assumed they aren't interested in us. I would like to find out all I can about your Party. Maybe I'll change sides."

"We would love to have you." Paula smiled at Abajoe, as if to say, 'This girl is a beginner. Why bother with her when I am so much more accomplished!'

Abajoe said, "Siti, take your time and don't believe everything Paula tells you. She's biased and exaggerates the help we can give you. We have a lot of inertia to overcome before we can accept your people as immigrants."

Siti looked at them in turn. "That's what I've found. The Middle Way Party does not understand Yamism. It seems to be terrified that it will multiply and destroy the Australian way of life and therefore they must oppose it. But Yamism is unstoppable. We assert our rights to spread Yahm's words. They are not a threat to Australian culture for we will assimilate into a multicultural society. We too want to preserve Australian traditions."

Paula frowned. "Some aspects of your Yamin lifestyle seem to clash with Australian traditions. It is not very compromising."

Siti shook her head. "No, it's not like that. Yamism has only been aggressive in defence of its rights. That is because the other religions have tried to bully Yamism and prevent its emergence. The prophet Numan's teaching tells us how to prevail against bullies, through centralism, hierarchy and rigid conformity to our codes.

"Our detractors criticise these methods as being un-Australian when they are merely a temporary measure made necessary by racist opposition to our evangelism. It is our response to insecurity. In locations where Yamism is secure, it has integrated into the local community, adopting local dress, mixed-race marriages, supporting community traditions and causes and promoting birth control by its members. Yamism is not a threat. The Middle Way Party's response has been paranoid."

Paula and Abajoe had listened intently to this.

Siti's criticism had raised Paula's hackles. "Siti, you shouldn't believe media reports. It's true that there has been some intolerance in a few electorates. We regret it. It is holding back our Party. Some of us have been trying to give Yamism a fair go," said Paula. "Our central policy has never been against Yamism. Our stance on immigration may look racist, but it's not, it's about resources. It's unfortunate that Sudarta's strategy is to turn our re-election into a racist conflict. Our campaign is to introduce voluntary population control because there aren't enough resources. We are not attacking Yamism."

Siti smiled brightly. "Then we really are on the same wavelength. A distorted message has been getting through. If you do accept that Yamism can grow, then I'm much more interested in the MWP. I think the MWP has done a good job in the past and that your ideas about Australian independence and sharing of resources by the people are far-sighted. If only you can break down the racial barriers and bring the whole nation together."

"I hope you'll join us," said Abajoe. "Many of our supporters are ignorant about Yamism. We could do with your help to get the message across."

When they arrived at Grove Island, they carried their bags into the resort reception. Abajoe asked for three single rooms and they arranged to meet on the beach for a swim in an hour. He changed into a beach shirt and shorts, then met with his team to work out a schedule for their overnight stay and conference the next day. The formal dinner would be that evening. He edited the speech prepared for him and then jogged to the beach with his security guard.

The two women were in the water and he ran in to join them.

They swam and chased one another, then trod water and talked.

"You guys are almost a couple..." began Siti.

Abajoe knew then that while they had been waiting for him, Paula had been claiming him, probably telling her how they had been together since they were children.

"...then why don't you share a room together?" she asked Paula.

It was a provocative thing to say and Abajoe realised that Siti's pose as an ingénue concealed a troublemaker. Paula looked at him expectantly.

He laughed and said matter-of-factly, "There is the possibility that we are not so much a couple as boon companions and want to sleep separately. There is also the possibility that we will both sleep together in one of the rooms. Does that satisfy your curiosity, Siti?"

"Oops, I'm sorry I asked. What's a boon companion?"

"Someone you have a good time with, isn't that right, Paula?"

"Whatever you say, Abajoe," she replied icily. She dove under and swam away. Abajoe followed her, grabbing her and kissing her. Then they swam side by side until they dived and met on the bottom.

"She wants you," Paula mimed, signalling with her hands and body, "and she doesn't care if she upsets me."

"You must not be jealous," he signalled back, pointing up to Siti, who was treading water above, jabbing a spearing finger at Paula's heart, then negating with a scissor cut of his hands.

"Do you like me?" Paula pointed to herself then to his heart and put her head on one side quizzically.

He nodded and kissed her.

Their lungs bursting, they swam up to the surface, where they rejoined Siti.

When they went to dinner, the three met at Abajoe's room. He was dressed in a black-tie dinner suit. Siti had removed her mantle and the mask of her rias, revealing fair skin, statuesque features and red hair. Paula wore a ruby, satin-pleated gown and Siti a low-cut kebaya over a pink silk sarong. They went down together, Abajoe with a beautiful and elegant woman on each arm.

On the hotel's terrace overlooking the beach, there was a Balinese gamelan band playing. People were watching the performance or nibbling tapas at tables under the palm trees as the sound rolled and crashed like ocean waves. Abajoe knew about the gamelan from his research into Citra. The players were seated cross-legged on a dais with their instruments: metallophones, xylophones, drums and gongs, built and tuned to stay together when played by striking them with hammers.

Abajoe had learned from Citra that gamelan music is built up in layers. At its centre is a core melody known as the balungan. Further layers, including singing in vocal pieces, elaborated on this melody in certain ways, but the notes of each layer of the balungan coincided at the ends of phrases called seleh. The instruments played in a colotomic structure, in which the rhythmic cycles of the fast-playing smaller gongs were nested in cycles by medium gongs that played once at intervals within the largest time cycle, marked by the boom of the largest gong.

Abajoe stood listening with the two women, watching the intricate performance, explaining to Siti, who hadn't heard a gamelan before and was fascinated. The waves of harmonious reverberation flooded and ebbed, with muted swirls and ecstatic splashes, in fractals that multiplied in complexity and intensity, until the whole harmonious sound rose like a breaker and crashed down around them on a silent shore.

When the band stopped for a break, Siti chatted with one of the musicians. Abajoe watched her from the other side of the verandah as he exchanged pleasantries with local Party members. She was different from other women he had known, more independent and less in awe of him. She treated him as an equal, her interest spontaneous, sometimes sceptical and sometimes discovering interests in common. Whereas most women, even Paula, deferred to him automatically, Siti's approval had to be earned, from her study of his inner self, rather than because of his position.

After a while, Siti came over and after being introduced, she stood listening to the conversations with Party people. When they were alone she said, "Don't you get bored doing this?"

"No. I like to relate to people. Everyone has an interesting story to tell if you can get to it. It takes time…I'm sorry that you are bored. Have you tried talking with them?"

"These are rich people – they're not interested in what Bhakarian guest workers want."

"It may be possible to get them interested. Perhaps you can persuade them…"

"You don't mind if I tell them what I think?"

"Of course not. You are my guest. You can be yourself."

"Thank you. Then I will do some campaigning of my own."

Abajoe noticed that Siti had become a little fearful and uncertain with him, as if her feelings for him were foreign and scary. He tried to gain her confidence by consideration and gentleness. He hadn't met a woman he wanted so much. She moved away, joined a group of mine owners and managers and began talking with them.

Abajoe pretended to listen to the people he met but he couldn't take his eyes off Siti.

"You don't have to be so obvious," Paula criticised.

He looked at her with a wry smile but said nothing. He met more people and then he took the two women into dinner, to their place of honour at the head table. Each table was set with a cascade of white orchids and finger bowls of floating frangipani blossoms amid glinting silverware.

Abajoe was seated with the local member on his right. Siti was on his left, with the President and Paula across the table. They started with crab soup, spiced with lemongrass, chilli and ginger. Then there were sates of tender meat marinated in peanut sauce. These were followed by poached fish, trevally, in a spiced herb broth. The layers of taste from the spices led perfectly into the delicate flavour of the fish. Finally, there was a layered tapioca cake, sweet with a gentle texture.

They talked about Bhakarian food and how little known it was in Australia.

"Isn't it strange how two nations that live so close exchange so little," Siti remarked.

The local member responded, "Bhakarians come here, don't they? The quota of guest workers is always filled."

Siti was abrupt. "Bhakarians wouldn't be so keen to come if they were fully informed how Australians will turn on them in a famine, with racial prejudice."

"It did happen but it may not happen again," he said.

"It is MWP propaganda," said Siti. "The Bhakarian Government should correct the misconception that Australia is well-off. Australia should be seen as a neighbour with shortcomings."

Abajoe said, "But that may make us seem weak. Bhakaria may have territorial ambitions…"

"Although we are isolated, we have friends in the international community…" the local member countered.

"We can't rely on them, as we found out in the famines. It is better that we present ourselves as strong," Paula told him.

"It is a cleft stick," the local member told her. "If we seem poor, we seem vulnerable to colonial ambition. If we seem well off, there is the threat of invasion for our resources. We can't win."

"We need to work on getting the Bhakarians' respect," said Abajoe.

Siti spoke quietly, "When there is a Yamin state here and a dialogue with Yamen countries, Australia will get respect."

There was an awkward silence.

"I disagree," broke in Paula. "The Yamen countries are so much bigger than we are. They would engulf us. It is our different culture that is keeping us apart and it should continue."

"I don't think so," Siti's voice rang out in the quietness. "What is needed is mutual understanding."

"That is okay," said Abajoe reasonably. "Australian culture has diverse opinions. Yamens can have a voice but it is not the only voice. I hope you will recognise that the Middle Way Party will preserve your rights first as an Australian and second as a Yamen."

"I'll be voting for the other side," said Siti. "My rights as a Yamen will be uppermost."

Abajoe laughed. When he had invited Siti to be herself, he had not expected such vociferous opposition. He wondered if the local member regarded Siti's behaviour as rudeness.

The President, who had been listening to this exchange quietly, shook his head. "You'll regret it when the immigrants start flooding in."

"We'll see," Siti said defiantly. "The domino theory is dead. It is time the MWP faced reality."

The others shifted uncomfortably, not used to seeing their Prime Minister challenged.

"Yes, Siti," said Abajoe patiently, "but our reality is to avoid another famine. Now, about the election…"

He talked with the others about local issues and local supporters' interests.

Later, when he was able to talk with her alone, Abajoe spoke quietly to her.

"Siti, I know you mean well in promoting the guest workers' cause, but it embarrasses me when you attack the MWP. Could you please not promote the Progress Party here?"

"But I raised this when you invited me. You said I could be myself!"

"Well, you are also embarrassing our hosts tonight. They feel unable to argue with you because you are with me. And you are not likely to make any converts here."

"People should hear the truth. The MWP doesn't have a monopoly on virtue!"

"Well, I am asking you to desist. I am talking about rudeness!"

"And when you tell hard-working Bhakarians to go home, that is not rudeness. Right?"

He didn't answer her and reflected that she was putting her allegiance to her people ahead of her allegiance to him. He turned away to talk with his hosts. However, he noticed that during the remainder of the dinner, she behaved well, heeding his request.

Then a dance band started playing and he took the floor first with Paula and then with Siti. Paula was slender and supple, following his lead with practiced ease.

He invited Siti for an Argentine milonga, a fast tango.

"I don't know this one but I'll try," she replied.

"Just follow my lead," he told her.

She was cautious at first but his lead was sure as they fled around the dance floor with light staccato steps, sudden reverses and dizzying spins. The second dance was a slower more romantic tango. She knew it better than him, from her dance class in the Workers Club at Mount Argus and she took the lead. She was poised and graceful as she cavorted around him enticingly. Strangely, he didn't mind being led by her and he learned the new movements and became her partner in body, mind and spirit. After the tension between them over politics, it was thrilling to discover such harmony.

Gradually their bodies touched more and he could feel her breasts and firm thighs. They delighted in how quickly they had achieved unity. He performed intricate steps that he had seen but never succeeded at before.

Other couples stopped to watch them. When they learned that their Prime Minister had never danced with her before, they were amazed.

Eventually Abajoe said he was going to bed and the three said their goodbyes to their hosts and went to the lift. They each took a corner. As they walked along the corridor, he talked with Siti with Paula following. When they arrived at Siti's room, Paula waited nearby. Siti didn't ask them in, thanked Abajoe, said goodnight and went inside. Abajoe and Paula were alone for the first time that night.

"Well..." Paula began.

"I'm tired," Abajoe told her. He kissed her cheek. "Goodnight."

Paula began, "You can..."

He hugged her close as he thought what to say. He had had other women before but he had come back to her always. But this was different and he wasn't even sure Siti would have him. He knew that he was torturing Paula. He had to stop doing that, for his self-respect. He had to choose.

"I am so sorry," he murmured in her ear, "but I am almost done. This will be the last one, ever, I promise you."

He held her at arms' length and smiled reassuringly.

Paula wouldn't look at him. She pulled away.

They went to their separate rooms.

Half an hour later Abajoe knocked on Siti's door. She cracked opened the door.

"What is it?"

He asked her if she had any aspirin.

She said she did not.

"I have a headache – I might have a fever," he replied.

"Are you hot?"

"Yes. Can I come in?"

"No, sorry. Do you want a cold shower?" she asked politely, with a straight face.

He smiled. "I want you."

"I don't do sex with men. Or women. You'll have to go now, I'm sorry."

"But I want you. It'll be different for you."

"Why should it be different?"

"With me, it will be different. You'll see."

"What sort of different?"

"You'll enjoy it as much as me."

"But females don't enjoy casual sex. We are not like males. We have a bigger picture and need the details filled in first. I'm not ready yet."

"Can I help you with details?"

She hesitated, looking past him, as if consulting an inner spirit. Her eyes were wide-set with green irises.

"Okay. Come in."

Sita seemed unsure of herself as she showed him to an armchair beside a round table. She sat on the other side. They talked about themselves and common interests for an hour. Then she got up, as if he should leave.

"Not until you tell me why you are scared of me."

She shook her head but he insisted and she tried to hide the tears starting in her eyes as she told him how, when she arrived at Mount Argus, a man had tried to rape her. She had never trusted herself alone with a man since.

"But that was years ago!" he said, from what Paula had told him. "Haven't you met anyone you liked since?"

"Yes, several times, through the Church. But I was too assertive for them. Yamen men want submissive women. Can't we just be friends? You can have sex with Paula. I don't want to have sex with you."

He stood up and knelt beside her chair. He held her hand.

"You can trust me. If I mistreat you, you can tell the media and they'll blow me apart."

He held her head in his hands and kissed her.

"Don't push your tongue into me like that. I don't like it."

"Sorry. Slip of the tongue."

They continued kissing. Gently he lifted her up and undressed her. Her body was beautifully rounded and firm, but soft. Her breasts were large and they overflowed his hands. They lay down on the bed and hugged. He massaged her back, then caressed her thighs and mound. She was moist and he touched her softness, searching for the place he called the 'sweet spot'. When she suddenly drew in her breath, he knew that he had found it.

He gave himself to her pleasure. She responded to his touch, arching her back and digging her fingers into his shoulder. His finger moved gently around the wonderful shapes his finger found in her clitoris, learning from her whimpers. His touch was rhythmical, varying from fast to slow so that time distorted and she gave herself to his touch, her body convulsing when the pleasure was unbearable, until she gasped, mewed and tore his hand away. Sobbing, she curled up and lay still. Then she laughed, with deep joy, straightened out and stretched. Then she kissed and hugged him, still laughing.

"Thank you," she gasped breathlessly. "That was wonderful. How come you are so giving? What about you?"

"You owe me," he said. "I'll catch up with you later."

Then she lay next to his back and they slept until dawn.

He woke with a painful erection. When she stirred, he whispered to her, "Good morning. This is room service. Would you like to go on a sexual adventure?"

She smiled and turned towards him. She felt his erection.

"I see," she said.

She lay on her back and he touched her again. She responded to his hand until her back arched.

"Are you ready?" he asked.

"Maybe. I'll try."

"Are you frightened?" he asked.

"A little. But I don't know what to do."

"Which way shall we do it?" he asked.

"You mustn't hold me down or get on top."

"No. I know a good way."

He raised her nearside thigh and pushed his knees either side of her pelvis, their bodies in a universal joint, at right angles, their genitals near.

"Are you sure you want to go ahead?" he asked.

She put him inside a little way. "Yes. Do it."

He thrust once, testing. She flinched, then biting her lip, nodded.

"Okay?" he asked. "I'm coming in now."

He pushed all the way in and the joint was made but each could move freely.

"Okay?"

"Yes."

Then they thrust together and away again, alternating, with growing pleasure. After a few minutes, he lay still.

"Why have you stopped?" she asked.

"To stop coming; I'm very close," he said. "How about you?"

"No...not yet."

"Do you want me to touch you?"

"I can touch myself. Do you mind?"

Abajoe thought about how he wanted her to depend on him. "You have been by yourself...I suppose it's what you're used to..."

"Yes."

"But I want this to be with me, not by yourself. Will you let me touch you?"

"I like to be in control. I'm a bit scared of you. Why should you want to touch me?"

"No, not to control you. So we are together, not by ourselves."

"I can't touch you," Siti said.

"You are holding me and moving and letting me know what you are feeling...and we can come together, simultaneously...accepting each other's gift."

"Yes. I like that. Okay. Show me."

He reached around and inside her, his fingers playing rippling arpeggios and delicate tremolos with flamenco spontaneity. Her body surged, drawing him in, then pulled away again and again, deliciously, It required all his self control to wait for her.

"How are you doing?" he asked.

"Nearly...Oh...oh..." she groaned.

The excruciating pleasure convulsed his body in waves until he could take no more and had to pull away gasping. He drew her to him and kissed her affectionately, with perspiration running down his face.

"That was fantastic," he said.

"For me too," she said, laughing with relief. "We did it!" She sounded surprised.

He lay panting and sweating as echoes of his ecstasy reverberated through him. His mind raced and soared, pondering that simultaneous orgasm was a taboo subject of conversation except in intimacy. He wondered at the purpose of this ultimate sensation and how it had evolved. It was the hallmark of true intimacy. It was hidden, and others could only deduce it from a couple's behaviour apart and together.

Evolution had adapted a human female to seek simultaneous orgasm with a monogamous, dexterous and attentive male. Her sex with him would be more pleasurable than any casual promiscuity with an uncommitted or anonymous male could be. When she could count on this reciprocal intimacy, she would have the security to consider taking on the rigours and commitment of reproduction.

He realised then that voluntary birth control had to fight against sexual intimacy that triggered reproduction. Malthus had been right. It was only the veneer of birth control technology, activated by socioeconomic constraints that kept the Australian population from exploding. He made a mental note to build into their population model the algorithms people used when considering having children and how local governments could influence outcomes.

A mist of goodwill, wellbeing and lazy relaxation temporarily obscured reality and he lay against her, fitting into the curves of her back. He was filled with an altruistic love, warmth, calm, bonding, tenderness, togetherness and sexual fulfilment. Sleep came with his arms around her.

They slept until midmorning, when they remembered the rest of the conference. His body tingling with well-being, he showered and dressed. They walked in together, flushed and late, all eyes on them. Abajoe sheepishly sat in the Leader's chair. Siti went to an empty seat next to Paula but when she sat down, Paula moved away.

CHAPTER 31

Paula Shoots Herself in the Foot

Siti had left them at Mirani to drive back to the mine. Their goodbyes had been amorous, with arrangements to see each other again soon. On the way home, Paula didn't speak to Abajoe. She had never been so unfriendly before.

"What's eating you, Paula?" he asked, although he knew.

She ignored him.

As they arrived at Family Fare Tower, Paula spoke to him. "Would you do a polygraph test?"

Such tests were common for couples experiencing difficulty but Abajoe was surprised. He had never felt his affairs with other women were disloyal to Paula. Their friendship had been forged as a convergence of interest that had begun with adolescent promiscuity. Abajoe had an eclectic appetite for female company. He believed in the medieval ideal that a man should have a social partner to whom he was betrothed and a sexual partner to satisfy his lusts.

However, although he was betrothed to Paula, he was unable to keep Siti in the bedroom. She had become more accepting of the MWP but maintained a critical distance that he found tantalising. He preferred her social company more and more. He neglected Paula by default and she was hurting.

"A lie detector? I haven't lied to you. Fire away with your questions and I'll tell you the truth. It's the same as I've been telling you all along."

"I want to know what you really think of me," she replied. "I don't think you have been telling me everything."

"This is about Siti, isn't it? Well, it's too early to know what I think of her. You'll just have to be patient."

Paula's voice had an edge of steel. "No. I'm not going to wait around for you in case your affair with Siti falls through. If you won't have me alone, you don't like me enough and I'm through with you."

"But I do like you heaps, you'll see. I'll do your test."

Later that week, Paula went with him to a Testing Centre where she had arranged for the Chief Psychologist, an old friend of hers, to carry out the test in secret. Paula waited in the Control Room, while the psychologist prepared Abajoe for the tests.

He fastened a heartbeat detector on his chest, a breathing rate detector on his abdomen, a blood pressure cuff on his arm and skin conductance cells on head, body and fingers. He shaved hair to fit them snugly against his skin and held them on with a helmet, moulded vest and gloves that hinged open. Then he fastened him into a reclining chair and strapped his arms to the armrests.

He was immobilised. The psychologist explained it was to stop him dislocating the sensors but he knew they had him at their mercy. He could ask him anything. Abajoe wasn't concerned because if they asked him state secrets he could call out to Paula. He went to the Control Room and his voice came through the earphones in his helmet.

"Now I'm going to ask you some questions. If you lie when you know the consequences are serious, you will show fear. Your amygdala in your brain will make you sweat and your heart speed up, both of which we will detect. Are you ready?"

"Okay," Abajoe had no idea what the questions would be and he was apprehensive, regretting his agreement to this test but it was too late.

"Firstly, we have some simple questions that we will use to zero the sensor signals.

"Is your name Abajoe Yabra?"

"Yes."

"What colour is your bedroom wall?"

"I don't know. Maybe grey."

"What natural colour would you have preferred for your hair?"

Abajoe laughed. "Do you mean, what colour would have stopped me from dyeing my hair? That is like, "have I stopped dyeing my hair?". It's a deceitful question. I don't dye my hair. I prefer my hair to be the colour it is, which is black. Have I fucked up your calibration?"

"Relax, Abajoe. These first questions are designed to test your involuntary responses to stimuli using all the five senses. Can we continue?"

"Okay."

"Try and create in your mind the highest sound you can hear."

"Okay." He imagined a shrill bat squeak.

"Remember what your mother's voice sounds like."

"Okay." He recalled her stentorian tones when he saw her yesterday.

"How does your handshake feel to others?"

Abajoe remained silent.

"Imagine shaking hands with your father."

He breathed deeply.

"Think about the taste of chocolate."

"Okay."

"Can you remember the taste of sour milk?"

"Yes."

"Remember when you last saw red."

"Okay."

There were more questions like these, then the psychologist asked, "Can you remember the taste of Paula's mouth when you are kissing?"

"Yes." But he couldn't. He remembered Siti's.

"Can you remember the smell of a campfire?"

"Yes."

"What smells better than a campfire?"

He didn't answer.

"Siti smells better than Paula."

He tried to get up but was unable to move. He struggled briefly.

"Let me out of here."

He felt he was in front of a ruthless interrogator and he was absolutely naked. For the first time, Abajoe was caught by surprise and felt anxious. What if the questions became even more intrusive? Should he refuse to co-operate? Then he remembered from somewhere that his responses could show only that certain items seemed to be associated with a greater change in behaviour than others were. The polygraph could only provide evidence that a particular statement caused him to react in a certain way. It couldn't show his actual beliefs. He also knew that lie detection could be foiled if he didn't react in the predicted ways. He could thwart the calibration step by pretending anxiety for nocuous topics. To an extent, he might be able to summon an anxious response or repress one at will. His relationship with Paula was not threatened and his responses would not register the fear that lie detection exploited.

Paula answered. "But you agreed."

He relented.

"No," he lied. He could remember the smell of Siti, fresh like carnations, unlike any woman he had ever had. She was unique and the memory of her smell flooded in.

The next question jerked him back to reality. The question was more subjective and fake behaviour was more difficult.

"You will stay with the Middle Way Party."

"Yes." He had no other plan.

"You will stay with Paula."

"Yes." His heart lurched with the lie. He might not stay with her.

"You love Paula."

"Yes." Again, his body involuntarily qualified his answer as a lie.

"You love Siti."

He didn't answer, but he relaxed. At last, it was out.

"Yes." He did, in a crazy way. He thought about her all the time ...often. In a different way from Paula, fresh, an adrenalin rush. If this is love, then it is an obsession, delicious but vulnerable.

Paula was suspicious that he was using her, which had never been his intention. All that she would learn was that he wasn't yet committed to her and had an infatuation with Siti. This would tell her little she didn't already know.

The questioning continued, looking for evidence of his feelings for both Paula and Siti. He knew that Paula was observing his responses and he suspected that many of the questions being put to him by the psychologist were her questions and that the psychologist was filling in the gaps.

When they had exhausted the topic of relative importances to him of Paula and Siti, his questioner took up a new thread.

"Do you believe it is possible for a person to love two people at the same time equally?"

He hesitated. "Yes." Whereas he knew most women would object to this answer, most men would agree. He knew that many men felt stifled in monogamous relationships and would prefer to live in polyamory, as had been usual in the past. Before becoming Prime Minister, his grandmother, Zelta, had lived happily with two men in a triad.

A group of women sharing a single man was quite usual in some countries and religions, but not in Australia. Cult leaders often aspired to a harem but Abajoe led a religion rather than a cult and he deplored male-centrism. He thought that polyamory had more opportunities to complement skills and share responsibilities than monogamy. Now that parenting of children was controlled by DNA testing rather than monogamy, sharing was possible. He wanted both Siti and Paula.

Afterwards, Paula was disheartened by his lack of commitment to her and was very jealous of Siti. She took his ambivalence about her amiss. She was definitely not interested in a triad with Siti. Abajoe's feelings had been revealed and her relationship with him was strained.

A few days later Paula made the next move.

"Has Siti had an affair previously?" she asked Abajoe.

"No, she had a bad experience in a brief encounter with a man and has been on her own ever since," he replied. He didn't want to tell her about the attempted rape.

"Well, her 'brief encounter' seems to have included living with a man for a year. Then she had an abortion, which he contested and lost."

Abajoe felt stung. He had trusted Siti and this was an unpleasant surprise. He thought about the publicity if this got out and said, "Who told you that?"

"An investigator. I've been checking up on your little friend."

Abajoe was silent. He had underestimated Paula. She was tougher than he had thought. It was lax of him not to inquire into Siti's recent past himself. Paula had recognised that he had an idealised view of Siti and their relationship might not stand the cold, hard light of reality.

"I don't believe it, Paula. But I'll ask her about it. I'll have to tell her it came from you. This could be the end of your friendship with her."

"Our friendship ended when she got her hooks into you."

"She will be hurt. She thinks highly of you."

"I am thinking of you. I don't want to see you hurt. Ask her."

"I will."

Paula's action had made a deep impression on him. She was tougher than he had thought. Perhaps he needed her after all.

He asked Siti that evening at his flat.

"Yes, it is true. But it is not important. Who told you?"

"Paula. She has been digging into your past. What happened?"

"I met Jorge at church. He was a teacher at the Yamen school in Mount Argus. I knew him for about two years. We were in love and we moved in together."

"But you told me a man had tried to rape you and you hadn't had a sexual relationship," Abajoe said. "You lied to me."

"No, after I finished with Jorge, another man was rough with me and I stayed alone for more than a year."

"But you pretended I was your first lover."

"You were. You were the first real man I had loved. Jorge was immature, a romantic boy."

"He wanted to keep the baby."

"But I didn't. By that time, I had finished with him. It was right to terminate my pregnancy. He wasn't my type, a hopeless dreamer."

"You haven't been honest with me, have you?"

He wanted her to know that if she was with him, he wouldn't tolerate dishonesty or even sleight of hand. His partner had to be 100% open with him.

"I have been honest. I have never lied to you. I suppose you jumped to conclusions. You haven't been entirely honest with me about Paula have you? I think you have led me to think you do not have a commitment to her, when you do."

"No, it is puppy love that has become a habit with her. But now I think it is over."

"Does she know that?"

"I'll tell her. Now what other skeletons do you have in your cupboard?"

"None. Jorge isn't a skeleton; he helped to make me the way I am. I've nothing to hide."

"I am shocked. If you want me to trust you, you will have to do better in the future."

"Sorry. You know everything about me now..."

He doubted that. He would watch her carefully until he was sure her game was straight. The doubt in his mind somehow made her more mysterious, more challenging. He would have her story about Jorge checked.

"...and I still like you," he said.

They kissed.

Abajoe found Siti a government job in Meannjin and she moved into a flat not far from The Tower. He spent more and more time with her.

"Would you have the decency to move away?" Paula demanded one morning when she passed him coming home next door after spending the night with Siti.

He was surprised. He had lived there most of his life and now he became aware of his surroundings full of memories. Perhaps he should move – he could swap with T One and Marko at the stadium. That was where the Prime Minister usually resided, because it had the best studios, communications equipment and offices for staff. He had been waiting until after the election to make the change. He didn't give Paula an answer. If anyone had to move away now it should be her. He would miss her, but it might be better for her. Paula was his reserve in case things didn't work out with Siti.

"Don't imagine Siti is permanent," he told Paula. "There's a lot between us that we have to work out. Anything can happen."

Paula poked out her tongue at him, scowled and turned her back.

One morning Peter came to see him.

"It's Paula. She spent last night in John's bed. I thought she was your girl?"

Abajoe was aghast. Paula had never shown any interest in John. He was sad. Perhaps he had so upset her that she had resorted to this to make him jealous. Alternatively, perhaps she had lost patience and involuntarily precipitated her relationship with him. All her life had been together with him. Paula had never gone with anyone else despite his frequent adventures with other women.

However, he couldn't imagine how she could believe her sleeping with John would bring them closer together, unless to make him aware of his double standards and his hypocrisy in their relationship. He concluded that she had finally rejected his ambivalence with a vengeance. She had tried to hurt him. It was a parting shot.

He thought she should have asked him if it was okay. He was angry that it had been with his best friend, John, because of the disrespect to him. He considered confronting John, but nothing he could say would undo the damage. He would never be able to trust either of them so completely again.

"Hmm. Thanks for telling me, Peter. Are they having an affair?"

"I don't think so. I think she was jealous of your fling with the Yamen girl. Are you having an affair?"

"Her name is Siti and, yes, I think we are."

"Perhaps Paula is punishing you. You know she regarded you as hers. You have hurt her and she wanted to hurt you back."

"Well it was foolish of her because I was very fond of her, but I won't trust her again."

Abajoe was sad because he had often imagined having children with Paula when he was ready to settle down. If only she could have waited a bit longer. His infatuation with Siti would probably end and he would have gone back to her. But not now. She had revealed that her pride was more important to her than their friendship. He had lost a lover. He hadn't thought of her as that before. Now he realised that he had truly loved her and regretted his selfishness but it was too late.

In the days that followed, he and Paula avoided each other. They were involved together in Party work, but they communicated only on business courteously and considerately. He was sad that after 20 years, they had nothing personal to say to each other. He wanted her sometimes but he knew she would mock any advance he made, telling him he wasn't serious, which was true. He was seeing Siti regularly. Paula moved away to a nearby apartment. They continued to see each other almost every day in Party work and she still came and helped with 'Family Fare' shows, the vegetables, poultry and the rossits experiment. Paula had been his closest friend and sometimes, he still imagined settling down with her. He could forgive but he would never forget.

CHAPTER 32

Gunyaba

One day, when he had an hour free, Siti said to him, "There's something I'd like to show you."

She took him to an ornate building with gracious lawns beside the Meannjin River.

"Eight generations ago, in 1892, my ancestor, Mary Donovan, aged 19, arrived here as an immigrant aboard the steam-assisted schooner *Villaneuve*."

"Was she a convict?" asked Abajoe.

"No. She left Ireland in a depression when she couldn't get a job of any sort. She saw an advertisement for a public lecture by Queensland's recruiting agent and signed up. She must have been desperate because she had little idea of what she was coming to. There were rumours that Her Majesty's garrisons in the Far East captured young girls as sex slaves."

"Is this true or speculation?"

"It is based on letters that she paid to have written to her family in Ireland. They told that she disembarked in Moreton Bay and took the steam packet up the Meannjin River to come ashore at this wharf."

Inside the embankment, holding back the river, stood a dilapidated jetty. Siti turned and they faced an historic symmetrical two-storey mansion with verandahs framed by cast-iron lace castings.

"Her first impression of Gunyaba was that it was the stately home of gentry. Mary and the other immigrants ate a sumptuous meal in the Main Hall. Single women were accommodated in a dormitory in the North Wing. Exhausted by the journey, she lay on her bed and sank into a deep sleep.

"Her awakening, with the sun already up, was an experience she never forgot and was passed on down the generations. Through the window, she could hear tropical birds in the trees outside, smell fragrant flowers, see ferries angling across the current of a broad reach of river in the foreground, with the colonial buildings of the city centre beyond.

"After all the agonising and anxiety about coming, she finally knew that this was a place worth coming to. It made her feel welcomed and valued. Now she felt they belonged here, where she was being given this generous reception.

"She spent a week there, tramming into the city centre and marvelling at the rich displays of goods in the shops. Then she started looking for work.

"She was interviewed by Patrick Flynne, from County Armagh, squatting at a place called Widgeroo Station. He had a run of 20,000 acres of bushland with 1000 head of beef cattle. He said he was looking for a housekeeper since his wife died. He asked her about her skills at cooking and keeping house and seemed unimpressed until she told him she could play the fiddle.

""You're hired," he said. "I need some cheering up." He told her about the rugged, lonely life and the independence and the beauty of it. "Either you love it or you hate it. Catherine was never happy there and in the end, it killed her. But I love it here...if only I could find a woman who would like it."

"Mary agreed to come for a visit. They left the next day with two horses each and rode inland. In a couple of days, the greenery of the coast became arid semi-desert. It was the driest country she had ever seen. After 15 days, they reached a house made from slabs of timber, cut from trees felled on the property.

"Mary's visit never ended and she was laid to rest beside him 62 years later, under a bottle tree. She bore him nine children and when she died, she had 58 grandchildren and eight great-grandchildren. She fell in love with the shimmering bush and learned its secrets from the Aborigines of the Gidgeree tribe."

"They were kin of the Wagarras," Abajoe added, "our lot. We let them hunt on our land during droughts. Otherwise, they would have starved. Their land had kangaroos, emus and small creatures that fed on the growth after rain. In droughts, they came down to the coast."

"So that's where you get your sharing from, is it?" said Siti. "Now, to continue, Mary learned to respect the bush and the Aborigines' experience. Unlike the other squatters, Patrick didn't clear his land but shared it with the Aborigines, who burned it through regularly to keep the pastures free of shrubs. There were usually kangaroos there and he protected the Aborigines from the Government, who were forcing them on to reservations.

"Every three years, except in wartime, the Donovans have had a reunion at Gunyaba and remembered Mary and Patrick and their meeting there, where the adventure of their life together had begun.

"Not long after having my identity on the National Database updated as the daughter of Jenny Craig, who was a Donovan, we were invited to the 52nd reunion of Mary and Patrick's first meeting at Gunyaba. There were 2500 people here, contacted by a descendant using the online genealogical search facility. One of the speakers told this tale of Mary and Patrick's meeting."

Siti was delighted to have discovered her ancestry. Until the previous month, she had thought she was an orphan, ignominious and inconsequential. The event had been spoiled for Siti when she learned that the Government had sold Gunyaba to a developer, who was planning to build blocks of flats alongside the old building. The facade of the mansion would be restored but the inside gutted to make 10 luxury flats.

"Why is the Government allowing them to destroy the interior?" she had asked the speaker. "That is where the immigrants stayed. It was purpose-built as a reception centre and is absolutely priceless!"

"They want the facade as window dressing for their concrete cubicles," he had answered. "People will pay a lot for a place with a bit of heritage."

"But this site and the main building are sacred," she told Abajoe. "Everyone of us non-indigenous people is descended from someone who stayed here at the beginning of a new life. These days, people want to connect with their origins and this is a disconnection. Can't you stop the sale going through?"

"I can see your concern," he said. "I'll find out why we are selling it."

Abajoe knew the answer but did not want Siti to know his true feelings. Gunyaba was a liability that he wanted off the balance sheet.

He spoke to someone on his communicator for a few minutes. He turned to her and shook his head. "The sale was done several months ago by Felix's National Works Department. The building wasn't being used and needed lots of money to repair it. He is waiting for approval of the buyer's development application before it settles. I'm afraid you're too late."

He thought that would be the end of it but Siti formed Gunyaba Action Group and mounted a publicity campaign demanding the Government renege on the sale.

Abajoe was most concerned at this time with getting a better type of urban development that was sustainable and what all the people wanted, as Australian cities repopulated. The decisions could not be made by partisan politics. There had to be independent and scientific evaluation of development applications. The MWP proposed establishment of local planning tribunals separate from Government, like the Judiciary. Following public debate, his Government held a national referendum.

"We have done it," Abajoe called her when voting closed. "We have changed the Australian Constitution! Here, read this," he said, sending her a news article.

TRIBUNES TO END PLANNING TRIBULATION
by Phillip Lascar, Oznews, 16/04/2260

In the national referendum today, 82% of Australian voters preferred creation of a new statutory authority, a planning tribunal, to decide development applications locally. Of the others, 15% wanted to keep the existing system of local government control, with 3% undecided

The referendum result has added a fourth pillar to the Australian Constitution. The planning tribunal has been separated from the legislative, executive and judiciary tribunals. It will take over and bring together the approval of development applications, which up to now has been done by the other three.

In this article, the old and new systems are compared. Tribunals will be set up in each local government area as required. Under the new system, objective evidence and the testing of hypotheses will take over from the rhetoric and fallacious disputation used in the past. The adversarial Planning and Environment Courts are to be replaced by inquisition into mediation, arbitration and compensation of objectors. The Science Method will have the upper hand in ensuring developments meet legitimate demands of all stakeholders

Developers' profits will be reduced by having to compensate or modify their plans to satisfy objectors. In the past, if the judiciary found in their favour, because their plans had been found in the balance of probabilities to be legal, they could proceed without meeting objections. From now on, they will only be allowed to disadvantage others through commercial competition. Individuals and communities in the vicinity of a development will be protected under the Bill of Rights, adopted in 2025, under which Australians have the right to freedom from all forms of incursion, pollution, heritage destruction and cultural dislocation.

The national planning tribunal will oversee the appointment of local tribunes and require certain planning codes to be followed, such as the Burra Charter, which recognises the cultural heritage that local governments have previously ignored.

In the past, objections were heard in Appeals Courts under legal jurisdiction. Scientific expertise was barely understood and took second place to legal interpretation. In future, a tribunal's interpretation of plans and objections in relation to central requirements will be heard in a scientific forum, where expert scientific inquisition is understood. The scientific staff of the tribunal will forecast impacts, get the developer to modify plans, and arbitrate compensation using transparent methods.

Whereas development approvals have been sought with secrecy and those disadvantaged often didn't find out until too late, the tribunals' work will connect objectors with the developer and with each other, bringing mutual advantage and voluntary modification. Any residual shortfalls from community goals will be addressed by the tribunals' scientific staff, who will undertake open-ended inquiries. When objections become disputes, unlike the judge of a Planning Appeals Court, who could decide one way or the other, persuaded by the skills of advocates, on the balance of probabilities, tribunals will promote mutual benefit by scientific evaluation, mediation and arbitration.

This additional work will not impose higher costs on developers because professionals, especially scientists and technologists, are expected to volunteer their work self-altruistically, that is, pro bono, once their position has been sustained. These voluntary contributions spearhead the Government's vision of a diverse, non-material, meditative society.

Developers' radical designs can be better considered by the new system. The adversarial legal system couldn't help but be backward looking, because it followed legal precedents, preventing imaginative designs. Tribunals will evaluate them for their scientific merit, replacing legal uniformity, consistency and reproducibility with these values in science.

In the past, a single property owner has been able to stop a development but it may be overruled by the tribunal if the objection is not congruent with community development goals or if compensation with a similar property that meets the objection is irrationally refused. If the property is valued by the community for its place in cultural traditions and the developer is unable to compensate, the tribunal would support the owner in blocking development.

Overall, the tribunals will result in cohesive communities, where their own kinds of development are allowed to flower and exploitive developments are weeded out. Their own heritage, cultural icons and uniqueness will be fostered locally and better respected by outsiders. In the past, developers have sometimes come into a community and destroyed it, with depletion of non-renewable community resources of land, water, energy, infrastructure, heritage, cultural icons, beauty, symmetry, order and ambiance, with very few offsetting benefits for local stakeholders. This will end.

Prime Minister, Abajoe Yabra, whose Government proposed the legislation, said in announcing the result of the referendum: "This is a victory that will strengthen living together in cohesive communities, untrammelled by avaricious developers. Parliament is scheduled to appoint Jennifer Ogama as our first National Tribune later this week. Development is sometimes marred by bitter disputes. She has had a distinguished career as a scientific facilitator, mediator and arbitrator in emotional situations. Hers will be an independent voice laying the ground rules for tribunals to apply throughout Australia."

The work of tribunals will be to inquire into impacts, including effects on the general public, evaluating them scientifically and proposing redress from the developer. There will be fewer developments but they will be higher quality. Community living will be improved.

Siti finished reading and put down the article.

"Congratulations! Many people did not fully understand what difference it will make, including me," she said. "You did well to get those people, from all walks of life, saying they were for it. That tipped the balance."

"It took a lot of work to get it through," said Abajoe. "Luckily Sudarta kept a low profile. If she had been seen as a mouthpiece for developers, she would have lost support."

"If only the development application for Gunyaba could be processed by a tribunal," she told Abajoe. "I'm sure it could be saved."

"I think you are too late, Gunyaba is about to be approved."

"Our YAG campaign has stirred up a lot of support. People do not like you selling Gunyaba. It is going to cost you votes."

"How many votes?" he asked.

"Almost everyone, except recent arrivals, has an ancestor that stayed at Gunyaba," she said. "There have been 14 generations since Mary arrived and if her descendants only had three children each, she would have 46,000 descendants alive today in 2260. Because about 200,000 immigrants stayed at Gunyaba, most people would have at least one ancestor who stayed there. Put the other way round, each of us today has 11,264 ancestors alive in Mary's generation. The Australian population in 1892 was about 3,300,000, so there would be a good chance that the 200,000 immigrants had descendants who intermarried into the general population to give everyone at least one ancestor who stayed there. YAG is contacting them and telling them what your Government is doing to Gunyaba."

"I'll see if Felix can do anything," Abajoe told her. He was overawed by Siti's tenacity. It was a characteristic he always found appealing but in the woman he loved, it was irresistible.

He called her later that day. "You're in luck. Felix is going to pull the Gunyaba development application out of council's planning office on a technicality. Ausland will have to resubmit it to the new planning tribunal."

"Whoo-hoo. We might be able to stop Ausland. Thanks man!"

A few days later, Ausland lodged their development application with the new planning tribunal. Jennifer appointed as Tribune, Theodore Mellin, Professor of Scientific Anthropology in Swan City, on the other side of the continent. He had a team of scientists prepared to work by self-altruism until the case was decided. They met online with Ausland, Meannjin Council staff, Siti and representatives of the other stakeholders and designed a survey form that sought evidence to refute the hypothesis that insufficient people were interested in any other outcome for it to be preferred above Ausland's plan.

Siti told them there was no other site like Gunyaba in Australia. Thousands of Australians had contacted her detailing their objections to losing public access to it when Ausland would fence it off.

According to Mellin, the iconic stature of Gunyaba was due to 'imprinting'. The phenomenon had first been discovered by Nobel prizewinner, Conrad Lorenz. His experiments had shown that newly hatched goslings immediately became dependent on the object they first saw. Immigrants' brains also became 'plastic', like youngsters' brains, while they rapidly learned to fit into their new environment by making neural connections. Consequently, they had a strong emotional connection with the place they first saw as a home in Australia: Gunyaba. The strength of this emotion would be passed down to descendants, who would value their association with Gunyaba. Interest in Gunyaba could be revived by restoring links to the ancestral experience.

When Siti told him about Mellin's theory, Abajoe was more concerned about what should be done with Gunyaba.

"We cannot afford to restore and maintain useless old buildings."

"How is the delight of arriving as an immigrant at Gunyaba to be explained to future generations of descendants of immigrants if they cannot go there?" she asked. "Australians are losing their memory. A society without a memory is a poor thing. Many people do not know who their original ancestors were, why they came, how they got here, where they arrived and how they were received. They think that they have sprung, fully developed as Australians, from the land as if by magic. They do not understand their origins."

"Why does that matter?" he asked.

"Knowing where you originally come from imbues your spirit with the characteristics of your forebears. Their strengths become yours when adversity tests your core values, your basic strengths. They give you resilience and the will to survive. How would you be without knowing your Aboriginality?"

"Lost," he answered. "It means a lot. I can see why you want a Gunyaba museum. The council should have money for immigrants to discover and maintain their origins."

The replies to the survey flooded in to the tribunal. The feedback showed the types of involvement with Gunyaba that people wanted. Ideas were submitted for a wide range of applications of Gunyaba, such as a memorial ruin, Ausland's development, a wall plaque memorial with public access, tours of a restored building, museum, family gatherings, educational tours, re-enactments, cultural drama and so on.

Next, the tribunal surveyed interest in the most popular facility options. Every option had some of its cost funded by Ausland, as compensation for their exclusive use, which had been agreed with the tribunal. The most expensive option required Ausland to donate the main building for restoration and adaptation as a tourist attraction that re-created the immigrant experience. Visitors would stand in the shoes of their ancestors and be educated and entertained by a succession of authentic simulations of conditions of the day. They would wear the clothes, talk the language and be processed as an immigrant pioneer. Ausland's funding would be augmented by donations of 100,000 seus per family that would be held in trust and returned if that option did not attract sufficient funding.

Siti campaigned to get YAG members to select one of the tribunal's options.

She was having dinner with Abajoe at her place when the videophone rang. It was Mellin, looking pleased. "You're going to get a tourist development. It was oversubscribed to twice what was needed."

Siti gave a whoop of joy. "Thanks, Mellin. Your people were great."

"Just doing our job. See you later."

Siti blew Abajoe a kiss. "Your tribunals are brilliant. They have turned corporate rape into civilised intercourse with no losers."

"I doubt that Ausland are rapt in it."

"I'll give them a call. On second thoughts, I'll wait until Mellin has their signature on the deal."

She told Abajoe later that Ausland had grumbled, "There's not much in it for us now."

"Never mind," she had replied, "you got off lightly from locals who withheld claims so that you would be able to go ahead."

"Bollocks. That's how everyone used to be!" Ausland's General Manager growled.

"They used to have no choice," she had told him. "Now they do. Choice is everything. No one has to be worse off!"

CHAPTER 33

Cause of a Fight

Abajoe was besotted with Siti.

'I think this must be true love,' he told himself. 'This is growing every time I am with her and even when she is not there.'

He had an erection that wouldn't go away, hour after hour.

After they had made love, his head would be spinning, his emotions stretched and disoriented, experiencing the world anew. At work he couldn't concentrate and would smile and laugh at inappropriate times, causing consternation.

"Excuse me. I'm in love," he apologised.

They predicted he would recover in a couple of days but it was several months before he forgot her for more than an hour and he never ever did get over thinking about her at inopportune times. Between the distractions, he became more focused. It was as if he had a new point of view that had to be recalibrated on her. She provided his test pattern.

But their relationship was balanced. He found himself agreeing easily and disagreeing just as easily. When he wanted to, he got his own way. They were like two peas in a pod, united but separate. He didn't know then how different they really were.

Living 2000 kilometres apart made being together difficult. Abajoe got together with Siti either at Mount Argus or at places where he was campaigning in-between or at Meannjin whenever they had the opportunity. When they got together, their talk would often include discussion of her campaign to allow the guest workers to stay. He helped her prepare the guest workers' case for consideration by the immigration authorities. He was happy working with her for something they both valued. It seemed a natural part of their relationship as lovers.

While drawn together by their political involvement, the power of his position came between them. He worried that she might be an influence digger. He was fastidious in limiting himself to positions of legal authority and regarded any other influence he might have as corrupt. It was a possible outcome that he wanted to avoid at all costs but Siti had skilfully drawn him into supporting the guest workers' application for immigrant status.

When she tried to conscript him into using the power of his position to obtain a favourable decision from the officials of the Immigration Court, he became suspicious that she was using him and he refused to participate further. When their application was rejected, he had preliminary talks with lawyers and identified a technical loophole that would exempt the guest workers from the Immigration Restriction Act. He helped her present an appeal to the Supreme Court.

Although he had appointed the judge who would hear the case, he had no intention of corresponding with him to obtain special favour. Therefore, he was at first surprised and then incensed when he received a call from the judge.

"Good morning, Prime Minister," the judge said, "would you clarify your position in the case of the guest workers. I have today received a petition presented by Siti Iftiqad, supported by a dozen elders, with your name at the head. Am I to believe that your Government does not want its own legislation applied in this case?"

He agonised about what to do. The longer he delayed, the more the ambivalence would seem to be corrupt. He had to act.

"No, of course not," Abajoe mumbled, embarrassed. "There has been a mistake. I want you to apply the legislation as you see fit. As for the elders, you may or may not wish to consider their point of view. They are certainly not government representatives."

"Ah, good," said the judge and that ended the call.

He was unable to contact Siti until that evening.

"I had a call from Judge Ellis today. You had no right to put my name on your petition."

"Why not? You do support us don't you? You helped us take it to the Supreme Court. Aren't you with us all the way then?"

Abajoe told her what he had said to the judge. She was furious.

"You bastard! What a turncoat. What you did was as good as giving the judge the thumbs up to find against us. Why couldn't you lend your name to our cause?"

"Didn't you realise my conflict of interest? We put through the Immigration Restriction Act that the case is being heard under."

"But you as good as said to me that the guest workers had a special case. You encouraged us to take it to the Supreme Court as if you would support an exemption. Now you have left us in the lurch. How dare you!"

Siti's venom hurt him. It was as if the guest workers were their only mutual interest. Again he looked for and found evidence that she was only interested in him for his influence. It was enough for him to withdraw his affection from her. The conflict had destroyed their relationship when they hardly knew each other.

"I want out," he said. "I don't want to have any further role in this other than as an ordinary member of your guest workers' support group. I do want to support them but I do not see why my opinion on this should count more than anyone else's. It is not a part of my mandate."

"You should have discussed this with me first, not countermanded the judge," she said angrily.

He thought, 'How could I have discussed it with her when this was tantamount to accusing her of using him?'

"A letter from you to the judge explaining my involvement will fix that," he said, evading the issue.

"It shouldn't have to be fixed. I trusted you."

"It wouldn't have happened if we had been living together," he said bitterly. He was hurt that she hadn't replied to his proposal that she move in with him at Family Fare Tower.

"You're not my type," she said.

Until then he had thought their relationship had something special going for it and would last. He lost heart and abandoned courtesy. His remaining interest was to vindicate himself.

"You shouldn't have put my name at the top of your petition without my permission. It seemed like a set up."

"Set up? How dare you! I thought we were friends!"

"We are friends. I am sorry if I misled you into thinking I would look after you and your friends. I never had any intention of doing more than helping you to get a fair treatment under the existing laws."

"Well you certainly led me up the garden path," she spat. "This is the end. I don't want to go on with this relationship."

She said he had betrayed her trust and there wasn't enough unity between them for the relationship to continue although they could remain friends. She would contact him in a month's time. The next day, she returned his door key.

Abajoe was devastated. No one had ever rejected him against his wishes before. They had enjoyed such good times together. Unless he would apply his influence to her cause, it seemed she had no further use for him. He had the power to do it but she wanted him to drink from a poisoned chalice. How would he ever be able to refuse her?

He began to look around for someone else. Then he realised he was looking for a partner the same as her, that she was unique. He would never get her out of his system and had no choice but to accept her terms.

He wrote to the judge saying that, in his opinion, the guest workers should be considered as the most deserving category of prospective immigrant. He sent her a copy of the letter but she did not reply and he waited forlornly for her to contact him. He threw himself into his work but time went slowly.

There are 720 hours in a month and he slept only 200, badly, during the month he waited to hear from her. Each of the others seemed like a lifetime of rejection for reasons he barely understood. She had pitted his duty to the nation against his duty to her and rejected his alignment. He was despondent and wrote to her several times because that was the only way he was allowed to contact her but she never replied to his letters. He despaired that their relationship was over. Perhaps she had left the door ajar so as not to dash his hopes with such finality.

After three weeks she wrote, saying she didn't want him involved in her campaign any further but they could meet to talk about their relationship. It seemed like a reprieve. Although something in their relationship had died, he took a gift of a ring with a large rose-coloured rhodochrosite stone. It signified amity, which he visualised as the overlap in their personal interests. Although there were real differences between them, he hoped they might get over them.

When they met, in secret from the media, they assiduously avoided talking about her guest workers' campaign.

"Let's talk about that separately in our next meeting," he said whenever she raised the topic. "We get on so well about most things; it is only your campaign that is coming between us."

She liked the ring. To make small talk, he told her about a scheme of personality assessment he had come across. According to it, they had significant personality differences.

"You are concerned with recognition, having an impact on people. You are impulsive, liking excitement and action. But you are disorganised and dislike details."

She smiled. "Maybe I am. What type are you?"

"I'm the opposite, I like details. I'm into analysing causes, needing correctness. I like expertise and inquiry but tend to be critical."

"Perhaps we are incompatible? Or do opposites attract?"

"I have checked that. Generally, there is no evidence that they do. In fact, there is some evidence that similarities attract, so it doesn't look good for us. People get together because they have similar attitudes and beliefs and they stay together if they have similar personalities."

"We have similar attitudes, don't we?"

"Yes – that's why we got together. But will we survive with different personalities?"

"There is not much hope for the long term," said Siti, resigned.

"I don't accept that our different personalities have to clash," Abajoe said. "We can make allowances for each other. If we agreed on everything, it would be dull."

"We can help each other with things we're not so good at."

"It would be good to have more unity," said Siti. "It is our separateness that is forcing us apart."

"It's worth a try."

The evening ended amicably, with agreement to meet and talk about her campaign. Abajoe was relieved that she wanted to continue their relationship.

Two days later, they met at his flat for dinner. As he finished the cooking, she told him the news of her campaign. There had been media interviews, publicity stunts and lobbying. She ran the organisation with megalomaniac zeal and, consequently, she controlled most of the activities, with little help from supporters.

After a curry, they exchanged views on the progress of her appeal in the Supreme Court. She lacked the funds to pay initial legal costs. Siti knew Abajoe was uncomfortable with his wealth and enjoyed sharing it with others. The irony was that he didn't really want to use the financial muscle he had inherited. If he had known how, he would have locked his cake away for any children he might have some day. But it was there, contradicting his beliefs in sharing. It demanded to be nibbled at, if not swallowed whole. Getting rid of it by doling it out to worthy causes seemed the next best alternative but unfortunately created an obstacle to equality and interfered with his relations with Siti. One way to limit the interference was to separate the money from the romance.

To pay the initial costs, he offered to match her seu for seu. She would be liable for the bulk of the later court costs and her supporters would have to raise it from donations and by running events. He supposed that a private action that opposes one's public position is not a conflict of interest and his donation need not remain secret. She accepted the donation but told him he could have no further involvement in her campaign.

As he would have no control over how his donation would be spent, he said he wanted a report on how the money had been spent. Immediately she stood up from the half-finished meal.

"I don't want your money," she said in a strangled voice and walked out, leaving the flowers he had given her and the apple pie he had baked for the occasion, her favourite food.

She wrote to him later that day. "I apologise for walking out. You insulted my integrity. I need time to myself to think about this. I'll call you later, in about three weeks. I'll tell you what I've decided."

Once again, her position eluded him. Whatever he had done, she seemed to him to be paying him back, for something that he didn't understand, by keeping him on a piece of string.

The days dragged by. He missed her badly.

Maybe she was using him for his money: wasn't that often a part of true love? After all, a person's prospects do count for something. Perhaps she was holding out for more – it had worked last time.

As she was obviously worrying about how to get enough money to complete the legal action, because he had started it, he felt obligated to help her. He wrote to her promising to give more money, matching her own donations.

She didn't reply.

He called her and they met. Their relationship as lovers resumed a day or two later.

Nothing had happened except that he had agreed to match her donation of up to half the legal costs, which might amount to a major sum. He had realised that his commitment to their relationship had to be made rather than said. Her commitment to him might then follow.

It was a solution that recognised his conflict of interest but also their incompatibility. She went by gut feel and spiritual omens whereas he calculated risks and selected strategies scientifically.

She had hurt him badly. He accepted that it had been his own fault. He should not have withdrawn support from her cause without discussing it with her. He was her main supporter and he had let her down. The money had seemed like a zero sum game but now he realised he could compromise with her when he had to.

When Abajoe considered his true position on the guest worker issue, he recognised that deep inside he wanted to keep Bhakarians out of Australia. It was ugly and not politically correct. He had to keep it secret. Whenever he met Bhakarian strangers, he knew instances of fear, deep within his psyche. These people were of a different, unknown kind. It was not logical and he regretted it but all he could hope for was that he would not transmit his prejudice to other Australians and to his children, if he ever had any. His support of the guest workers was an apology for a guilty conscience.

A few months later, he signed a cheque for half the initial deposit required by the lawyers. He was acutely aware that he was squandering the inheritance entrusted to his prudent care on trying to change his own Government's policy. But he put a brave face on it because he knew he had no choice: his relationship with Siti depended on it.

He wondered why he had given in to her. There was the carrot of his fulfilment with her and there was his reaction to the stick of her veiled threats that unless he supported her, they were finished. Nevertheless, the donkey of his compliance had been kept going by his ambivalence over the guest worker's issue and his weakness in not declaring his secret bias and opposing her directly.

In terms of power in their relationship, he guessed that she had lost as much as he had and they were equal. She had wanted him to shoulder all the costs, political and financial, but had obtained only a half of the latter. He had wanted to pay none and lost a half too. He had also lost control of his donation and took no further part in her campaign. Their relationship had achieved a balance but it was inherently unstable.

The wrangle with Siti had been the tip of the iceberg of their relationship. Most of it had floated enjoyably below the surface. He was considering how he could get her to live with him, while retaining enough independence for himself, with equality between them. Sharing of this magnitude could not be given and he waited for more harmony before he would suggest it to her. He had realised that sharing would only confer equal power in so far as giving to her would change her behaviour in the way anticipated.

Disappointment from their conflict lingered. It seemed ridiculous that he, as Prime Minister, could have personal fears. But he feared that Siti would take advantage of him if he gave her equality. When it came to getting her commitment to him, he hoped that something good for both of them would hatch from his golden egg. His fear was that it was addled.

CHAPTER 34

Guest Workers' Debate

IN the national interest, Abajoe was empowered to call in Siti's appeal from the Supreme Court, for resolution by Parliament. He did so because of the controversy she had stirred up, in order to protect the Supreme Court, at the request of the unanimous bench of judges. Sudarta was backing Siti's appeal against the Government and the issue had become too partisan for the judges.

Abajoe's donations to her campaign were a secret between him and Siti, paid in cash. If known, they would have ended his political career. He very much regretted his sponsorship of her court case and was uneasy about his vulnerability to her discretion.

The technical loophole forming the grounds of Siti's appeal had been that the Immigration Restriction Act was being applied in a racially discriminatory manner to the Bhakarian guest workers. Therefore, their exclusion was invalid. If she had won in court, it would have been a severe embarrassment to him and his Government.

Cabinet decided to resolve the issue in the virtual parliament by a full debate. The proposition was, 'That guest workers be allowed to immigrate'. Instead of affirming their exclusion, identifying the MWP as xenophobic, they chose the less racially discriminatory task of negating their inclusion on grounds of insufficient resources. It was a test case for their election platform. If they failed to get public support, they would drop the immigration policy from view and choose another plank for their platform.

"If we win," he told Siti, "I hope you will accept what I have been telling you all along, that it is Australia that is against the guest workers, not me. In my job, I have to consider the national interest. I have not been able to come out in your support for that reason."

"You have caved in to Sudarta. You didn't have to call in the appeal. We were winning in court and now our supporters' money has gone on useless legal costs."

"That was your own doing. You should have stopped campaigning when it was sub judice."

He hoped the debate would resolve his confrontation with Siti, from which he still had painful bruises. He hoped that the debate would vindicate his limited support of her campaign goals. She would recognise that it was public opinion rather than his leadership or his politics that had thwarted her.

Winning the debate was therefore very important to the MWP. There would be three speakers on either side in Oxford style. Abajoe would be taking a back seat, as this could be a close-run thing. If he took the lead and they lost, his leadership would be tainted. His position was already weakened by the irony of his commitment to sharing of resources and his opposition to immigration. He would not share his nation's resources with foreigners. His sharing seemed parochial and it flew in the face of globalisation. He was vulnerable and he thought it would be best if he sat this one out.

Paula, his Deputy, would lead the Government team in the debate. Since she had moved away, they had stayed friends. She had thrown herself into Party work and was the prime mover in his re-election campaign. She had taken over several responsibilities from Abajoe and become indispensable. He gladly accepted her offer to lead their team. That afternoon he found her in the Party's studio under the stadium, being made up for the debate, which would be broadcast on the national network. Her head was enclosed in make-up machinery as he spoke to her.

"Most of our people are already with you, but you may be able to get some independents to swing over," he told her. "If you can get them to imagine a severe recession or a drought, when there would be sharing out of food and essentials, they won't want guest workers to stay."

"Once they imagine a drought, they won't want them to come here in the first place," she replied, her voice muffled.

"Yes," he said, "but if they don't come and operate the mines, then they will be even worse off, without the essentials that mining taxes will provide. The issue is not whether they can benefit us, because they can, but whether in hard times their presence will cause racial division."

Paula thought for a moment. "That's a good question. What do you think?"

"It's Newton's third law; the action will be cancelled by the reaction. If our action is to let them immigrate, there will be an equal and opposite force to send them home. It may not surface until we have a drought or recession. But in the end, nothing will be gained by letting them stay."

"Then there's no point in doing anything at all about racism...or anything else for that matter," Paula concluded sadly.

"Exactly," he enthused. "Most problems go away by themselves. If we were to let them immigrate, it would be discriminating against other races. The prejudice would eventually come back to haunt us. We should stick to the agreement they came under."

"The Yamens will be for letting them stay, recession or no recession but what about the Jandus?"

"I've no idea," Abajoe said.

"Shall I appeal to their fear of a Yamen takeover?" Paula replied, but her voice was muffled by the headstall, which held her make-up robot and the brushes, palette and colours.

He didn't hear but he wanted to seem agreeable and nodded vaguely, not realising that he had pulled the pin on a political grenade that would destroy their campaign to win Yamen votes.

When Paula was ready in her war paint, she took her place before the cameras, soft and alluring. Abajoe and Siti observed at the bank of monitors, whispering to each other. Siti had managed to get time off work. The white face paint of her Yamen rias hid her expression. Abajoe was glad that he had asked Paula to takeover. If he were speaking, he would be directly in conflict with Siti.

The chair gonged and Parliament hushed. "Honourable Members, this afternoon we will vote on the proposition, 'That guest workers be granted residency'. Proposer for the Affirmative, are you ready? Would you begin?"

Sudarta's Shadow Minister for Resources spoke first. Siti clapped him on. The Party's office staff heard her with surprise. They had poured into the studio and stood around the central island with Paula in the Leader's chair, with Siti and Abajoe to one side. They knew that the Prime Minister's female friend had her own campaign but they hadn't realised how opposed to them she was until that moment. Nor had they realised just how tolerant he was. What a great man! Or was she just his weakness?

The Proposer for the Affirmative began and defined guest workers as unskilled workers, who had been granted temporary work visas in neighbouring countries, limited in number by quotas. They were admitted for three years and then were returned home at government expense. Their case would be that guest workers should be allowed to stay because they filled skilled positions, which were limiting production. He listed biological, economic, trade, security, cultural and religious advantages of accepting immigrants.

Then John, Abajoe's Minister for Resources, opened for Abajoe's side. His rift with Abajoe had healed. He accepted the Affirmative side's definition but outlined his side's case that immigrants would fill the vacant jobs less satisfactorily than guest workers would. Guest workers should be allowed in and then sent home to develop their own country. This would build bridges between the two cultures and create greater security for Australia.

It seemed to rest on whose data you accepted. Keeping one ear on the debate, Abajoe researched the world database on his communicator. He gathered data to test the hypothesis whether immigrants from Bhakaria to Australia returned to Bhakaria frequently. There was an avalanche of statistics and research findings on both sides, with the conclusion that the hypothesis was refuted at the probable level of confidence. Immigrants to Australia seldom went home after cheap air transport ended. He flashed the conclusion on to John's screen and John was able to use it to drive home his argument.

Next, Sudarta's Seconder denied that immigrants would carry Australian culture to Bhakaria if they returned. Guest workers suffered prejudice. Bhakarian investors would see their acceptance as immigrants as symptomatic of respect, so that their capital would be secure in Australian projects. There would be more integration within the region, creating larger markets, humanitarian respect and more prosperity.

Judging by the applause, their opponents seemed to have the lead.

Siti smiled at Abajoe jubilantly.

Then Abajoe's Population Minister seconded, refuting that immigrants built bridges. It had not happened in the past between the two nations. The consequences of continuing population growth caused by immigration would be another famine.

"It's neck and neck so far," Siti whispered to Abajoe.

The Affirmative Concluder said that Australia's role in the region was rather like the precarious position of an old couple's run-down home and mineral access in the middle of a shopping complex. They should welcome in immigrants as workers to develop it and obtain the highest value for their property to leave to their family.

She sat down to loud applause.

"Paula will bring us home in front, you'll see," said Abajoe.

Siti shook her head. "Fat chance."

The Opposition had done well and Abajoe could see the desperation in Paula as she waited to make the final speech. However, she disguised it with her clear, confident and persuasive voice.

"Mr Speaker, fellow Australians, you have heard us make the case for sending guest workers home after the agreed time of three years. The Opposition has attempted to show that we have nothing to lose by changing their visas and letting them stay. There are bigger issues than visa conditions at stake here. I will argue that the Opposition is wrong, that they have ignored our advice. Our Seconder told you that our Government's main concern is to avoid famine by limiting population growth. On the other hand, the Opposition's Proposer has stated that immigrants should be allowed to enter freely. Our Seconder replied with a question: "By what right should they be able to come and take a share in Australia's resources? They have no right," he said. Do we have a right to the resources in their countries? Their Seconder never answered but the answer is obvious: Of course not! Foreigners have no right to come here and share in Australia's resources."

Siti whispered to Abajoe. "No. They do have rights – as global citizens."

Paula had been speaking indignantly but quietly. Now she raised her voice.

"Our Seconder reminded you that property rights in Australia belong to its citizens under commune law. A survey last week showed that most communes in our 149 council areas do not want immigrants. They cannot allocate land and water to immigrants because there is not enough for a 200-year drought situation. However mining communes want guest workers and will allocate them land and water to grow food temporarily. Guest workers are more than welcome.

"I reject their Seconder's claim that guest workers suffer major prejudice and treatment that is inhumane and unfair. This used to occur before communes set aside land and water for them, when their presence threatened others' security. A little of those attitudes may have lingered but they will soon disappear. The guest workers have been requested by our communes to come here and they are regarded as assets to their communities."

"Not at Mount Argus," whispered Siti.

Now Paula changed her tone, becoming pleading.

"Our Seconder told you there is a positive reason to send guest workers home. They will help develop their homelands into better neighbours, as places where Australians are understood and respected. If they stayed here, that wouldn't happen. When they have immigrated, Bhakarians seldom return home and when they do, they stay too briefly to transfer our culture. For transfer of culture, the guest worker scheme is better."

Siti shook her head. "But Bhakarians may not want to know about Australian culture."

"I rebut the Opposition's suggestion that 'we owe it to guest workers to let them stay'. Certainly, their law-abiding hard work is appreciated but that is no more than their original contract. When we are pleased with a product, do we pay the seller more? In some circumstances, we leave a tip, but the granting of residency would be far more than a tip."

Paula became self-righteous.

"But the Opposition's most ludicrous charge is that we of the negative team are playing on an outdated fear, the fear of a 'yellow peril domino effect', that Australia would soon be swamped with immigrants from neighbouring countries, who would destroy our culture. We don't believe our immigration control would be so ineffectual. We do not fear immigrants, quite the opposite. We respect them and their need to have the security we cannot offer. We just don't have resources for them. Nor do we accept the charge that guest workers are being kept out as the 'thin edge of the wedge'. They have dug up a skeleton from their own past and tried to set it up as a straw man to tear down. Well it won't work because the facts tell a different story. We are dealing with the immigration problem, not hiding from it with our heads in the sand."

Siti looked at Abajoe and grimaced. "Rubbish. Sending guest workers home is not respecting them!"

Abajoe grimaced. He was concerned that Paula had raised a straw man of her own and gone too far. Her dismissal of the possibility of any immigration at all would alarm any Yamen voters who were swinging their way. Too late now, he reflected. He had thought Paula would have known not to raise the spectre of racism and he would ask her about it. Then he was jerked back to her speech.

Paula finished to thunderous applause.

"Bastardry," snarled Siti, glaring at Abajoe. She got up and pushed her way through the crowd and out of the studio. He stood up to follow her, then went back to talk with Paula. He was concerned that she might try to reverse the result by exposing his duplicity and conflict of interest in the call-in.

The Chairman asked members to vote within the next 30 minutes. The parliamentary network disintegrated into dozens of private conversations and the studio crowd went back to work talking excitedly.

"Great speech," Abajoe told Paula. "You put us on the front foot nicely. We could win this. One thing, why did you bring up the 'destroying our culture' issue?"

"I was trying to win the Jandu vote. We talked about it and you agreed."

"Oh? When was that?"

"Just before, when I was doing my make-up. I asked you and you agreed. Is there a problem?"

"I must have misheard you. For every Jandu voter we win by bringing up the threat of a cultural takeover, we probably lose ten Yamens who see it as racism. We have been trying to avoid polarising the vote because we'll be the losers."

"Shit. I never thought of that. Sorry."

"We'll have to wait for the result."

"Do we have a chance?"

"It'll be close. We'll have to wait and see. You did a great job."

He thought that he still found Paula very attractive and if his relationship with Siti fell apart again, he would try to take up with her where he had left off, if that was possible.

When voting closed, the results were available instantly on the monitors.

Results for proposition that 'Guest workers be granted residency'.

Affirmative 70
Negative   75
Abstention   4

It was a very narrow win but Abajoe was delighted. T One came over to congratulate them. He hugged her away from the cameras because he was trying to develop a political image that was independent of his connection to the dominant Yabra family.

He spoke to his communicator. "What was the vote, by Party?"

Proposition that 'Guest workers be granted residency'				
Party	*Affirmative*	*Negative*	*Abstention*	*Total*
Middle Way	*0*	*72*	*1*	*73*
Progress	*63*	*0*	*0*	*63*
Independent	*7*	*3*	*3*	*13*
TOTAL	*70*	*75*	*4*	*149*

He discussed the figures with Paula.

"The Independent vote will be crucial in the national election," she said. "We could need all their preferences."

"Let's see how the Jandus voted," he replied. "What was the vote, by culture?" he asked his communicator.

The following table appeared on the screen.

Proposition that 'Guest workers be granted residency'				
Culture	*Affirmative*	*Negative*	*Abstention*	*Total*
Indigenous	*0*	*6*	*0*	*6*
Crucian	*1*	*31*	*0*	*32*
Jandu	*13*	*5*	*3*	*21*
Yamic	*53*	*0*	*0*	*53*
Other	*3*	*33*	*1*	*37*
Total	*70*	*75*	*4*	*149*

"The Jandus have sided with the Yamens against us," Paula said.

"They are threatening our stewardship," Abajoe muttered. He drew breath through his teeth. "If they are against us on immigration, they could be against us on other issues. We could lose them to the Yamens. We need to wedge them away. But what can we use as a wedge?"

"You'll think of something,' Paula replied.

When he returned to his flat for a meeting with the others, they were talking about the results. They had listened to the debate and were apprehensive.

"That's too close for comfort," said John. "We are dependent on the Jandus. What else are we going to run on?"

"Not joining the SEU."

"That's very negative. Can't we turn it into a positive?"

"Keep Australia independent!"

"Home rule for Oz!"

"It wouldn't appeal to the Jandus."

"What's the Jandus' attitude?"

"According to Muller, they are still making up their minds. Our Jandu support is hanging by a thread."

"Heck. Surely they can see..."

"They fear Yamen extremism here. We don't want to have to make racist concessions. There are many different problems with SEU membership and we need to bring these to his attention. Paula, could you look into the centralisation problem? John, would you do resources and I'll do cultural effects."

"What about Peter?"

"He's not here, again. Peter used to be reliable. Is there a problem?"

"Maybe he has given up. This is the second time he's let us down."

"No. He's just not motivated at the moment."

"Perhaps something's bothering him. I'll try to find out."

"We need all the help we can get."

"What about Siti?"

"We're out of favour with her since the debate. Her friends, the guest workers, hoped we would be defeated and that would change our tune. It was close. Perhaps we should try something else?" He looked at Abajoe questioningly.

Abajoe shook his head. "No, it's a pivotal issue. If we show weakness, support could tip the other way. We could lose our majority."

John said, "Siti was looking pretty upset. You could be on the sofa!"

Abajoe laughed. "We get on okay so long as we don't talk politics. Fate seems to have pitched us on opposite sides."

"How long have we got to decide about the guest workers?"

"This time next week," said Paula. "We need to finalise our platform."

CHAPTER 35

Betrayer

Despite their differences and living apart, the two of them had become closer and closer. However, their political interests severely limited their time together. Some weeks they met only for a night or two at the weekend and he would joke that he was a 'sleeping partner'. Abajoe yearned to spend more time with her, to have her company to enjoy when they weren't tired. He asked her if she would live with him.

Siti preferred living by herself. He was disappointed at first, but he valued his own independence as much as she did hers and enjoyed having his personal space. Although sharing would have been good, their different interests would have clashed. The main problem was that they had little experience of seeking mutuality and compromise with each other. Nevertheless, he was disappointed that she didn't give him the option.

Their affair was headlined in the media. Her campaign for guest workers to be allowed to stay in Australia permanently opposed Middle Way Party policy. Her political allegiance was the subject of speculation. When asked about this, Abajoe said, "Her politics are her own affair. You'll have to ask her."

She worked in the government job he had found for her and observed his one string that she did not go head on against his Government in public. So far, she had kept her activism separate from her work.

Although the guest workers had not obtained Parliament's support for their immigration, Siti continued her campaign, dedicating her time outside work to their cause.

"We think this is a matter of humanity that should not be subject to Party politics or personality attack," she said. "Guest workers benefit the whole community."

Bhakarian miners came to Meannjin for conferences and stayed with her in the unit she rented in an almost empty building near Abajoe. She used her savings to set up a studio where she could conduct meetings across the nation.

One day, when he was visiting her, she asked him if he would speak to her supporters about the MWP's policy on immigration. He looked around the mean furnishings of her place. The guest workers were poor and he wanted to give in to them but it could fatally undermine his Party's election platform. His mind raced as he tried to find a way to say no without upsetting her. He decided to tell it the way he saw it.

"We haven't got much for them at present, only hope for the future. But I doubt that will keep them happy. I could be stepping into a hornets' nest."

"Well, you don't seem to have the courage of your convictions!"

That stung him. He agreed to do it, sat at the rickety dining table and planned what to say to defend their policy. He wanted to take a hard line, but by the time he had written his speech, he had come over to a view that guest workers could stay permanently once they had fully contributed to provision of the water and energy infrastructure they would need. When he told her of this proposal, she rejected it outright.

"That's absurd. The Bhakarians don't have any spare money. They are supporting relatives in Bhakaria. Why can't you give them what they want without making such a song and dance about it? You are supposed to be generous and a sharer!"

His answer was to talk about his responsibility to Australians.

"I call it racism," she told him.

It was a contest of two iron wills. He saw the tightening around her eyes that betrayed her anger and noticed how his own voice had a sanctimonious, hollow ring. There should have been compromise but neither of them was willing to give way. All he conceded was that he would help the guest workers if he could.

Usually they got on well and she shared his attitudes on most matters. However, there was a fundamental rift between them concerning the guest workers. It was unfair of her to use him to advance the guest workers' cause. Perhaps it was her only interest in him. He wondered if her agreement with him on other matters might be a ploy. Perhaps she would like him more if he would make some concession. Perhaps a few guest workers could be accepted by a lottery. He proposed this to her but this, too, was unacceptable to her and compromise seemed impossible.

When it was evident that there was a stand-off, she said she wanted to be alone and it was clear to him that she was sanctioning his non-compliance. He became concerned that once she had finished using him, she would probably dump him. It worried him that she could be concealing negative feelings for him. His instinct was to say "No." He wouldn't do it but he told her he would see what he could come up with after talking with the others. She dismissed him impatiently and they spent the rest of the day apart.

Their relationship continued but as the days became weeks and the election got closer, prompted by Siti's agitation, he considered the guest workers' situation very carefully. However, capitulation would have been inconsistent with the MWP's other policies on population and resources management and he held fast. His discussions with Siti became strained. She wanted to know what he was going to do to help her. She had manoeuvred him into a corner where he had to commit to her cause or face her wrath.

Then Paula, who was aware of Siti's representations, proposed that local governments could decide for themselves whether to allow guest workers to settle in their area. Immigrants would be welcomed in some places but not in others. The idea had merit because she knew that councils would discriminate anyway, even if the national government approved it. It would replace the central immigration quotas with a local case-by-case determination.

"I think it needs to be more centralised. There could be mayhem," said Peter. "One council could bring in guest workers, who could then abscond to the council next door that has refused them."

"They could keep them out – a ban on immigration could be from anywhere."

"It would be difficult to enforce. I still think we need a central policy," Peter persisted.

"Centralisation stinks," said Paula. "Compared with the failed attempts at communism in Russia and China, we devolve issues for consideration by ideologies that are home grown in the communes rather than imposed from higher up. It will work. Individuals can take care of their birth rate themselves with commune support and with the council's safety net to prevent discrimination."

Peter had no further arguments and he gave in gracefully.

'Paula is so attractive,' thought Peter. He would try to crack on to her now that Abajoe was seeing Siti. Her night with John had turned out to be a flash in the pan. He hoped she would move out from The Tower as she had threatened. It was strange how well the two girls got on together.

"This could be the breakthrough we have been looking for," Siti said, adopting Paula's proposal.

Now it all depended on whether Abajoe would support it.

Abajoe was not impressed. His gut reaction was to reject the idea. He had not liked it when he had looked at it before and nothing significant had changed except that, unless he agreed, he would be shown to be two-faced. That was too bad – in politics, you had to keep your options open. He suspected Paula's intervention was motivated by a desire to split Siti away from him. He was not normally a centralist but devolution of immigration would undermine a cornerstone of their platform, population control. There was no way he could accept it and there was no possibility of a compromise. Remembering the last time he had arbitrarily withdrawn his support from her campaign, he knew he should first talk it through with Siti but there was nothing to say that they hadn't argued about before. To avoid an ugly scene, he wrote to her telling her of his decision.

'The people have given my Government a mandate to decide immigration. We can't pass it back to local government. Our decision is no immigration by guest workers.

'The good news is that the Kurilpa planning tribunal has stopped the proposed Gunyaba development, so that the guest workers will continue to feel welcome.'

She did not reply and the next day Parliament renewed the Guest Worker Policy under the Immigration Restriction Act.

Siti had been away at Mount Argus and when she found out, she was furious. Her face loomed large on his communicator and it wasn't smiling.

"Why did you put the Bill through without discussing it with me first? You promised to help us. I trusted you and now you have gone behind my back."

"It was government business, approved by a committee. It was my duty to the Party. I had no choice. You could have expected that."

"Bullshit. You could have changed it if you wanted to."

"I was in an impossible situation," he said. "It seemed like a set-up."

"A set-up?"

"Like you were using me. I went out on a limb for you over Gunyaba. Yet you weren't satisfied with that. You wanted more and more."

His gallantry stopped him from saying he was suspicious of her motives in their relationship and that they seemed to be based on emotional extortion. If he had said that, she would certainly leave him and he didn't want that. After all, people did use each other and take advantage of their affections.

Siti's voice was hard with anger. "How dare you! As if you are a god on a pedestal! You were thinking only of yourself and your precious Party, all along. You didn't consider me or the guest workers at all."

When most men have to choose between a lover and a career, they attempt a compromise. Abajoe had chosen the Middle Way Party, because he was prepared to lose Siti to test her loyalty to him. She already could destroy his career over his Gunyaba donations. He would risk that to simplify their relationship.

He wanted there to be two separate arenas. In the first, their romance would be decided by mutual affection. In the second, the guest workers' issue would be decided by political science. Behaviour in each of the arenas should not affect the other. No longer would he allow her to use their romance to lever his politics. He would separate the two and find out whether they would still have a romance.

But it wasn't that simple. He realised too late that the guest workers' hopes had been pinned on Siti. They would expect her to have influence with her lover. He should have given her face. They would see she had let them down and her leadership of the group could be jeopardised. It meant everything to her and he should have supported her better.

When he replied to her, his voice was bitter. "It wouldn't have happened if we had been living together!" He was hurt by her lack of response to his proposal to live together. Why should he show commitment when she had shown so little to him? If they had been living together, they would have communicated better.

"Why would I want to live with you, when you behave like this? How could you go behind my back, knowing it meant so much to me!"

"It was just business. You were just one of several players. You shouldn't take it personally. I will help you after the election," he replied.

"It's too late. I am taking it personally. I want to meet with you face-to-face to talk this through. Our relationship is probably finished."

His heart sank. He had taken a risk but hadn't realised the consequences until now. He agreed to meet with her in their local park that evening.

All that day, in a meeting of the Cabinet, he was distracted by the prospect of facing her anger and hurt.

"Hey, Abajoe, what's up?" John asked.

"Nothing," he lied. "I didn't sleep well, that's all."

But it wasn't nothing. Siti was very special. He knew how much she meant to him and it seemed like everything. He tried to visualise her feelings and that afternoon he turned to Lani, John's partner, for help. He went around to their place, a glorious, old wooden house on stumps, where he had coffee with her on the verandah. He explained the situation to her.

"How will she see it, Lani?" he asked her.

"You have betrayed her trust that you would help the guest workers. She has lost face as their representative. You have also accused her of being underhand with you. You have scorned her and her pride has been insulted." Lani counted off on her fingers. "That's five mistakes."

"What if I tell her I'm sorry?" he said, sipping his coffee.

"I doubt that an apology will be sufficient. You must give the guest workers something. On the other hand, if her main interest is to exploit your affections for her cause, then it is probably best that you finish now. Are you sure she's trying to manipulate you?"

He was indignant. "I think she wants me to accept that her feelings for me are conditional on my support for her cause."

"Then if you don't provide that support, your relationship will be over."

It saddened him that Lani hadn't denied his suspicions. Lani hardly knew Siti. She had tried to be friends but Siti had always seemed preoccupied with her campaign. Lani had confirmed his worst fear, that Siti might be using him.

"She has shown no commitment to me."

"But she seems committed to your cause, the Middle Way Party. She has helped you quite a bit..."

"Yes, she has..."

"And she seems committed to your election."

"Yes..."

"Perhaps you need to suspend judgement on the narrowness of her motives and acknowledge the breadth or her involvement in your life. Has she betrayed your trust in any way?"

"No. She's been very considerate, apart from luring me into conflicts of interest over Gunyaba."

"I thought you had worked that out...as a misunderstanding?"

"Yes...you're right."

He wouldn't tell Lani about the donations. Only he and Siti knew. Lani poured him more coffee.

"Then perhaps you should ask her forgiveness for your indiscretion."

"Isn't that going a bit far?"

"That's how much it might take, at least. And you need to have something for the guest workers too."

"That's difficult...all she wants is capitulation...we are locked in."

"Could you jump them forward to the front of the immigration queue?"

"Now there's an idea..."

Abajoe waited for her in the park, on the bridge over the Japanese fishpond. He wore a disguise of a hat and sunglasses to avoid the media. She kept him waiting for 25 minutes, as if she might not come. She recognised him instantly.

"You look like a detective...Peter Sellers' Inspector Clouseau," she laughed.

"That's about how competent I feel," he replied.

They strolled side by side along a bush track, pushing aside branches. The Japanese garden was empty. Its carefully manicured, precise forms had beauty that had been appreciated in their thoughtful restraint. The whole matched their relationship perfectly. They sat down in silence and looked across the lake to a gazebo on an island.

"I want you to explain why you did what you did," she said.

He said he had wanted the matter decided in the national interest. He apologised for not consulting with her but his mind was made up and a discussion with her would only have resulted in a dispute.

"You believed I was setting you up?"

"Not you. When I said I was set up, I was not implying that you had created a situation deliberately. I am not holding you culpable, denying trust in your motives, or pre-supposing billiards was being played. Our involvement with each other is more like lawn bowls, with each of us playing separately for the same side."

"But you went ahead and played your shot, ruining mine."

"I didn't mean to spoil yours. I didn't think about your situation. I just wanted it to be decided."

"You put yourself first."

"Yes. My job seemed more important. I was wrong."

"I suppose you thought you had to consider more than the people I represent. After all, you're a Yabra with a vision for the nation and they're just Bhakarian workers. You can destroy their hopes without thinking twice!"

"If I had let you win this time, what next?"

"Your turn next."

"We have no basis for a quid pro quo. There wasn't enough overlap between us. We don't even live together."

She glared at him. They got up and walked along a path to a cactus exhibit. The plants existed in isolation, braving the harsh environment alone, with their spikes to repel enemies.

He told her then about jumping the guest workers to the front of the immigration queue.

"It's not much," he said. "But your supporters would get something." They looked at a plant with spiky forks.

"We don't want your paltry hand-outs!" she spat.

He told her that if they won the election, he would reconsider the guest workers. But for now he was locked into his decision. A large spherical cactus caught their attention.

Siti turned and faced him. "As for living together, you're not my type." She handed him back the key to his flat. "Words mean nothing to you. Your actions tell me everything. I don't want to go on with our relationship. I hope we can one day be friends. I'll call you in a month's time."

She started to walk past him.

"I hope you find someone you like," he said bitterly.

She walked briskly away, back the way they had come through an avenue of self-contained forms.

He was dismayed and puzzled at this turn of events. Here we go again, he thought. She was the only woman he had ever known who kept him at arm's length for weeks at a time. He didn't know why he put up with it. He tried to imagine how she felt from his betrayal. He had once been betrayed in love and he had lost his trust in that person. If it were the same here, Siti would never trust in him now. It seemed unfair because he had not meant to hurt her; it was a conflict of interests and there had been no room for compromise.

The sadness he felt seemed hopeless. Then he remembered that she would contact him. She had left the door ajar again. When he finished with someone, it was final. Last time he had got back by supporting Gunyaba. This time perhaps he had to let the guest workers stay. It was extortion. She was a dangerous person and he had had enough. He should finish with her.

Paula was different. She didn't make demands. He wondered if he should call her.

That afternoon, Lani brought back his things from Siti's unit. There were his dressing gown, pyjamas, slippers and toothbrush. It wasn't a lot but they had shared so much. He was caught by a heavy rain of sadness in a place that had no shelter.

Some of her Bhakarian friends were going home on holiday and she had decided to go with them.

Gradually, over several weeks, his anger left him and he began to forgive her. After all, the woman-manipulated man was a stereotype. In any case, he was being hypocritical, because he had required her to support his MWP cause. He had to talk to her.

He wrote to her.

Dear Siti

I hope your visit to Bhakaria has been/is enjoyable.

I have been soul searching and come bearing the fruits of my labours for your possible interest.

1. I sometimes think that we have a communication problem. I know you can be wonderfully lucid and I am literate enough that I doubt we are held apart by verbal incompetency. Rather, I think we have chosen to reveal only a part of ourselves to each other. We are both partly in hiding.

2. You may not be aware that I disapprove of some things that you hold near and dear. You won't like me any more and probably less for telling you. If you do not mitigate, compromise or otherwise acknowledge these charges, we'll know that it is incompatibility, not misunderstanding or inopportunity that has come between us.

He then listed a dozen incidents where their differences had surfaced. Then he continued his letter.

3. You wanted me to pay for more. I believe there is no obligation on better-off people to share their resources with the less fortunate except by law. If we lived together, I would share much more with you until, eventually, we have equal shares in everything.

4. You believe I am mean in not giving to your cause. I believe that humanitarian action requires care, not money. Money merely creates dependence. I believe that unreciprocated gifts and those without strings come between people and destroy amity.

5. You believe I go back on my word. I believe that in a relationship, amity is born of actions and empathy rather than verbal consistency. True partners should be able to explore ideas together rather than be pinned down to negotiation behaviour.

6. I think you may be hiding other concerns, I haven't been able to guess at. I hope you'll have the courage to tell me. If there is serious antipathy on some of these points, then we could talk about why we have those differences, where they come from and how our different perceptions make us feel.

7. While I have been writing the above, I have become convinced that our verbal relationship has been lacking in something, maybe honesty. I would describe our verbal relationship as terse. I don't feel we have explained ourselves to each other adequately. Do you see that too or is it my imagination?

If we can be more open and honest with each other, I believe our differences would be a healthy diversity. If we were both the same, it would be very dull. Small chance of that!

If you would respond to this by coming out of hiding, then I would do the same.

With love
Abajoe

He sent the letter and waited anxiously to hear from her.

A week passed slowly. She should have been back if she had kept to her travel schedule. Perhaps bad winds had delayed her ship. Or she might be ignoring him so he would stop contacting her.

He ordered a large bunch of red roses to be delivered the next day, Valentine's Day, and waited to hear from her. He was on hot coals, fearing it was over. Then she called him. He received it beside the swimming pool, where he was mixing liquid fertiliser for the gardens.

"Hello, Abajoe. Thank you for the lovely flowers and your message."

"Will you be my Valentine?"

"We have some talking to do. Anyway, how are you?"

"All the better for talking to you. Where have you been? How are you?"

"I'm good. I came back from Bhakaria on Sunday and I've been back at work."

"How was Bhakaria?"

"I loved it there. It's so different. People are considerate, social and cultured in Yamism. They are immersed in it. It protects them from despair. They don't have much, but their lives are rich."

"Did you feel they would be better off if they had our lifestyle?"

"What, population control, fewer people and more space? They wouldn't like it. They felt sorry for me, that I lived so isolated and alone."

"A healthier, outdoor, sporting lifestyle?"

"They are envious of our opportunities to play sport and enjoy nature. But they're not unhealthy. Epidemics affect mainly poor districts. If you are checking your assumption that the guest workers will return and help bridge between the two cultures, I doubt that they'll have much effect. The two cultures are eons apart."

"Did you get my letter?"

"Saying that we don't communicate enough…I have always let you know how I feel. I think you have too – I already knew your attitudes to those issues and you know mine. They are not a problem. We are just different."

"What did you mean when you said I was not your type?"

"I don't remember that," Siti replied.

"So there isn't a communication problem?" he answered.

"No. The way you do things is the problem. I want more consideration."

Abajoe thought, 'Now this could lead to a breakthrough. I will not go on being manipulated.'

"I think you mean we have had power problems," he replied. "We have found it difficult to compromise. I don't want to continue like that. The last few weeks have been miserable."

"They have been difficult for me too."

"I've done a lot of thinking but I'm not sure what to do," Abajoe said.

"You have been doing what's best for you and that's no criticism," Siti told him. "But I need more than that. I need more consideration."

"If I don't look after myself, I won't be there for other people. There's a lot to talk about and we should meet. How about dinner at 'The Interior'?"

The following evening, they met at the restaurant and enjoyed a traditional dinner of kangaroo fillets, sweet potato, Chinese greens and strawberry strudel. Their conversation was nervous and both were reluctant to address the real issues between them. When they had eaten, Abajoe delivered a short speech he had prepared that he hoped would mend his betrayal of her cause.

"I apologise for leading you on about helping the guest workers. At the start, it was a possibility. We could have changed our policy. But the debate results ruled it out. We can't do a U-turn – the politics of the situation have made it impossible. My loyalty to the Middle Way Party rules it out."

Siti's voice was sad. "It is clear to me now that your loyalty to your Party is more than your loyalty to me."

"Yes, if it goes right down to the wire, I suppose it is," Abajoe admitted. "I will not compromise my political career because my family are counting on me. They have nurtured me for this job. I suppose my loyalty to them is greater."

"But my career requires me to be loyal too," Siti objected. "I never expected it to be diametrically opposed to yours."

"No, it is not a zero sum game," he said. "We can both be loyal to our people and still overlap in other things. Only the issue of the guest workers has split us apart. We have so much in common. We both believe in personal independence – we have big personal spaces but we believe in self-altruism and community with others."

"We do share interests in history, culture, art and transcendental meditation, don't we? We are both optimistic and existential."

"It would be terrific to have you on our campaign team," he enthused. "If you like, I will give the hot potato of Immigration to someone else. That will avoid friction between us."

"Hmm. Better the devil you know...leave it where it is, thanks."

"I am sorry for leading you up the garden path. I won't do it again," he promised. "Can we get back together?"

She accepted his apology. In future, he wouldn't make promises to her that he couldn't keep and she wouldn't seek from him political results that were outside his control. He needed to be flexible. A little reluctantly, she agreed to resume their relationship.

It was a separation of their trajectories and it strengthened their relationship. But his doubts about Siti's motives continued. Her affection for him had not been thoroughly tested. The evidence he now had overwhelmingly supported her using him and he should finish with her. He would be wary and look for an opportunity to decisively test her affection for him.

CHAPTER 36

Inertia Testing

Paula and Abajoe had met at Party Headquarters under the stadium to finalise some policy details. They looked in at a studio where John was making a publicity piece.

"Well, will you look at that!" said Paula in disgust.

"What?" Abajoe spun around.

"Over there, on that monitor," Paula pointed, her hand trembling.

She was looking at a monitor where a news camera showed miners holding 'Elect Sudarta' placards. Standing shoulder to shoulder with them was Siti. They were rowdily protesting during a speech by the local Mount Argus MWP candidate. It was a live news look at election events in provincial centres. He couldn't hear the sound but he guessed that the story was about the contradiction of his well-known partner's participation in the protest.

"Shit!" said Abajoe, thinking what his reaction should be, if any. This had always been on the cards.

"Yes," said Paula.

There was silence for a few moments.

Paula said softly, "Well?"

"Well, what?" repeated Abajoe, biting his lip.

Paula's voice menaced. "What are you going to do about it?"

Stalling for time, Abajoe said, "Do?"

"Yes, do!" snapped Paula.

She stood glaring at him. Although she was resigned to Abajoe having finished with her, she still cared for him in a sisterly way and was concerned that Siti was taking advantage of him. Now she had gone too far and Paula's patience had snapped.

'This is the last straw,' he thought. He could not have his lover actively campaigning against him.

He confronted Siti when she called him on her return to her Meannjin flat that evening.

"What were you doing at Mount Argus?" he asked, trying to sound casual.

"Trying to get my lot to vote for us."

"Not for us. For Sudarta. I saw you on the news. It looked as though you were leading a protest against the local candidate," he accused.

"What? It must have been some pretty fancy editing..."

Abajoe felt his pulse quicken. He could not tolerate dishonesty. Instead of helping their campaign, she spent her time lobbying for the guest workers. It was making him look foolish.

"More like double-crossing!" his voice was just short of a yell. "I want to talk about this face-to-face. I'll come over..."

When he arrived at her place, she greeted him silently.

"This looks like the end," she said, seeing the grimness in his face.

He didn't reply. She gave him a bowl of soup she had made. It was good. They made small talk while he ate but the atmosphere was strained. When he had finished, he put down his spoon.

"Tell me, what were you doing at that rally?"

"Trying to get the miners to support the MWP."

"It looked like the opposite. You looked as though you were demonstrating against the MWP! All you seem to care about is your precious guest workers! You should be helping us to get elected. You don't seem to care for me at all. This has gone on long enough."

He hoped that she would refute his words, showing she cared for him but he was disappointed. His mistrust had stung her. Her eyes were cold, daring, goading.

"Why don't you end it then?"

Her tacit acceptance of his accusation and the indifference of her challenge hurt him. He couldn't accept them. His anger rose and spoke for him.

"Okay...I will. I'll leave now."

In slow motion, he stood up and she held the door.

Neither of them said anything. They had been together for three years.

He walked away sadly in slow motion, noticing details of her place for the first time. Now it was too late. Without her, everything had suddenly changed. His senses were reeling, disoriented.

He needed support and he immediately thought of Paula...how he had used her but hadn't meant to...how she had gone with John...he would forgive her and trust her again. It was his own fault. Now he would make it up. When he got home, he would call her.

She answered him in her quiet voice.

"I've finished with Siti," he told her.

"Are you sure?"

"Yes."

"Why?"

"I think she's been using me." Paula had told him this previously. Now she said nothing. He had thought she would be pleased.

"What do you think?" he asked, to say something.

"What does it matter what I think?" she countered.

"I want to get back together, permanently," he said lamely.

"Oh no, that isn't possible. Is that why you finished..."

"No, not exactly. But we used to have a good thing going, before..."

Siti had taken him away, after a few days, he remembered, from Paula who had been with him for a lifetime. Paula, who would not allow him to have a mistress.

"No!" Paula said with bitter finality. "You are too late. I'm not going back to that again."

Rebuffed, he ended the call. His commitment wasn't enough. He had hurt her and she had vengeance within her. He was numb. She had been his insurance when he had risked everything with Siti. His job made him so exposed. Paula had been his backstop in case Siti wasn't suitable. He had been counting on going back to her if it didn't work out. He thought she would wait for him. She had loved him before. She meant so much more than an adopted sister to him. He knew that her rejection was final. He had lost her...the two important women in his life had gone. He had never been totally alone before and he could hardly bear it.

Siti was gone from his life. It seemed like the end of all joy. She had injected a passion for life into his veins and he had been hooked. Could he keep going without her? He tried to imagine how he used to feel before they got together but he couldn't.

He wandered aimlessly through his home. The rooms seemed empty. A tap dripped noisily in the cavernous silence. Angrily he turned it off. He listened to his breathing. It came in gasps, unevenly. He could feel his heart pounding in his chest. He might forget Siti better if he ate something. She had left half a bar of dark chocolate in the cryolyzer. He chewed greedily. It was bitter with a little sweetness and he ate it all. It didn't matter if he got fat. No one would care.

In the dining room, she had left a scarf draped over the back of a chair, a memento of her presence. It was bright orange and he remembered the orange chiffon outfit she had been wearing and her appearance, on the surreal side of flamboyant. He held the scarf to his face, remembering the feel of holding her when he had hugged her earlier that evening. Her body had quivered and throbbed like a wild bird. She vibrated with energy.

The silk of the scarf was soft and smooth, reminding him of her face and hands. He sniffed it and her smell, a pure flower note, flooded his senses. He sobbed, grieving for her, because she was gone from his life and nothing would ever take her place. He sat down and held his head in his hands as his lungs convulsed, air grunted through his larynx and hissed staccato from his nose. He gasped, blinded by tears and sobbed again and again. It didn't matter if she was using him. It didn't matter if she wasn't perfect, he loved her the way she was. But it was too late and she would never have him back.

He knew Paula would never tell. Perhaps Siti might forgive him if his explanation was honest, leaving out Paula. What if he begged her to have him back? Siti would not like it that he had used Paula to cover his exposure to her, but that had fallen through. He didn't have to mention it. It was too late tonight and she would have turned in. He had time to think it through calmly so that he could explain to her and recall the occasions of her neglect that had multiplied in his mind. They had been sufficient then and he wanted her to know exactly how she had upset him.

He went to bed. Before he fell asleep, he remembered that Siti had shown she cared for him. She was attentive in her own way. He had been unduly suspicious of her. He felt foolish and regretted his hasty action. He had changed his mind. Now he was too tired to think what to do. Perhaps he could undo the damage tomorrow when his mind was fresh. Then he fell asleep.

He had been half-awake, with a letter churning in his mind, when he got up and wrote to her. He wasn't used to being ignored he told her. He had been hurt when she seemed to have cut him off. He had thought he was addicted to her and had wanted to be free of the habit, without a dependence on her that was not returned. But now he could see that they had depended on each other and usually there was a balance. He had judged her harshly and foolishly. She had obligations to the guest workers that required her to side with them. He hoped she would be able to forgive him.

It was a letter of abject and genuine apology and he signed it 'With All My Love' and sent it.

She should feel sustained by his addiction thesis. The problem had been his excessive need for her presence. He hadn't mentioned the other reason, that he wanted to test her true feelings for him and that her challenge, that he end the relationship, had been fatally drawn in the heat of the argument, like a bull to a matador's rapier. He had wanted to measure her affection by comparing her loyalty to him as opposed to her mission. Now he saw that her independence was more important to her than their relationship and, curiously, it made him want her even more. He realised that her independence had attracted him all along.

Her reply came that evening.

"I am shocked," she told him. "My feelings are in turmoil and I don't know what to think. I don't want to see you, at least for several weeks."

As usual, she was using time ostensibly to assuage her wounds, but really to test his commitment. He thought her reply showed that she wasn't using him. She must care for him a little. There was hope.

He waited impatiently and, as usual, suffered without her. He didn't bother to open the windows and the acrid smell of sweaty clothes suffused though his mouldy apartment. Dirty dishes built up at his kitchen sink and swarms of tiny midges came in through the flyscreens.

He performed his role in leading their election campaign automatically, without his usual brilliance. His lacklustre performances drew comment from his disciples.

"Are you going to be okay?" John asked.

"Yes, but she is always on my mind," he admitted.

After two weeks, he wrote to her explaining that it was her inertia, her tendency to keep on doing the things she had been doing before he met her, that had led him to suspect that she was using him. She was too intent on pursuing her own concerns at the expense of his. In his position, women tried to use him, he said. He had resented that he had so little influence over how she spent her time. She had seldom joined him in activities, except in bed. In contrast, he had had to be so flexible that he felt vulnerable. She had been dominating him, fitting him in to her very full life besides which his own life seemed unsupported and empty. In a way, he had finished with her to find out just how much she cared for him.

She replied that she hadn't realised that he felt like that but needed more time to consider.

The days crawled emptily by. He remembered fondly their conversations and her amazing skills that balanced his own perfectly. As each day passed, Abajoe realised his love for her with more conviction. After two weeks, he sent her a bunch of red roses with the message 'I love you'.

Two days later, they met and he proposed a compromise that they should spend less time together. She would continue to spend much of her time on the guest workers and Gunyaba, where she was involved in restoration planning. He would be campaigning for re-election. She would cease to dominate his life and their relationship would be better centred. The inertia of her busy life would be balanced by the increased predictability of his life when she had less involvement.

Siti seemed to forgive him but Abajoe wasn't sure that he hadn't hurt her so deeply that she never would recover the trust she once had in him. They resumed a less involved relationship but for a long time afterwards, she was sensitive to the possibility that he might terminate their remaining relationship on a whim.

CHAPTER 37

The Last Supper

There were 12 of them besides Abajoe. Some of them had given up good jobs to join his election campaign. Their bonds from working together in the MWP for more than three years ran deep. They were all now gathered in a restaurant near Party Headquarters to finalise policies for the election in four months' time. The atmosphere was expectant, for they had spent the last week together planning and they knew that this was their final gathering before the election.

From Meannjin there were Paula, John and Peter. From Warringa had come Lani and Rajah. From Flinders there were Andrew and Cassandra, from Swan City Jake and Rafi, from Alice Njeri and from the north Alwin and Siti. Siti was an outsider who had quickly become influential in the Party through Abajoe. She had recently been nominated as the Party's candidate in the rice growing and mining towns in the electorate of Mount Argus. They were all sitting around a long table chatting.

Their reverence for Abajoe holds them together. They suspect he is supernaturally inspired. Even though they are not Christians, they believe he has the Jesus spirit prophesised as a second coming.

John and his partner, Lani, discussed him one day.

"Did you ever know anyone so able to lift you up?" John asked.

"No," Lani answered. "He's a very special person."

"Have you ever seen him down?"

"No. He has a vision that keeps him going..."

"...as if he has a higher purpose..."

"...to help people."

"Like Jesus?" asked John. "Do you think?"

"Jesus claimed to be supernatural," Lani replied. "Abajoe doesn't."

"He says he is quite ordinary but he isn't, is he?"

"No. He's amazing. He knows it too," Lani said. "But he keeps quiet about it. It comes out in his sharing and his skills."

John thought for a moment. "What if he went around saying he was special?"

"People wouldn't like it. They would pull him down like they did Jesus."

"Instead he works from inside the system. He's in a good position because of his family."

"Maybe he's starting something that will improve human behaviour for ever," John enthused. "Technology has not changed people. Human lives have been nasty, brutish and shorter than they could be. We have been mired in a dog-eat-dog competition and it is not improving. He is showing us another way."

"He respects people for what they are, not their position or their possessions."

"Not always, he treated Paula badly," said John. Lani didn't know how Paula had gone to him in despair or what he had done. She had not told John how Abajoe had come to her when he had been fighting with Siti.

"It's not Abajoe's fault that women want him and he has to choose," she said. "It's difficult for him to know if they are using him for his position or money."

"I suppose so," John replied. "Do you think Siti is good enough for him?"

"Yes, because she is so independent, like him. They balance each other."

"He's the dreamer and she's the realist," he said.

Lani nodded. "Together, they may make his dreams come true."

"Let's hope so," replied John.

The disciples never tired of recounting the legends of his self-altruism, his ingenuity and the brilliance of his vision. Although Abajoe was at pains to dispel the image of a cult leader and abhorred his own charisma, their admiration was devoted and uncritical. They would do anything for him.

When Abajoe stood up to address them, there was immediate quiet. They could hear the poultry squawking in the egg-laying boxes on the floor below. As usual, he was dressed in a saffron coat over an ankle-length white robe.

"This will be our last supper before the election," Abajoe began.

"Are you going to be crucified?" asked Myrtle.

Twelve pairs of eyes bored into his face. He gave a light, relaxed laugh.

"Don't expect us to win the election by divine intervention. We will win by the example of our civilised behaviour..."

"How do you know that New Science will work?" Jake asked nervously. "Do you have...er...divine inspiration?"

Abajoe responded with a smile. "I have been trying most of it for years, with success. It works. People want more say in how they live. As for divine inspiration, I have self-altruism instead of a religion to inspire me. Self-altruism is a moral code that will ignite and lead our nation forward." He faced the group, with his hands apart and palms towards them. "I wish I did have divine inspiration and then I could say, 'Believe in self-altruism, which has been revealed to me'. As it is, self-altruism is an application of Aboriginal practices from the past to governance of devolved collective living. Its inspiration is atavistic. Learning from our past should not be scorned because Aborigines developed it to survive the harsh conditions and to avoid famine. They had the same purpose, as we have today."

Bang! A distant explosion got them on their feet and moving as one towards the door. Gunfire was a signal for fleeing or rallying. It had saved their lives more than once.

"Relax," said Abajoe, beckoning them back. "That was just gas...probably an air leak into a biogas generator. Not sharp enough for guns. But you are right for thinking it could be Sudarta's thugs."

They went back in and sat down.

"I don't plan to be killed but if people vote against us, much of what we hold near and dear will not survive. You've all seen Sudarta's election manifesto. Sudarta would be a SEU puppet and will slash, burn and destroy the civil society that the MWP has nurtured over the past 150 years. She will exploit our spiritual community. She will grow demand for materials to levels that cannot be sustained. She will turn the clock back to an old-fashioned, material economy, where poor people have to work their fingers to the bone making stuff for rich people. All this will happen and if the MWP opposes it, we may not survive. Our lives could be in danger. This election is not for the faint-hearted and if you want to pull out, then do so now.

He paused and looked around the table, making eye contact with each one of them.

"Good. From now on, it is all for one and one for all. Now I want to check that each one of you supports our beliefs: our faith in self-altruism, devolution and New Science. Afterwards, we are going to swear our loyalty to upholding this platform."

From beside him, Siti spoke. "How can we get people to be altruistic when the Progress Party is offering new individual choices, products people want and selfishness?"

Rajah added, "Siti's right, Sudarta is promising new help for people who are struggling. Big Brother SEU will pay."

Abajoe said, "That is the main plank of their platform. We must make voters realise that the SEU will give with one hand and take away more with the other. They will take away the rights of minorities. The Jandus will not have the SEU for that reason. The SEU is Yamen-controlled and the Jandus will lose power. They do pretty well with us."

Andrew shook his head. "It's not as simple as that. The SEU seems okay at first to poor people."

Abajoe agreed. "Yes, that's true. Famine victims and immigrants, who are alienated from government control, have a cargo cult mentality about the SEU."

"Their numbers are growing...the minorities have more children," said Andrew. "It is their way of surviving. How can disadvantaged people be better off under our voluntary population controls?"

"By compensation for abortions," said Abajoe. Everyone laughed. "No, really. The Jandus and other minorities would like that especially: they complain that whereas they marry at 30 and have two children, the Yamens marry at 18 and have at least six. It would be expensive. But we should look into that...it may be possible."

"What about compensation too for obeying water restrictions?" said Jake, who was from a dry area with a large river nearby. He was often negative and there were rumours that he leaked MWP secrets to Sudarta.

Several voices said no.

Abajoe answered him. "No, we couldn't give out compensation for that because everyone would be eligible," said Abajoe. "People only have a natural right to a portion of the water harvest. Taking beyond that is theft. There is the same benefit for everyone from complying: protection against famine. We wouldn't compensate them for preventing famine."

There was applause.

"If only the Yamens would accept that logic..."

"They think our policy is biased against Yamism" said Jake.

"We have to get them to read our manifesto," replied Abajoe, holding up 'The New Science'. "Next, I want to go over our policy. It has been a year since it was published and there has been time to find out if it works on the ground."

"Your little-read book," said Jake caustically. "The thoughts of Prime Minister Abajoe. How do you know that New Science will work?"

"The thoughts of the Middle Way Party," Abajoe corrected him. "We all contributed. Anyway, it's read a lot – it's a bestseller. We know it works – ask Siti about Gunyaba."

"It works beautifully," Siti said. "I'll tell you about it sometime."

"Our main activity now should be campaigning for New Science. We can show that scientists are more truthful than politicians by publicly correcting politicians' misuse of scientific reports.

"We can correct the perception that science is esoteric, centralised and elite by publishing reports that can be readily understood, with a devolved viewpoint and accessible by ordinary readers. The failure of the Soviet experiment with science was due to elite centralism, which would be excluded from our experiment in Australia. Communism threatened and persecuted people because of ruthless central control. We have a new type of communism where communities' social purposes are those selected by local people.

"Neither will we condone Westminster dilettantism. We would not have large British bureaucracies led by people without understanding of the technologies they employ. This error can be demonstrated by contrasting leaders who speak knowledgeably about their technologies.

"Our governance would be by elders with seniority in that technology, who would lead the group to a consensus on issues. Our people won't be exploited by self-seeking representatives or systems of voting that pander to ignorance, lies and artificial drama. We can do without representatives employed to kowtow to the media, hide the truth and apply spin dishonestly."

It was a revolutionary campaign. Abajoe summarised the philosophy of New Science and they listened intently.

"New Science is a faith in investigating proposed changes by modelling situations, conducting controlled experiments and analysing consequences. New Scientists engage in self-altruism to support the work of tribunals that ensure change disadvantages no one. A material collectivism emerges that frees individuals from material worries and enables them to transcend."

"How shall we present it to sceptics?"

"Get your community to try it and they will find that people are able to meditate more and will be happier."

"Is New Science just a strategy of self-altruism?" asked Njeri. She was a small farmer who grew fruit and supplemented her income as a casual labourer.

"Yes, that is how everyone can contribute. It seems to work. The projects that tribunals are approving have self-altruism supporting them. Public interest will replace private greed. Australian society will be held together by the objectivity of New Science rather than by any idealistic central control or by the exclusive access of the wealthy to the judiciary."

"Is it communism?" asked Siti. "Many of my constituents' ancestors sought asylum here to escape persecution of communists in Bhakaria. Even if they are still communists, they may not want to break cover. People have bad associations about communism from what happened in the past."

"Communism was threatening and persecuted because of ruthless central control. We have a new type of communism where communities' social purposes are those selected by local people. Each community is different except in its common use of scientific evaluation. The nation would unite for an objective common purpose, such as repelling an invasion. There would be national rights of individuals. There will be no central censorship or controls. New Science encourages individuals to follow their own beliefs so long as they don't impinge on others.

"For example, a commune will not be able to ban the sale of sheep meat unless it is shown that it is unhygienic to eat it. Some religious customs are logical but others are not and they cannot be imposed on others."

"Is New Science radically different or just the application of managerial methods to public sector development problems?" John asked again.

"Very different, a new mindset," Abajoe replied. "People doing science are aware of and declare their own biases, whereas managerialism assumes the organisation has established goals. It does not empower stakeholders who have different goals. They present hypotheses and tests results rather than so-called proofs. Science is the dominant public policy-making discipline, not politics, economics or law. Does that answer your question?"

"Yes, thanks," said John and that seemed to resolve the matter. There were no more questions and Abajoe summed up.

"Sudarta and the Progress Party are saying that New Science is an election gimmick. Before the election, we will put through the legislation for councils to use our model to co-ordinate their compulsory water management and voluntary population control."

He stopped and looked around the table. "Which one of you here will betray us by leaking our plans to Sudarta?"

"Him," said Peter, looking at Jake.

"That's unfair, Peter," Abajoe said. "We have an open group and just because someone questions me, doesn't mean they'll let us down. Quite the opposite: they have wanted their questions answered. There may be some of you here, who haven't felt able to present your objections tonight. I hope you will take them up with me or with one of the others afterwards."

"Some of us doubt that people are as good as you suppose," said Peter. "Self-altruism won't work. People are petty, selfish and prejudiced. They won't share with others, even when they can afford it. People are not generous enough."

"With great leadership, people will be great. I won't let you down. We will all pull together and people will join us creating a new powerful force for change. I predict you, Peter, will pull against me three times before we're elected. But in the end, you will join in with a will to succeed."

That caused a stir. Peter went red.

'He deserves that,' Abajoe thought, 'because he has been wavering all week. Hopefully, that will sting him into mending his ways or leaving the Party. I haven't been able to get him to tell me about what is bothering him. He is an embarrassment to me because he has been so close to me, yet he is showing such disloyalty publicly. I would prefer that he leaves the Party rather than stay and generate disunity from within.'

Conversation broke out around him and he let it run for several minutes. When he spoke, it was quietly, with resolution.

"It's only natural that each of us has his own perspective on our platform. However, we have to pull together as a group or the media will pick us off one by one and destroy our campaign. We have to stick to what we have agreed and keep our reservations until our next meeting.

We'll meet like this again after the election...whether we win or lose. We'll learn from our mistakes and, together, we will eventually succeed.

"What you must do is spread these ideas and activate our Party. It is moribund. Get acceptance of the need for New Science, self-altruism, tribunals and a diversity of lifestyles. Use these ideas in campaigning; explaining the reforms we are planning. Confront Sudarta's ideas publicly. Are you agreed?"

The disciples pounded their approval on the tabletop until the cutlery rattled.

Siti said, "I know some of you believe Abajoe is a messenger from a higher power. I've got to know him quite well and he certainly is a very special human. I have talked with him about each one of you and your friendship and support means everything to him. He has told me that your support makes him special. We have been through some tough times with him and we know his plans are brilliant. Now he has a great re-election plan. If we keep going the way we have been, we are going to shit it in."

More applause.

"Thank you very much, Siti. I'll try to live up to your over-estimation of my abilities," Abajoe told them.

"Let's eat," said Siti.

The food was brought out. Abajoe carried around a basket of bread and as each of them took a roll, he said, "This is the body of knowledge called New Science. Eat this and remember the Great Famine. That it may never be repeated, through the actions we will take."

Abajoe took a carafe of red wine and carried it around the table, pouring each of the 12 a glassful.

"Drink this and imagine New Science is in your blood," he said.

They drank and their glasses were refilled. Following Abajoe's example, they ate in silence, reflecting on the week's experiences. Afterwards, they talked quietly with each other until Abajoe and Siti rose to leave. They came around and shook hands with each of them. "Thank you for coming. I am counting on you," he said. "See you later."

As they watched, Jake slunk out after checking he wasn't being followed. They felt sure he would be reporting to Sudarta. It was going to be a difficult campaign with his opponent informed of his every move.

CHAPTER 38

Election Diary

In the first six months of the election year, Abajoe travelled widely throughout Australia to speak at gatherings, visit workplaces and talk with people in their homes.

When relaxing after spending all day campaigning, Abajoe liked to reflect and keep a diary of his thoughts, as he had done for many years. He considered this introspection as essential for his learning and was his way of preparing for future events.

Below are his diary entries with the number of days left to the election.

DAY – 150

In Swan City staying at Rafi's. Great views over river.

Tonight I have self-doubts and wonder what I am doing here. Am I a good PM? Am I the best person to lead us into the election? Will I be a winning leader? I have a big personal following, more than anyone else in our Party, but it will take more than that. Am I enthusiastic enough in spreading our ideas and getting support?

I haven't had much time as PM to show what we can do. Since taking over from T One, the national election has loomed larger and larger until it affects my every decision. Not that I have had many big decisions – just co-ordinating local governments on small problems, administering our few national policies and taking a lead with a few new ones. Paula looks after the virtual parliament. I spend about half my time in meetings with Heads of State. Rather than winding back for our election, they are coming to bring up issues they think we should include in our election platform, such as renewal of trade agreements. There is little prospect of that as it is local authority business and has to wait until after we are elected, but I am polite.

Today we announced the election date well in advance, so that the novelty of a real alternative, the Progress Party, has worn off. Our main problem is that we have been in power for so long that many voters are looking for a change, any change. Hopefully, by Election Day, the attraction of a change to the Progress Party will have worn off and they'll see that change for change's sake doesn't make sense.

The election game has been transformed into a thriller and that suits me well. I'm in politics for the adrenalin rushes of policy-making on the run, nail-biting debates, media hyperbole and polling landslides. The final contest beckons with vindication of all our feverish preparations.

I have to be exceptional to replace my mother. People are finding I'm very different. My immediate priority is to replace our old Party machine with a new one capable of meeting the challenges. Yabras have always run the Party like clockwork but what we want now is responsiveness to the Opposition's deception, creativity in presenting our proposals attractively and collective decisions that transform us into a vibrant fighting force. The old machine has to be put out to grass but the power brokers want to keep it going. I have to explain why we need to replace it and with what.

People pretend to have read my book and understand it but many don't realise it takes the nation in a new direction: social planning. The media have described our plan as communism, trying to link it back to the state planning disasters in Russia and China three centuries ago. But what I am proposing is a new discipline of self-altruism in local planning, not central planning. There's a world of difference.

The big issue of this election is Bhakaria. Australians fear they will come back despite the Independence Referendum in 2223. Bhakaria's population is bursting at the seams. We are countering boatloads of illegal immigrants by detecting, arresting and returning them to their country of origin unless they have a special case for compassion and redemption.

The MWP has steadfastly declined to develop relations with Bhakaria for fear of attracting attention and this is what the Progress Party would change, beginning with joining the SEU and allowing a tide of immigrants in.

Whereas the Progress Party would centralise governance of Australia by the SEU in Seutosa, the Middle Way Party's plan is for devolution. I marvel at the foresight of my great-great-grandparents, Arnhem and Marta, in devolving the infrastructure of parliamentary control to local government. We consider change first in local planning tribunals. The national government is only for disagreements, with representative voting the last resort.

Some people want Meannjin to be our new capital. There is no need for a permanent national seat of Government. I will work from Meannjin until the election. If we retain office, I will rotate between the other major population centres during the four years until the next election, borrowing staff and office facilities from local governments. They will bid for national programmes in their areas of interest and expertise. For example, Flinders Council's consultants might advise the national government on control of fisheries.

Today, people wanted to know how I would prevent corruption in local government elections and in the allegiances of my central team. The way I see it, some people presently get more than one bite at the cherry. They first have a vote like everyone else votes but band together and pay the media to give their policies a second bite. Then they make promises that buy support and get them a third bite. Along come other groups, professional lobbyists, unions and industries, whose support gives them a fourth bite. Some of these get a fifth, hidden bite by donations under the counter. Finally, they may have to pay off independent politicians, to achieve a majority, with a sixth bite. This is a far cry from democracy where everyone has an equal vote.

All these higher order inputs subvert the democratic process and should be outlawed. Ordinary voters' wants are paramount. If people want to inform the political system, they should approach it with information, not block-voting support or donations. Donations to political parties are cheating and the Middle Way Party is unfunded. Supporters are able to donate their time but that is all.

Without sponsors, candidates have only their own funds and a means-tested allowance. I have my savings from the 'Family Fare' work over several years but I am not as well off as Sudarta's candidate, who is supported illegally by developers. Our followers are often minimalists and meditators. Our candidates seldom have jobs, whereas the Progress Party is led by materialists and developers who have more resources for campaigning. The public regards their campaign spending as fundamentally corrupt and they gain nothing from it.

Whereas we are attacking the Progress Party with concrete evidence of their financial corruption, they have a vigorous campaign of discrediting our candidates with misinformation and malicious innuendo. They have lowered the tenor of the competition and I am concerned about what they may try next.

I am missing Siti badly. We talked for an hour tonight. She is magnificent, spending all her time campaigning and organising the others.

DAY – 100

Flinders, at Andrew's place. It's huge – I am in a self-contained flat he has built, which has a comfortable meeting room where I have been working.

We have picked our team and published the budget we propose if elected. Ours is the leanest of all the Parties because we have only a token national programme. The Progress Party has a fat budget to implement SEU policies in every aspect of daily life. They will have to tax everything that moves to pay for it. With our budget, there is only a handful of us involved and the cost is mainly for Defence, overseas aid, population control and global pollution control. Only a small tax on incomes will be enough to pay for this. Everything else is under local councils.

Local councils will set their own income tax on individuals. We believe taxation of personal incomes is the most just and fairest method of raising public funds, whether the income is consumed, saved or ploughed back into corporations. With this collection method it will be apparent the extent to which high earners are carrying non-earners. An individual's income should determine how much they should share with less fortunate people in the community. Our tax regime is transparent and without lurks and perks, doled out to various groups, as in the past.

The media have been busy trying to show that I am self-interested and our team corrupt. They know their audiences and show them aspects of our lifestyles and policies that seem to conflict, creating a sensation. To poor people, they show me being extravagant. To rich people, they show me being a Robin Hood. To prudes, they show me being immoral. To feminists, they show me favouring males. To males, they show me being effeminate. To heteros, they show me with gays. To gays, they show me with heteros. To dumb people, they show me with the elite. To the elite, they show me with dumbos. To nationalists, they show me with foreigners. To foreigners, they show me with rednecks. To the media, I am fair game. To me, the media are inconsequential and their access to me is the same as a private citizen's.

People expect a lot of a leader. The media's thesis is that I am a sectarian leader in a sectarian society. They have no interest in promoting unity and harmony. As Marshall McLuhan said, "A medium affects the society in which it plays a role, not by the content delivered over the medium, but by the characteristics of the medium itself." The media are subjective, bigoted and self-seeking and this is how voters are encouraged to behave. The media are the enemy of intellectual freedom. The content they deliver is biased and so consequently are the members of their audience. Lest they drag us down to their level, it is best to ignore them.

Goodwill is lacking in the media's spume and under their sustained criticism, we will be lucky to survive.

It is impossible to ignore the Progress Party's campaign against our candidates, which has lately turned to harassment and disruption of rallies by a plethora of dirty tricks. We have responded by exposing their tactics to public disapproval at every opportunity.

I have wondered why Sudarta is playing a dirty game. I suspect that we have upset her by our tactic of diminishing her importance, dealing with her as a SEU lackey. We ridicule her policies by saying those matters would be decided by Seutosa. We suggest she is a traitor under influence of Bhakaria and the SEU. These emphases, sent to all our candidates for use in their campaigning, may have annoyed her.

Siti has gone up north to her electorate but continues to keep the others together on our campaign. John and Lani are running the office. Siti has some tough competition from Sudarta's candidate. Our stance on immigration is making it difficult for her with the Bhakarian miners and rice farmers but Sudarta's racism is not appreciated. Hopefully she'll win. Still missing her terribly.

DAY – 50
At Warringa with Myrtle and family looking over the harbour. Have spent last month in Karrawa and southern interior. Tired and looking forward to getting home.

The Progress Party has announced its policies under the SEU, with centralisation of economic, social and political power in Seutosa. Australia would be regulated rigidly by an army of remote bureaucrats. There would be a barrel of handouts to disadvantaged regions and our local councils would be replaced by agencies of central control. It is the reverse of the empowerment I am proposing with New Science. We are trying to build up trust and compassion between people whereas the Progress Party are removing it. We will attract community-minded voters but a worrying number are being lured away by the SEU gravy train. A surprising number of voters want to have a remote big brother looking after them.

I met up with Marko today. He is down here campaigning our policy on water resources. Warringa is in drought and people are very sensitive about change. He reassures them to support equal rights and fairness.

He said that people are concerned that we are not taking strong central control of water and other resources. Sudarta will move into the vacuum.

"Water allocation should be decided by an expertise like yours," I said. "You are the best qualified to resolve all the competing interests."

Marko shrugged. "Then politicians wouldn't have anything to do. So they oppose that."

"Politics is shit," I said.

The media have whipped up a public debate about how the nation should decide various issues. We had planned that the national government would devolve issues to local government but Sudarta is having a ball exploiting our lack of policies. Morale in our Party has plummeted and there has been an outbreak of factionalism and infighting for positions of spokesperson to match the Progress Party's policy areas, where we have had no one previously. Some members are demanding that we introduce policies that equal the best of the Progress Party's, white-anting our plans for a devolved structure. I have been spending my time explaining why we want a devolved structure and why the Progress Party's policies would destroy Australians' easy-going lifestyle.

The devolution we propose gives out responsibility and authority while retaining accountability. We will encourage local problem solving, local learning and independence. The SEU structure makes locals responsible but doesn't give them authority, retaining dependency on the favour of the centre. I believe this is unnatural and results in alienation and social problems, even if it is not corrupted.

We virtmeet as a Party every week to consider campaigning and policy issues. I try to get a consensus but there are always cases of disobedience and leaks to be dealt with. Invariably these are by candidates who place their own interests above loyalty to the Party. It is discouraging when our Party, which champions collective interests, is thwarted by the selfishness of its missionaries. It is a conundrum that voters want personal attention to their local wants but also want powerful representation in the central arena. In my experience, these wants are mutually exclusive. By plumping for local wants, our candidates appear ineffective in the national context. Sudarta is magnifying implications of this to our detriment.

Sudarta's people include psychopaths. The Progress Party has turned to illegal tactics, with a spate of break-ins and fires at Party offices. We hope the culprits will be identified and linked to them in the next few days.

Siti is still up north but will come back when I do. Am so looking forward to it.

DAY – 30

Arrived back yesterday. Great welcome from Siti and the others.

I'm worried that the Progress Party's policies seem fresh and promising, whereas all we have is the same people touting New Science. It is perceived as an election gimmick and they say if it was any good, we should have done it before. It's a no-win situation for us.

We may not have central programmes to brag about but we are proposing a revolution in the processes of local government. Journalists are suspicious of my book: they are unable to read, and rely on hearsay. It is macho to be anti-intellectual. I am a tall poppy and they try desperately to cut me down. The media focus is on my record, which is rather slender and privileged.

It is evident from their campaigning that the Progress Party does not respect fair democratic processes. If elected, they would probably replace the MWP's democracy with a dictatorship. There is more at stake in this election than being the winner this time round.

DAY – 14

Spending a week in Mirani and the north with Siti, staying at hotels on the road. Mirani now has half a million, many of them Yamens. Local government struggling to cope with rapid growth servicing the new paddies.

The Opposition here claim that the planning tribunal needs a large central authority, as the local government isn't much support. When development is really wanted, self-altruism will provide. It's a fail-safe brake on greedy developers in these frontier settlements where the environment is readily damaged.

Six of our candidates have been physically beaten up by Progress Party thugs. I now have two armed bodyguards on continuous roster.

DAY – 9
Back in Meannjin. election fever. Media demanding and hard to resist.

It's agony this campaign. I sometimes wish I had never become a politician. The enmity, disloyalty and selfishness of the media and personal character attacks by Opposition politicians are very wearing. There is a self-fulfilling lack of respect within the profession. How I long to have time alone with Siti, my family and friends.

There are still swinging voters out there flaunting their apathy. But more people than ever are interested in politics, wanting collective action rather than personal favour. Their hopes lie in collective action. Australians have experimented with collective governance since William Lane and other socialist idealists established a communal settlement called New Australia in Paraguay in 1896. There have been several bursts of social revolution since then. Now we have New Science to take a bold step forwards.

My indigenous inheritance was in focus today and I have explained where my collective philosophy has come from. Although our family have ownership of land, we are careful to allow others access for legitimate purposes, the same way we respect others' rights for their property. We demand that others acknowledge our ancestral rights. We have always sought friendly relations with neighbours. Their support has been our main defence. When challenged, we have sought to assuage others' hostility with persuasion rather than with physical or emotional reactions. When persuasion has failed, even when it is scientific, we have had to resort to assertive action in support of our declared rights.

This approach has been well received, for it contrasts with the might-is-right dogma of opponents of collectivism. Our family has always fostered persuasion and assertive action privately but I am the first Yabra to take it to the ballot box as our method of national control.

We have discovered a plot for corruption of the electronic ballot processing system. We hope to link it to the Progress Party.

I am spending every spare moment in my electorate, going around the commune headquarters. Sometimes Siti comes with me – we always have a great time together.

DAY – 7

I am thrilling with the chase. My blood surges in the spotlight.

In the Primary vote today, we came in with 36%, only 2% ahead of the Progress Party. The 30% vote for minority parties was quite unexpected and we are worried that their votes will be distributed to the Progress Party in the final round when there will just be the two of us running.

The result is a disappointment after our campaign ran to plan. But the Opposition has been scoring points with its expensive advertising. We must score some back by modifying our policies towards bigger Government, a compromise. Many people seem to want welfare to be centralised. Education, too, needs a steadying hand rather than being kicked around in local politics. If we appoint new ministers from the minority parties and they bring their voters with them, we can kill several birds with one stone, but I need to negotiate this quickly.

Paula has taken the lead in putting a public face on the awful outcome of the preliminaries. She is appealing to our strays not to desert us in our hour of need. It seems to be reasonably effective and it may be all that stands in the way of defeat, an invaluable contribution. She has played a huge role in our campaigning and I have appreciated her friendship and support everyday.

DAY – 3

Sometimes I feel predestined but it is a trap. I have to force myself to be self-critical and avoid entrancement by my own utterances. I am resisting fatalism. I have to make my own good luck. Although I am tired of this campaign, I have to keep to my schedule on the stump and bring freshness and magic into people's lives.

My personal following is very strong, much stronger than Sudarta's. I am perceived as a prophet. But I am less outspoken than Sudarta and lead by example rather than through invective. I play the role of the PM of a devolved nation. It is a difficult role because devolution can be mistaken for indifference or even benign neglect. They say my western intelligence and indigenous wisdom combine into omniscience. My weakness is a tendency to righteousness, with preaching and admonishment, which I must curb.

This week John has been wheeler-dealing with the minorities. He has the skills of a Dutch auctioneer. He has compromised our demands to get a taker for the Ministry we are offering. He has almost brokered a coalition with the National Party but they don't have our commitment to devolution and collective decision-making and want us to bring in big Government spending. Apart from our antipathy, there isn't time to agree an acceptable programme. So all we have with them is Minister for Regional Development, who will look after a couple of areas where their vote is strong.

Siti has been very active, talking to women and Yamen groups. She speaks powerfully and has been doing wonders for our support. Our candidates are crying out for her visits and if I didn't know her so well, I would worry about a leadership challenge. It would be good if we could share the leadership, as we complement each other so well. But primacy is necessary and Siti will make an ideal Deputy.

According to polling by the media, it's neck and neck. The nation seems to have polarised on the SEU membership issue but 20% of the voters are swinging. I just have to keep my nerve, show confidence and keep making personal contacts with voters in marginal areas.

DAY – 2

The situation is very tense. I like the adulation, the way people back up into doorways to watch our motorcade pass by. I like the way they try to touch me and how supporters chant my name wherever I go. I don't mind when the media wait for me at all hours and follow me with cameras. It amuses me that they are so misguided, for my philosophy is collective empowerment and it is contradictory and surprising when my leadership is elevated to a pedestal like this.

It is too bad that elections polarise the electorates to extremes rather than moving towards a compromise. It is a flaw of the democratic process that there is no convenient halfway house between devolution and centralisation. We are going to the polls on a false dilemma. People can identify the two positions but are unable to imagine the gradations possible. Consequently, whoever wins will have the challenge of representing the whole electorate, applying the new skills of holocracy, of devising a policy folio attractive to the spectra of interests.

Interest in our policies is wide but everyone gets an equal vote. We have resisted the trend to weight votes by the amount of tax paid. A large proportion of our population lives outside of the economy and has an equal right to be heard.

I am tired and losing patience in explaining our policies to opponents. On virtual visits with voters, I quickly establish which side they are on and hear their reasons. Often they are so entrenched in their thinking that I don't bother to reply but move on to someone else. I am concerned that so many voters are against us but I hope that our supporters will outnumber them.

It has come to light that the Progress Party intimidated at least a few voters in the Preliminaries, threatening reprisals against MWP voters. The police are investigating. The story has not appeared in the media and there is nothing we can do. They can be expected to repeat this in the election.

My debate today against Sudarta's proposition to join the SEU was a litmus test. I felt uncomfortable forced into the stereotype of a parochial and reactionary nationalist. There is no easily identifiable opposite role. The audience's response showed she has enough support to win. Tomorrow's debate will have high stakes and I feel more nervous about it than at any time since I have been in politics.

Siti is a tower of strength. I think she is thrilled by the situation as much as I am. She is tougher and less deterred by setbacks.

DAY – 1

Our situation is getting desperate. Most media attention is turning away. They seem to have sensed us losing and their coverage has an arbitrary bias with many swinging voters climbing on to the bandwagon. The Progress Party can do no wrong. I can't believe the media are so fickle and plumping for a change that will put many of them out of a job when Australia is governed from Seutosa. Perhaps they see that as the lesser of two evils, as we would have little time for them.

T One came on a visit and her presence was reassuring. She was positive about our campaign but I think she believes we have to face the inevitable that people want a change.

The Progress Party's concept of the position of Prime Minister is quite different: Sudarta would spend most of her time heading a large bureaucracy planning and administering programmes by SEU rules. When I point out the difference to people, to their shame, many consider it would be an improvement. It is being brought home to me that a significant number of voters see our devolution proposal as running counter to achieving a stable national role in the region. They are wrong because they have not taken into account the religious divisions within Australia that will resonate with foreign interest, creating instability.

Privately, I am less than optimistic.

Siti thinks we have a chance.

Today's debate with Sudarta could turn the tide.

CHAPTER 39

Science not Politics

It was Abajoe's first election since taking over as PM from T One. Voters would, the next day, choose between Sudarta's new way, with Australia becoming a territory of the South East Union (SEU), and his new way, which would be to replace politics with New Science.

There was a tradition of election-eve virtual debates between the two major Party Leaders, to be broadcast to a national audience. The day before, he had debated with Helen Sudarta her Progress Party's proposition that 'Australia should join the SEU'. During the debate, polling had indicated that Abajoe and the MWP had a small advantage. For today's final debate, they had agreed on the proposition that 'New Science should come before Politics'. He hoped the debate would showcase the constitutional change that was the MWP's major policy initiative. He knew that Sudarta would relish the opportunity to take a reactionary position, since Australia had enjoyed an era of political stability even if her Party had been kept in opposition. But in doing so, she would be inadvertently supporting the MWP's continuing incumbency.

Their host was producing the broadcast from a national network studio hooked up to their home studios. Abajoe was at Party Headquarters at the stadium. There were two robot cameras on each of them, one fixed in front, the other on an overhead arm and able to move around them freely. They could view the broadcast. With a third camera they could watch their opponent continuously, simply by focusing their eyes, causing brain transponders to pull the focus onto each other's face, or push back to study their body language.

They had agreed that neither of them would use this occasion as a platform to espouse their own wider policies. The only issue would be the motion that 'New Science should come before Politics'.

When prompted by their host, Abajoe took his place in his studio chair. The broadcast had started but Sudarta's studio chair was still empty. Abajoe's waiting face was being beamed to 30 million Australians. He welcomed the shot, feigning indifference. Sudarta's late arrival would be seen as rudeness by the more intelligent viewers, whom he was targeting. His research had concluded that only an elite few would change their minds tonight. Yet he had to do the debate to show the flag.

He was obviously ready to engage. He was dressed in a kaftan and relaxed in his chair as he flipped screens, stopping now and then to have a few words with Party colleagues in the audience. When she strolled in late, open, confident and unapologetic, it was evident she meant to show she was used to keeping others waiting. Neither did she acknowledge the Prime Minister, declining to show the customary respect between adversaries. She adjusted the back of her chair, as if her preparation for this event had been minimal. She sat down and ran her tongue over her lip gloss, as if unconscious of the millions of eyes critically watching her, and studied a page of notes. Her thin lips, narrow eyes and aquiline nose underlined her sour temperament. She sat upright with downcast eyes displaying the calm detachment for which she was famous and feared. It belied a lightning-quick mind and her detractors had nicknamed her 'Snake Heart'.

Their host's rotund face filled his monitor. He was well known for his biographical interviews with famous people on his weekly show.

"Ladies and gentlemen," he announced, "welcome to a debate of the motion that 'New Science should come before Politics'. It is between Australia's best-known public figures, Prime Minister Abajoe Yabra of the MWP and against him is the Leader of the Opposition, Helen Sudarta of the Progress Party. The rules tonight are that our speakers will take turns of up to three minutes. We will pause after 20 minutes for home polling, so would our audience register and get ready, as you will only have one minute to vote."

Abajoe had earlier won the roll of a dice and had chosen to speak first.

"When you are ready, Abajoe."

"As you know, we in the MWP have been working towards Australia becoming a spiritual and meditative society," Abajoe began, speaking in a warm friendly voice. "I will show that to rid ourselves of materialism, New Science must come before politics." He spoke forcefully, leaving no doubt that this change would be made if he was elected. "I will explain New Science's strengths and politics' weaknesses to get the future we want."

He looked over to his opponent, giving her the cue to speak.

Her appeal was that of an ingénue who had strayed into the territory of a predator. "Politics has always come before Science and should continue to do so." Her voice was thin and reedy and although her face was too vulpine to be called pretty, she was not unattractive in the same way that a bird of prey fascinates by its deadly purposefulness. "I will show that you would not want to have scientists running this nation. They must stay in the back room where they belong."

It was a blunt attack, trying to draw him into argument on his weakest point at the outset. As reformer of a party that had been in power for 150 years, he had to criticise his own Party and his ancestors who had been its leaders. He was not calling for a complete U-turn, as the MWP had already adopted science in some areas. In clinging to the past, Sudarta too would be in the unusual position of having to extol the virtues of a system that had kept them out of office during all that time.

He began in the traditional way, defining his terms and outlining his case. "New Science has a prescribed method, whereas politics, according to the Dictionary of Empirical Australian, is 'the profession devoted to governing, often involving intrigue to gain authority or power'. I will maintain that we no longer need this self-centred and devious profession."

Sudarta's face had the sharp awareness of a fighter from her ruthless campaign of the past four months. She replied with absolute confidence, rebutting his terms. "Political democracy is a tried and true method of making collective decisions on leadership, in which everyone can participate, whereas scientists think their way of knowing is the only true way, excluding all others. Science is an instrument of autocracy and tyranny."

He responded disdainfully, using each word as a bludgeon. "On the contrary, it was democracy that brought tyrants to power and kept them there. National politics has been a carnival procession of crises that has diverted attention away from solving injustice and poverty. It has been an arena for parades, pageants and ritual contests. Elected representatives apply dilettante, prejudiced and bought reasoning. Politics is entertainment for millions. Always the best entertainer has been elected leader and thereafter run the whole show as a re-election campaign. We in the MWP want the Government to improve conditions without the hindrance of politics. Our Government would be devolved and inclusive, unlike the Opposition's centralism."

Sudarta shied away from his directness. She lowered her eyelids momentarily, then gazed directly into his eyes, an unwavering stare as she spoke, a concentration of hostility with a mesmeric quality.

"You would know better than anyone that people know what they want. They want their politicians to please them. Don't throw the baby out with the bathwater. The MWP has grown tired of elections. Now when they are about to lose, hey presto, they want a dictatorship." She was spitting out clichés like a real estate salesperson. "Democracy is a shining ideal for development of civil society. It has delivered a good and free life to generations of Australians. On the other hand, scientists tend to be narrow-minded and dangerous. It is not by accident that most of them work in back rooms. Scientists do not..."

Abajoe interrupted rapid-fire. "Rubbish. They are not less but more capable. Politicians have stunted their leadership. Politicians have kept them few in number and out of the limelight to stop them influencing voters with non-PC recommendations," Abajoe replied. "Politicians nurture a stereotype of the scientist as an inhumane, dithering person who cannot see the wood for the trees. The reverse is true. New Scientists are more humane and wider in their thinking than most of the population, especially politicians. It was politicians, not scientists, who ordered evil weapons of civilian destruction to be made. Politicians blame science for their failures and claim science's successes as their own."

"No, it is politicians who have curbed scientists' excesses," she answered. "Scientists are good at creating new technologies but it has fallen to politicians to make them take responsibility for unintended consequences and take corrective action. For example, without politicians, scientists would have had us overrun by cyborgs."

When she spoke, her words were evenly spaced in a monotone like a robot. It had been rumoured that she herself was a cyborg. Her face was pale, with a floury look of make-up powder, like a mime artist whose expression is solely by eyebrows, eyes and mouth.

"That is totally untrue. Cyborgs were ordered by the military and deployed by politicians, not by New Scientists. New Science is always sceptical about the benefits of new technologies. It has consistently warned of adverse consequences of cyborgs and scientists tried very hard to stop their development."

"Science merely serves market demand. It is incapable of leadership."

"New Science serves people as individuals. Democracy has been sufficient to create market conditions that have delivered a welter of inessential and wasteful products while ignoring massive poverty. It has not brought better living conditions for the poor. Millions die from starvation every year. It has corrupted professionals as instruments of government policy. Professionals have left societal problems, such as poverty and injustice, for politicians to dabble in, like a flock of zoo ducks. They turn up at feeding times for a generous share of the public purse. They contribute little of value and always manage to look hungry for sponsorship. They woo support. Such a display of servitude wins over many voters. Once elected, a politician is a parasite and reduces the well-being of society."

Sudarta had no ready answer but changed the topic.

Their exchanges came quickly in undefended torrents, an exchange of accusations. They were truths and there could be no defence. They both knew that the debate would be carried by the weight of evidence on one side rather than by any single point of politics, science, logic, ethics, justice or belief. Abajoe continued to list the deficiencies of politics.

"Politicians raise spectres of evil, to gain kudos from delivering us from them. Bipartisan politics has ritual contests like this one. Rather than inquiring and deciding about any real differences in what the candidates are likely to deliver, many voters simply prefer to get on the media's bandwagons. Few voters apply critical thinking skills. Voting is a lottery. We can do without it."

"Democracy is much more than voting." Her face gave nothing away. She eyed him carefully, wanting to catch him unprepared for her next serve. "Its principles of participation and 'one person one value' are unifying. It has held this nation together through some hard times.

"Science is too slow! By the time scientists have concluded their studies, disasters will be upon us and opportunities will have passed us by."

It was an extreme opinion but she presented it as commonplace. So far, they had been playing tennis, with serve and reply, volley and smash, drive and return, trying to force a mistake. He had run steadily through his arguments and Sudarta had kept up. He wondered how much longer he could hold service.

Abajoe's voice rang out with determination.

"More haste, less speed. Politicians like you always exaggerate and try to extract sensational conclusions before results have been obtained and analysed. Politicians like you turn an uncertainty into a crisis and then strut your idiotic leadership. Look at the climate change fiasco. Voting won't elect an accurate leader...just a media sycophant. The media have power over ignorance and they give it to those politicians who have the largest advertising budgets. How incestuous is that? Voting is only good for deciding things like who is to jump overboard from a sinking life raft, for choosing dates for public holidays, daylight saving and public hanging. Such issues are few and far between."

Sudarta tried to dispute this but she did not answer the point and her opposition seemed to be melting away.

Abajoe felt his cause gathering momentum. "For most matters," he spoke bluntly, his words slapping the air, "voting is a method of partisan control over ignorant voters. The people get the Government they deserve and with compulsory voting, the election is especially an ignorant and dangerous process. It is deeply irrational as a problem-solving tool. Voting puts authority in the hands of a person whose only skill is in fronting a political party. Voting devolves responsibility to electors while awarding all the authority to the Government. After election, a politician's grasp of reality may be tested only by other politicians, until the next election. Their reality is inward-looking and dilettante, except in the art of politics."

While he was speaking, Sudarta pulled faces into his camera. He knew she was trying to annoy him, to bring out his overbearing self. She wanted him to be disparaging, dismissive and abrupt. He kept himself from being distracted by her antics.

When the broadcast switched back to her, she quickly adopted a neutral expression and tried a new thread. "To be re-elected, a politician has to listen to advisers, experts...scientists. They..."

He held up a flat hand to stop her words.

"No, they don't. If politicians did take expert advice, I wouldn't be sitting here. History shows that leaders listened to sycophants who pluck half-truths out of context from unfinished scientific studies. National leaders have seldom followed the advice of disinterested scientists. On the contrary, they have tried to intimidate their critics by withholding funding from them, even whipping up a convenient dogma into a quasi-religious fervour and accusing them of heresy, as they did with global warming."

She gave him a pinched, acid look and pursed her lips. "Why should we believe that when New Scientists get into office, they will produce results that are any better than politics?"

It was a nice point, he thought, but if he kept smiling, the audience may not give it much of a rating. "Science will be less corruptible than politics because it has transparent methods and doesn't require arbitrary leadership."

She shook her head. "That won't wash! How would science find a leader to deal with a national emergency, for example, to negotiate with an invader?"

"Well, we wouldn't rely on military advice alone as they used to in the old days!" He swallowed, making time to think. "Response to an emergency should be co-ordinated and decided by a scientific council. They would act unanimously, without the need for politicians."

"That's called a dictatorship," she shot back.

"No, there wouldn't be..."

Their host interrupted.

"Excuse me, folks. Our speakers have had about 20 minutes and we'll pause there to test the water with some home polling. Would our audience now tell us which side of the motion they are on? 'For' is Abajoe Yabra with the proposition that 'New Science should come before Politics', or 'Against' is Helen Sudarta with her opposition that it should not. You have one minute, then polling will close and we will look at the result before continuing."

Three meters filled the screen, FOR, AGAINST and UNDECIDED with a clock face above. The numbers were a blur but slowed as the hand reached the minute and stopped. FOR was 2,368,049. AGAINST was 2,558,776 UNDECIDED was 3,602,421

Their host spoke with excitement. "We have a close-run fight here, ladies and gentlemen. After 20 minutes, we have a cliffhanger, with a huge audience of eight and a half million, breaking all the records. I have never seen an undecided vote as large as this – Helen has a small lead but it could go either way. Now we will continue and poll again at the 40 minutes' mark. Helen, it's your turn."

Buoyed by the polling result, Sudarta seized the initiative.

"Science solves material issues," she spoke quietly, confidently, moving into the attack. "Emotions also have to be considered. People have opinions that should be taken into account."

Abajoe was slammed into a brick wall. It was a killer of an argument. The difficulty he would have was to prevent willingness to compromise seem like overall weakness. Disappointed by the poll, he felt the result slipping away and there was nothing he could do but fight it out, point by point. He nodded, acknowledging the importance of this issue. "New Science knows quite a lot about emotions, their causes and effects," he said proudly. "It can set the ground rules for participation, where personal qualities need to be injected logically rather than accepting the open slather that politicians like to create for their self-aggrandisement. The national parliament could consider matters requiring a uniform response, as when they debated guest worker immigration. People's opinions will be considered every five years in elections, just as they do now, to establish leadership."

"So what will be the difference?"

"Politicians will appoint scientists to run things and then take a back seat until the next election."

Her voice was querulous. "So politicians would win power for scientists to take over...like gridiron with an offensive team of politicians and then a defensive team of scientists...?"

"No! New Scientists are not the defensive. They are the offensive. They hand over to politicians to defend their actions by putting on spin and getting public support for their proposals."

"Let's get this right," she said. "You will have politics, but only at elections?"

"Let me repeat what I said before. There will be voting for representatives but politicians will appoint scientists to run the country. They won't have the opportunity for any pork-barrel spending or other corruption."

"Why will you end voting on issues," said Sudarta, appearing to lose her temper. "It is the basis of liberty, equality and fraternity. If politics is so bad, why don't you get rid of politicians altogether?"

Zooming in on her face, he could see from her irresolute eyes that she was upset and he was delighted. This debate could win the election but he had to show enough humility to avoid provoking those who thought the Yabras were arrogant.

"We will still need politicians, but in a more limited role," said Abajoe, stepping around her false dilemma. "Representatives won't be needed because plebiscites will be a part of daily life. Instead of passive reception of the news, unbiased scientific inquiries will inform voters and measure their attitudes so they can be acted upon."

"What absolute bullshit!" spat Sudarta. "The idea of unbiased inquiry is a myth. Every investigation begins with a point of view, someone's problem and it is therefore biased in his or her favour from the start. Scientists would run the country based on the polls!"

He continued in a hard voice, slicing the air. "No, our surveys will be about personal values rather than affiliations and preferences. Scientific reports will have to declare to whom the problem they are investigating belongs and who may be adversely affected by the scientists' bias. New Science will be the master tool of one or more visible stakeholders...not the exclusive tool of central authority, Government or corporations."

"I am glad you recognise that science reports have been biased. But I don't think anything can be done about it. Under your proposal, reports would become elite, esoteric and beyond people's understanding."

"No, you are wrong," he said, shaking his head. She was choosing her rebuttals carefully as if she was nearly out of ammunition and saving it for points she could win. "There will be a revolution...a resurrection of the objective spirit. It has been buried since the middle of the twentieth century. New Science will reclaim the attribution of causes from the subjective and blinkered methods of politics, law, religion, ethics, economic arts, anthropology, sociology and psychology." He listed them sardonically as if they were endlessly awful and nothing could be done except throw out the whole lot with politics, kit and caboodle.

"Is that all?" she asked sarcastically. The audience had professionals in these disciplines who would be concerned for their future. She was trying to ridicule his proposal to reduce their roles.

"Ultimate causalities are unknowable and belong to God," he heard her saying.

"Rubbish," he declared. "Science can find out the cause of most practical problems. Many scientists meditate to discover ultimate causes."

Unintimidated, she kept on in her flat voice. "Your scientific agencies are going to be in a quandary. Causalities are always tentative, subject to falsification and qualified by confidence. There is no gain without risk,

349

as every businessperson knows. Deep analysis is a waste of time. Governments are elected to solve problems, not test hypotheses. We prefer a can-do approach..."

He felt the full force of her disdain blocking his persuasion and momentarily despaired of ever having his proposal accepted.

"It's an approach that has to be canned!" he said. "You have asserted that we should accept fatalism. Now listen. Science denies that causalities are unknowable. Governments should not take risks with people's welfare and with community resources when they can afford to wait for investigations to reach conclusions. I prefer a can-get-it-right philosophy. We should delay to be sure that the cause is real. God, all Gods, will have to defer to ecumenical science, a least common denominator of beliefs."

At last she had yielded and he was free again and gathering momentum. But his ascendance was halted when they stopped for a commercial break. Both he and Sudarta stood up and walked about, sipping water. The monitor showed an advertisement to recruit workers to a vegetable producing commune. It showed people working together, picking up the carrots turned up by a plough. The workers were chatting happily.

"If they have common roots, they'll share anything," their host joked. The three of them laughed.

The next advertisement was by a company selling agricultural robots.

"How would you train a robot to harvest carrots?" Abajoe asked.

They shrugged and looked at him.

"Negative reinforcement," Abajoe said drolly. "Offering a carrot won't work."

"You would have to stick it to it," said Sudarta.

They laughed together.

'Sudarta only seems like a reasonable person as a front,' Abajoe thought. 'Underneath she is a dangerous psychopath.'

Then their host asked them if they were ready to go on. They eyed each other, waiting for the other to speak first.

"Please continue," their host said.

Suddenly they were both talking at once.

"Okay," their host said. "Abajoe, you go first. Helen went last before."

"New Science will reconcile the present with the past, not just write on a tabula rasa," Abajoe said, launching his flagship issue. "In the past, developers have been able to get away with murdering people by theft, pollution and destruction of human and natural habitats. They have had their scientific lackeys front their dirty work. When scientists are in control, science will not be used to steamroller communities. Compensation will have to be fully paid for the change to be approved. It will prevent social policies that redistribute value and wealth but reduce overall community welfare."

"Can scientists measure winners' and losers' value and add them up?" asked Sudarta.

To find his point unopposed, after bearing the full force of her sustained opposition, was liberating but unnerving. Was she genuinely persuaded? Had she given up? Was she egging him on to recklessness? If only he could see behind her mask!

Abajoe spoke with passion. "What local communities value is progress towards their goals. New Science will provide a national vision for achievement of those goals without them being sidetracked by adversarial party politics. Politicians care most about looking good and being re-elected. They have learned their trade at university in an elite, clubby context. They have learned how to factionalise contests, how to ritualise character attacks, how to distract with arguments that lack relevance, how to give the appearance of logical correctness and how to work behind a smokescreen of technological ignorance. Their rhetoric reeks of fallacies to deceive an ignorant public audience. New Science will rescue the public and empower them with truth."

Her tone was acrid. "Science wants to corner the market in truth. Scientists will get the power and no one else will have a say."

He shook his head emphatically. "New Science's power is open, not exclusive like politicians. With science, you don't need to be voted in..."

"...more's the pity!" she interrupted.

"New Scientists' power rests in their expertise," he ignored her. "Not in belonging to an exclusive club of deceivers!"

"Bah Humbug," she scoffed. "Scientists have to have a doctorate. If that's not exclusive, I don't know what is!"

He frowned. "That's a myth. Anyone can be an expert under New Science – a doctorate is not required. The accuracy of their data and arguments qualify them, whereas a politician has to have psychopathic ambition to join a party, get nominated, pay a deposit, win an election and then do it all over again within the party to become a faction leader and have a say. A politician is not the sort of person we want solving issues. A politician is deception personified. A politician is centralised, uncompromising, divisive and makes his or her appeal to rhetoric and emotion rather than to objective measurement and logical analysis. Instead of a cost benefit analysis of competing proposals, you get candidates lambasting each other with scurrilous character attacks. Who wants that?"

"We do!" replied Sudarta. "A politician has the drive to be a leader. Democratic leaders are held accountable for their actions every few years by elections. Their decision-making record is scrutinised in a contest for re-election and if they have been reckless, voters will withdraw their support. How will you ensure that New Scientists have public support, except by democratic elections?"

"By voting, but not by politics," Abajoe appealed with both hands open. "That's why we will retain national and local government elections. Democracy will be a tool applied at intervals to legitimate the tenure of top officials. The representatives will merely appoint scientific bodies, with voting as a last resort, when collective commitment is wanted."

"When would that be?"

"When an issue appeals to the emotions, such as the brain enhancement issue."

"Then for other issues, New Scientists won't be accountable to anyone!"

"The merit or otherwise of an expert's scientific work is visible to co-workers," he explained patiently. "Reputations will be made and lost depending on a New Scientist's contribution in his field. This will be the criterion applied in appointing scientists to the organs of state, such as tribunals. This will bring unhurried reason to bear on development applications. The national tribunal itself will be appointed by Parliament. The work of the tribunals, commissions and review committees will be evaluated when the Government seeks re-election."

"Nevertheless, politicians are skilled in logic," she said grasping at straws. "Politicians are skilled in media..."

"Competing ideas should be evaluated by a tribunal rather than by the drama of trial by the media," he continued. "The media cultivate unduly strong emotions, focus on sensational perspectives, create illusions and marshal them to access the confidences and funds of politicians. They encourage the king to appear in new clothes and record it to use against him when he would go his own way. The media's role in democracy contradicts New Science...we want transparent and logical consideration. The media and democracy have aims that conflict with New Science. They should take a back seat."

"I agree about the media being less opinionated but not that democracy is at fault. A few politicians are show ponies but most are honest and hardworking. Their skills hold the community together and keep development happening."

Their host interrupted. "We're at the 40-minute mark and we'll pause there for our final poll tonight before you vote in the election tomorrow. The debate will continue afterwards for another 20 minutes but there will be no further poll. If we were to have a final poll tonight, it might weight tomorrow's voting too much on the performance of the Party Leaders in debate on this single issue. Now, cast your votes. You have one minute."

When the meters stopped, FOR was 4,766,391. AGAINST was 4,343,812. UNDECIDED was 1,439,026

"Abajoe has taken the lead but it is only 4% of the total vote whereas 14% are still undecided," said their host. "The number of voters in the audience has greatly increased as people have heard about the excitement and joined us. This is the largest voting audience we have ever had and it shows that this issue and the leaders' debating skills are of tremendous interest to people, but tomorrow the election could be decided quite differently. Now we'll continue for another 20 minutes."

Abajoe was pleased but he knew that the polling in this pre-election debate indicated little other than leader preferences. These had contributed less than 50% to votes cast in election voting. Voter preferences for the Parties and their policies on issues would be more important in casting their votes tomorrow.

"Okay. Abajoe, it's your turn."

He had some big points left. He would try to hold the initiative by delivering a series of broadsides that would finish Sudarta off.

"Politicians operate in gangs, with opportunism that is random, sudden, arbitrary and decisive – a type of mob rule. To be successful, a politician must toe a party line rather than pursue the interests of electors."

"Scientists won't deal with the public at all. They won't even exhibit their methods to public scrutiny. They won't let you even ask a question unless you have a doctorate. They will be a law unto themselves."

"Most people want someone honest and expert to make the hard decisions for them."

Sudarta, who was lying back in her chair, linked her hands behind her head. "Isn't that why we have parliamentary representatives, to test the local water, talk with the experts and input into a central debate?"

"Most parliamentary representatives now do not have enough science skills to make an objective assessment or to input to a reasoned debate. In future, politicians will depend on scientists rather than scientists on politicians."

Sudarta laughed. "What nonsense."

"New Science will relegate politics," Abajoe continued. "The Middle Way Party's faith in science will displace the historic traditions of religion, law, ethics, economics and psychology. There is a tool bag of empirically validated scientific methods called management science or managerialism. It uses techniques such as econometrics, statistics, modelling, simulation, operations research, behavioural and cognitive science and neuroscience to solve problems. New Scientists will use them to run the machinery of government, allocating work to the tribunals, commissions and review committees. Issues will be decided by reason and ecumenical values rather than by a partisan head count. Real problems can be solved by scientists when people allow them to concentrate and don't distract them with politics."

It was the nub of his proposal but his answer had been irritable and short rather than persuasive. He was feeling spent. He had been campaigning or travelling every day for months and needed to rest and catch up with himself. She was getting to him, wearing him down. He knew that was her game.

"A politician is a leader who relies on advice by scientists, lawyers, business people, Government administrators, clerics, educators, military analysts, welfare agencies, NGO leaders and religious leaders. Why should one advisor, science, be empowered to take over the leadership and do away with all the others?"

A muscle ticked in Abajoe's temple. He felt self-conscious. He was aware that all eyes were on him. He shunned the limelight as he had always cherished his privacy. He knew that the eyes were willing him to make a mistake, to show weakness. He had to stop watching himself in a mirror or he would make a mistake. He felt fear of this woman for the first time. She could win.

"Scientists are able to apply the expertise of all the others to problems. They would be there in the background. The politician does not have the necessary epistemological understanding to obtain and apply scientific knowledge or to reach valid ecumenical agreement."

The cords in Sudarta's slender neck tensed. She smashed back with her defiance. Her tone was ridicule. "Science does not have any ecumenical qualifications. You are trying to throw out religion and authority and expand the role of science to take their place. It can't be done. In most problems, cultural meanings are religious meanings. New Science has no way of taking them into account. Their cultural effects are emotional and can't be impartially observed. When science tries to include these, it imposes its own religious authority in the guise of 'objective' science. Is Abajoe saying that his New Scientists will be better judges of cultural meanings than our leaders? Our religion goes back 1000 years, longer than science. Science is a Johnny-come-lately. Surely our leaders have more experience?"

Sudarta leaned back confidently. Abajoe knew that as long as the debate kept to the abstract, Sudarta would be able to sustain her assertion that New Science had little to offer. He had to ground the issue in a concrete example where Sudarta's cultural values could be reduced to reactionary dogma.

Sweat coursed down his forehead. He shook his head vigorously. "The Aboriginal component of our leadership on this continent goes back far longer. For 50,000 years, our civilisation lived in harmony with the land, the vegetation, the kangaroo and other marsupials. Kangaroos adapted to the harsh and uncertain climate with control of their own fertility. Like the vegetation, they could survive drought with little water and multiply rapidly when the rains came. We understand the problems of population, water and food here. We have learned to use the firestick to maintain kangaroo forests and limit defoliation and death of trees. We have learned to limit our fertility too. We have learned to limit our children to the replacement rate of two per couple.

"Your Progress Party has refused to engage with these problems. Yamen cultural leadership asserts religious values from a foreign environment when the earth was almost empty of people. Now, it directs individuals to have children they do not want even when there is over-population. Quite clearly, the cultural values they hold so important are nothing more than a device to promulgate their religion as a competitive strategy that ignores the welfare of their followers and imperils the rights of the rest of the community. We will be better off if Yamen extremists consider the whole of the community, not just their own members."

As Sudarta listened to this, her face became red and her voice was raised in anger.

"We have a right to expand our religion," she asserted. "We encourage our members to have as many children as they can afford. Who do scientists think they are, trying to impose birth control? You say that our leadership is following a competitive strategy but are you not doing the same in advocating population control? We both want more followers. Which is worse; the possibility of famine or denying people the right to have children? Who will feed us when we are old if not our children? When you preach population control, are you being any less dogmatic than the ancient scriptures? The word of God confirms that individuals have the right to have children. That dogma has stood the test of time. New Science is trying to tamper in cultural matters of which it has no experience. The people won't accept it!" Her voice was a yell.

"Stop," said their host. "You may not shout. Cool it, please."

Sudarta lowered her voice and spat out her words. "You are setting yourselves against our religion and you will regret it."

'No," said their host. "You may not make threats. If that is repeated, I will have to stop the debate."

Abajoe knew the threat would not have done Sudarta any good. She had not refuted his community responsibility argument and had merely asserted the authority of the Kitab. It was a weak argument for non-Yamen people. Abajoe decided to deliver his knockout blow.

"New Science is not against your religion," he said. "We want all Australians to consider which is best: to follow your advice to keep having children as long as they can afford to buy food, or to voluntarily adopt birth control before the food starts running out."

It was a false dilemma and Sudarta fell for it. She had lost her self-control and with it the possibility of compromise. He thought he could hear a slight quaver in her voice but he couldn't be sure.

"This is blasphemy and if you impose New Science on us we will begin a holy war against you. Our community lies..."

Their host stopped her. "I said no threats. If you make one more threat, I will cancel the debate. Now continue."

Sudarta gripped the arms of her chair. Speaking precisely, she aimed her words at Abajoe like bullets. "We will not have you dictate to us. Our community lies within our religion and we will not have scientists tell us what we need. We are guided by the holy Kitab and that has decided how we live."

It was empty religious dogma. Her rational opposition had fallen away. He was in the clear and gathering momentum as the winner.

"New Science believes disputes should be solved by reason rather than by war."

"Well, New Science is not in control, thanks be to God. Why should science be accorded such a privileged and powerful position?" Sudarta asked despondently.

Abajoe wondered if this could be a trap.

"It is just another philosophy," she continued. "Why should it not be one of the several voices that politicians listen to?"

"Science is a voice that embraces all others," he said cautiously.

"No. Not Yamism. It is a religion that believes in the evidence of the senses without moral control, by science or by any other system of beliefs..."

"What evidence do you have for your beliefs?"

"Spiritual evidence of a controlling God ..."

"These are delusions...your evidence does not really exist. Science has objective evidence with which everyone agrees. It is an enterprise for the systematic gathering and organising of knowledge, or cognition. Humans are cognitive animals and science serves the motive to know and to understand."

"Not everyone has deified that particular motive the way scientists do. Curiosity killed the cat. Some humans are also religious or ethical believers and they would rather be directed by moral precepts. They don't want to know or understand. For them science is an anathema."

Abajoe felt tired. He regretted agreeing to take part in this and wanted it to be over soon.

"Time is almost up," said their host. "Helen gets to choose the final topic."

"Why does science want to go public?" she asked. "It is influential working behind the scenes. What has happened that it needs to come out from hiding now?"

"Science has been mighty influential in explaining the worth of projects, with the build-up of projects seeking funding being unblocked by the log-rolling skills of politicians. Politics was okay for the rough and tumble of materialism, but it was usually corrupt and it has ridden roughshod over communality, culture and diversity. With materialism disappearing, the materials that remain have shared uses and that is where our society is growing. Scientists want to explain the essential uses of materials with the kind of honest zeal vegetarians have for preserving animal species. Scientists have the skills to do this and politicians are fresh out of a job. New Science will take the lead in providing the material security necessary for spiritual lifestyles."

He saw fear in her eyes but she set her jaw and brazened on without answering his criticisms, as if all that counted was an appearance of certitude amid a snowstorm of words.

"If science really has a better way of leading Australia, it would already have taken over naturally," she said. "The MWP is seeking a mandate from this election to make scientific advisers into decision makers. But scientists make lousy decision makers. Science needs politicians to be in control. Public policy is not simply a matter of rational objectivity but of doing what people want as judged by the ballot box. These so-called New Scientists would not have to answer to voters. They would decide what the truth was and what moral values could apply. Debates like this one could be deemed unscientific and adversarial politics would be ended. If we lose, we will have nothing to do in opposition. No one would be there to keep the Government on task and honest. We might have to disband. That would leave a dictatorship. Make no mistake, if you vote for the MWP, who have governed for 150 years, you will be voting for a dictatorship. We..."

"...That's not fair! It's a downright lie..." he said hotly, overcoming weariness to expose the straw man she had erected. "We believe in devolution! People will have more..."

"We will have to stop there, unfortunately, as time is up," interrupted their host.

In her final rejection of his proposal, she had cleverly harnessed the authority of tradition, as if the weight of centuries of political governance were on her side. She had been a skilled opponent. His conviction had been tested again and again. Although his case should have been able to convince voters, he had taken them into uncharted waters and conservatives would not have been won over.

"Well, there we are: Democracy versus New Science. Our national leaders are widely apart, with opposing philosophies. There is neither a middle way nor agreement to disagree. Tomorrow, one of them will be chosen to take us into the future. I hope this debate will have helped you to make up your mind. Emotions have run high here. You have seen your Party Leaders in action and they have done a very good job of presenting their side's case. Abajoe Yabra's MWP is promising a new direction ruled by New Science, with a new kind of Government without politics. Whereas Helen Sudarta's Progress Party would rule a Yamen state by political democracy. Which one has the future you prefer? Now, it's goodbye from us and over to you as voters. You have a lot of arguments to weigh up."

Abajoe realised the debate was over. He felt thwarted that Sudarta had come through relatively unscathed and her last punch had been a big one. He wondered if the debate would have changed anyone's mind. It hadn't turned out to be the walkover he wanted and he was disappointed. The topic was too complex for most people to judge fairly and they would align themselves on religious grounds. Science wasn't yet trusted to seek community goals fairly. He had been goaded into coming out against Yamen ideas of community and leadership and some would accuse him of racism. The election was now a religious confrontation between tradition and the Yamen interlopers. He knew that if Sudarta ever gained power, she would mute him and the MWP, using as much force as it would take. On the other hand, if he won, he might have to do the same. Australian unity was in peril.

It was not the outright win he was hoping for. The debate had conformed the MWP's intention to change the Constitution and appoint planning tribunals if elected. He had not let Sudarta sustain any major objections that were not due to uncertainties about the new system and suspicions about the MWP's motives for the change. The problem his Party now faced at the ballot box was that most Australians were unaware that, under the MWP and the Yabras for the past 150 years, they had enjoyed the best of political democracy. The Aboriginal brand of devolved leadership had left little real cause for complaint.

Unfortunately, there was a groundswell of support for change for change's sake. If Sudarta won, they would soon experience centralised and corrupt politics. Then they would realise they wanted science not politics. But they might not get another chance, as Sudarta was likely to declare Australia a Yamen State and cancel further elections.

He hoped that enough voters would foresee a dictatorship and warn others to keep Sudarta out. Once the MWP had brought in planning tribunals, they would be a bulwark that would thwart dictatorial ambitions and sustain free voting in the legislature. It all depended on tomorrow's election.

CHAPTER 40

Election Result and Aftermath

D*AY 0*
Today is the day of reckoning, the run-off between the MWP and the PP. We were close last week.

Polling opened at 6am and we went straight into the lead. We are more popular with early risers, travellers and country people who vote before going to work. The votes are not locked in until the final hour before 6pm. Swinging voters come in late to get a fair idea of which way things are going before committing.

It was a hassle having my communicator take a voice sample. I hope that people will see this as centralisation and vent their annoyance by voting against the SEU. Our local elections use our PIN.

Campaigning is banned today. I am spending the day at the football stadium watching the tally with Siti and the others.

As the results poured in this afternoon, it looked like we were losing. Shit! We have misread support for famine prevention. People don't want water reallocation and birth rate austerities. They want to have their cake and to eat it too. How stupid they are! But we have been even more stupid in believing that rationality could win! The other disappointment is that the established churches have seen state ecumenism and rejection of materialism as competitors and therefore regarded us as a threat. They have voted for independent candidates, another case of Lenz's Law, with our action to include their beliefs being cancelled by their reaction to reject ours. The churches have shown they want to pick up victims of materialism rather than finally get rid of it. When Sudarta creates a Yamen state, they will realise their error.

Our people here are sinking into a quagmire of defeat and hopelessness. It is 5pm and 80% of votes have been locked in. We are behind 54 to 66 seats. It is a substantial swing against us. Now, at closing, there has been a landslide, with 41% of votes to us and 55% to the Progress Party, with a record low of only 4% abstaining or not voting. They have 81 seats to our 60.

We had thought most of the alternative lifestylers would vote for us, and the Middle Way Party had tended to ignore them, being tolerant and allowing them to do what they wanted but this has turned out to be a mistake because now they have voted for the benefits of SEU patronage.

I have won my own seat but only just. I can hardly believe this awful result and suspect corruption. I have been crucified, killed in public while impaled on my election promises.

Oh, Lord of Fates, why hast thou forsaken me?

Chagrin...an unfamiliar feeling of humiliation, disappointment and failure. We have been decisively beaten. How can I live with this loss of face? I've let our Party down, by stealing the limelight, then failing to convince. I have let Australia down – now we have a bad Government and it's all my fault. I can hardly bear the responsibility, I must escape from it. I am emotionally exhausted. I want to get drunk and then sleep for a week but I owe it to my supporters to get through the next few hours coherently.

Siti has been very supportive and has taken my mind off the onslaught for hours at a time. She has been diverting me by telling me all about her life at the orphanage, putting our difficulties today into perspective. An election loss is small beer compared with the hunger and brutality she suffered.

DAY +1

I'm out in the cold, rigid in my cave. I can't believe how suddenly I have been sidelined. The media hyena pack is still here. They have picked over the bones and are hanging around hoping for some drama. They want my plans but not my ideas.

There's only the analysis of what went wrong to do – it'll probably go on for months. It's a way of healing our wounds.

We were doing okay until the Progress Party put out that 'The SEU-will-embargo-us-if-we-don't-join'. What rot! In any case, so what if they did: we could live without their rice – we can grow rice ourselves; we can make water available for that.

The other surprise was the strength of support for accepting the Bhakarian guest workers as immigrants. Although we had tried to be scrupulously fair and treated them exactly the same way as guest workers from other countries, we were seen as xenophobic in our attitude.

I look at Siti and wonder which of us is hurting most. It helps to be together, to know that she understands my suffering. My love for her is positive, stopping the negatives.

DAY +3

I am beginning to recover but it will take a long time before I cease to grieve for the death of my dream and another takes over. I am going through the motions of evaluating our loss in a daze.

I think more people than we expected sided with the Yamens to get freedom of movement to and from Bhakaria. The immigration barrier was a mistake: at first, many people liked it but when they saw what we were up against, they were too faint-hearted. In interviews, voters wanted immigrants to develop common aspirations, rather than focusing on the least common denominators of Yamen assimilation, as we had done.

Now our loyal supporters without a seat are out of work. Politics has been their whole life for the past year and they are shocked and grieving. They blame themselves and are sinking into depression at the very time when they need to be positive and seek alternative employment.

Some of our people see themselves as victims and are focusing the blame on others. There has been a bout of blame on me as Party Leader. I have been accused of everything from dominating policy to taking too low a profile in getting policies adopted. Everything has been fair game, from my own behaviour to our electoral system, even to my relationship with Siti, which they said made me seem less resolute about stopping immigration. It is unfair, to her especially, but I am considering resigning.

I met with the elders and learned that our loss was tactical rather than outright rejection of our ideology. It is a setback and I should gird my loins and take up the fight again.

DAY +5

It should be Easter. Today my spirit resurrected when the body of the Party supported my leadership with a vote of confidence 110 to 39, although there could be a challenge at the Party Conference.

I have offered to continue my leadership because I believe people will vote for us again when they have experienced the SEU system and realise that our entry is a mistake. Siti and others have persuaded me to stay on and lead a vigorous Opposition. In four years time, or sooner, voters will understand our ideas, restore us to Government and we will put the costly failure of SEU membership behind us.

Already, our Opposition has strength. It seems more likely that the Government will be forced into another election, perhaps within two years.

But it is more likely that Sudarta will tear up the rule book and stay in power. Then, if not before, the MWP will be banned. If I am too effective, I could be imprisoned. Let fate decide.

CHAPTER 41

Opposition Leadership

Abajoe reluctantly handed over to Sudarta the job he and his ancestors had performed for the past 150 years. They had regarded it as theirs by right as custodians of the land and its resources for all Australians equally. Now Abajoe was out of work and spent his time growing food for his family and for sale in the community. Even the 'Family Fare' show had ended. Its slot had been replaced with government propaganda advocating the opposite message of migration from subsistence in the country to factory work in the cities. The MWP's careful dismantling of the centralised economy was being undone. Abajoe was furious.

"Sudarta is in the pay of investors intent on becoming rich by restoring wage slavery and urban poverty," he told his disciples. "Australians don't need another dose of materialism but Sudarta is determined to take away their independence and dignity. She is a despot and will rule by force."

Initially, the MWP could do nothing to oppose the destruction of everything they stood for. Even their elected parliamentarians were shocked into silence. Nevertheless, outrage grew and a month after losing the election, the Middle Way Party met in virtual conference to decide their new direction. MPs from the Party's 58 winning electorates and candidates from the other losing electorates had been invited to log in, making a total of 149, one from each electorate, online for the three-day conference.

Their first business was to elect the Party Leader.

"You must get your nomination in today," Siti reminded Abajoe.

"I'm thinking I won't run," he replied. "Someone else can have a go."

"It's not like you to quit," said Siti. "Don't you want to finish what you started last time?"

"Maybe we need a different platform. I'm not the person to do that."

"Hell...your's is a very good platform. Sudarta seduced people with paternalistic change. It wasn't that the changes we were offering were inferior. We've invested a huge effort in developing and getting understanding of your platform. I'm not going to be at all happy if you waste it. You have to run."

"When you put it like that...will you nominate me?"

"John would be better."

Abajoe's stalwart friend was widely respected and had his own following. "I will run for the leadership if you don't," he had told Abajoe.

"His nomination would bring his supporters to you," Siti reminded him.

"Maybe he wants to nominate?"

"He can't. He's chairing the conference."

He had told her John would be Chair and control the speaking schedule of nominees for the position of Party Leader.

"He may want to be seen as neutral."

"Okay, I'll ask him then," said Abajoe.

John agreed to nominate him.

The next day, John was ensconced in the Party's main studio at the football stadium, running the virtual conference. A technical person was in the Control Room managing the cameras and collection and presentation of voting statistics. John's head and shoulders were resplendent in an authoritative collar and tie, whereas many members appeared on the monitors dressed in their work clothes, pausing to watch or to vote as they came in from their fields or while doing their domestic chores. His image was backed by displays showing the agenda items, with graphics displaying results of continuous voting for the nominees. The technician supervised the biometrics measurement system that authenticated Party members for cyber voting.

The four nominees could each speak for 20 minutes. Usually the online audience was quiet but occasionally it erupted in applause, booing or chanting. Then there were 40 minutes for questions.

By tradition, Abajoe, as the incumbent Party Leader, would speak last.

Andrew was a house builder and led a conservative faction who wanted growth and a special relationship with the SEU. He was a formidable opponent.

Next was Cassandra, who was an anarchist and wanted an armed fight against the Government to prevent them joining the SEU. Only a small, extreme left wing group supported her.

Darjeel was a Jandu opposed to SEU immigration and determined to curb growing Yamen power through compulsory population control. He wanted passive resistance against the Sudarta Government. He had the support of the small Jandu contingent at the conference.

By the time it was Abajoe's turn to speak, the majority already looked to him as their Party Leader. His voice had changed from before the election, when it had been clear as a bell with a certainty that attracted givers but repelled takers. Its hubris had metamorphosed into humility. He spoke quietly but there was no doubt he would eventually take the Party into the uncharted waters of insurrection should that be necessary.

"My goal is to stop the Government taking us into the SEU. The election result was close enough that Sudarta does not have a mandate. Her support is already falling away. Like the incumbent capitalists who tried to oppose the socialist revolution in Chile, we have lost at the ballot box. We may have no other avenue for three years. By then it will be too late. Opposing a large and hegemonic force is dangerous work and we have to be careful even when most of the people are with us, as Ghandhi found out to his cost in India. I reject national strikes, hunger strikes, sabotage, terrorism and assassinations as these are uncivilised and could hurt our own people indiscriminately without much success, as the IRA found out when they tried them against the British. If I were to stand here and advocate passive resistance, that would be illegal. Mahatma Gandhi organised passive resistance in secrecy and in the end, he prevailed. When Nelson Mandela's patience ran out, the majority asserted their rights and they too prevailed. Now it is our turn to prevail and we will. First, we must unite. After me...Middle Way in!" he intoned.

With one voice, they repeated, "Middle Way in!"

"SEU out!" he chanted.

"SEU out!" they shouted together.

"Middle Way in! SEU out!" they thundered, stamping their feet.

"Middle Way in! SEU out!"

"Local in!" he confided to them.

"Local in!" they replied.

"Central out!" he yelled.

"Central out!" they yelled back.

Siti took over from him.

"Guest workers in! Famine out!" she led them.

"Guest workers in! Famine out!"

"Community in! Greed out!"

"Community in! Greed out!"
In a show of unity, Andrew took the lead.
"Volunteering in! Selfishness out!"
"Volunteering in! Selfishness out!"
Darjeel was not to be outdone.
"Passive in! Violence out!"
"Passive in! Violence out!"
Thwarted, Cassandra showed loyalty to the Party platform.
"New Science in! Politics out!"
"New Science in! Politics out!"
Finally, Abajoe implored their hoarse throats.
"Middle Way in! Sudarta out!"
"Middle Way in! Sudarta out!"
Voting for Abajoe was almost unanimous. He appointed Siti as Deputy Leader. The conference ended with unity and confidence.

Afterwards, Abajoe and Siti relaxed in The Tower swimming pool. They were satisfied with the day's proceedings.

"Anyone would think we had won the election!" said Siti.

"People are pleased we have a formula that can win next time. It's a matter of getting it widely understood."

"When people realise what Sudarta wants to do, then they'll appreciate us!"

The final day of the conference was spent planning the way forward. Abajoe could be charged with incitement if there was evidence linking him to illegal member action. Therefore, he spoke to the assembly in these words.

"In history, an unpopular Government in India was once opposed by passive resistance. Indians in 1938 were seeking independence from Britain. British control was undermined by non-compliance with British directives by a movement of government workers. Some argue that the movement was spontaneous and unorganised. Eventually Mahatma Gandhi took responsibility and was rewarded with house arrest. Such a situation should not arise here."

Although it was almost certain that Sudarta would have informers present at the conference, there were insufficient grounds for Abajoe to be charged with incitement. He went on to give details of opposition by the usual means of presenting the electorate with a viable alternative. He announced a Shadow Cabinet and schedule for preparing policy statements.

"The secret of success is organisation," he said. "Your organisation will have two kinds of business to be centrally controlled. The first is public opposition in the legislature. However, Sudarta has the numbers and the Middle Way Party is devolved – opposition at the centre is not our prime business. The second requires your active involvement in a centrally concerted campaign, following the example of Gandhi." When he abruptly sat down, they realised that he would not risk being accused of incitement and would not reveal his plan in this forum because Sudarta would not hesitate to arrest him.

The conference continued for another day. One of the inner groups contacted each delegate to confirm his or her participation in a passive resistance movement, to be clandestinely organised. The delegate would be contacted by a secure communication route, with guidelines for infiltrating government bureaucracies.

After the conference, Abajoe was prominent as Opposition Leader in the virtual parliament, where he criticised the Government's performance and plans at every opportunity. He led a large group of MPs that opposed the Government's application to join the SEU. Their arguments were winning more and more support and Sudarta's support was steadily whittled away as independent members deserted Sudarta's Government, to where a referendum on joining the SEU would not have succeeded. Sudarta lost no opportunity in denouncing Abajoe's opposition as un-Australian. She defamed Abajoe as an arrogant Yabra with a megalomaniac flaw.

Abajoe's popularity increased with the general public. He received many invitations to speak and he and his entourage travelled widely. Wherever they went, they visited the sick and troubled, providing help and money in the surrounding neighbourhood. On their return to their homes, they often followed through on contacts made, providing information or practical help and registering people as members of the MWP.

The richness of Abajoe's vision of self-altruism attracted an ardent following of young idealists, who clung to his every word. However, it was difficult to pass on his enlightenment to them in public because hecklers sent by the Government now marred his public appearances. As his organisers gained experience in responding to and controlling his appearances, the disrupters became increasingly hostile. It was evident that the conflict was escalating and heading towards personal violence against him. Sudarta was using the police and the military to squash opposition.

He travelled from one public engagement to another escorted by a phalanx of followers in brightly coloured costumes on ornamented electrobikes, causing a sensation wherever he went. They wore a different colour for each of his appearances, so that he was surrounded by the colour of his own gown and indistinguishable to a sniper.

"I wish I could do without a security cordon," said Abajoe. "It is cutting me off from the people."

"Sudarta knows that," said Siti, "and there is real danger. Your death would set the Party back years."

"Sudarta knows that too," he replied.

CHAPTER 42

Rainforest Rally

Under Abajoe's leadership, the Middle Way Party recovered from its election defeat and went from strength to strength. Sometimes, the Party would meet for a rally where participants would study, plan, socialise and meditate together. The rallies attracted hundreds of supporters. The rallies were so successful that they posed a threat to Abajoe, who could be assassinated or imprisoned for incitement by a ruthless Government.

After about six months in Opposition, supporters wanted action and the Party held rallies across the nation to instigate passive resistance. The leadership had established a hierarchy of secret organisers to select targets and schedule actions.

Abajoe and his disciples led supporters in Meannjin to a rally at Mount Beacon in the scenic hinterland. To prevent the Government from blocking their route, he gave only a few hours notice and supporters set off without food or camping equipment. Streams of hitchhikers converged on Mount Beacon from every direction. He was surrounded by 50 guards in orange. When they arrived, they spent the first day and night at the campgrounds in their makeshift tents. The next day, when they were all assembled, Abajoe announced they would trek up into the mountains to a sacred site, where they would hold a retreat for several days in scenic, natural surroundings.

"What food and shelter is there?" someone asked.

"We will fast and sleep in the open, celebrating our oneness with the land," Abajoe replied. "There is a mountain stream nearby. The site is in a rainforest and we can shelter under fallen trees and in caves."

They set off on foot, walking up vehicle tracks into the foothills. The trail became narrow, winding in single file around precipitous cliffs. Conditions varied from scorching sunlight and dried vegetation along the lower escarpment to wet mud and mossy rocks under rainforest canopy, where winds from the coast blew up the escarpment, cooling and condensing their moisture into rain.

It was evident that few trekkers came this way and the procession was thrilled to observe the fearless animals they came across in the pristine forests. Rock wallabies grazed peacefully as they passed by. At one place, they had to step over a large carpet python coiled on the trail. Bowerbirds scurried furtively near their nests. The walkers were quiet and respected the sanctity of the environment.

Eventually, they reached a cairn of stones in a large, sunlit clearing that was their destination. It was very hot and they were perspiring from the climb, when Abajoe took off all his clothes and led the others to a rock pool filled with icy water. Siti, Paula and the others undressed and plunged in. Couples clung together, making love underwater in the shadows. Soon the pool was crowded and the others sat around on sun-dappled rocks and conversed convivially.

The talk was about the Party's plans, how to recruit new members and oppose the Government. They discussed the events in Parliament, dwelling on the successes of their Party Leaders in debates. There was excitement about the camp and they made arrangements to share shelters and campfires.

After several hours in the pool, Abajoe, Siti and Paula returned to the fallen fig tree, where they threw down blankets between the root buttresses. Abajoe spoke to Paula and she nodded and walked away. He lay down with Siti on a ground sheet and they made love slowly, with only the lash of the whipbird's call disturbing the quietness. Then they slept entwined until evening shadows stole over them.

Paula's eyes were red and she wouldn't speak to Siti. She had started a communal fire in a clearing and as it grew dark, people came to it bringing logs from their own campfires. Soon there was the crack and spark of a roaring fire with a sea of faces upwind from the smoke.

There was a full programme of speakers, who used a megaphone to present topics varying from Party policy initiatives to how to achieve self-altruism. Abajoe spoke last, asking people to be prepared to co-operate when their organisers approached them to take part in passive actions. He emphasised the need to protest peacefully, involving as many people as possible.

After the talks, there was singing of revolutionary songs. When the fire died, they went to their shelters. Abajoe lay down with Siti and Paula and they slept.

The camp continued for two days and they became very hungry. Hunger made them light-headed and Abajoe and Siti were in high spirits when they dressed and set off to trek down to a village to get some food for their group.

They reached the village two hours later and were delighted to see a group of topless women with children in the swimming pool.

"Great. A nude swimming pool. These people are really cool!" said Abajoe. He had always envisaged an idyllic, transcendental society in which clothing was for protection rather than morality and seldom worn.

Laughing with exhilaration and hunger, they stripped off and jumped in. Then a man, who was bathing with his family, called the attendant over and spoke to him. The attendant looked across the pool to where they were and then went into the kiosk. About 10 minutes later, two burly policemen arrived and beckoned Abajoe and Siti over.

"Get out and get dressed," they ordered.

When they had done this, the police told them, "You are under arrest."

"What for?" Siti asked.

"Indecent exposure."

"But those people are naked too!"

"No. The women's breasts are bare but everything else is covered. The Chief of Police," he indicated the man in the pool, "has complained about you."

"Uh-oh," the two looked at each other in dismay.

When they had dressed, they were ordered to get into the police car and were driven to the police station and questioned. When the police discovered that they had arrested none other than the Leader of the Opposition and his partner, they called a local journalist, who got the scoop of a lifetime. The Government portrayed the incident in the media as depravations of perverted leaders of a cult.

They were held in jail until night-time fell, then marched out of town in the opposite direction from their camp and released. They were able to double back along the trail to the others. On the precipitous sections, in inky blackness, Abajoe and Siti had to hold on to each other. The one behind held the one in front's belt in case they fell off the path. It took them five hours to reach camp and they arrived weak, exhausted and without the food supplies they had gone for. When they heard what had happened, the others convulsed with laughter. "It just goes to show that it's dangerous to make assumptions about people," joked Abajoe. "You have to look below the surface."

The others hid their disappointment that they had failed to bring back any food. Hunger tested their serenity and now they couldn't think about anything else except food. The whole group struck camp the next day. By the time Abajoe and his guards had walked out and reached the shops and restaurants, they found they had no food. Abajoe went into the last restaurant and sat down.

He asked the waitress, "What do you have? We're hungry."

She knew who he was and he was like a god to her. "Nothing...only some bread and fish fingers we have kept for our family to eat," she replied, wanting to help.

Abajoe looked around the crumby joint, at the grey peeling walls, the window-netting thick with dust and the broken furniture.

"Could you spare some of it?" he asked. "Your kindness will be passed on to others."

She brought two boxes of fish fingers and three loaves of wholemeal bread.

"That'll do nicely, with plenty of tea," he said.

She put a box of a dozen frozen fish fingers into a thermoducer. When they were done, he broke up the fish into pieces, wrapped each in bread and passed them to the back of his group outside the door.

"There's plenty for everyone," he announced.

They were amazed because the pieces were so large and there was some for everyone.

Afterwards, when he was peeing over a fence into a field, John, who was alongside, asked him, "How did you do that with the food? Are you a new Jesus?"

"If you want something enough, it can happen," Abajoe told him. "I sometimes think, 'What would Jesus have done?' and copy him. If people believe there will be enough, then there will seem to be. To a person who is starving, a morsel is a meal."

"It was a miracle!"

"If you like, yes, I agree."

They travelled back to Meannjin in a huge procession. They mixed freely with the crowds who had turned out to see them, generating a carnival atmosphere and publicity that conflicted with the exclusive cult label the Government tried to pin on them. But people knew Abajoe was the democratically elected Leader of the MWP who had an effective campaign run by dedicated followers. He was a prophet, not a cult leader. His opposition to the Government gathered strength daily.

CHAPTER 43

Broken Rules

In the following weeks, Abajoe's stature increased but sometimes he travelled incognito, without his bodyguards even though there was imminent danger. Party members were being attacked, beaten up and, in one case, killed. Sudarta's people were suspected and he had to restrain groups of young Party members from reprisal attacks.

"Our passive resistance is being tested," he told them. "They hope we will retaliate and then they will be able to ban our activities and imprison us. We must avoid that but we won't stand by and have our people attacked indefinitely. Our elders, Zelta and Hugo, are against it because it could lead to civil war but I see no alternative. If their provocation continues to escalate, as a last resort, I will unleash insurgency."

The rich feared Abajoe because he owed allegiance to no god or man or faction that could be corrupted. He could not be bought, nor intimidated, nor castigated. From his policies of self-altruism, non-materialism, collectivism and local planning tribunals, they inferred that their wealth was under threat.

"Whether wealth is redistributed or continues to have opportunities for growth will be up to each local community. Each commune can have a different outlook on capitalism. Wealthy people may find some places to live more profitable than others."

One morning, he was driving with Siti to a meeting. They threaded their way along a potted highway between acreages where families subsisted happily on the little they could grow, supplemented by gifts of food from neighbours. Houses had been built back-to-back, with neighbours around a refectory where they shared food, appliances, chores, communality and love. Their lives had a dignity and purpose shown in their planted gardens and tidy houses. Their children attended virtual school, tutored by the adults. There were only a few cars, and children learning horticulture waved to them as they passed.

Suddenly a vehicle blocked their path and four hooded men in overalls got out. The two quickly locked their doors but the thugs smashed the side windows, opened the driver's door and pulled Abajoe out. Passers-by, who had been watching helplessly, backed away. Abajoe thought they were going to kill him.

From inside the car Siti screamed, "No! Help!"

One of them got into the car and wrapped his arm around her neck, smothering her cries. The other three started kicking him, in the body and head. Then they brought an iron bar and chopped above and below the knee, breaking the bones in his legs. Siti bit the arm restraining her and the thug released his hold on her neck for a moment. She screamed, "Help," but he renewed his hold, almost throttling her.

They continued kicking Abajoe until he lost consciousness. Then her captor released Siti, gave her an envelope and got out of the car. The thugs walked to their vehicle and drove away.

Siti rushed to Abajoe, who was lying facedown in the dirt of the road with his shattered legs twisted under him. She called to him but he was silent. She rolled him onto his side and felt in his mouth for obstructions. There were none. She held her cheek next to his mouth and nose and put a hand on his abdomen. He didn't seem to be breathing.

"Get an ambulance," she yelled to the bystanders.

She ran to the car and brought the first aid kit she had packed. There were defibrillation pads, a control box and long wires with plugs. She started the car, opened the hood and plugged in the box. She turned him onto his back and rolled up his shirt. Then, peeling back the covers from the sticky pads, she fastened them at the sides of his chest. She stood back and pressed the button on the box.

There was a short delay. Abajoe's body jerked with a shock that convulsed his quivering heart and restarted the beat. There was a smaller jerk every second as the pacemaker imposed a steady rhythm. Siti held his nose, tilted his head back and blew breaths into his mouth until he resumed breathing. He regained consciousness.

"Fuck. Fuck Sudarta," he mumbled.

Soon afterwards, an ambulance arrived.

The nurse handed Siti the defibrillator. "Where did you learn to use that?"

"Mine rescue training," she said.

"You saved my life," groaned Abajoe. "Thanks."

"I'm only sorry I couldn't have rescued you from those thugs." Then she remembered the letter. She brought it from the car and opened it. There was a message printed in untraceable encryption.

Stop your campaign or she will be next.

There was no name.

She read it to Abajoe.

"Just as you thought," Siti said. "Sudarta is behind this. She can't compete with you so she is trying to stop our passive resistance campaign by violence and threats."

Abajoe's pain-filled voice was determined. "It's a helluva threat. They won't get away with it. But we have to protect you. I have to regain my walking – I'm going to be out of the limelight for a while. Would you get John to contact our people and get them to call it off for a few weeks?"

"Let's get you to hospital," said Siti.

Three weeks later, Abajoe came home in a wheelchair. Siti and Paula took turns to look after him. His days were filled with exercises to grow strength in his legs so that he would be able to walk again. He had a stream of visitors who marvelled at his disregard of pain. His face, which had been soft and peaceful, had hardened with determination.

"I'll be running around in a few days," he groaned as he hobbled back and forth.

"You have more willpower than anyone I have ever known," Siti told him. "Where do you get it from?"

He looked into the distance and spoke quietly, as if she too could see.

"I sense that...something out there...has plans for me," he said. "I feel that I must save our people from Sudarta."

The attack had frightened her badly. She felt that under Sudarta the people were doomed to servitude and drudgery. It was her hope in Abajoe that had kept her going these past weeks of nursing him back to health.

"The people believe that you are a saviour with special powers," she told him.

He smiled wryly, with the charisma of his wrinkled eyes.

"And what do you believe?"

"I believe in you. It is my mission in life to follow you, do your bidding and call others' attention to your greatness. I would willingly give up my life for you."

"Wow. You are my most loyal supporter! Please don't die for me!" He kissed her passionately. "You know I love you," he murmured.

"Do you want to possess me?"

"Sometimes."

"When?"

"When you are kind to me. Often these days."

"Then there is hope. That is all I want."

Siti devoted herself to looking after him until he had healed and regained use of his legs. She supported him as he battled with the painful exercises. Abajoe finally trusted her completely. He committed his life to her in his mind and from then on, they were as one.

The MWP's campaign of passive resistance had faltered.

CHAPTER 44

Handicaps

A year after the election, Australia formally acceded to the South East Union and was renamed Austrasia. Immigrants flooded in, mostly from Bhakaria because people could move freely between Union countries.

Parliament had ceased to meet and Abajoe's Opposition watched the Government metamorphose into an instrument of SEU control with growing concern. However, Sudarta was enjoying the honeymoon of her ascendency and there was little Abajoe could do as he recovered from the brutal attack by her thugs. Under the threat of an attack on Siti, the MWP had ceased even passive resistance. The Party had lost momentum and Abajoe despaired of it regaining its former influence with voters.

When Abajoe was able to walk unaided, trained and armed supporters guarded him and Siti night and day. Forced out of the limelight, Abajoe met secretly with his supporters and the MWP resumed its campaign of passive resistance. They were angered by the attack, and speculated that when Sudarta's popularity waned, she would govern by tyrannical oppression unless they could successfully oppose her. Under the influence of elders, Zelta and Hugo, Abajoe would not condone violence, despite the terrible provocation of his broken legs. Only when other methods of protest had failed would they allow violence and then only against perpetrators of violence, away from innocent bystanders.

Government reprisals for the MWP's passive resistance escalated and Abajoe wondered when Sudarta wouldn't bother about evidence and would dare to arrest him and hold him without charges being laid. He was a very prominent figure and she didn't have the strength to do this within a democracy but Sudarta might move to a dictatorship with SEU approval any day.

Now Abajoe concluded that they had to undermine the Government. He raised this in a meeting with the disciples. "I want you, like me, to use your skills to compete for and win a job so the Government cannot target you as a dissenter, or a loser from the election, locked in the past. We need to lower our profile to survive. I want you to become respectable citizens who prepare quietly to white ant government planning. Disaffection from SEU control is growing daily and our voice will be loud when the time to rise up comes."

Peter protested. "Faking it seems like a sellout to me. What are we waiting for? Why don't we come out and lead a revolt now?"

"We would lose because the people aren't ready yet. I understand your impatience, Peter, but the people who voted for Sudarta wouldn't support us in a revolt now. They've voted to join the SEU and it will be some time before they will accept they have made a mistake. It's too soon after we lost the election."

"There are plenty of people who voted for us."

"There's not enough yet. We need a majority or we could end up with what we're trying to avoid – civil war. If we divide the country now, it may take generations to heal and recover the sense of community we had going. We must wait."

"We need to have our people in positions where they can prevent adherence to SEU guidelines. We need to infiltrate the new centralised bureaucracy and when the time is ripe, block Sudarta's Government from within. We need to get jobs."

"Will anyone hire us?" asked Peter. "We're hardly factory fodder. We're definitely not for human consumption."

"Can you pretend to be normal for once? You can work...I saw you once."

Everyone laughed.

"I hate to cross the floor on this," said Abajoe. "But the SEU's employment handicap system does give everyone a fair chance of getting a job, even immigrants. You may have to compete against Bhakarians and some will have more experience. You will probably have to accept low pay at first."

The disciples faithfully set about lowering the MWP's profile and began seeking government jobs. Sudarta was pleased by the show of compliance and relaxed her persecution of MWP members. It was a strategy Gandhi would have endorsed as necessary to keep the peace while the Government was undermined.

Abajoe was visiting his parents for Sunday lunch. He had been starting to complete a government job application form but was now helping them prepare food for a hundred people from raw ingredients in their commune's kitchen.

"The Government want to know everything," he said, as he set the utility robot to peeling potatoes. Another couple were also rostered on and when they had gone to set the tables in the hall, he caught T One and Marko's eye and mimed a person outside the building, wearing headphones, listening to their conversation. He held his finger up to his lips, signalling caution. They nodded.

Marko aimed the temperature-probing gun at the rows of roasting rossits. "Hmm, 75°...about half an hour. So you want a job as a social advocate, helping the disadvantaged to get money from their communes?"

"I may not get short-listed." Abajoe tipped the skinned potatoes into a hopper feeding a chain conveyor into the oven. "The ad didn't say how much experience was wanted. This is my first work for someone else and my education has been informal so I don't have qualifications. They may not consider a homegrown intellectual like me."

"But you are a household name," his father said. "You were Leader of the Opposition until recently. It must be pretty humiliating for you to have to compete for an ordinary job. Surely you can get something higher level through your contacts?"

"The Government wouldn't allow it. These days, they have to approve every appointment and they won't let me do anything influential. I have to fall back on my basic skills. I could do the work of a facilitator or advocate but I don't have any relevant experience registered. They regard all that reconciliation work as political."

"How badly do you need a job? Can't you make enough at The Tower to support yourself?"

In answer, he took Marko's arm, led him into a freezer room and closed the door. He threw a switch. "That starts the interference cage," he said. "They can't hear us now. They have this place and my place staked out. The answer to your question is that I want to get a job where I can disappear into the woodwork, as a front for running the Party."

He shivered. Marko wrapped his arms around himself. "So you think you will be able to run it from where you work? Good luck!"

"It won't be easy but better than from here or The Tower. I have heard they have new technology that can penetrate and listen inside these cages. In the job I'm going for, I would be able to set up a pseudonym and use the government communication system anonymously. By the time they have located it in cyberspace, I will have shifted."

"How will you fake the biometrics?"

"I won't. I'll piggyback on someone else's."

"They'll be watching you like a hawk. Why do you have to get a job with the Government of all people?"

"It's a Trojan horse. We have our people everywhere and they'll be able to warn me if they're on to me through the communications system. I'll be at the centre of things to concert our actions. At the same time, I'll be modelling the infiltration I want all our members to copy...except that I won't be able to take part in passive resistance myself because they will be looking for me to step out of line..."

"You will be like a general who stands behind his troops directing the action."

"Exactly."

"What job did you say you were going for?"

"Social facilitator."

"Why are you going for such a lowly job?"

"I don't want to be in the limelight. It's a job where I'm supervised remotely and will be able to work for the cause unobserved."

"It sounds dangerous. If they catch you, you will be imprisoned or even killed. Is it worth it?"

"We Yabras have opposed outsiders for centuries, risking our lives."

"Why?"

"Australia is our land that we hold in trust for our children and theirs ad infinitum. Now Sudarta is giving it away to foreigners. She is seriously in my personal space and I intend to get rid of her."

"Be careful, won't you?"

"Yes, Dad. Don't worry. I know what I'm doing."

They went back inside. Abajoe set the robot to shell the peas and pass them through the oven. When this was done, Marko opened the oven door and stepped back to avoid the blast of heat. "If they do give you a run, you'll be an outsider for sure. But you could romp in on handicap. It depends whether you're prepared to start on a pittance." Together they lifted out the hot trays of rossits and stacked them in the warming oven.

"I'm getting the hang of the handicap idea," said Marko. He had talked with government employees in his work as a water resources consultant. "You have to show the best combination of qualifications and commitment to get the job. Your qualifications go into calculating your handicap and your commitment by how cheaply you'll tender to do the work."

"I get it," Abajoe opened a pod and ate the peas. "It's like in a sailboat race…the winner is the best, considering some individuals have started with better experience and others have sailed well. Is it good to have a high handicap or a low one?"

"High of course, to make the salary you are asking for seem lower."

"But you don't need a big salary," interrupted T One. "You have your own money."

Abajoe caught her eye and cupped his ear, shaking his head vigorously. If the Government knew he had an ulterior motive to bid cheaply for the job, they could infer he wanted it as a cover for political activities.

"No, Mum. I need the money… to go overseas for a year or two."

T One was sitting at the kitchen table beside them eating from a bowl of dried fruits. "I fail to see," she announced, "why you shouldn't be paid the going rate for the job." She had discussed this with them before. She believed that the new handicap system would foster competition and this was anathema because her Government had promoted the spiritual dimensions of good jobs that would be highly valued by demand.

"There's no rate for the job," Abajoe replied. "It's more like auctioning yourself. The better are your qualifications, the more money you can ask for. Your handicap depends on what skills and experience you have, how good at the job you are likely to be. A contract rate is negotiated. There will be applicants with twice my handicap trying for twice as much pay."

"How can anyone have twice your handicap? How could they decide that?" scoffed T One. They set the dining tables with white tablecloths and cutlery.

"Give the signal," said T One.

A resonating, low tone sounded and people came out of neighbouring houses and walked towards the dining room.

Abajoe poured the fat into a pail and stirred in gravy powder. "They will rate my form compared with people throughout the country already doing this kind of work. They'll work out how much a person is likely to earn in jobs like this at this location if they have my education and training…also, with my previous, relevant experience and responsibility…and my rate of pay increase or decrease from my previous position. Then there's my degree of support by referees…and my ethnicity."

"What's ethnicity got to do with it?" asked T One, passing the gravy boats while he poured from the pail. "An indigenous person should get the same pay as anyone else."

"You're right, it shouldn't matter but it could make a difference," said Marko. "Abajoe, their regression analysis will show how significant it is, when they will increase your handicap to take out any racism. For example, Bhakarians sometimes suffer prejudice and this is corrected by raising their handicap."

"What do they do with the handicap?" asked T One.

"They will tell me what it is before the interview and I'll tell them how much pay I want. If I'm low enough, I'll be short-listed." They carried the food out to the tables, which had filled with people. "My handicap will be low because I don't have much experience."

"So your pay rate is calculated before they interview you? What's new about that?" T One queried as she sat down beside Marko.

"No, my pay will be negotiated with the panel at the interview. They'll talk up the job and try to get me to accept less if they want me," Abajoe said, looking up from carving.

"Now…dinner is served. Take your seats please," Marko called to the others in the kitchen. "It seems like a fair system, what do you think?"

Abajoe pursed his lips. "A lot of people think it's an improvement on the old system. A graduate and a person at the peak of their profession now compete on a level playing field. For example, the graduate would need training but accept less money."

When the last of the kitchen people were seated, the people at the tables began serving the food.

"Usually there's an ideal type. If they want someone, they'll be able to get them," sighed T One, helping herself to roasted sweet potato.

"No. Not if they don't show commitment by tendering low enough. It's a transparent process."

"They'll be pretty keen to have you, Abajoe," Marko said, taking a rossit leg.

"The greater the connections, the fewer the privileges," said Abajoe, quoting a family motto. "They wouldn't dare give the job to me unfairly."

"No. It's more likely that fame will be your handicap," said T One. "They may decide your politics have disqualified you. You may never be able to get a job."

"I think they'll be pleased to have him," said Marko. "His entry into the workforce will show that he has ceased to oppose the Government." He winked and they smiled.

They ate hungrily, in silence. Afterwards, Abajoe went to the communications room, completed the job application form and sent it in.

Ten minutes later, his communicator beeped with a message:

Your initial handicap is 0.75

He read it out to the others as they cleared the tables.

"Is that good?" he asked.

Marko responded, "If the top earner with a handicap of 1.00 would do the job for 60 million seus per year, they would only have 60 million divided by 1.00 equals 60 million points against. If you would do it for 60 million seus too, you would have 60 divided by 0.75 equals 80 million points against, significantly more They would get the job."

"Is that all there is to it?"

"The interview panel would give you the opportunity to reduce your offer. If you would accept as little as 30 million seus or just below, giving 40 million points against, you will be winner. Will you go that low?"

Abajoe pressed a button on the dishwasher. "Not for this job. I think I'll go in high. Social advocacy is not my ideal job," he winked at Marko. "I would rather be a collaboration facilitator."

"I agree. That would be a job with more challenge," said Marko with a wink.

Abajoe put in an offer of 40 million seus. The next day he was notified he had been short-listed and given an appointment for an interview later that week.

A few days later, Marko and T One arrived on a surprise visit to Abajoe's place. He came to the door wearing a business suit and was looking in a mirror as they came into the lounge.

"Where are you off to?"

"Interview."

"Oh yes. Social advocate. The SEU process. What is supposed to happen in an interview these days?" asked T One.

"The panel make the job seem attractive so that you will lower your offer," said Marko. "Isn't that right, Abajoe?"

"Yes, that's how it works. They have to sell the job to me. Get my price down. It's like a reverse Dutch auction, to get the lowest price."

"What if they lie? They could make the work seem exciting when it's not."

"It's illegal. The interview will be recorded and I will get a copy..."

"I don't get it," said T One. "So they're trying to get you to accept less money and you're trying to get more from them without pricing yourself out of competition. I suppose that is when you trot out your experience and qualifications to convince them you're worth more."

"No. It's not allowed," he said. "My handicap measures my past performance. I can only talk about how I would go about doing the job."

T One sat down. "But how can you convince them you would be good at it without going into the past. Wouldn't an interview become a field day for a bullshit artist?"

"Not at all. Most interviews have a series of tests that simulate working conditions. For example, I could have to do a social assessment of a client, using a simulation robot."

"Could you do that?"

"Yes. I've studied assessment techniques and practiced on a training robot."

"Well, good luck with the interview."

He was made to wait in a room full of applicants for various jobs while their genetic make-up was measured and their heredity established. All available records of their kind were combed through and their handicaps calculated. They went back as far as they could, many generations through every parental branch and checking siblings' records, looking for evidence of positive and negative contributions to the community. They looked at earnings in relevant positions, property ownership, rates payments, responsible community work and any convictions or even arrests. They were particularly interested in religious and cultural affiliations. Every aspect of hereditary and acquired behaviour could be considered in a person's handicap. He was strongly against reverse discrimination and didn't want his indigenousness made into a liability to the community. If some indigenous persons were low contributors to their employers and were lowly paid, this should not lower other indigenous persons' handicaps. Caucasian sub-groups also had low handicaps and these were not imposed on the others.

His initial handicap of 0.75 could be increased or decreased on closer inspection.

The atmosphere in the room was tense as the applicants waited for their handicaps to be finalised. Sometimes an applicant was called to verify a record or supply missing data. The process appeared to be impersonal, with a complex system operated by a large number of low-ranking officials but Abajoe suspected that it was under the control of powerful individuals who remained invisible. He wondered how much political influence was being exercised. Abajoe didn't know how his family's prominent position would be rated, nor his leadership of the Opposition.

He suspected that his employment would revert to the old hidden biases of his indigenous ancestry. They had suffered centuries of discrimination by similar processes. The transparency and equality of opportunity that his great-grandparents had brought in had disappeared. Now he was forced to accept the equivocations of a vast bureaucracy under a culturally opposed Government. He suspected it would discriminate unfairly against him, with no process of appeal. All he could do was wait and hope.

"What happened?" Marko was still reading when Abajoe returned.

Abajoe shrugged and took a chocolate biscuit from the coffee table. "My final handicap was 0.80."

"Was that fair?"

"It was higher than I expected for that job because I don't have much experience. I had put in an offer of 40 million seus, making 53 million points against me, the most that would be likely to be considered."

T One said, "You want 40 million? For a first job! You are hopeful!"

He waved a hand around the unseen listeners and with a finger drew a smile on his face. "I'm more interested in facilitating than doing case work. That was the lowest I was prepared to go for that kind of work!"

"Did they know who your family were?"

"They probably did, but they never mentioned it. You know, *'the greater the connections, the fewer the privileges'*. They were very proper and neutral throughout. They tried to get my offer down, first by putting me through some simulation exercises. They were fun. They showed how a social advocate could affect people's lives. I was given a case to deal with. It seemed like a real case. I had to interview a person, discuss it in a conference with other professionals, write a letter and make a verbal presentation to the panel. In addition, there was a heap of psychological tests.

"They pointed out that I had too many points against and I needed to reduce my price to be competitive."

"How did you go?"

"How did they know you were uncompetitive? Had the winner been interviewed already?"

"Before I was short-listed, I was asked how much I wanted. I guess we all had and that's how they picked the short list. I must have just got on it. A lot of people have applied."

"You must have been quite competitive then."

"Yes, but other people caved in during the interview."

T One snorted. "The winner will be the one prepared to do the job for least, allowing for experience, or the most easily intimidated. Not like the old system where it was the one judged most capable who got the job."

"When will you find out?"

"Later today."

They were having tea when Abajoe came in.

"Did you get the job?" Marko said, passing him a tray of sushi.

"I was third. The winner had 45 million points against, just a tad fewer than me."

"Was it an experienced person?"

"No. A beginner. Her handicap was 0.50."

"I'm sorry, Ab. Do you think it was fair?" T One asked him.

"Er...yes. She'll only get 22 million seus. If I'd really wanted it, I could have had it."

"But would you have got as much as you deserved?"

"The handicaps put candidates in fair competition. The one qualified and hungriest for that work will be the winner. It was fair."

T One shook her head. "No, I don't agree. They can't reduce individuality to a double-digit number. This SEU system assumes that someone with a handicap of 0.50 is worth paying half as much to as someone with a handicap of 1.00. It assumes that they'll be half as productive or profitable, when really they'll be worth many times less. It's ridiculous." She stabbed at her food.

"Not at all," Marko said evenly. "It means that they get someone with lower qualifications who is prepared to do the job for much less. It favours beginners."

"I disagree. It does give beginners a fair go but the system is elitist," Abajoe said. "The elite are open and accessible at every level. The system offers hope of fair treatment and job satisfaction. I like it."

"But it pits worker against worker," said T One. "I thought you were in favour of strengthening communities of mutual interest."

"I am," Abajoe replied. "But selfishness comes first, then altruism."

"I must say, you are taking part in this job-finding system in good spirit. Do you reckon it is okay then?"

"Yes, it seems like a step forward. We'll keep it when we get rid of the SEU."

"Hmph."

His mother didn't say anything, but he knew that T One was one-eyed about this Government that had beaten them in the election and their few innovations were automatically bad. He hoped he would be more open-minded when he reached her age. The handicap system was a fair system for selecting outsiders to join an organisation. It dovetailed with his scheme for evaluating contributions scientifically for rewarding existing employees.

Two weeks later, Abajoe won a position as a collaboration facilitator. He would be working for local government, getting communes to work together in developing supply of essential services and industrial products. His salary would be only 20 million seus but it was his ideal job. He would be practicing his skills of politics and leadership. His fame would be a distinct asset. Most importantly, he would be able to lead the national resistance movement under cover of his daily work.

CHAPTER 45

Centaurus

Abajoe went to work at his job in the enemy camp with the sole purpose of using it as cover for his leadership of the MWP. He was very careful and within a short time was trusted to work away from scrutiny. He was able to receive and transmit messages that conducted the actions of the collaborilla army effectively.

Chronic resistance within the Government to SEU takeover became acute. Although leadership had not been identified with certainty, Abajoe was suspected of being the mastermind and the MWP of preventing the takeover coming into effect in all government departments.

Sudarta responded by outlawing the Party. MWP members could not take their seats in Parliament. Police destroyed the Party's virtual headquarters and seized its records. Party members could not meet, nor participate in events. They could not have offices, communications or records. Nor could they seek public support. Sudarta was intent on silencing opposition.

Abajoe considered their position and was particularly influenced by Nelson Mandela's experience. They had many supporters in the community and they could wage a clandestine war of passive resistance. He and his disciples left their jobs and went into hiding. They moved into neighbourhoods where they were not known, adopted disguises, obtained new identities and broke off contact with people who had known them, except other Party members who they directed by hidden communication methods.

One evening, local representatives of the outlawed MWP virtmet at a secret location. Abajoe audio-conferenced with 250 sites around Austrasia, keeping everyone's identity concealed and merging the communications into established patterns. There were no visuals and none of those present knew the identity of the others taking part except by their code names. To avoid detection of such a large communications event, a supporter, who was a religious leader, had disguised it as a regular church service.

"We'll miss our Sunday service," he said. "No one will know that your conference is using our booking. Access is closed except to members and to know the difference they would have to listen in. We have a list that we call to assemble members."

"We have a list too. Are you sure they won't notice the change in lists?"

"It's unlikely, but by the time they have your conference will be ended."

"Won't they be able to trace our people from the call list?"

"You'll need to warn them to change their numbers just before and after the conference, letting you know their conference numbers at a new address."

"What if they have a stooge who participates in the conference?"

"The damage will be limited. He or she won't find out any permanent identities."

"Great."

"You'll have to find some other organisation to front you next time. It's too risky to try it twice."

"We'll manage. We have supporters in several organisations that hold big audio conferences. But maybe we'll try other media as well."

"Radio?"

"Maybe. There are several possibilities, including holding a real meeting."

"Good luck."

"It's more a question of good planning. Thanks for your help."

Abajoe, began the virtmeeting, using a voice scrambler to conceal his identity. He was at the religious leader's studio, with members' password names arrayed on a video screen so he could see individuals present, mute them to hear their questions in advance and sequence their requests to speak. He spoke into a microphone using notes on a screen. Other screens held notes passed to him from participants that he responded to in private asides using a voice to text converter.

"Good evening, everybody. My name is Apple and I'll be chairing our meeting. Everyone today has been assigned the name of a fruit as a password. You can request to speak and I'll put together a speaking sequence as we go."

He then gave news of various actions, meetings and members, with their identities concealed.

"We have been active in almost every electorate in resisting the Government's capitulation to the SEU. This has delayed the hegemonic takeover of our markets and production and discouraged development of industry where it is not wanted. There has been less immigration than expected. Growth has been mostly in areas of the country with Yamen-controlled governments.

"Already, the Government is in difficulty thanks to your efforts," he summarised. "It is time we decided what we're going to do to remove them from office. I'd like you to listen to a story, an analogy, that I hope will help crystallise our thinking. It's about relations a nation has with its neighbour and the regional government. You've got it; relations between Austrasia, Bhakaria and the SEU. The analogy will let us predict stereotypical behaviour, without getting bogged down in recent history."

He began the story with his voice cold and distant.

"Let's imagine a galaxy of nations with a constellation, Centaurus, which is a group of stars, like Austrasia which has eight sub-economies. Compared with the other national economies, Centaurus is small but wealthy, like Austrasia. The Centaurians are concerned about their national security and, to obtain the protection of the regional government, they have to allow immigration from Proxima, the nearest star, which, like Bhakaria, is much larger and more crowded than Centaurus. Let's consider the relationship between Centaurus and Proxima."

Abajoe paused a moment for his listeners to think about this hypothetical situation. His voice climbed to a higher, more urgent note.

"The inhabitants of Proxima have a culture that clashes with the Centaurians' culture. There are many immigrants from Proxima arriving in Centaurus and they are destabilising its Government. Centaurus is polarised between the two cultures and there is civil war. Collaborators with Proxima in Centaurus invite Proxima to invade and it does, establishing colonial rule. Now, how does colonial rule affect Centaurus?"

Siti interrupted him.

"My name is Quince. Is this like when Bhakaria invaded us during the Great Famine, or is it a future possibility?"

"It's in the future. You're right; the Proximans did invade Centaurus in 2242, because they were invited by the Progress Party. The Proximans are expansionists. However, they weren't there long enough to establish a colony. Five years later, T One led Centaurus to independence."

"The Centaurians hated being subservient to the Bhakarians," said Siti. "In a colony, the invader is dominant and the locals are subjugated. What type of relationship would there be between the Proximans and Centaurus?"

John spoke up. "Guava here. Colonisers send a military force, convicts, settlers and emigrants, whereas the way that the invader exercises power over the locals is called imperialism. It is control exercised informally via influence."

"Yes, there was informal control. First there would have been imperialism, followed by colonialism," Siti concluded.

Abajoe's voice took on a note of urgency. "Correct. I'll continue the story. Imperial Proxima established a colony. For many years, Proxima bought or rather took minerals from Centaurian mines, maintaining a military force in Centaurus to support the Government and sending settlers to relieve its own overcrowding. Centaurian locals resented the presence of the Proximans and an independence movement started with locals sabotaging Proximan interests and fighting with settlers and collaborators. The situation deteriorated into a bloody civil war.

"The regional capital, the star Alpha, like the SEU, sent its troops to Centaurus and Proxima brought its own home. Alpha took minerals without payment and imposed a regime of state socialism that reduced Centaurian's wealth to the same level as that of people in other undeveloped nations in the region, which had half the population below poverty level. Within a few years, Centaurus had been reduced from the wealthiest nation in the region to one of the poorest.

"The Centaurian locals continued to seek independence. For many years, Alpha troops in Centaurus suffered guerrilla attacks until eventually they withdrew and once again, Centaurus was independent. Except now, it was impoverished.

"There, what can we learn from my analogy?"

"That we're up to the Alpha intercession bit."

"Correct. What else?"

"Pomelo. Why did Centaurus allow an influx of immigrants in the first place?"

"To have Alpha's protection they had to…it was one of their cultural rules…free immigration."

"But this brought a problem far worse..."

"Yes, the Centaurians' culture was destroyed..."

"Instead they ended up ruled by Alpha under state socialism..."

"...wasn't that a failure in Russia and China?" Paula interjected.

"Yes, but people wanted to try it again. Communication technology had improved, allowing more voting."

There was silence as they considered the analogy for its depiction of the SEU's role in Austrasia.

"Persimmon. Why did Alpha insist on free immigration?"

"Quince. It followed from wanting to have labour available for development anywhere, to create competition between local governments. Developers could attract workers from near and far. Conversely, if a country had unemployment, people could emigrate to other countries where there were jobs."

"What if Centaurus has fewer job opportunities than Proxima?"

"Then immigrants would stop coming, or would return home again. But Centaurians' wealth meant there were jobs providing personal services for wealthy people, care, personal development and education."

"But Centaurians are accumulating communal wealth, with individuals having little property, a low standard of material living, in a subsistence economy."

"Some people could be wealthy enough to employ cheap immigrant labour."

"It doesn't seem a very humane policy to plan for immigration into sub-marginal jobs."

"The SEU argues that once employed on Centaurus, they will gain experience to be self-sufficient. However, many immigrants always get stuck in submarginal positions whereas they would be better off at home. I think it is an inhumane policy. Alpha has no right to force free immigration on Centaurus."

There was a pause as the participants considered Austrasia's immigration situation. It was broken when Abajoe spoke again.

"Apple. Shouldn't the Centaurians have shared their hectares with the newcomers?"

"Monsterio. Not if that would reduce their ability to make a living," said Paula. "That would just transfer poverty from Proxima to Centaurus."

"If Centaurians won't share their wealth, then there wouldn't be as many immigrants."

"Obviously. Centaurus can only absorb a few."

"So if Centaurus had had strict immigration controls from the start, it would have been able to stay independent," said Siti with finality.

"Yes," agreed Abajoe. "Centaurus could have remained a curiosity, a primary economy with wealthy citizens. The territorial ambitions of Proxima and Alpha would have been thwarted. In retrospect, Centaurus would have been better off without Alpha's protection."

"Alpha didn't protect them at all," Peter objected. "Not even when Proxima attacked. Alpha did nothing to stop them."

"Maybe there was bad blood between Centaurus and Alpha. Like between Austrasia and the SEU. Austrasia was in the SEU from 2050 to 2102 but then left because of the SEU's racism. The SEU's racist policies subsequently collapsed. They have tried to get us back in ever since. They helped make the Bhakarians go home and we were supposed to join the SEU then. But T One was suspicious of their motives in taking over our mineral resources. So we reneged and they may feel we owe them."

"The upshot is that Centaurus should not have sought protection from Alpha and should have remained independent," Siti reasserted. "We reject regional control. We will be better off looking after ourselves."

"Persimmon. But we cannot look after ourselves in a stoush, can we? We have hardly any defence force."

"Pomegranate. For defence, Centaurus could have had a nuclear deterrent. It worked for Austrasia in 2168." *

"Nuclear weapons will deter a distant power but you are hardly going to use them to stop a neighbour from invading, to rescue our Government from the bloodbath of a civil war," said Abajoe.

"Austrasia is friends with other nations who will come to our aid. That is where our defence must lie. We must be a good friend in the neighbourhood, helping others where we can. We must share our good fortune through self-altruism. Resources not needed to sustain us in the long term should be made available to be shared with others. They are the basis of our defence."

*(*In 2168 Australia confronted a foreign power, Eurany, that was exploiting Austrasia's minerals through monopsony, a buyers' cartel. Australia threatened to deploy nukes in her defence and stopped Eurany's invasion, ending the Coal Wars. See Carbexport Ozsanction 2168 by the same author.)*

John said, "The problem is that most foreigners don't understand how limited our water and food-growing capacity is. The difference between Centaurus and Austrasia is that in the analogy, Centaurus could choose whether to allow immigration whereas in reality an invasion by Bhakarian immigrants is being forced on us by our own Government through the SEU."

"Your analogy is unfair. Immigrants from Proxima, or rather Bhakaria, aren't wholly bad as you have suggested," said Peter hotly. "A lot of what passes for public debate about Bhakaria and Austrasia is based on profound ignorance and stereotyping of the country, including the xenophobic ranting of people who claim to value human equality, respect and dignity. For them, Bhakaria and its problems have little significance in their own right, but are only a canvas upon which Austrasian political battles can be played out and Austrasian fears and fantasies projected. We have a responsibility to the region..."

"If we choose to accept it," said Abajoe. "But we won't. Self-altruism requires we look after our own long-term interests before we help others."

"The canvas is already laid out, Peter," said Siti. "The situation is not an open choice. Centaurus has a treaty with Alpha. The Centaurian Government is ruthlessly crushing opposition...us."

"Perhaps there's nothing we can do?" said John.

Others voiced similar concerns. There was a general feeling of hopelessness in the group. When all seemed lost, Abajoe spoke again. His voice was persuasive, confident.

"Comrades, we will prevail but it will take some time. In ice hockey, they say you shouldn't go to where the puck is now but to where the puck is going next. Soon we will have the commitment of the people to obtain independence from the SEU and we need to get ready to mobilise their support. We have to build influence within the new society that the Government is creating and work through the channels that are open to us to show the problems of uncontrolled immigration and SEU membership. We must be invisible. Then, on the day when we are ready, we will propose our alternative and overthrow the Government. This will take time and there is no time to lose in preparing for that day."

Abajoe closed the formal meeting and participants chatted with each other until they left the virtual conference on a random schedule. They

departed one by one, each by a different electronic route to avoid
government attention.

CHAPTER 46

Long March

The MWP campaign Abajoe co-ordinated from under cover of a government job was being met by harsh reprisals and progress was slow. He wanted to preserve the system of government but get rid of its political masters, just as Gandhi had done in India, Mandela had done in South Africa and Mao had done in China. Mao was the most militant and the best organised. Abajoe knew they couldn't win in armed confrontation through lack of funds to acquire superior weapons. Because Mao had sought armed confrontation, whereas Abajoe sought to avoid it, he had taken Mao's Ten Principles of War and worked out opposites to each of his Ten Principles of War, with the results listed below.

1.   *Infiltrate strong government offices first, infiltrate isolated government offices later.*
2.   *Target big cities first, then towns and rural areas later.*
3.   *The main objective to subverting hierarchies without wiping out the Government's strength.*
4.   *Infiltrate government offices even if they cannot be completely overcome.*
5.   *It is worth entering contests even if you cannot win.*
6.   *Fear confrontation and have courage with self-sacrifice and fatigue.*
7.   *Infiltrate the government offices when they are at work.*
8.   *Wait and study before infiltrating even weakly defended systems.*
9.   *Do not use new collaborators immediately to spearhead infiltration.*
10. *Rest, train and consolidate to sustain infiltration. The Government should be permitted sufficient breathing space to prevent their panic.*

These were Abajoe's secret principles of Passive Resistance to counter the SEU takeover actions by strengthening reactions. Based on Lenz's Law, the passivity would be attributed to weaknesses in the SEU policies being introduced.

He communicated them to every local member via a commercial communicator service offshore having no traceable connection with Abajoe. The MWP was actively recruiting and training members for passive resistance. They were eager to begin. From the concealment of their jobs, Abajoe and his followers slowly but surely organised recruits into a nationwide resistance movement. The movement trained 'collaborillas' who would appear to collaborate with the Government but who would render it ineffective from within, until SEU control would be paralysed.

When the MWP was ready, he called for passive resistance that would bring provincial hierarchies of government throughout Austrasia to a standstill. Following these Ten Principles, collaborillas in growing numbers infiltrated and blocked the bureaucracy. SEU and Bhakarian agencies suffered administrative chaos across the nation.

The Austrasian Government had difficulty implementing SEU policies. There was a groundswell of opposition and people continued to use traditional methods even when threatened with arrest. For example, the SEU required that food producers market their produce under central auspices at set prices but they continued to distribute it locally by bartering.

In a few suburbs there was a predominantly Yamen population that collaborated with the Government and these became known as the 'seuburbs'. Bhakarian immigrants, rejected elsewhere, were accepted in the seuburbs and they became Bhakarian ghettos. Even so, there was periodic sectarian violence where communities tried to expel Bhakarians. Yamen leaders instructed their followers to meet racist force with superior force and the Government became absorbed in quelling racist conflagrations.

Persecution of the collectivists was stepped up and informants were rewarded handsomely. Nevertheless, collaborillas maintained passive resistance to SEU centralisation and immigrant processing. MWP comrades and new recruits gathered in secret urban encampments near large government offices. When the police discovered them and attacked them, they moved out of the city to safer secret bases from where concerted passive resistance was instigated. For example, sympathetic workers would give SEU matters their lowest priority, causing delays that wreaked havoc.

Unable to countenance the Government's loss of control any longer, Sudarta requested help from the Bhakarian Government. The Bhakarians had sent troops to Austrasia earlier, during the Great Famine. Many Austrasians had Bhakarian ancestry, including Sudarta. The Bhakarians regarded Austrasia as a potential province and were eager to reassert their control. Large numbers of troops arrived the following week and set about finding the MWP bases and capturing insurgents.

The MWP response to military occupation was to meet violence with violence. Guerrilla attacks escalated and the Bhakarian troops engaged in reprisals on innocent civilians. There was arrest without trial, and traditional freedoms of education, speech, movement and religion were removed. Local governments were placed under military rule by the Bhakarian Army and the police swooped on known MWP members. Prisoners were tortured and killed. Many more simply disappeared.

Abajoe reflected on the fate of Celts, Bretons, Basques and Tamils who fled repressive regimes to remote and difficult terrain where they survived. Abajoe fled with the Party core to the hills of the Noomben district, where the local people had routed the Bhakarian Army after the Great Famine. There his rebels could openly foment rebellion against government tyranny. The Party's hierarchy concerted opposition throughout the nation.

Living frugally in supporters' homes, barns, caves and tents, the protestors grew in numbers to 30,000. There was safety in numbers and Sudarta's militias would not venture into their midst. Although committed to passive resistance, the rebels met steel with steel and would use guns for their own protection when there was no alternative. Abandoning hope of quelling the insurrection, Sudarta requested the Bhakarian Army to drive them from the area. The MWP did not have the technology to match their robot attacks and evacuated, leaving hundreds of dead where they lay. They carried their wounded to safety and left them in supporters' homes.

Despite their losses, the MWP force grew to outnumber the Bhakarian troops and they were confined to picking off isolated stragglers. He had read about Mao Tse Tung's epochal role in opposing the Chinese nationalists and how he had transformed a rout into a victory march. They needed to retreat slowly, gathering recruits to a more remote and more easily defendable place, where they could get food and train to become an armed force to liberate the nation. Copying from history, their rout became his Long March.

Led by Abajoe and organised by the disciples, the MWP migrated south along a route inland of major river crossings, which could be defended by the Bhakarians. Following the Great Dividing Range, 50,000 collectivists braved bitter conditions in which 2000 of their number died. Those that continued emerged with their resolve hardened, ready to sacrifice their lives for the good of the group. They spread out to avoid Army ambushes at bridges and in road cuttings. The Bhakarian Army had control of the major roads and very few of the rebels had access to a vehicle. They walked through the alluvial lands where food was produced, the most populous part of the nation. Many local people were inspired to join them and their number steadily increased.

Abajoe walked tall and proudly, in the footsteps of his forebears, who had been persecuted and driven into captivity and near extinction. He was a warrior from a long line of warriors who had given their lives so his people might live the way they wanted. Now again, their culture was under threat and he would do his utmost to save it. If he had to make the ultimate sacrifice of his life, he would willingly do so.

The marchers were unarmed but sections had armed guards backing them up. They avoided presenting a target for a Bhakarian Army attack and kept apart, blending into the places they passed through. At night, they came together in encampments. Supporters brought cooking equipment to them from their previous camps, hidden in local people's vehicles so as not to attract attention. Each encampment was guarded and well organised. When a raid was signalled, a squad would oppose the raiders while the rest dispersed.

During the daytime, the marchers had used different tactics to get past the Army. When a Bhakarian Army platoon confronted them, marchers in hundreds surrounded them within minutes, more than they could hope to shoot and the platoon's escape was cut off. The marchers had moved in on the soldiers, who had panicked and started firing. As they fell, other martyrs pushed into their places and they kept coming forwards until the soldiers had pleaded for their lives but the marchers had trampled them underfoot. The Army was nonplussed. They knew that if they tried to stop their progress, they would be crushed by weight of numbers. They adopted a harassment role for a while but Siti made sure they were punished for any interference in their progress. Gradually, they changed to shepherding the marchers.

Several times each day, Abajoe, Siti, Paula and John, disguised as tourists, surveyed along and across the line of march in a borrowed electrocar. In a village about halfway between Meannjin and Warringa, they stopped in the main street beside the highway and were having coffee at a pavement table.

Marchers came sporadically, a few minutes apart on both sides of the street, in ones, twos and threes, distinguishable by their steady progress through the local shoppers, by their walking clothes and by their backpacks. They were in every main street of every village, along every country road and in every town up to 20 kilometres inland. They would be passing by for the next week, over 60,000 individuals with the same purpose. It was a migration that swarmed past obstacles, stopping only to eat and sleep, always moving south.

Abajoe was awestruck by how many marchers there were, exultant that so many people had left their jobs and their homes spontaneously to join them. But the weight of responsibility for their welfare now lay squarely on his shoulders. Food and shelter had to be provided for every day of the march. Keeping the bellies of the marchers filled was a challenging task, which he had assigned to Peter. The Party had funds and he went ahead of them purchasing supplies to be ready for delivery when they made camp.

Stress tightened bands across his brain and down his spine. He had an unerring sense of danger and he was quick to call on the others to help him deal with it. He knew his limitations and confronted problems rather than denying or hiding from them. If they failed, Sudarta's militias would hunt them down and kill them like vermin. The march led inexorably towards a new future and their lives depended on its success. He would have to get his organisers to takeover some of his responsibilities. They were good people and although they would make mistakes, so would he if he tried to keep control to himself. The burden of responsibility was too much to bear alone.

While the marchers captured media attention, like the tip of an iceberg, the hidden MWP force throughout the nation continued its passive resistance to the SEU takeover. For example, in Meannjin, bank workers delayed processing of all SEU and Bhakarian transactions. Sudarta found that the Bhakarian Army could not recover her control of the nation nor stop the marchers and her leadership faltered, never to be regained.

The marchers were the focus of opposition to the Government throughout Austrasia. During the trek, which lasted two months, Abajoe attained unchallenged command of the Middle Way Party, ousting rivals, evading militias, escaping Army assassination squads. He inspired collaborillas to daring feats of passive opposition. The marchers' legendary discipline increased Party prestige. As the movement grew in size, it collected sufficient funds to sustain the rebels on their long march.

Abajoe and Siti bivouacked together and shared leadership of the march. Abajoe, for the first time in his life, was monogamous and became closer to Siti daily. They had complementary skills and shared the decision making. Abajoe concentrated on the goals for the day's marches and how they would overcome obstacles, such as Sudarta's troops, and where to set up camps. Siti commanded the marchers and communicated Abajoe's plans. When they were under attack, they worked side by side, with Abajoe deciding strategies while Siti maintained contact with the leaders and decided tactics.

Siti decided the bluff, bluster and bribery needed to evade Bhakarian platoons. She was a people person who liked coping with new situations. Her lieutenant was John and the two walked near the front of the column, talking with the others by communicator. Abajoe was by nature peaceful and a details person. He worked to ensure the marchers were taking the best routes, were properly fed, rested and supported in action. He co-ordinated the specialists who organised security, defence, camp sites, food, kitchens, ablutions, hospitals and recruitment.

The organising group was split up between different sections of the march to provide continuity of the leadership in case a group was captured. Abajoe and Siti stayed together but looked after a different section every night, co-ordinating them and maintaining their morale.

One evening Abajoe and Siti relaxed together in canvas camp chairs by their tent.

"We made 50 kilometres today," Siti said proudly.

"It went pretty smoothly," Abajoe replied, "and it wasn't easy." He knew that recognition meant a lot to her. The column had avoided an ambush by having scouts go forward and the column diverted at the last minute.

"We lost a man and had two stretcher cases, didn't we?"

"It's about what you would expect. The Bhakarian Army isn't trying to wipe us out, just demoralise us so we will turn back."

"But we aren't demoralised, are we Ab?"

"No. We were in good spirits at dinner."

"That was the curry and red. Peter spoils us rotten."

"An army marches on its stomach. We eat well when we have the money."

"How's that going?"

"We're right for the next week and I think there's more on the way. Support is growing. The collaborillas have been so effective that the SEU takeover is in total disarray."

"Great."

T One and Marko, who had gone ahead secretly by train, joined the march as they arrived in Warringa, bringing with them a contingent of 20,000 supporters. The marchers walked six abreast and blocked the Harbour Bridge for four hours unopposed by the police.

Although the recruits were welcome, they were an additional responsibility for which Abajoe had to plan. The marchers were headed for the South Coast, where they would be hemmed in between the following Bhakarian troops and the sea.

CHAPTER 47

Trial by Sea

As they neared the South Coast, the marchers came together in columns that were pushed forward by those behind. Nevertheless, their retreat from the pursuing Bhakarian Army was hopeful because they would be sailing to freedom in Bassland. Sudarta had hired militia to persecute them but the tentacles of the national government decreased in effectiveness the further they were from Sudarta's headquarters in Kambarra. The Bhakarian Army slowed its progress with identity checks and the occasional arrest of a straggler. Now, only the sea crossing stood between them and freedom in Bassland.

The marchers poured on to the South Coast beaches at 30 coastal villages. The beach was crowded with tents of those waiting to cross. They bought food in the villages but many marchers had little money and lived off shellfish collected along the shoreline. Abajoe, who had watched a movie of the Dunkirk evacuation in 1940, deployed the disciples to enlist the help of local boat owners. They unmoored or launched an armada of small sail craft and they came into the beaches, loaded up with marchers and set out for Bassland 400 kms away. The boats took a week there and another week back and it took three months to clear the beaches.

Abajoe watched the embarkation with anxiety at Lanport, a fishing village, where he and Siti were in a supporter's home. Most marchers were impoverished and they lived in makeshift shelters on the beaches and relied on the food Peter's group provided. After a week, Abajoe paid for himself and Siti to cross on a steamboat. They left John to oversee the exodus from the mainland. Too much was at stake for them to take the risks of a small boat crossing. They needed to get to Bassland quickly to oversee arrangements for those arriving. It was important that they visited the encampments and dealt with any difficulties at living places on which groups might have to depend for more than a year. They were determined to bring the Party through these difficult times to success.

Sixty thousand marchers eventually reached Bassland after several months. They landed at various places along the North Coast and the marchers made their way to billets and encampments on supporters' properties.

The Party established a new headquarters (near Launceston) and their people were billeted either singly or in small groups, with supporters dispersed across Bassland. Local organisers co-ordinated with them.

Abajoe and Siti had been loaned a cottage in a village with a small harbour. They borrowed a boat and fished with boat rods when the weather was fine, catching fish for themselves and their guests, for they often received visitors from the mainland and they hosted meetings to organise the exiles. They had a vegetable garden and a barn where visitors could stay and they were self-sufficient. He and Siti loved living there and after two years were very sorry to leave.

On the mainland, Sudarta's Government had lost control of the nation. As passive resistance took hold in every government office, SEU programmes were halted and the Government staggered from crisis to crisis. The Bhakarian Army tried to maintain law and order, but their presence was resented and this made matters worse. With such a level of defiance, Sudarta had to compromise but she refused to lift the ban on the Middle Way Party or hold elections.

CHAPTER 48

Rebels' Camp Demands

When a detachment of the Bhakarian Army was sent to Bassland to look for the leaders of the insurrection, it was met with such hostility that it returned to the mainland. There it watched for a D-Day invasion or for return of the MWP leaders by checking passengers and inspecting small craft arriving from Bassland with a cordon of patrols along the South Coast.

Abajoe and Siti were headquartered at a supporter's farm at Truganini on the North Coast of Bassland. Their host was able to disguise their presence and the coming and going of their visitors amid the busy traffic of produce, farm supplies and machinery associated with the horticultural part of his business. They spent their time orchestrating by radio the resistance on the mainland to Sudarta's dictatorial Government and the Bhakarian occupying force. They had established a covert network, secured by a member's device, for secret signal coding and decoding that enabled them to broadcast to all the agents of the MWP resistance or interact privately with individuals. They had with them a small group of aides to help with communications, analysis and tactics. Because of their leading role in the confrontation on the mainland and the fear of discovery and assassination, the situation had become tense.

Sudarta had planted agents in the MWP, who received broadcasts and were aware who was leading the resistance, but she was unable to identify members of the collaborilla army. She had advertised a huge reward for capturing or killing Abajoe. He knew the MWP had been penetrated, from raids consequential to broadcasts and he had reduced the broadcasts to misinformation, while increasing private communications. This required more time but the MWP had robots it could programme to personalise, compress, code and transmit messages continuously.

Sometimes, to escape the pressure of leadership, Abajoe and Siti were able to put in half a day helping on the farm, harvesting or packing vegetable produce for market. It was a luxury to engage in work with a set routine and they could relax and chat together as they worked. They exulted in each other's company and explored their pasts in detail that

407

they had never had time for before, discovering skills, traits and foibles with delight.

The two enjoyed more time together than they had ever had and in beautiful surroundings. Some evenings they strolled together through forests where the Antarctic beech trees shared their Gondwanaland ancestry with almost identical trees in Chile. They had separated 80 million years before, as the continents broke away from each other and drifted apart. With hats, sunglasses and scarves concealing their identities, they walked along the sea beaches looking for useful items of flotsam among the piles of seaweed. They fished for trout in the farm dams with cunning fly hooks they tied themselves. Quickly the summer passed and the leaves turned golden. Their days were filled with togetherness and love.

"If I was pregnant," Siti said one day, "would that be fair?"

They talked about it. Abajoe badly wanted a child to fulfil his duty of passing on the Yabra heritage but their life was too uncertain and dangerous to have a baby with them. They must wait until their lives were more secure.

Siti accepted that it was a sufficient reason at present but because of their involvement in politics, their future would probably always seem uncertain. They should take the risk as soon as the ban on the MWP was lifted and there was not the immediate threat of arrest.

Inspired by the rebels in Bassland, mainland opposition to the occupying force grew, as had happened before in Austrasia in 1788, in 2170 during the Coal Wars and in 2220 after the Great Famine. Abajoe's underground army of collaborillas had infiltrated most government bureaucracies and brought many to a standstill despite persecution by the Bhakarian Army. The takeover by the SEU had been stopped. Soon, only the seuburbs and Yamen localities under SEU control had government offices that still functioned.

Fearing civil war, citizens loyal to the SEU and Bhakaria migrated to the seuburbs. Sudarta's Government partitioned the nation despite vigorous MWP opposition. The rest of the nation stayed under Bhakarian military rule.

Abajoe recalled Gandhi's opposition to partitioning and Eamon de Valera's prophetic role in opposing the partitioning of Ireland in 1921. Following his example, Abajoe campaigned for withdrawal of the SEU and independence from Bhakaria. He demanded scrapping of the name

'Austrasia' and return to the old name, 'Australia'. He called for establishment of a presidency that would stand above sectarian issues and for restoration of the Australian language and culture.

Abajoe adapted Eamon de Valera's message to British Prime Minister Lloyd George as a message that he sent to the SEU leadership in Seutosa.

By condoning Bhakarian troops outstaying their welcome in Austrasia, the SEU has added another horrid chapter to the already bloodstained record of relations between imperial powers and our multicultural people. First Britain declared terra nullius and helped herself to our land in the 19th century. Then Eurany came for cheap coal 80 years ago. Now the SEU is supporting the colonial ambitions of our neighbour, Bhakaria. Bhakarians are responding to Austrasia's dire circumstances by helping themselves to Austrasia's resources.

Can your Government not accept that Austrasia has the right to political independence? Will it not respect our right to determine how we dispose of our land, coal and minerals? Will it not call for Bhakarian withdrawal? If not, will it allow us independence from the SEU?

Will the Government in Seutosa not acknowledge that this island continent has since time immemorial withstood the ravages of rapacious invaders who have come, taken and departed? An island continent that regularly suffers famine, drought and disease and then recovers? An island continent that has never surrendered her soul but has adopted democracy, peacefulness and humanitarian values to persevere against heavy odds.

We, of our time, have pledged ourselves to preserve intact and pass on to future generations our glorious heritage and unblemished traditions. Will the Government in Seutosa please support us by requiring Bhakarian withdrawal?

Seutosa's immediate response was to encourage the Bhakarian Army and pro-Sudarta militias to even more harsh treatment of MWP dissidents. For a year, the two sides grappled with each other but slowly the MWP won the support of the people and the Bhakarian Army became ineffective. The nation was polarised and the Yamen inhabitants fearful of retribution if the Bhakarians left.

Abajoe followed the example of the ANC under Mandela and allowed sabotage and violence against the Bhakarian forces. The MWP fought a guerrilla war of attrition from its stronghold areas. The SEU, fearing a protracted civil war, announced a referendum to find out whether Austrasians wanted to be independent of Bhakaria. Abajoe and Siti were delighted because the civil wars they knew of in the UK, USA, France and Vietnam had left an indelible mark on the national psyches of those countries. A referendum could lead to withdrawal of the Bhakarians without further bloodshed.

However, Abajoe was doubtful that there was a majority sufficient to send the Bhakarians home. The situation seemed to him to be like the confrontation in Vietnam, with an invader staying to protect a minority who were kindred followers of their religion. Following the IRA and Vietcong's example, he ordered a campaign of terrorism in the seuburbs, to foreshadow events that would follow from continuance of the Bhakarian military presence.

A week later, they watched a news story about the referendum by a well-known journalist, Hilary Tensing, from Channel 077 Independent News. She was sympathetic to their cause and had made contact through a collaborilla friend. She had interviewed Abajoe by communicator, with Siti holding their host's camera, against a background that would not give their location away. The news story, 'The Austrasian Referendum', began with a video collage of Bhakarian soldiers fighting and later patrolling in the streets of Meannjin, with Hilary's voiceover as follows.

Title graphic map of Australia. 'AUSTRALIANS TO CHOOSE GOVERNANCE'.

"Austrasia will shortly have a referendum on the future of relations with its more populous neighbour, Bhakaria. The SEU, which is conducting the referendum, is confident that a majority of Austrasians will want to become an autonomous region within the Bhakarian Republic.
"On 15th July, 25 million Austrasian voters will be asked two questions."

Close up shot of referendum questionnaire. They read:

Do you accept the proposed autonomy for Austrasia within the unitary state of the Republic of Bhakaria?

Do you reject the proposed autonomy for Australia, that will lead to Bhakaria's withdrawal of support from Austrasia?

Medium shots of Progress Party and Middle Way Party faithful at congresses. Hilary's voice continued:

"Abajoe Yabra is the former Leader of the Opposition – the Middle Way Party. He lives in exile in Bassland, with an army of supporters estimated at 60,000 who marched there to escape persecution by the Sudarta Government and Bhakarian Army."

Shots of lines of marchers arriving on southern beaches.
Shots of Bhakarian Army confronting marchers.
Head shot of Abajoe, who says:

"There is no doubt that if Austrasians choose independence, they will be plunged into a tumultuous period of change and uncertainty and quite possibly political instability. Control of the new nation will be retained by the SEU but governance will be contested at least by the ruling Progress Party and by the currently illegal Middle Way Party.
"The Progress Party invited Bhakaria to provide a peace-keeping force when opposition by the MWP made the nation ungovernable shortly after they were elected nine years ago. Those who want independence point to the devastating effect that Bhakarian occupation has had on Austrasian morale and culture, comparing it to East Timor and Tibet at the end of the 20th century."

Medium shot of Bhakarian soldiers executing Australian MWP rebels.
Medium shot of exhumation of East Timor mass grave.
Medium split-screen shots of Abajoe at a western barbecue and at a Yamic feast.
He says:
"The easygoing, outdoor lifestyle of Austrasians is being displaced by intensive living under Yamic law," said Abajoe Yabra, Leader of the Middle Way Party. "There is a need to merge the two cultures to a

degree where governance is stable and this will take time, not compulsion at breakneck speed."

Long shots of coal mine. Narrator speaks.

"If Austrasia goes with Bhakaria, they will control natural resources which are considered strategic or vital to their foreign affairs, monetary and fiscal policies and national taxation."

Abajoe, face shot, says:

"If people vote 'Yes', they would retain very little control over their lifestyle and development. Austrasians will get very little from the plundering of their resources. Their heritage will be bulldozed and shipped out. The troops will stay and people have had more than enough of their biased intervention in our affairs."

Medium shots of marchers loading into boats. Hilary says:

"The Bhakarian military expelled Middle Way Party supporters to Bassland in 2270. But supporters of the ruling Progress Party believe Bhakarian supervision is needed to stabilise the deep schism in Austrasia between the traditional Austrasian and Yamen cultures."

Long shots of burning churches and gerejas. Voice-over:

"Austrasians are polarised into groups of Yamen newcomers and traditional Austrasians."

Close-up shot of journalist narrator Hilary Tensing standing in front of an ecumenical church. She says:

"Most Austrasians want an ecumenical Government like that being offered by the Middle Way Party, which is banned under Sudarta's Government. The leadership and devoted followers are living in camps in Bassland.

"All observers agree a 'No' vote could bring pain from a confrontation between the Bhakarian military and the rebels who have

become increasingly violent with terrorist strikes against them. Austrasians will soon find out who is going to be responsible for stopping it, either Bhakaria as a colonial power, or by a new democratically elected Government that melds both Yamen and MWP influences. Both roads forward seem thorny but an 80% majority is needed for independence.

"This is Hilary Tensing in Meannjin returning you to the studio."

Credits made by Channel 077 Independent News.

Abajoe switched off the screen. "Hilary's done a good job," he said, "but she doesn't mention the problem of the SEU moving into the vacuum when Bhakaria leave. One day we'll have to get rid of them too."

"That will be easier," said Siti. "We just have to reneg on our SEU membership, like we did in 2102."

"It was not easy," said Abajoe.

"But we did not need the terrorist back-up available."

Siti referred to the bomber who had been ready to blow up the Seutosa Parliament building in full session if it had refused to accept Australia's withdrawal.

"Next time we won't need it either. Once was enough."

"Sudarta never had a mandate to seek membership in the first place. She has a lot to answer for."

"Let's hope she doesn't manage to corrupt the referendum."

"The SEU won't let her get away with it."

"At least they're useful for something."

A few days later, the referendum showed overwhelming support for Austrasian independence. The immediate effect was a rampage of destruction as Bhakarian troops withdrew. Additional SEU forces were brought in to support Sudarta's Government but by the time they arrived, most public infrastructure built by the Bhakarians had been destroyed or damaged, allegedly by the departing troops. Yamen militias were also suspected of destroying infrastructure in areas opposed to Sudarta.

The nation's bureaucracy was blocked and the nation had become ungovernable. Sudarta lifted the ban on the Middle Way Party but did not set a date for an election. Abajoe, Siti and their supporters made their way home from Bassland openly, using public transport. They had been away for four years.

CHAPTER 49

Gone Home & Arrested

In the power vacuum left when the Bhakarians went home, Sudarta, supported by SEU troops, adopted draconian measures to assert government control. She set up an intelligence unit to monitor the Middle Way Party's activities. When the heroes from Bassland joined in the opposition on the mainland, the subversion was rooted out and viciously suppressed. Many supporters were tortured and imprisoned without trial.

Soon the channels for peaceful protest had disappeared and the situation seemed hopeless. People were angry that they had been duped by the lifting of the ban on the MWP. There was no democracy – only a takeover by the SEU. The MWP's militant youth wanted a national strike. However, now that the Bhakarians had gone, all the majority of Austrasians wanted was to avoid civil war and they accepted Yamen rule by the SEU.

Abajoe researched Nelson Mandela's struggle against racial discrimination in South Africa in 1961. In the end, passive resistance would not be enough. At a strategy meeting, John and his faction won a policy vote 'to embark on violent forms of political struggle and to form an Anti-Immigration Action Group'…the Government had left them no other choice.

At first, Abajoe was against any form of violent action. He warned the meeting, "Don't be violent except when your peaceful protests have been ignored, or to protect yourself or your companions from direct attack."

"So we can't strike at a militia who have raped our women and burned our homes?" retorted John.

Abajoe shook his head. "No. You must pursue your revenge legally. We will not sink to their level except when they are attacking us. Then it is an eye for an eye. But we will support the legal system as long as it acts effectively and with fairness."

Despite the hot bloods who wanted attacks, reluctantly, it was agreed.

At first Siti had tried to persuade Abajoe against actions opposing immigration. "You promised the MWP would let the guest workers in after 10 years," she reminded Abajoe.

"That is up in the air now. We are caught up in racism and have to take sides."

"Why?" she asked. "The MWP should stand above racism and unite the nation. Your stand against immigration will only divide us."

"I agree, privately," Abajoe replied. "But it is what the Party wants now. We can act to unite the nation later."

"I can't go along with this."

"Please, do it for me. Support the Party. If you are not for us, you're against us. Our relationship will be finished. I couldn't bear that."

She didn't answer for several days. It was a test of her loyalties but in the end she decided to make her future with Abajoe and acquiesced, albeit reluctantly.

"I think the MWP is making a mistake. But I'll go along with the crowd because the sooner they find out and reverse their position, the better."

She allowed her representation of the Mount Argus guest workers to wither although she kept in touch with her old friends there. But her relationship with Abajoe and the MWP had taken first place.

In the weeks that followed, Abajoe and John, anticipating an armed struggle, developed guerrilla training for the militant left of the Party to be deployed in Anti-Immigration Action Groups. 'Doing a Mandela' he went underground and travelled around Austrasia living with supporters and initiating the training of all members. He was compelled to live indoors during the daytime and could only venture out under cover of darkness. He had to disguise himself and adopted the fictitious name of Christopher.

Their most decisive actions prevented the Government giving Austrasians' property to immigrants. The Government was inspecting private property for the purpose of compulsory subdivision to provide homes for the burgeoning numbers of immigrants. If they assessed a family's wealth and income as providing an excess of self-sufficiency, half their land could be forcibly annexed and given to an immigrant family. Abajoe authorised the use of force to prevent these hated SEU-inspired inspections that stole Austrasians' lands. He deployed the Action Groups armed with hand weapons to stop the inspections.

The resistance to inspections quickly resulted in an escalation of violence. The situation was brought to a head when a government militia sent to protect an inspector was ambushed, overpowered and their weapons taken. Abajoe was trying to popularise the MWP's opposition to the Government. He wanted immigrant housing to be decided by local governments. Immigrants should be invited by local governments, not dumped on them. Sudarta's inspectors were unnecessary.

Not long after, Abajoe was arrested and charged with incitement to violence. The Government had evidence of his guerrilla training activities. The ban on the MWP was re-introduced.

He decided to conduct his own defence and used the trial as a forum for democratic rights. He applied for the reconstitution of the jury since there were quite a few immigrants and persons of Bhakarian extraction who very likely would not be impartial.

He prefaced this challenge with an affirmation based on Mandela's statement in court:

"Although I am opposed to immigration, I detest racism, because I regard it as a barbaric thing, whether it comes from an indigenous, oriental or Caucasian person. What I object to is the free entry of immigrants, who are accommodated by theft of land from the most thrifty of our citizens."

His challenge of democratic freedom was not sustained by the court. He was convicted and sentenced to five years' imprisonment. He was martyred and his name became the rallying call of their cause. "Free Abajoe" was chanted at pickets and protest gatherings.

Two years later, in 2257, he was charged with the sabotage of Gunyaba three years earlier. His inner group were arrested too and Abajoe was charged with leadership of the bombing and brought from prison to the dock with Siti, John and Peter, to stand trial.

Abajoe recalled that at that time, the MWP had regarded Gunyaba as a threat to the survival of local culture, with its operation counter to their immigration restriction policy. They requested that the national government stop encouraging immigration, but they were ignored. Peter had proposed they bomb Gunyaba. Going against the advice of elders, Zelta and Hugo, he had taken his proposal to Abajoe for decision.

"No, Peter," Abajoe had said. "Siti would be very upset. She spent a lot of time stopping us from selling it for conversion into flats."

"Yes, I know. I talked to her," Peter said, "but she's living in the past. The way the Government is using it could be our undoing. The future of Australian culture is on a knife edge now. We have to shut it down."

"Hmm. How else could we shut it down? Contaminate it with something…?"

"They might continue regardless…" Peter said.

"Make it so immigrants won't like to stay there… Could we infiltrate the staff with our unfriendly members?"

"No, it wouldn't work. The Yamen community would confront them."

"Can we damage the building just enough that it is unusable?" Peter suggested. "Or could we damage some immigrants?"

"No, Peter. People wouldn't vote for us."

"What about a small bomb?" Peter replied.

"Hmm…would the damage be enough to shut it down?"

"How about three very small ones: one in the front entry, one in the admin office and one on the stairs?"

"Okay," Abajoe had said. "That should do it. We will have to get the others' agreement."

Siti had reluctantly agreed but insisted on placing the bombs herself. She hid them in the crowded building one night. Then she set off the fire alarm and when the 500 immigrants poured outside, got away. Peter detonated the bombs remotely. The building was damaged enough for the immigrants to be relocated and the building did not reopen.

The Prosecution had portrayed them as acting against the public interest. They said that Gunyaba had been restored to its former use as an immigrant reception centre at public expense. Immigrants were accommodated until they could get work and find a home of their own. Gunyaba's welcome had brought more immigrants, most of them Yamens. The Yamen community was bolstered by the arrivals and looked forward to gaining majorities in the local and central parliaments against the MWP. Because of the MWP's rivalry and racist prejudice against the Yamens and opposition to immigration, they had tried to stop it by bombing the building.

Abajoe and the others were charged with very little evidence of their involvement. The maximum penalty allowed for sabotage was death. The case was brought to trial in Newtown, a suburb where there was scant support for the MWP. The jurors were Sudarta supporters and when the MWP lawyers requested they be changed, the replacements were even more biased but there was nothing the Defence could do. The MWP's defence was that there was neither evidence of their participation nor a motive, since the MWP had striven to save Gunyaba not long before. Their defence lawyers discovered that the Prosecution's case was to be based totally on the false evidence of witnesses they had bribed. There was a chance that they could persuade the jury to free them.

While Abajoe waited for his trial, he studied Nelson Mandela's strategy in his trial for a similar offence at Rivonia. His defiance had brought international opposition to the Boer Government and had been a turning point in the struggle against Apartheid.

In a speech to a packed court, Abajoe caused a sensation by admitting his involvement. He was hailed as the voice of the Austrasian people, calling for self-determination.

"I do not deny that I planned sabotage. I did not plan it in a spirit of recklessness, nor because I have any love of violence. I planned it as a result of a calm and sober assessment of the political situation that had arisen after many years of tyranny, exploitation, and oppression of my people by the Sudarta Government."

Abajoe told the court that the Anti-Immigration Action Group was formed to bring the Government to its senses before the desperate state of a civil war was reached. Attacks were to be against the symbols of colonial oppression, such as public buildings and the supply lines of economic exploitation. The MWP only attacked when buildings were empty and this was not terrorism. These acts were designed to provide an outlet for those people who wanted adoption of violent methods and would serve as a source of inspiration to maintain the hopes of the people. The sabotage would be vindicated by the nation rising up and overthrowing Sudarta.

When his words of defiance were broadcast, protestors jammed government frequencies for the following week. Sudarta called out the Army to quell rioting outside the court and stop demonstration marches throughout the nation.

He denied he was a communist and said he was an Austrasian patriot, attracted by the idea of a classless society. This society would acknowledge that the land was the means of production and belonged to the community, as indigenous people had owned it in the past. Once there had been neither rich nor poor, and there had been no exploitation. This could be achieved again by self-altruism, New Science and devolution. The Middle Way Party had provided a century and a half of fair governance, until losing office due to promotion of sectarian politics and population growth by the Progress Party and Yamen religion. Since then, Australia had been mired in regional centralism, Bhakarian expansionism and cultural dilution.

Abajoe made an impassioned plea for science to determine public policy issues rather than politics.

The next day, Sudarta invaded disputed territory in Antarctica in response to a trumped-up pretext and distracted the nation's attention from the trial. This created a crisis with the northern superpower, Eurany. Austrasia needed Bhakarian support and the MWP's confrontation was an embarrassment to be glossed over as quickly as possible.

His final words from the dock were:

"I have fought against immigration and I have fought against closing our borders. I have cherished the ideal of an open, democratic and free society in which all persons live together in harmony with equal opportunities. It is an ideal, for which I hope to live and to achieve. But if needs be, it is an ideal for which I am prepared to die."

Abajoe's confession saved his life but, for his defiance, he was sentenced to life imprisonment. His testimony inadvertently incriminated Siti, John and Peter and other members of the group, who had taken part in the organisation and training for the sabotage. Peter denied leading the bomb squad and Abajoe was held responsible. Although they denied involvement, his evidence had betrayed them and they too received life sentences.

The others accepted his explanation that if he had remained silent, the movement would have been crushed, whereas their defiance was now being held up as an example, to millions of Austrasians, of opposition to the Government. Their bonds developed on the long march and in Bassland were strong. They knew he had done it for the good of the Party and had gambled on overthrowing the Government. He had underestimated Sudarta. As they served time with him, they never held his protesting confession against him, as his motivation had been to publicise the injustice the movement acted against and the invalidity of the court.

Abajoe, John and Peter each served 15 years in prison together at a tiny island prison, where few visitors ever came to see them. Siti had also received life but Abajoe didn't know where. When the other men were released, Abajoe served another three years, the remainder of the sentence for his earlier conviction.

Through patient inquiry, he found out after a year that Siti was serving equal time at a women's prison for dissidents, also at a remote location. His lawyer obtained for him the right to one exchange with her of heavily censored letters each month. This slender thread of correspondence kept their relationship alive.

Noogoon Island Prison – 7/7/2261

Dear Siti

I hope you are well and free. I have received nothing from you since your letter of 12/5/2257, although I have written every six months as I am allowed. I have requested a visit from you too but perhaps they are keeping us apart. Paula came first, then T One.

Their visits were a tonic and I am in good health except for hypertension. As I write, I glance at the photograph of you reclining by the pool at Minjerribah Island, that adorns the wall behind the desk in my cell. I look at you many times each day and have a fantasy for almost every pixel. How I miss the wisdom and humour of your company and long to feel your beautiful body against mine. My love for you tries to burst my heart, with aching sobs and regretful tears not far below my surface. When I think back to our intercourse, with every passing month the sensations are fading, like awakening from a dream. But the significance of the dream and its pleasures is being magnified the longer we are apart.

My sorrow at your incarceration does not fade, but at the same time keeps my hope alive. News of our men and women, who are standing up to be counted, is vindicating my decision to speak out at the trial. John and Peter have forgiven me. I am also grateful to our (sentences deleted by censor).

The garden that I told you I had started in my last letter is a great success. John and Peter help me supply the kitchen and the warders with tomatoes and green peppers. I spend several hours a day there and we talk about what we will do on release. (Sentences deleted by censor).

My other pastime is studying the politics of oppression. I have been reading biographies of the Mandelas of South Africa, de Valera of Eire, Mao Tse Tung of China and Mahatma Gandhi of India. These leaders sought to unite their nations against oppressors in several different ways we could copy. There is no benefit in reinventing the wheel. Nelson Mandela's example makes my every day here more meaningful.

I have also been studying the SEU and Bhakaria to 'Know thine enemy.' One day, we will want to negotiate with them to effect a compromise. Their wants need to be met to get a united Austrasia.

Although times are dark for us, our cause is just and we will prevail. I have copied below the last stanza of William Henley's 1785 poem 'Invictus'.

> *It matters not how strait the gate,*
> *How charged with punishments the scroll.*
> *I am the master of my fate:*
> *I am the captain of my soul.*

May this letter reach you and bring a reply soon. You are always in my thoughts.
With all my love
Abajoe

For the men in jail, the days crawled past with a numbing routine of chores that included growing their own food. Abajoe exchanged his other chores for gardening, to which he brought a wealth of experience. As they worked in the gardens, they would discuss politics and prepare a campaign for when they were released.

Learning to put remorse behind him, from Gandhi, Abajoe lived each day in prison a day at a time. He drew his strength from Siti's rare letters from her cell. He kept his mind alive with secret messages to Paula and the MWP outside. With the enthusiastic John and the taciturn Peter for company, he spent as much as possible of his time gardening and experimenting with plants. He was allowed one visitor every six months.

His parents and Paula came individually, their faces lined with age and concern.

While they were in jail, the MWP members remained committed to the fight for SEU withdrawal and Abajoe became their prophet. His writings, smuggled from jail, were the inspiration of a large resistance movement.

These were not wasted years, nor did he become bitter. Abajoe adopted Mahatma Gandhi's principle of 'ahimsa', meaning non-violence. It meant that members may not offend anybody; nor may they harbour uncharitable thoughts, even in connection with those whom they consider their enemies. They had to meet their enemies with passive resistance.

The men also spent time in meditation. He prepared for leadership on his release by developing his philosophy and rehearsing in his mind how he would deal with the situations that would confront him. Austrasia was in the hands of a tyrant and traditional culture was being destroyed and replaced by materialism and selfish competition. He would pick up the pieces and continue developing self-altruism.

Siti's letters rarely reached him but kept him going. Her letters revealed she was essentially alone but had kept alive her dreams of political success. She was studying law and economics in prison and he heard from visitors that she smuggled out learned papers, which were published anonymously by the MWP. She had become the Party's intellectual dynamo, while he was its martyred icon.

Family Fare Tower – 25/2/2273

Dear Abajoe

I have just now received your letter of 7/7/2271 and hope you are still well and in good spirits. They released me two months ago and I am back living at The Tower and growing food. I wrote to you several times before that and several times since, so it seems like they are holding up or stopping our communication. My MWP work is a thorn in their side and they are trying to dissuade me by illegally removing your rights as a prisoner. I have applied every month to the minister to visit you but he hasn't replied.

My condolences for the loss of your great-grandfather Hugo. One hundred and thirty three is a good age to reach if you have good health, which he did not. The virtual funeral brought the nation to a standstill. I miss him and have visited Charlotte several times since.

I am well and healthy but, without you, I am existing rather than living. You are my joy and soul mate. Our separation is a cruelty that I am unable to forgive and prison has left me with a deep sadness. I regret very much not taking the risk of having a child when we had the opportunity. By the time you are released, I will be 61. Medical advances have extended female fertility and I still want to try to have a child with you immediately, even if we are not secure. Our freedom will have to be enough security.

You should not have any regrets about Newtown. The publicity you achieved by your confession vindicated our silence to a puzzled nation. There are 12 of us 'disciples' but there are 50 million Austrasians who know, or will learn, of our cause as your speeches are broadcast and when our protests act as a prompt, they will be broadcast again and again.

Thanks to your self-altruism, the plight of Australia's traditional people has become known throughout the world and sanctions applied to end Sudarta's tyranny.

Could your study of oppression include Suu Kyi of Myanmar, whose strategy of passive resistance eventually prevailed, although she lived most of her adult life under house arrest? I have copied below the beginning of her 'Freedom from Fear' speech.

> *It is not power that corrupts but fear. Fear of losing power corrupts those who wield it and fear of the scourge of power corrupts those who are subject to it.*

Your fearlessness is an example to us. We are not letting ourselves be intimidated and are focused on getting a fair election that will unite our polarised nation.

It seems that I have become a gardener like you. The rossits have been kept going by Zelta, Hugo and Charlotte and number about 800, in all the rooms. It seems a long time ago when that number bred in one small room called 'Bhakaria'.

The censor has covered up your working party talk but I'm very sure it would not be about central control. Here we talk about democracy,

On release after 15 years in prison, Siti was not banned from politics. She led from their home the Party's passive campaign for a national election. Her strategy was to offer policies different to the Government's, such as restriction of immigration. The immigration issue had become tense, with feelings against immigrants running high due to a drought and food shortages on the East Coast.

When he was imprisoned, Abajoe had time to think at leisure about the hectic years of political campaigning. One day, he thought over the rossits' experiments and how they had made a hole between the pens, just larger than the size of an adult rabbit, and blocked it with a grill. They recorded rossit activity at the grill with cameras from both sides and tried to relate activity at the grill with conditions in the two pens, such as population and food availability.

They had a robot analyse the camera recordings and showed that there was little activity on either side, even when living conditions were dissimilar, until one pen suffered from acute hunger. Then rossits tried to get out into the other pen. Suddenly, he remembered seeing young rossits, not long after leaving the nest, squeeze through the grill and obtain food. Their bellies swollen, they were too large to return through the grill. Abajoe was surprised to find that their hosts accepted them and they grew and bred with them as fully integrated immigrants. When he had seen this, he had barely noticed, as he was more interested in adult behaviour at the grill. He alone had seen rossits move between the Australian and Bhakarian pens. He hadn't thought about the implications of what he had seen until now.

He recalled that the same acceptance of young refugees had operated in reverse. When hunger struck the host pen, a few young rossits migrated through the grill in the other direction. Thus the two communities shared resources and formed one population, with their young migrating through the opening to obtain food and living space when forced to do so by inferior conditions at home.

Abajoe knew that his people, the Wagarra tribe, shared what they had with kin. This was reciprocated within family groups, defining who was included. If you shared your resources with the group, you were given protection, shelter and social acceptance by the group. When kinfolk were in need, even if they were strangers, they allowed them to pass through their territory, with access to water and permission to gather food. At other times, females were exchanged to diversify the gene pools.

It was evident that the rossits in the two pens recognised each other as kin by sharing with each other and by accepting refugees from famine. Emigration helped those left behind to survive. It also diversified the gene pool in both places, welcoming the genes of adventurous immigrant types that had been hardy enough to survive adverse conditions and prosper.

When he realised that immigration between Austrasia and the countries of the region would be reciprocated and relieve food shortages, improve survival and diversify heredity, Abajoe's heart sank. He had spent 15 years in prison for bombing Gunyaba when he should have supported its important role in processing immigrants. He had wasted the most productive years of his life in prison for nothing. In the excitement of taking office and campaigning, he had focused on their precarious position from unrestricted immigration and overlooked the benefits of emigration until now, when he had a more distant perspective. After some careful thought, he concluded that Austrasians would benefit more from reciprocal immigration than Bhakaria because Austrasia's food supply was more threatened by a higher incidence of drought.

Lest he seem foolish, he decided to keep his retrospective error quiet, but on his release, he confided in Paula. They talked about MWP policy. Were Austrasian living conditions, he asked himself, truly harsher than Bhakaria's? He concluded Austrasian Governments had always acted as though Austrasia had superior living conditions. People had wanted their Government to fill them with nationalistic pride. They supposed that an open border policy would threaten that, with more mouths to feed and smaller shares in Austrasia's bounty. Under this assumption, the MWP had discharged their responsibility to the Austrasian people by restricting immigration.

Now he had concluded that the Austrasian community had living conditions no better, and probably even worse, than those which prevailed in the other countries of the region. Austrasians would benefit from the pooling of resources and unrestricted movement, allowing hungry Austrasians into Bhakaria.

CHAPTER 50

House Arrest

After serving 20 years in prison, Abajoe was released in 2275 into house arrest. For three years, Siti had been waiting for him at The Tower. When he came home, they lived together.

The ban on the MWP was lifted due to public demand and international sanctions but Abajoe was forbidden from participating in politics. On the day of his release, Abajoe was brought before the Austrasian Chief of Police.

"I have a message for you from Prime Minister Sudarta," he said. "The Government forbids your active leadership in the MWP," he read. "You will be arrested and charged with incitement at the first transgression. The penalty for incitement is brain clearing."

Abajoe and Siti were forbidden participation in the MWP and had to report to their local police station daily. Paula led the Party in virtmeetings with Party officials, received petitions, spoke in media interviews, managed the Party's daily business and dealt with the external world.

Paula met with John and Peter and explained Abajoe's observations from the rossits experiment.

"The stupid bugger! If only he had realised earlier!" said Peter. "We need never have gone to prison! Poor Gunyaba! We should never have stopped immigration in the first place!"

John objected that Austrasians might not behave like rossits. There was racial prejudice. Austrasians might not accept Bhakarians as kin. Neighbourly sharing would not be possible. They agonised over how to U-turn the immigration policy smoothly. They decided that the MWP should maintain the myth of superiority but gradually lower immigration barriers as largesse.

The meeting decided that the MWP should about-face on immigration and authorised Paula to make the announcement immediately, promising a new era of exchange with Bhakaria, if they were elected. In the Opposition's weekly broadcast throughout the nation, Paula told of the policy change and the reasoning, as follows.

"The Middle Way Party's view is that our population has increased to a point where Austrasia needs to share her resources with her

There was a public debate in the following weeks and agreement
reached with Sudarta to allow a plebiscite on the motion 'There should
be free movement of people between Austrasia and neighbouring
countries'. It was passed with a large majority.

Having solved the immigration issue, the MWP focused on restoring
elected Government, opposing industrial development and preventing
population growth. At the first MWP conference to be held for 30 years,
with virtual attendance from nationwide, Paula was voted in as President.
In her acceptance speech, she said:

*"Now that the Middle Way Party is able to participate openly in
Austrasia's public life, our immediate goal is to have fair elections. The
SEU knows that when we win, Austrasia will withdraw from the Union
and that is why there has been no election for 30 years. We must work
tirelessly until all Austrasians can see the urgent need for democratic
elections to legitimate Austrasia's governance."*

While in prison, Abajoe and Siti had studied the life and works of
Mahatma Gandhi and now, at the ages of 60 and 61, they enjoyed a
serene, ascetic lifestyle, as he had done, when under house arrest. They
adopted routines of purification and health, food preparation, gardening
and meditation.

They woke up each morning at 4.30am, exercised and massaged each
other. Then Abajoe would shave and shower, while Siti did her yoga
routine. He made porridge and put out sliced fruit with yoghurt. They
would eat together, reading and chatting. After breakfast, he would tend
the garden, using water recycled from the bathroom. She harvested

vegetables for the kitchen and he planted out seedlings to maintain their food supply.

At midday, they were sometimes allowed to go for a walk, visiting people in the village, taking food to the sick and aged. They would engage secretly in MWP business in the afternoon, including control of the underground organisation. They would study political history throughout the world, discovering alternative systems and campaign logistics. To maintain the necessary pretence of an apolitical life, they kept no notes but relied on their memories.

In the evening, they would reflect and write their thoughts for the day. Then they would prepare dinner together, sometimes entertaining guests and talking into the night.

They would retire around 11pm and, when they felt like it, which was often, they made love, fuelled by the passion accumulated during 20 years of enforced separation. In sating their passion, their love had rekindled.

He and Siti were allowed out for walks and were visiting nearby, when they received a call from a neighbour that the fire brigade had broken into their apartment. They ran home and when they arrived, there was a fire engine outside. Their front door had been smashed through and uniformed firepersons were in every room searching through their papers and looking for hiding places for illicit materials. Paranoia of discovery of their clandestine activities surged through them, but they had been scrupulous in destroying evidence and they dismissed their fears and became indignant. When they asked the intruders what they were doing, they stopped and slunk out. As they left, the squad's indolent captain tried to conceal the real motivation behind the raid.

"You are lucky," he told them as they surveyed the wrecked apartment. "A neighbour smelled gas. Your stove was leaking. There could have been an explosion."

They had never before had any problem with the stove and the captain wouldn't reveal who had smelled gas and had called the brigade. They never did find out who it was and they were certain the story had been concocted to conceal an illegal raid. The so-called firepersons had behaved more like undercover detectives.

Some of their papers went missing – lists of Party contacts, their addresses and a file with coded reports of local actions. Siti immediately warned her organisation of the breach in security and ordered a change in addresses of contacts and adoption of new codes. Abajoe complained about the break-in to the police but it was soon evident that they were unsympathetic and didn't hide that they were complicit in the break-in.

Undeterred, Abajoe and Siti focused the dissent within Austrasia over SEU rule on to one particular issue – water recycling. They decided to confront the Government, as individuals rather than through the MWP, over the water recycling law brought in by the SEU. It was a SEU law that a gardener's own grey water recycling equipment had to be shut down and the water allowed to flow into a contractor's collection system. Recycled water had to be purchased at a high cost.

The Government argued that this minimised potential for disease and insisted on disconnection of recycling facilities, even if the private hygiene practices already in place were more stringent than those of the government contractor were. It was an unpopular law and the MWP campaigned to end it and allow supervised private recycling with government inspection.

The effect of the new law was to decrease irrigation and reduce the amount of food grown. People, who had previously bought the excess food grown with home-recycled water, were mostly people too poor to have gardens and went hungry. The MWP highlighted it as an example of SEU tyrannical interference.

Abajoe and Siti decided to copy Mahatma Gandhi in confronting the Government by legal processes to ridicule its oppression of the people by a law forbidding extraction of salt from the sea. The water recycling laws appeared to be a suitable issue. Abajoe followed Gandhi's example in writing to the Prime Minister as follows.

Family Fare Tower
Kurilpa Commune
Meannjin

6th July 2275

Prime Minister Sudarta

I wrote to you on 19th May and, as I have received no reply, I am writing to you again, as a home gardener requesting amendment of the laws preventing owners re-use of water in home gardens. If my letters *make no appeal to your heart, on the 15th day of this month, I shall proceed to disregard this provision of the Water Laws. I regard this regulation to be the most iniquitous, from a poor person's standpoint, of many, unfair SEU regulations. Poor people want independence from the SEU. As the Independence movement is essentially for the poorest in the land, the beginning will be made with overcoming this evil.*

In telling you of my plans, I am a home gardener rather than a political activist with the MWP. If I am a lawbreaker, then it is the law of recycling water that I am planning to break. My family will join with me, because the law has already incited them, not me.

Abajoe Yabra

Abajoe was confident that his letter did not lie within the ambit of MWP politics forbidden to him. This would be a family action. Nevertheless, there was bad blood between Abajoe and Sudarta and he would have to tread warily. The 15 years he had spent in prison had not changed Abajoe's mind about devolution and empowerment of the people. The water recycling issue was a test case.

When Siti read his letter, she was very concerned.

"You will be arrested for incitement," she said.

He denied it. "The letter does not align me with the MWP and denies incitement."

Siti was reassured and he sent it. There was no reply. They discussed going ahead with a protest.

"We must be very careful that the protest is not construed as a MWP action," Siti said.

"They may see anything we do as a MWP action. Nevertheless, we must not be intimidated. Politics is our life – if we shut down completely, what else is there?"

She had no answer and they set a date for the protest in about a month's time.

Abajoe arrived home one day to find Siti lying on the settee in the lounge looking at images from her communicator on the wall. Normally she was in the study sending messages or composing a media release or speech.

"How are you?" he asked.

"Excellent," she replied. "How are you?"

He didn't reply but walked over to her and sat down beside her.

"Why are you excellent?" he asked.

"I am very happy," she said.

He waited for her to explain but she was keeping it from him. She seemed to be absorbed in using the communicator.

"How's the protest looking?" he asked.

"The same," she replied.

That wasn't it. Perhaps she had heard from her family, or from her guest worker friends.

"I think I'll call my dad," he said. "I haven't heard from him for a while."

"Uhuh," she answered, scrolling down.

She had not responded to the prompt. It seemed unlikely that news from family or friends had made her excellent. She could have met someone, someone she wanted to keep secret. Suddenly he was jealous. He regretted not having been kinder to her lately. He got up and went into the study. He wanted to check her mail but didn't. He thought he should do something about it but what could he do? He would make tea – that would keep his mind off it for the moment until he was sure.

"Good book?" he called from the kitchen.

"It's okay."

"What is it?"

"Chinese zodiac signs."

He was amazed. Normally she was so rational. He went into the lounge. "Why are you looking at that?"

"A person's personality depends on the year they were born, on a 60-year cycle," she replied. "The year you were born, 2216, was the year of the Fire Dragon. By coincidence, it will be again next year. You will be 60." She read from the wall, *"Fire Dragons are natural leaders: it says here they are downright electrifying. Fire Dragons breathe vigour and power..."*

She continued, listing characteristics until Abajoe interrupted.

"...It is a bit of everyone. No one could have all those. I am no more like that than any other of your predictions."

"It isn't your birthday I was thinking about."

"Who is this Fire Dragon you have met?"

"I'm not absolutely sure they are a Fire Dragon yet. I'm not sure of their birthday, except it's around February," she looked at him and smiled.

He was right. She had met someone. But how could she be 'not sure' of their birthday? Either you knew someone's birthday or you didn't. It didn't make sense. He gave up.

"Are you hungry?" he asked.

"Hmm...yes, very."

"Which would you prefer, tandoori chicken or tandoori rossit? We've got both, I marinaded them overnight."

"I hope you don't mind but I would prefer some kangaroo."

He was hurt. He had grown the chicken and rossit but now she wanted bought meat from the bottom of the freezer.

"What's wrong with tandoori? I thought it was your favourite."

"It's the chemicals you use in growing them. I want natural foods."

His heart sank. He used an anti-coccidiosis medication in the rossits' water, steroids in the chicken pellets and artificial fertilisers for the hydroponic vegetables. He used chemicals for all their foods and they had never had any problems from them. His methods had been broadcast as a model for Austrasians to use. Without these chemicals, the amount of food he could grow would be severely reduced. Why had she suddenly turned squeamish? Perhaps she had wanted to object to the chemicals all these years and now had turned against him under the influence of the Fire Dragon she had met.

"What's the matter?" he asked. "You haven't minded the chemicals before. Is something wrong?"

"I have a medical condition that may be sensitive to the chemicals."

She was unwell! That explained some of it. But she had said she was 'excellent'. It didn't make sense. "What medical condition?" he demanded, full of concern. His mind raced. What condition could explain her relaxation and investigation of horoscopes for someone whose birthday she wasn't sure of? Perhaps the birthday wasn't yet... Oh, yes. She must be pregnant! Thanks be to Yahm – may peace and goodness be upon him!

She was watching his face with amusement.

"You're pregnant," he said. "This is a miracle."

"No, the cause is earthly and well-known...you. You have been rather slow to take responsibility for my condition," she laughed.

"How stupid of me...I guess I had almost given up. This is the best news possible. You are very clever! Will it be a boy or a girl?"

"They can't tell yet. Which do you want?"

"If there will be wars, I would want a girl, for her to survive when boys are killed. If there will be peace and growth, then I would want a boy, for him to have many wives and father many children. But hopefully our child will live in a world free from wars, or growth, or population, or territorial, or material concerns. I also hope our child will meditate on our parental influence, acquire our unique family lore and pass it on. I don't mind what gender it is, provided it understands, appreciates and transmits our experiences, validating the concerns for posterity that have led us to make the sacrifices we have. It will be the inheritor of our genes and our teaching and I hope it will replace us by teaching our lore to offspring and strangers when we die."

"Then there will be much to do in raising such an individual."

"He or she will be our magnum opus."

Siti stopped her political activism. It had sometimes brought rough handling by the police. Paula took over from her as the fighting President of the Party. Siti continued to manage the Party's activities behind the scenes.

Siti's prison sadness was dispelled. She was radiant, thrilled at her enlistment in ultimate creation. Her happiness was transmitted through the Party and their members became hopeful and dedicated to achieving a democratic election soon.

With the prospect of fatherhood, Abajoe regained the spring in his step that he had lost in prison. He felt potent, with his vision for Australia within his grasp. His new vigour inspired the Party.

Government informers looked for evidence of clandestine activities to incriminate him and recorded his every move. They suspected him of masterminding the underground movement. They wanted to imprison him but he was too prominent to jail without compelling evidence.

The day scheduled for their water recycling protest neared.

"Perhaps we should pull out?" Abajoe asked her. "We shouldn't take any risks now you are pregnant."

"We're committed," she answered. "The family are counting on us to be there."

"How many of them will come, do you think?"

"I don't know," Siti replied. "Only a few. We haven't gone public on it. It's not an issue that's in the news."

"Sudarta won't be upset by a few dozen of us. They'll overlook it. The exercise will do me good."

"Me too. I think we should go."

So, that settled the matter.

At first light on 22nd August 2275, three generations of Yabras – Abajoe, Siti, T One and Marko, elders Zelta and Hugo and a handful of home gardeners from the Kurilpa Commune gathered at Kurilpa Hall. Siti told them their purpose was to show the unfairness of the water-recycling ban. They set out as a small, determined group with Abajoe, in a white robe walking in their midst, holding a staff like a shepherd or a drum major, as Gandhi had led his non-violent Salt March to the sea in 1930. A broadcaster heard about the prestigious group and sent a reporter. The story hit the headlines and their numbers rapidly increased, some coming from afar to join in. The procession was soon two kilometres long, walking four abreast. Thousands were marching resolutely, knowing they would be defying the Government by breaking the law.

As Abajoe walked with Siti near the front, he was at first surprised, then exhilarated by the growing number of marchers, but as the protest took on the proportions of a popular uprising, the spectre of government punishment rose and cast a shadow. He knew they wouldn't be allowed to get away with it; only the form of the Government's retaliation remained in doubt.

That night, 20,000 people slept on the beach at the river mouth. The next morning, they broke down a fence and assembled beside the water contractor's reservoir at Underton, where they each filled a bottle to recycle their gardens. Abajoe spoke to them from atop the dam wall, with Siti beside him, hips forward, celebrating the life within her.

Fellow gardeners

We are here on behalf of the thousands of Austrasians whose food supply, from gardens like ours, was cut off when our recycling was prohibited. Few of us can afford to buy expensive water recycled from this reservoir. The water here is no better for your health than you could produce in your own backyards. Sending it here is senseless and expensive. The law must be changed.

Our protest is only a beginning. We should be grateful for the happy ending of the first stage in our final struggle for freedom. I am thankful to the Government for not opposing our march but it remains to be seen whether they will tolerate the actual breach of the Water Laws by countless people when you return home and recycle the water on your gardens.

If we are arrested, then the struggle for justice must continue with other protests, but resistance must be passive. Two wrongs don't make a right. In the end, the people will get the Government they deserve and we must make sure that the people show they deserve fair laws, as we have done here.

Good on you for coming and may your return be peaceful

He had made sure his speech did not contain incitement. The walkers dispersed back to their suburbs and villages, carrying the stolen recycled water which, when they got home, they would pour on their gardens. They did so with joy, the very act symbolising their liberation. Their defiance of the Government was magnified by the media. In the days that followed, an outbreak of lawlessness followed, which gathered momentum rapidly throughout the country.

The media attributed the initial action that triggered the uprising to Abajoe and Siti's iconic presence at the march. Their euphoria was replaced by fear. They had sought anonymity but they had inspired the nation illicitly and government retribution was sure to follow. They waited, resigned and sad. Abajoe realised that his vision for Australia had arrived at its Waterloo. He had confronted Sudarta and only one of them could win.

Abajoe and Siti were in bed when a platoon of SEU soldiers burst in and arrested them. Abajoe was pulled away from Siti, his hand keeping contact as his hand was dragged away down to her fingertips. She was weeping.

"I love you," he said as she was bundled away.

She puckered her mouth into a kiss.

Abajoe learned later that John, Paula, Peter and Margo had also been arrested and locked up in different police stations, unable to communicate with him or each other. They were charged with breaking the water recycling law, whereas he and Siti were charged with sedition for which the maximum penalty was brain clearing.

CHAPTER 51

Prisoners' Dilemma

Outside the grill of his cell window there was wire mesh and behind that a high brick wall topped by electrified razor wire. He had been there a week and had never been out of the cell. Meals were pushed through a hatch. He had not seen anyone. A guard came three times each day with food. Abajoe called to him to bring paper and pen but there was no response.

It was only a month since Siti had delighted him by falling pregnant. Although she was 61 and the pregnancy would be risky, it was not unusual these days for a woman to have a child in middle age. They had been apart for 20 years while they both served 15-year sentences, plus his preceding five years. Their political lives had been too hectic to have a child and too dangerous; then it had become physically impossible while they were in jail. Their child would give their lives fresh meaning and be their heir. However, the tranquillity they had looked forward to had been shattered by their arrest. Now long prison terms for Siti, himself and their child threatened his family picture horribly. The other possibility was clearing of his brain. He could live without his memory of the MWP and its struggles for justice but the clearing would remove his mature intelligence and ability to speak.

Isolated in prison and pondering these alternatives, he longed for Siti. He didn't know where she had been taken after their arrest and whether she and the foetus were safe. He missed her, as if a limb had been amputated. The hours passed with grieving. He wondered when, if ever, he would see her again. With this abyss as his companion, he filled the lonely hours by writing a mental diary of his thoughts. He would imagine reading it from time to time.

Every minute of every day, he was stuck in his drab cell with little to hope for. Through supreme effort, he kept his thoughts objective and fended off depression. The reality of his situation was awful enough, without exaggeration.

He had previously been threatened with brain clearing for the Gunyaba sabotage and knew what it entailed. He had accepted instead a long prison term, 15 years. It had been devised to be a logical consequence of political deviance by the Government's heinous behaviourists. His brain's motivational area, the hippocampus, located in the medial temporal lobe of his brain, would be cleared by an electrical shock. It would destroy the neural circuits that accessed high-value information from a lifetime of memories. He would be reduced to the verbal skills of a two-year old, simply reacting to the world, unable to create coherent speech. It was possible for a person of his age, 60, to slowly reorganise his thoughts but he could not ever expect to recover formal verbal expression, even with the best of teaching and an ideal environment. In the experientially sterile government rehabilitation centre, his recovery would be slow.

He had escaped brain clearing by confessing to the Gunyaba bombing. Because his confession had been in defiance from the dock, they had reneged on the deal to let him off with a light sentence for confessing and his sentence had been commuted to 15 years. The others had not admitted to any crime at Gunyaba. If his confession had been honest, Siti and Peter would have suffered brain clearing for their roles in the sabotage but he implicated them only as accessories. Nevertheless, his confession was enough to get them 15 years, like himself.

Had he not confessed, they might all have got off scot free. His confession had caused dissension among the others, their families and friends. Abajoe reasoned that the trial had provided a platform for denouncing the Government and fomenting resistance and the Party had been invigorated and spawned new proactive leadership instead of fading away. His confession had been a sacrifice that had served the Middle Way Party.

Eventually, the others came to understand that he had been right. During the 15 years in prison together, they realised the wisdom of Abajoe's decision, his self-altruism to the nation that made his sacrifice sustainable. Had he not been there in jail too, their loyalty would have faltered but in the end, he was vindicated.

Siti, in a different prison, had understood why he had confessed and sided with him through her monthly letters. Although few had reached him, she had been his strength through those long years, planning her leadership role for when she would be released.

He doubted he would escape brain clearing this time, unless he betrayed Siti and the others again. Now the MWP had sufficient publicity without needing a court drama. He did not have the same reason to confess this time.

His isolation was invaded when he received a visit from a prosecution lawyer.

"How are you?" he asked Abajoe.

"What do you want?" Abajoe demanded.

"I want the best outcome for the future of Austrasia."

"Is Siti okay?" Abajoe asked.

"Yes, she's in a cell like this one in a building near here," he replied. "I am visiting her this afternoon and I am offering her the same deal as I am offering you."

"What offer?"

"We'll come to that."

The lawyer told him that after his arrest, there had been protest demonstrations in every major city. The trial would be the centre of national attention. If he was convicted and sentenced to brain clearing, there would be riots and possibly bloodshed. The Government was making plans to head off civil war. Did he, Abajoe, really want to cause so much pain and suffering? If he confessed, the sentence would be lighter and the people would accept the fairness of the court.

Abajoe remained silent.

Then he read out the police report on the incident. It documented his incitement, or persuasion of the protestors at Underton Reservoir, of citizens to break the water recycling law and his publicity encouraging the breaking of other SEU laws. There were recordings of his speeches, interviews with citizens and copies of the publicity material.

"We've a record of almost everything," the lawyer said. "Now tell us, do you believe Austrasians should place their own interests higher than those of the SEU?"

Abajoe didn't answer. He knew this was sedition and they wanted him to confess.

Then the lawyer confirmed what he had feared.

"We will be seeking the brain clearing penalty," he said. "It's pretty straightforward. We have enough to send you both down to have your brains cleared."

Abajoe shook his head. "I don't believe you. That is what you promised last time. But I got 15 years...not an acquittal. The Government ratted on me."

"That was because you were defiant – you didn't make a proper confession, at the proper time. This time, if you keep to telling what you did and who was doing what, we'll let you off with a charge of trespassing. The maximum for that is one year inside. You might get off scot free. You don't have to make up your mind now but when you're ready to tell us about it, send a letter to me in this envelope and we'll talk. I'll keep the deal confidential and no one will ever know."

"What if Siti confesses too?"

"Then you'll each get five years. That kid of yours will get a chance. He will be able to go to school normally. It will be much better for you."

"I'll think about it."

"Remember, after brain clearing your kid will be smarter than you are."

"Bastard. Piss off."

Abajoe was left alone with his options.

Now the uncertainty was what Siti would do. If only he could communicate with her. The situation was familiar, that of the prisoners' dilemma, which he knew about as a classical gaming problem from his guerrilla interrogation training. Each prisoner of a crime decides whether to remain silent or betray the other. Betrayal of the other would get the betrayer off but the other would get life. However, if neither confessed, they could only be convicted of a minor charge and get maybe one year. If they both confessed, they would get five years. There was no best choice: it depended upon them both acting in a spirit of co-operation with each other and not confessing.

Abajoe had learnt to play mental chess against himself during his 20 years in the island prison. He could concentrate for hours, recalling all the positions and predicting the results of moves he might take. Now he applied these skills to his predicament.

Siti's pregnancy was now up to month four. He didn't want his kid to spend its first few years in an impoverished prison environment. The first five years would be a big part of their child's life. Spent in prison, their child's life would be stunted. If it was the first 15 years, the child would be disabled. He would do anything to avoid that. He would give anything for Siti to go free and have their child in a normal environment where she could carry on with their campaign. If he confessed, he would be taking a terrible risk.

The difficulty was to know which way she would jump. He had been fascinated in the training, where an academic mathematician proposed that the best play in repeated Prisoners' Dilemma play was to do what the other had done in the previous play, resulting in their co-operation in either denial or confession. It assumed that the other would have a tendency to repeat their first position. Thus, they would both confess, or both would deny and neither would suffer the maximum penalty. Abajoe had mentioned this to Siti at the time but she had shown little interest and he was not sure that she had been listening.

He wondered what she would choose to do this time, whether it would be what he had done last time at Newtown, when he had confessed to sabotage and they had chosen to stay silent. Their sentences had been reduced from brain clearing to 15 years because the Prosecution had shown that the Action Group was a quasi-cult and they had fallen under his influence. If they had deserted him and blamed him, he would have had his brain cleared. They admitted nothing and he was let off from brain clearing.

Now he and Siti had to make their choices again. If she stayed silent again, and he did too, which was what their Newtown experience had taught them was the safest thing to do, they would soon be freed and their child could have a normal upbringing. The first year in prison would not disadvantage him or her. After walking age, freedom was needed.

He cursed his stupidity in telling her the mathematician's advice because he couldn't now assume she would repeat her Newtown choice. If she complied, she would instead copy his lead from Newtown and confess. And if he remained silent, as she had done last time, their child could be born free.

Either way, he should remain silent. If she confessed, as the academic had advised, he would be sacrificing his mind for their freedom. He expected that she would follow the academic advice because she was observant; it was the strategy they had most recently discussed for this situation and she would be consistent with his commitment to New Science, which respected academia and rational reason.

Then, he should take the advice and do what she would expect, following the advice to do what she did last time, which was to remain silent. It meant he would pay the ultimate penalty and have his mind taken from him. He accepted it was necessary. His whole life was testament to his belief in service to others: self-sacrifice was his highest moral duty. He was a self-altruist and he would proclaim his faith, even if the course he had to choose would sustain little more than his life, rendering his life worthless to others. He would trade his roles as father, husband and political leader for Siti's and their child's freedom.

It was a dreadful dilemma. It was agony to choose between achieving his vision for the Australian people or his loved ones' freedom. He examined it from every angle until he was satisfied and then his mind was made up.

When the prosecutor visited again, Abajoe stayed silent, even when the lawyer produced additional evidence of his guilt. He wondered if he might have obtained it from Siti – she might have confessed. If she had already confessed and incriminated him, it was as he expected. The finality of it came as a shock and almost made him change his mind and confess too. Alternatively, they might be trying to trap him into a confession that incriminated her. Should he take that chance? He dwelled on it and retreated into a world of his own for a few days. He was aware that the effect of his solitary confinement could be the Stockholm Effect, where a prisoner wants to help his keepers and proffers undue compliance. He resisted and kept to his earlier decision to stay silent.

The trial took place about a month later.

He pleaded not guilty. Fearfully, he waited to learn of the decision.

CHAPTER 52

The Trial

He had been entirely alone, except for visits from his lawyer, for two months. The courtroom was packed and when every eye focused on him, it was intimidating. He raised a hand and waved. The room erupted in applause. His eyes searched around for familiar faces, which he acknowledged with slight nods. Then his eyes alighted on Siti. When he saw her sitting with the Prosecution, he knew she had accepted the plea bargain and agreed to confess. It was as he predicted. She could get the most freedom for their child if he remained silent. At the same time, he dreaded the consequences for himself. His subconscious had been hoping that his plan would fail and she would remain silent to protect him.

His lawyer told him later Siti had confessed, thinking Abajoe would confess too, the same as he had done at Newtown. Except this time, it was sedition, which was a worse crime. She thought the police probably had enough evidence to convict them both, even without their co-operation. If they both confessed, it would mitigate his sentence from brain clearing to five years of imprisonment. She remembered his enthusiasm that night for the gamester's advice to copy his partner's previous play. Abajoe would expect her to confess and she would do that. Her sentence would be reduced because she carried their child. It was Abajoe they wanted. He wouldn't risk copying her Newtown silence, despite the gamester, because he could be condemned to brain clearing. She thought that in the cold light of day he would realise that following the gamester's advice, which was for him to stay silent like she had at Newtown, would be an error and he would confess instead and be saved.

Despite three months apart and no communication, there were no smiles between them as he looked at her. The fear in his face, as he sat in the dock, told her he had remained silent. Siti's heart sank. She suddenly realised they meant to use her to betray him.

"No!" she said quietly, sobbing.

Her truths would indict him and then his brain would be wiped clean by electric shock treatment. She would be providing the evidence to destroy him and her feeling of guilt was overwhelming. He was her lover, her best friend and her world revolved around him.

They dragged her towards the witness box, despite the swelling in her belly. Weeping, she clung to the rail with her chest heaving over her bulge.

"She's pregnant – have a bit of respect!" yelled Abajoe.

When they persisted, he tried to go to her aid but he was quickly overpowered. The guards lugged her like a tree root, with awkward projections to be patiently unhooked. They weren't rough with her but they were forceful. Her fingernails broke and a finger bled from her struggles.

She stole another glance at Abajoe. How she had longed to look into those visionary eyes that had softened for her alone. Now she couldn't meet his gaze. She tried to speak to him without her words giving him away. She called out to him, "I'm sorry, man. I thought you would claim it." She hoped it sounded like the offence could have been pinned on anyone. Only she and Abajoe knew the truth.

He shook his head. "It's okay. Do what they want. It's for Alfons." It was their name for the unborn child. Abajoe grimaced and shrugged as if to say 'Just go along with it'.

She couldn't accept that this was what he really wanted.

"I won't do it," she sobbed, jamming her legs against the witness box gate. Because of her condition and the watching reporters, the guards made little progress with her and the judge signalled to them to quit. She sat down at the front of the courtroom to recover.

The judge called Paula to the stand and she was cross-examined by the Prosecution. Siti thought that her and Abajoe's rejection of Paula, which had affected Paula so badly, might influence her, but she said nothing to incriminate either of them. Her evidence supported the protest being spontaneous and led by the grassroots rather than fomented by the Party leadership. When she stepped down, Siti clapped. She felt like cheering but then she remembered her betrayal of Abajoe and how it contrasted with Paula's loyalty. Despair flooded through her at the cruel injustice that fate had dealt them and she wept silently.

The judge called a recess and her solicitor came and led Siti to an interview room outside.

When they returned to the packed courtroom, she didn't look at Abajoe. When she took the stand, she went willingly and answered the questions mechanically with the truth, providing evidence of his guilt.

Abajoe stayed silent. His lawyer told him what he had already suspected, that Siti had confessed in a plea bargain for her and her child's freedom. It was what he had wanted but his heart skipped a beat as the implications came thundering.

"Terrific, she'll get off...I'll have my brain smashed but I don't care so long as she gets out to raise our kid."

She testified she had masterminded the Water March but the Prosecution told the court that her confession was an attempt to reduce Abajoe's role and that they didn't believe her. After that, they were able to prise the truth from her. He was not ashamed of it. He did not resent it being told. He could have changed his plea and admitted it but he wanted the Prosecution case to rest on her evidence so that they would feel bound to honour their deal with her. He was secretly pleased by every revelation they extracted from her.

In the courthouse, he passed Siti in the corridor, her belly bulging. He choked with emotion. She cried, "I'm sorry," when she passed him. "I did the same as you did at Newtown," she sobbed. He knew then she had remembered the mathematician's advice. She had been loyal to him to the last. He had made his choice assuming she would do this, sacrificing himself for her and their child's freedom. If only he had never mentioned the academic's theory, she would probably have remained silent too, achieving the co-operation they had lacked at the Newtown trial, which had kept them apart for 17 years. Her forgetting had been worth taking a risk for, he mused. Too bad, she had remembered and it hadn't worked out.

He shook his head. "It's for the best," he said and smiled at her. She was pulled away.

He was found guilty. He wasn't surprised. His defence had been that he had not been a leader, just an ordinary marcher and had not committed any seditious acts. But the Prosecution had argued that he was a leader and therefore he was exercising leadership just by being present and therefore had been seditious.

There was time for reflection. It had been like stepping stones across a creek which you ran across to keep your feet dry. Every stone had been in just the right place. Everyone had been necessary.

Before sentencing, he made the following statement from the dock.

"I am expecting to be sentenced to brain clearing.

"You may not see me again in my old life. When you think of me, I want you to love one another, as I have loved you, for I have lain down my old life for my family and friends. Some people hated me because I stood aside from the SEU and criticised their selfishness. If you feel hated, remember that they hated me more because I told them their mistakes. Now they cannot hide them.

"We were arrested because the people in millions began to defy unfair government laws. I am the whipping post through which the Government is attempting to quell this movement. I was merely the messenger and yet the Government wants to destroy my life. These are oppressive times but my life is a small thing and civil society has come a long way when we have the opportunity to be honest as individuals as I am doing now.

"The Government will argue that I was the instrument of liberation and my treatment will be a deterrent to others. If I am sentenced to brain clearing, then the Government must know their punishment is a terrible one. Brain clearing may not be so terrible for me as for the woman I love, Siti, whom I chose should give evidence against me, for the freedom of my unborn child, who may never know me. Forgive me, Siti, for that choice.

"My offence is that I have revealed the power of neighbourliness. The present Government of this nation is not seeking mutual benefit. I showed them how technology could solve problems without selfishness. But they hated the strengths of collective living and hated me for providing a structure on which it could grow. If you have evidence of the importance of community, would you share it with others?

"Soon they will make me into a burden to the community but the community will not, I hope, be too repelled by my dependent state. You have my example to follow in opposing this cruel Government. My new dependence will be hurtful to my parents, who raised me to be independent. Let them know that the community values me for freeing them from tyranny. For the fire that we have started is burning more vigorously each new day.

"Remember me as the voice of community. I have tried to have Austrasians live by sharing their resources and their future. I have tried

to stop selfishness and diversity that harms the community. I have made my stand against subordination of the community to outside interests.

"My legacy is your awareness that Austrasia's population number has to be limited. My experiments have shown that contrary to expectations, couples do not voluntarily restrict their reproduction in an uncertain environment such as Austrasia's. Population growth results from the uncertainty it creates and can spiral out of control. Population control has to be accepted by every local council and will enable planning to avoid famine. Survival of Austrasian culture will be made possible by collective decision making using New Science, with its respect for systems, emotions and democracy.

"I am hopeful that we are passing into a new spiritual age in which communities are self-directing, nurturing, non-material and diverse.

"As the top down has today triumphed over the bottom up, does not mean that a hierarchy with natural justice has prevailed. It is more natural that aggregation should prevail with local interests pre-eminent. As this has not happened is indicative that tyrannical political power is at work. It is unpopular and I predict it will soon be overthrown.

"I am being tried for sedition. It is not sedition when I urge you to seek governance by New Science. I want you to provide evidence that centralisation does not improve people's lives. I want you to demand that decisions should be economically and emotionally rational. I want you to insist that donations to political parties do not corrupt political processes. This is not sedition.

"If you do these things, my old life will not have been in vain. Now I commit myself to the whims of my captors. I have respect for them for having permitted me to make this address. I forgive them for their error in carrying out these cruel orders. May Austrasians learn and prosper. My remaining thoughts will be love for my family, Siti and our baby.

"My absence from our family will be hurtful to Siti, who confessed to ensure our child has freedom with one parent, but will feel she has betrayed me, and caused loss of the other. This was my decision, not hers. It was my choice, not hers, that has brought this fate upon me. She played her part as we had agreed and she should not blame herself. Support her, as she has supported me. Our Austrasian destiny is being betrayed but I hope with the passing of my old life, a new way has opened up.

"Farewell."

He sat down to thunderous applause from the crowd packed into the courtroom. A chant started, "Free him! Free him!"

After deliberating only briefly, the judge sentenced him to brain clearing. He had expected it because Sudarta blamed him for her unpopularity. As a dumb martyr, he was less dangerous than as a living and leading prisoner.

Abajoe waved to the shocked and hushed courtroom as he was whisked away before a mass revolt could be organised to liberate him.

In the following weeks, his guards told the media of his defiance and established his legend. Although he was to be mutilated and condemned to a humiliating life as an antisocial deviant, his dignity, heroism and even joy in the face of his punishment challenged and ultimately defeated the values of the society that had imposed them. How could a guilty man be so morally superior, so certain of the justice of his cause? The brutality of the resolution reduced Sudarta to a dictator, who was tolerated only by force of arms. His martyrdom undermined Sudarta's authority.

Later on that week, his lawyer told him that Siti was tried. The sedition charges against her were dismissed through lack of evidence. They had honoured their promise to let her off if she would co-operate. She was allowed to go home.

She pleaded to visit him one last time before enforcement of his sentence. He was being held at the Armed Forces' Neurosurgery Detention Centre on an island in Quandamooka Bay. She crossed on the supplies' ferry. They were allowed to be together for an hour.

She cried and told him about her plea bargain and why she had testified against him.

When she had refused to take the stand during his trial, her lawyer had taken her into an interview room. She had sat down, her belly resting heavily on her legs. She had felt the child move inside her and had hoped it hadn't been injured. Her arms had felt bruised where the guards had held her. She had wept silently. She had turned to the lawyer. "How did this happen?" she had asked, bewildered.

"It's okay," he had said simply. "Abajoe knows what he's doing. He's going to take the rap so that you and Alfons can have a normal life."

"But they'll destroy his brain…the best brain in Austrasia. He's done so much good and can do so much more…" she had broken down, sobbing.

There had been a knock on the door and the Prosecution's solicitor had come in.

"How are you?" he had asked her.

She had looked up at him.

"No, I won't do it," she had said.

"But we have an agreement," he had reminded her.

"Fuck you," she spat. "I didn't know it would be like this. I won't give you the ammunition."

"Then you'll go down with him. What's the sense in that? What about the child?"

"I can't do it to him. I couldn't live with myself."

"If you can't do it for yourself, then do it for your child. It's what he wants you to do."

"You're asking me to destroy the man I love!"

"He may get life."

"Not with Sudarta in power. Abajoe is a threat," Siti had told the lawyer. "He's becoming more and more popular, a martyr whether he's in or out of jail. Abajoe's message is 'Independence for Austrasia' and they want to stop him. Sudarta will make sure he's taken out. Sedition is a serious offence, that'll be their excuse. They'll shock his brain. He'll be lost to me…to all of us. It'll be a tragedy. I can't do it."

"All you have to do is answer a few questions and tell the truth. We already have your statement. We just need you to tell the court that he called the shots, not you. For an intelligent man like him, brain clearing is better than life inside, less frustrating. He'll be as happy as Larry relearning his skills, instead of wasting away his prime years in jail, leading half a life."

"I don't know…"

"Think about Alfons. If you don't co-operate, he'll be brought up in jail. Abajoe will be in a different jail and he won't see him at all. Being raised in a prison is very limiting. He may even be taken away from you. Abajoe wants you and the child to have a normal life together."

"What other questions will you ask me?"

"Here, I'll read them."

He had read several questions about where Abajoe had been and what he had been doing at certain times. He had continued, "Did he announce that the marchers should bring with them a jar of waste water, even though they knew that would be illegal?"

"Yes," Siti had said, knowing it would be easy to verify.

"Did he issue an instruction that if they were opposed, they should continue to march, using force if necessary."

"No," Siti replied. "That's not true. Abajoe believes in passive resistance."

"Well, what did he tell them to do if they were opposed?"

"I don't know. I suppose he left it up to individuals."

"But the marchers behaved as one. They overcame the Bhakarian Army. Someone must have issued instructions. Is it possible Abajoe did but you didn't know?"

"No. He wouldn't give such an instruction."

"You can't be sure."

"I am sure."

"Well, to say you are sure would not be co-operating with us and we would appeal against your acquittal. You would be retried and this time you could get life. All you have to do is say you are not sure."

Siti had looked out the window, with her hands resting on her swollen belly as time had hung suspended. Her mind had been far away, remembering how they had laughed together. Now their thinking lives would finally be separated. She hadn't been able to prevent it.

"Okay." She turned to face him, resigned. "I'll do it. What are the other questions?"

With each question, they had halted to agree what she would say. Always the questions they had wanted cast doubt on Abajoe's passive role, until she hadn't been sure herself. She knew she had let him down but she had felt powerless to prevent it because she had agreed to confess.

She told him her love for him had never faltered as she was forced to testify against him. The evidence they extracted from her was damning. She never compromised the truth and this lessened her feeling of betrayal. The anguish she suffered was lessened as his child continued to grow inside her and kept her mind occupied with hope.

He said that he forgave her and they hugged and kissed.

They knew this was the last time they would be together as equal partners and they told how much they meant to each other, between hugs.

"Don't tell Alfons that I sacrificed myself for his freedom," said Abajoe. "My self-sacrifice must not be a burden to him, as a way of subjecting his life to my misery. I have sought merely to have you, who I love, to be able to bring him up naturally. I wanted the best I could manage for you both. For me, it was an easy decision because of my belief in self-altruism. My life has actually been sustained by this, for my days in opposition to Sudarta were numbered. I expect to enjoy peace and happiness even with my brain cleared.

"When you are sad for losing my company, remember how I was and what I wanted for you, to be your wonderful self and free of dependence on me. If you are lonely for a real man's company, then take a lover and divorce me. That is only fair because I will be inadequate for that role. I may seem to become dependent on you, but I will not be and will just be taking advantage of you. My belief in self-altruism requires that you sustain yourself before you extend help to me. Sustain yourself, my darling, be a mother to Alfons and provide him with a real father if you want. Don't worry about me. I am going away and I will be okay without you."

Then they took him away.

Later that day, the words of his familiar protests rang out through the empty corridors of the prison as they took him to the prison hospital, knowing that these were the last words he might ever speak, to cover his fear.

"Say yes to recycling! Say no to illegal government control! Stop political repression! Stop the tyrant Sudarta! Stop SEU takeover! We want an election! Vote the Middle Way!"

The sound of the other prisoners hammering on the metal doors of their cells was deafening.

"Free him!" they shouted. "Free him! Free him! Free him you bastards!"

His escorts tied him into a straitjacket and gagged him. He had been defeated. All his hopes and his life of striving for diversity and individual freedom had come to nothing. The only solace he could find was that Siti and his child would not be imprisoned.

CHAPTER 53

Self-altruism

They took away from Abajoe his language skills. Somewhere he still had his name but he could not access it or speak it. Sudarta's law enforcers were behaviourists who applied consequences to those whose non-conforming behaviour undermined the regime. They matched each type of offence with a corresponding consequence. Abajoe's opposition had been verbal and so they silenced it.

The Government's standard treatment for racketeers, embezzlers and blackmailers, who had used their memories deviously, was to kill the brain cells of the hippocampus, the part of the brain that organises a catalogue of memory records like a librarian. An electrical treatment destroyed the catalogue, removing access to the information in the cortex, so the person even forgot their own name and their skills, both legal and illegal. Reduced to babyhood, the cheat had to learn a new scheme for living.

For sex offenders, they killed the cells of the amygdala, destroying the emotions. They were left with no feelings about sexual activities, legal or illegal. As they recovered, they were conditioned to clockwork-like fear of unlawful sexual activities.

For political prisoners like Abajoe, they killed the brain cells of Broca's area, which controls speech and language. Language comes before thought, according to Chomsky, and without language, there can be no thought. Abajoe lost his political thinking and beliefs. He was left with the capacity to relearn word concepts from scratch. Like a person surrounded by a foreign language, he had to learn to communicate again, beginning with the simplest concepts. It was only by relearning to speak that he would be able to make sense of what people told him and have his own thoughts.

He was held at a government rehabilitation centre at the discretion of a review board. He received language tuition and played with other political prisoners whose speech had been cleared. The environment was sterile and his progress was slow. Siti could only visit him weekly and she used every minute to give him the immersion in language that he needed to regrow his brain capacity.

Neuroscience has shown that when a person has a stroke and loses the use of a limb, brain cells are killed, but if the skills lost are demanded, other cells will grow to perform their function. The disabled limb must be worked, if necessary, by immobilising the good limb in a sling or cast to stop it being used instead. Abajoe had to develop speech in contexts where he could not succeed by silence or non-verbal communication. The so-called rehabilitation centre provided few of these.

When Siti was allowed to visit him, she brought Tani, their baby daughter, but he was unable to find words or much in the way of feelings and was disinterested. She made him respond to Helen with words rather than with signs or gestures and reinforced his attempts at new words. As Siti talked with him about their child, his disinterest was gradually replaced by curiosity and affection.

After a while, he could speak of simple things hesitantly and tersely. His learning was made difficult because her visits with the child were restricted to a bare visitor's room with few objects to talk about. He was unable to show her the verbal skills he had learned in using the building's amenities and playthings.

One day he told Siti, "You ...book."

"Do you want me to bring a book?"

He nodded.

"No, you must say, "Please bring me a book.""

"Please bring...book."

"Good. What book?"

Siti's heart leapt. Could he mean his own book 'The New Science'?

"Picture book."

"Okay. What picture book?"

He shrugged, not caring. She tried not to sound disappointed. He would spend hours with children's picture books, learning the names of the objects and the language that went with them. His recovery would take a long time, perhaps many years depending on how much help he received. She persuaded the rehabilitation centre to allow him to wear a fourth generation wrist-robot that could reason and talk with him like an older child. It became his constant companion as he learned to talk with it and it applied higher and higher abilities.

Tani was learning at a pace similar to Abajoe and there was rivalry between them for Siti's affections. She tried to treat them equally, but they found ways to gain an advantage.

"Tani live in your house?"

"Yes, Abajoe, you know that."

"Can I live in your house?"

"No, darling, you have to stay here."

"Why?"

"Sudarta is punishing you."

"What is punish?"

Siti fought back tears. "You called them names and now they want you to be frightened of them so you won't do it again."

"I am not frightened. They are mean."

"When you understand what they have done, you will be frightened and not call them names again."

"Tani calls me names. I will hit her so she will be frightened of me."

"No. Punishment is bad. You should reward her when she speaks to you politely."

"What reward?"

"You could talk with her nicely."

"But I want to talk with you."

"You should talk with her too. She's your daughter. She loves you."

"She has to love me because I'm her father. But I love you because I want to."

"Me, too."

"Do you love me more than her?"

"In a different way."

She hugged him and he hugged her back.

Although he led the half-life of a childlike adult in an adult world, he remained positive and seized every opportunity to talk with people. He followed his jailers around and as soon as he had a smattering of language, he helped fellow prisoners with rudimentary lessons that forced him to acquire and search for new skills. He became the leader in his group and organised games. However, the environment was very limiting and it was difficult for him to find new situations to talk about with the others. His speech steadily improved but it seemed impossible that he would ever be able to talk about matters beyond that narrow world.

Siti tried to organise his disciples and friends to visit him. His verbal abilities so contrasted with his old self that they were horrified. Although he recognised them, he was unable to say anything that connected with the past. They had loved a man called Abajoe, but he had become a stranger, a child.

"What do you think of the people who gave your brain electric shocks?"

"I don't know who they are. The people who work here are kind to me."

"What about the people in charge, who did the shocks?"

"They work somewhere else."

"Well, did they change your life at all?"

"Yes. I have the mind of a child and I have to stay here."

"Why did they make your mind like a child?"

"They punished me for calling them names."

"Is that fair?"

"I don't know."

"What if the names you called them were true."

"Then it was not fair that they punished me. But if they didn't think they were true, then it would be fair."

"Even if you knew they were true?"

"They didn't think they were and they were in charge."

"What do you think of them then?"

"They were in charge and they have punished me."

"Will you call them names again?"

"No."

"Why not?"

"They would punish me again, except worse next time."

"Get better soon," John told him in despair. "If you are truly inspired, then now is the time for your higher power to help you recover."

The disciples did not believe he could recover and felt unable to help him. On the other hand, he might disclose their past activities. They feared for their own safety and freedom and did not return. Peter never came.

From hiding, they denounced the Government that was holding him captive and used his martyrdom to spearhead their campaign. His policies were iconic in their propaganda.

"His spirit is free," Siti told them. "It is only his body that is imprisoned."

After he had been sentenced, when she was at home, the sadness of giving evidence against him was gradually transformed and reborn as anger against Sudarta and a thirst for justice. After every visit with him, Siti came away determined to oust the Government that had perpetrated this outrage. She decided to seek leadership of the party and to achieve the success for both of them that had been thwarted by their arrest.

Within a short time, the mantle of his inspired leadership fell upon her and she became Leader of the Middle Way Party. Their child became the Party mascot. She would unite Austrasia, rejecting Sudarta and the last vestiges of Bhakarian colonialism. Carefully she was planning for his revenge. Austrasia would enter a new age.

The speeches and conversations he had made while in opposition were published and widely read. New Science was the central tenet of Party policy. Sudarta lost popularity and her regime became more and more oppressive in clinging to power. The nation was polarised and in turmoil. Siti forced Sudarta to hold an election. Infamous for brutalising Abajoe, she lost her own seat and quit politics.

Siti became Prime Minister and Austrasia withdrew from the SEU and changed the nation's name back to 'Australia'. Local parliaments drew up plans for diverse sustainable futures, commencing with zero population growth and a voluntary programme of birth control and fair allocation of water for a 200-year drought. The Government fostered an ecumenical spirit of self-altruism with Abajoe as its icon.

Plans were also made to restore and preserve Australian culture and at the same time to introduce and develop Bhakarian culture. Relations with Bhakaria recognised the nations' different resource needs and the two nations signed an agreement to help each other in emergencies such as famines.

These changes were achieved after local debate following New Science methods rather than by central edict. Economic development forced by the Sudarta Government was only continued where there was local government support. Australians developed non-material communities. Collectives came together from self-interest and altruism equally, in the spirit of self-altruism. However, politics and economics were of secondary importance: Australians self-fulfilled outside the economy with diverse lifestyles of meditation, spiritual achievement and care for disadvantaged people. In the dry centre and south, nomadism eventually returned.

When Sudarta was ousted, Abajoe and the other brain-cleared political prisoners were released. He went home to The Tower and lived with Siti and Tani.

Now that he was immersed in normal living, his learning proceeded in leaps and bounds. At 67, he had a very active curiosity. The electrical treatment had closed off certain neural pathways but fibres that connected together now accessed his earlier knowledge and understanding. After two years, his thinking left juvenile concrete thought behind and became adolescent, then became adult and formal. Although his libido had atrophied, his recovering Broca's emotions caused a second adolescent infatuation with Siti, which she reciprocated. His love affair with Siti resumed, intensified by the separation they had suffered. Their sexual relationship revived with a passionate honeymoon.

Gradually, his memory returned. Like Mandela, Abajoe was not bitter after his 30 years in detention. He had spent a total of 20 years in prison, three under house arrest and seven in government-controlled rehabilitation. He was surprised when he realised he had got what he wanted: Siti had been free, their daughter Tani had been raised happily in freedom and the MWP was ushering in his vision of society. He wouldn't have achieved as much without his sacrifice.

Despite the treatment he had suffered, Abajoe's legendary sharing behaviour returned. He shared his wisdom in advising a stream of visitors and his advice was to pursue win-win outcomes. His self-altruism was revolutionary but although it's purpose and meaning spread everywhere, Australia teetered on the brink of accepting it. The selfish gene clung to people's psyches.

He had emulated famous political leaders in history and brought Australia through revolutionary social change. There had been opposing reactions to those changes, further cases of Lenz's Law. Like Jesus, he had taken upon himself racial hatred and suffered. Now he had become what he advocated, a superordinate leader above nationalism and secular politics, an open-minded scientist.

Tani and Abajoe became inseparable, playing and learning from new experiences together. Within a few years, she took an interest in the rossit experiments he had revived at The Tower. Siti, as mentor to them both, followed the experiments closely. One day Siti noticed an old buck in a pen with a group of younger does and bucks.

"What experiment is your father trying now?" Siti asked the child.

"He is testing if the old one will tell the young ones about the famines."

"What about them?" Siti asked her.

"How to have no babies. He doesn't want them to be hungry."

"Has he told them what to do yet?"

"He has started, but it takes time. He couldn't tell them before because he has been kept in a pen by himself for a long time."

"How do you know he is telling them?"

"They have stopped having so many babies, so when there isn't much food, there won't be too many of them."

"How do you know?"

"Dad told me."

"How does he know?"

"He said he did a test, a long time ago."

"Then it must be true."

"No. But it could be. That's why we are doing it again."

When Siti recounted this story to the nation, it kickstarted the self-altruism that Abajoe's leadership had primed. There was an explosion of sustained generosity, with an abundance of joyous giving and volunteering, going beyond kin and community, even to complete strangers. There was steady growth in the spiritual quality of Australian lifestyles.

Abajoe became a very wise, young-minded elder, esteemed for his counsel. He led national social reform, bringing objectivity and religious tolerance to the nation. Local councils adhered to voluntary constraints on population, water, land, usage of resources and industry. The spectre of famine was finally laid to rest.

One day Siti brought Abajoe a letter she had received.

Gataka
Bhakaria
4 April 2285
Dear Prime Minister Siti and Elder Abajoe
You won't remember me but I was a guest worker at Mount Argus and met you on your visit in 2240. Thank you, Abajoe, for supporting the

guest worker scheme and to Siti for making the Government give us money for the fare home. I wanted to stay in Australia but now I am glad I was sent home to Bhakaria. I have had a good job here training people in the skills I learned in Australia at the mine. Now we have here a better life, like in Australia. My dream of a worthwhile life has come true. I hope Abajoe is okay now and your family is happy together.

Best wishes

The signature was scrawled and unreadable.

"I don't know the signature," said Siti. "So much for our immigration campaign."

Abajoe read it again. "It could be from Citra," he said. "She must really exist. I wanted to help her and maybe I have."

"Who is Citra?"

He ignored her question. "If there hadn't been a grid over the hole between the two pens, the results might have been quite different," he said. "Rossits could come and go."

"But people can't; immigrants get stuck here. We aren't in the petroleum era now; if people then had only realised..."

"...What? To learn from rossits?"

"Yes...not to fear immigrants...and not to panic in a crowd," Siti replied.

"Maybe I could knock-in some echidna, so they would roll up into a ball. Rossits are too fearful...hysterical."

"They are more rabbit-like than rabbits."

"They are almost as panicky as a crowd of lemmings. But adding echidna won't solve it. Balls and pricks actually cause the crowding in the first place...they're not a solution," she laughed.

"Sometimes they are," he chuckled, taking her by the hand and leading her into the bedroom, "when they're not a sacrament."

"That sounds like you are going to start a new religion."

"No. A commune or two may worship me for a while."

They lay holding each other close.

"But you could ... you suffered for longer."

"I wasn't cut down in my youth." He turned on to his back. "I'll see my vision realised. I'll die fulfilled. It's less dramatic."

"I guess there's no profit in your story, then," Siti quipped from beside him.

"No. Nor a Holy Ghost. But I want to share it."
"Why?"
"It could happen."

THE END